Water Must Fall

For my parents, who made me,
and Glenda, who sustains me.

Water Must Fall

Nick Wood

NewCon Press
England

First published in the UK by NewCon Press, April 2020
41 Wheatsheaf Road, Alconbury Weston, Cambs, PE28 4LF

NCP235 (limited edition hardback)
NCP236 (softback)

10 9 8 7 6 5 4 3 2 1

ISBN:
978-1-912950-60-7 (hardback)
978-1-912950-61-4 (softback)

Cover Art by Vincent Sammy
Cover layout by Ian Whates

Edited by Ian Whates
Interior layout by Storm Constantine

If you split the heart of a single drop of water,
One hundred pure oceans flow forth.
— *Mahmud Shabestri, fourteenth-century Sufi poet.*

Chapter 1
Graham — The Dry Falls

The Rainy Season, 2048, near Livingstone, Zambia

The rains were late.

Nothing here but drifting smoke and ashes, as if some giant dragon has blasted this terrain into cinders. Light face mask on, I boot-crunched across dull grey embers and black earth to the high razor wire of the LRE, the Livingstone Relocation Encampment.

The wire was electrified, so I kept a safe distance from the heat of its fizz. The acrid smell of burnt savannah grass leaked through my mask, tearing my eyes painfully. The brown grass inside the encampment was shiny with fire retardant, the eight or so mud-brown prefab buildings jumbled together, as if hastily dropped from the sky.

A sign hung from the fence, picturing a small black girl drinking water, the message in blue droplets underneath her open mouth: 'All water donated charitably by FreeFlow, where Water is Wine'.

But behind the fence, several men and a thin woman eyed me listlessly from under a scorched tree within the camp, seemingly squeezed of all will to move, in that burning heat.

I wondered if they'd seen their food shipped overseas as biofuels for SUVs and military tanks. No drones hovered overhead, and I'd heard FuelCorps had censored the overhead sats. *Anyway, there's no market for video clips of this sort of thing any more, not even from the last of the official news agencies.*

No money to be made here… So why have I come?

<Hey, what the fok are you looking at, Graham? I'm paying you to stick to the job, man — go get me some foking awesome pictures of the 'Falls.>

The Boss, chirping at me from Durban through Cyril, my neural Rig.

A boy of about eight or nine approached me and had his left hand through the electric fence, holding an old plastic Gameboy. I stared at the dead screen. *Needs new batteries?* I shook my head and pointed at the sky. *Everything is going solar.*

Slowly, he pulled his hand back. His Manchester United T-shirt smelt of smoke and dirt. He was crying. His shoulders hunched as he sobbed, just like Mark used to do, when he'd cried inconsolably as a young boy.

This is Africa. Get going, Mason, before the Boss rides you again.

I marched back, across that mini-Mordor, to the car park and entrance to the Victoria Falls, one of the last great wonders of the world.

One thing I knew for sure: the rains were damn late.

Inside the park, I scrambled across to the Zambezi River.

Scanning the ridge of grey rock towering off to my left, I could see there was no vast, unified surge of water pouring over the edge as I remembered only five years ago – just sparse, thin water curtains dropping from the escarpment into the sludgy green river, over a hundred metres below me.

Gone was the towering spray of vapour above, no water cloud sweeping overhead. Deep in the wooded Batoko Gorge, the sluggish river struggled through the trees. Good old Queen Vic – although she was long dust, her namesake waterfall here in Zambia was drying quickly too – this was no longer 'Mosi-oa-Tunya' either, no 'Smoke-That-Thunders'.

"Record," I said reluctantly, closing my right eye simultaneously to activate my neural cam. Du Preez was going to hate this.

A black-uniformed guard with an AK strapped across his shoulder stood nearby, clicking on his digital palm-slate. The payment request bleeped in my cochlea; with a muttered command, I sent the amount in Chinese yuan from the Office account in my head.

No, Du Preez would go absolutely mad, absolutely bedonnered about this.

The guard moved on, accosting a young black man with an antiquated mobile phone cam. There were only five other people circling the viewing platform; none jostling for a view. I licked my lips, ever thirsty as usual.

<Is that all it is now? What a fokin' waste of time and money!>

Hell, I had no idea the Boss had joined me again, watching through my eyes like a mind-parasite, and tickling my cochlea with his electronic croak.

I closed my eyes. In the reddish darkness of my interior eyelids I spotted the green light flicking on the right, virtually projected by Cyril 'the Rig's' neural cybernetics. *The Office was online, the bloody Boss definitely in.*

But there was still only a dull red glow behind my left eyelid.

Where are you, Lizette? What are you doing right now… and are you okay? You must know I hate having to leave you; but I've got to pay the bills, especially the damn water.

<So what happened about the fokin' rain forecast and the Vic Falls deluge that we flew you out for?>

"Blown away, I think, gone."

I spat the words, each one drying my mouth further. Eyes closed, a faint tingle of water from the falls sprayed onto my cheeks – a tantalising tickle onto my dry protruding tongue. I pulled my tongue in before the sun could burn it into biltong steak. The water from my hipflask sizzled sweetly as I swigged, but then the ever-present tongue-throat ache was back.

Always thirsty, I took a final frustrated gulp and opened my eyes. I stretched my arms and fingers across the wooden railings of the viewing platform, but I couldn't feel any faint spray.

The sky was turning darker blue – still clear, as the bloating red sun dropped onto the horizon.

No, there was no 'Smoke-That-Thunders', no constantly roiling crash of water any more – all that's left is an anaemic spattering of water, me, and a few other tourists scanning the ridge for a riverine surge that would never come.

<That's your new job, my boy, find me who's stealing the water. Get me that fokin' thief.>

"Global Boiling," I sighed. *Sometimes Du Preez could be so literal.*

Beyond the weak Vic Falls, surrounding green GM bio-fuel fields stretched to the horizon, leeching the river.

Wonder how much they've *siphoned off the mighty Zambezi too?*

<Hell, man, I'm off to ask Bongani how we can jack up your visuals on your clips, to get any of our online Avatar subscribers to pay for them. Not even our Chinese Stanley will want to meet Livingstone, with the crappy shots you got there. Du Preez out.>

Ach ja, shit, and the Leech Boss too, of course, who's constantly siphoning off me. I winced at the sharpness of his tone in my ear. I had no energy to reply – he never waited for one anyhow – and swigged another guilty sip.

A bleep in my cochlea – a Bluetooth neural kit requested contact.

I ignored it; it wasn't Lizette.

"Hey, have you got the latest C-20 model?"

I looked at a man in a khaki Smart safari-suit, skin reddened by the sun, despite the generous smears of what looked like factor 100 white sunblock. His accent was vaguely Pan-European, the wispy greying hair underneath his dripping pith helmet disguised its original colour.

He grinned at me and tapped his head. "I've had the latest C-20 model inserted, no need for vocal commands, it's all thought operated."

"Mine's an old C-12 model," I said, scanning past him, along the escarpment and eastwards to the vast maize fields below, which looked as if they were encircling to attack the shrinking strip of green riverine bush and trees.

Perhaps I'd edit the clip later; momentarily too embarrassed to audibly cut my shoot. *From this angle, no sign of the LRE.*

The man kept talking, breathing hot meat and beer onto me, and I wondered briefly whether he'd heroically Safari-Shot drugged game before eating it: "My Rig's compatible with the latest web designs from China and is wired into the optic nerve for six-factor zoom capability."

"That's good to hear, I'm afraid mine just does a job."

Ah. There.

Scattered on the edge of the riverine trees, before the fenced maize fields, were mounds of white. They looked as if they'd died seeking cover from encroaching razor-wire and thirst, cordoned off from the river.

I knew the Boss would kill me, but I had to keep filming – it was the biggest elephant graveyard I'd ever seen, and it had been months since *anyone* had last seen an elephant. Huge piles of bones, like stranded and stripped hull-wrecks of ships, some of them arching their white curves in neatly laid out patches – as if their death had been calm, deliberate, and careful to acknowledge an individual, elephantine space for dying.

Jan du Preez may only want Live Game – me, I take what I can get.

The man turned to follow my gaze and grumbled with disappointment: "Bugger. Just bloody bones, I thought you'd seen some real wildlife for a change. Did you know the C-20 also has full amygdala-hippocampal wiring, that allows synchronous ninety-three percent recall of emotion?"

"Really?" I looked back at him. For the past few years, it had felt as if my own feelings were desiccating; the barest husks of what they had been – *what must it be like, to pull out old video clips saturated with the original feelings, rich and raw with young emotional blood?*

The man dropped his smart-shades and tapped his ear, "Give me some elephants, Bok Kai. Now."

Now? There is no now.

Sweat trickled down the man's pasty cheeks, funnelling through shades of bristled beard.

It's been over two decades since we watched hand-held video-clips of us and baby Mark, now three years gone to a software career in New Zealand. Three years on from the hijacking that left Mark without a car outside our gates, but crying with gratitude he was alive, physically unharmed.

No.

Here exists, the tremor in that man's cheek exists… But everything changes, nothing can be held onto – so, no now.

The tremor in the man's left cheek vanished as he broke into an open shout. "Elephants!"

I leaned forwards against the railings, scanning the embankments along the sludgy Zambezi banks. A few cormorants fluttered, but nothing large.

Nothing?

"Where?" I asked reluctantly.

The man laughed and tapped his shades. "Here," he said, "What a magnificent matriarch at the front. Bok Kai has given me a vision of the past, superimposed perfectly on the now. No one at home will know the difference."

Why watch phantoms? And what kind of a name is Bok Kai for an AI? It's been just two years since Du Preez contributed to the Rig in my head – to 'Cyril', who has helped to sharpen and hold my most recent memories.

But post-operatively, I'd been left enduringly thirsty. They sure as hell buggered up my thirst centre, at the same time they did the Rig neurosurgery – but the insurance disclaimers had been twelve pages long, the surgeons in denial.

'Not radical neuro-surgery, Mister Mason', the Chief Surgeon had sniffed, 'the cheap option, a few enhanced neural nodes feeding the brain kit into your left cochlear.'

Cheap.

The pith-helmet man opened his mouth again; sweat dripped off the end of his nose, as if his Smart Suit was struggling to adequately regulate his temperature.

I smiled, and turned away, not wishing to say goodbye. Maybe old feelings should be left alone after all, left to dry and wither like fallen leaves.

I prefer emptiness and absence, to seeing faked images from never-when.

'Command – cut!' Cyril responded to my words, at least.

Okay, so his Rig is better (bigger) than mine… big bloody deal. He's not an African, just an effete tourist in a harsh land his skin can't deal with, filtering it through his foreign money, fancy implants and clever clothes.

And me?

Red blinked behind my eyelids on shutting my eyes, so I let Cyril randomly cycle a babble of blogs over me as I headed back to the car park, the public toilet, and the chilly airport hotel, before the early morning flight home.

Time, before flying, to update my VLOG: **Mason: *Building a Better World.***

Screams in the distant across the charred savannah. Fresh smoke rising from within the Livingstone Relocation Encampment. A wildfire kicking up again? Shit. Should I help? What about Game-Boy Boy?

Nah… What can I do, I'm just one man?

This is Africa.

I flicked open the door on my self-driving SUV, relishing the burst of aircon chill from the interior, as the rear door swung open.

<*Someone's scanning me,*> said Cyril.

I glanced across the burning glare of the roof. A tall man in a white juice-suit stood at the entrance to the 'Falls, but clearly watching me.

'Command: Who is he, Cyril?'

<*No One.*>

Jumping into the car, I snarled, "So why does he look like Josef fucking Stalin, then?"

But, through the one-way window, I could see that No One was gone.

Chapter 2

Lizette Basson — The Gardener

Someone was at the gate.

I jumped again, at the insistent sound of the front door buzzer.

On my own. Alone. As usual. Graham, you, you… swine.

Despite the pressure of ever-present pain in my lower stomach, I moved with smooth practice, from chopping carrots, to selecting a firearm from the rack by the front door.

Keeping the knife in my left hand – good for close quarter stabbing – I chose a small lethal handgun for my right hand.

Best keep any necessary killing at a distance, given a choice.

Hands full, I pressed the gate-cam button with my right shoulder.

Graham's told you just to ignore the bell. There's enough automated security to keep most threats at bay. But I need to know who's there. Just looking…

So why you already thinking of killing, then, Lizzie dear?

The screen above the door flickered into life – yet another stinking hot day outside, so it took me a moment to make sense of the parched view of grey gate, brown earth, blue gum tree and…

A little girl was sagging, in her tattered yellow dress, against the gated iron railings.

Don't choose electrify option… yet.

Who else is there, beyond the honey trap?

"Zoom and scan." I kept a taut grip on both knife and gun.

The camera panned in on the girl's face – *young, about seven or eight – and with a glazed, broken expression on her face. She can't close her mouth, her tongue's too swollen and cracked; she's bleeding between her new teeth.*

"Dear Jesus," I said, "Scan wider." I choked on the last word.

The camera panned over nearby bushes and the blue gum tree, but there was no sign of anyone else.

"Open door, Harry," I said, placing the knife down into the one empty gun space, having to jostle a bit with Graham's old R-1 automatic rifle from the Angolan War, for space.

Open the door for no one, Graham had instructed me.

Tough. Dying girls are someone.

I shoved on my floppy cricket hat, The KZN Dolphins, and stepped out warily into the drive, gun held in front of me.

A Beretta – Graham knew the model number and specs – *big damn deal.* At least he had given me some good training with it.

But, if I get ambushed, Mister Graham Bledy Mason, there will be hell to pay.

Nearing the gate, I could tell the little girl was barely conscious, keening in anguish from a parched throat. Flies were settling on her lips, as if seeking residual moisture.

I thumbed gate permission into the solar-pad and the railings creaked open. The girl tumbled forward onto the gravel, not even putting her hands out, to break her fall.

Scooping the semi-conscious body up with my left arm, I backed away cautiously, gun still cocked and ready.

There was no way to close the gate, with a steadied gun and a surprisingly heavy girl, so I dragged her quickly towards the open doorway, calling out for the Three H's; Home Help Harry, to seal the gate.

Behind me, the gate clanked shut, just before the door banged shut as well, in the breeze.

I thumbed the safety and dropped the gun, needing both hands to carry the girl over to the couch, where I laid her down.

The girl was on her back, still faintly keening through her biltong tongue, face browned with dirt. She was bleeding above the right eye, from a recent abrasion.

"Poor thing," I said. "I'm Liz. Let me get you some water."

But the girl, although she could sit up with support, could barely swallow or move her tongue.

I held her gently on the couch – just like I had held Mark, many years ago, when I had breast fed him.

With this little girl, though, water just spilled off her choking face.

So, instead, I tilted her head back slightly, slowly dripping water from a mug into her mouth, moistening the base of the tongue and lubricating the mouth, to enable the start of a swallow reflex. All the while, the girl never took her eyes off my face.

She coughed and choked, looking terrified, but I shushed her calmly. "*Ag ja, my kind, ek sorg vir jou ne, net tot ons kan jou mamma vind.*"

The girl looked blank and I laughed, switching to isiZulu, telling her I was just looking after her, until we could find her mother.

She sat up with difficulty, as I dabbed dirt off her face, applying some antiseptic above her eye and sealing it with a plaster.

The little girl finally closed her mouth, continuing to stare at the mug placed nearby, on the coffee table.

"Thandi, missus," she croaked, in response to my question about her name.

"Here you go, Thandi," I offered her the mug, "Finish it. I'll get some more. I also need to call someone, so we can find your *mammie, ne?*"

The girl had gulped the last drops of water from her second mug by the time I finally got a response from Traditional Leader Dumisani's office, on the 3-di mat screen that Graham had installed in the lounge for me.

The young man representing the Chief, was dressed lightly in white cotton shirt and trousers and frowned at me, through the sound of a big office solar fan behind his head. "You want us to come over there to fetch the girl – *and* you have some other news of use for us?"

I nodded, turning to the girl standing next to me. "Thandi Mavuso, say hello to Jabulani. He will be sending someone around to take you home and find your *mammie.*"

The girl just raised the mug I'd given her.

I switched off and went to refill the mug.

The water jug in the fridge was empty, so I thought for a moment. *Tap water is damn expensive; FreeFlow monitor it like diamonds. How can they afford it, in the townships, even with a hard-fought sliding rates allocation?*

The screen buzzed at me, playing the ancient Carpenters' song 'Close to You', so I knew it was Graham, calling via Cyril, his neuro-Rig. *Always so full of old cheese, mister – but never here, when I need you. Fat lot of good you can do me, from over a thousand miles away.*

"Thandi," I called the little girl over and bent down to whisper in her ear, "If I show you a secret, do you promise not to tell?"

The girl nodded, smiling.

I put my hat on the girl's head, so large for her it almost covered her eyes, and held out my hand. "Come then, we have to go outside into the back garden."

In my other hand, I carried the well module.

Graham would not like me doing this. Not one little bit.

I hesitated – but Thandi pulled on my hand, so we stepped outside, into the humid heat.

The garden was well away from prying eyes, surrounded by high walls, with orange drought resistant *Strelizias* decorating the wall tops. I had only a few non-indigenous plants, a purple snapdragon here, for its beauty alone.

I pressed the lever on the man-hole cover in the ground near the back wall and Thandi jumped in surprise as it swung away, revealing a deep groundwater well, with enough space for a large man to fit down.

I tapped a command on the palm-set and the small automated scoop trundled to the top, brimming with water – together, we shared another drink, from a nearby purifier jug.

The girl peered down the well hole again, as if fascinated by the sight of water, deep down near the gloomy bottom.

I held her gently by her shoulders. "Careful, little one, that's a long way to fall – and it's almost below the ladder line, so it will be hard to climb out. Can you swim?"

The girl shook her head. Didn't think so. *Not many township kids can, no opportunity to learn.* I knelt and pulled the heavy well hole shut, scuffing some Matabele ants away with my foot.

Harry boomed out an announcement that Traditional Leader Dumisani's Chief Representative had arrived, so I asked him to let her in and hollered from the back garden.

The rep was a large imposing woman by the name of Saartjie Baartman – her grizzled, close-cropped grey hair and lined face reinforced a sense of gravitas, that she seemed to carry before her.

Saartjie held her hand out, "I've come to take you home, little daughter."

Thandi went across to her, without a word.

"It is not good to be on your own too much, *sisi* – is your man away?"

It took me a moment to realise Saartjie was talking to me.

I was used to pretending with so many – oh, my man, he's in the backroom, or nearby out for a walk, or at a rugby game, or just around the corner – *a woman on her own is vulnerable indeed.*

But you, woman who carries your weight with such comfort, you I trust.

Slowly, I nodded.

She smiled. "Then you must visit us in Imbali, Mizz Basson. So, what is your news?"

I hesitated again.

Graham would not like me to say anything. This is Africa, he'd say, too big to fix.

Thandi smiled at me, briefly, through chapped and painful lips.

Now she, and possibly others like her, I should *help.*

"We have well water we might be able to share, but I will need to speak to my partner first."

"Of course," the woman said, "*Nkosi.* You look after us; we look after you. *Sala kahle.*"

The child did not even look back when they left, but I didn't mind.

Empty. Alone again. My friends have drifted away since I became ill, and I've lost the will to stay engaged. It's just Graham and me – and these bledy *ants.*

Come on Lizzie, keep busy.

I watered a few dying plants, with pale piss from the toilet.

The pain was back, of course, a grinding ache in the lower abdomen, courtesy of endometriosis. An old friend – or enemy – constantly haunting and fatiguing me. I've stopped doing so much, because of the incessant drag of pain.

I've been through countless therapies and pain clinics.

Pain, you never get used to, you can never welcome with completely open arms, no matter how much they tell you 'acceptance' helps.

A high-pitched buzzing penetrated my thoughts, coming from the sky, and I glanced up, fearing a swarm of flies or locusts.

It was a drone, flying in low over the walls, but it stopped to hover, about ten metres or so above my head.

I chilled, despite the late afternoon heat, as I read the lettering on the under carriage.

Du Preez Enterprises? Graham's boss – what does he *want?*

Somehow, I knew it wasn't anything good; so I looked away and hurried inside, suddenly finding it very hard to breathe.

Chapter 3
The Art of Data Sweeping

"Breathe," says father, "swim."

I breathe, but it's cold and burning wet and I choke and sink, scrabbling at nothing.

A man watches me, eyes open, saying nothing, bubbling briefly from his bum. His foot is trapped in the window of a drowned car.

Arms float above his streaming hair and darkness comes for me.

Darkness pulls me up and out, throwing me onto a roof. Scrabbling at tiles, my feet get purchase on a gutter. I look up at noise from the sky.

My mother is sitting straddled on the roof, crying, on her phone, waving at me, choking too. "We need help... we're on our house roof – where? North Shore..."

I scream as a man climbs onto the roof next to me, soaked, puffing. A dark man, but not the dead, bubbly man.

My father.

He turns to me, as I vomit water.

"I told you to breathe, son, and next time, God Forbid, swim harder."

He grabs me by the scruff of my coat collar and hauls me up the slippery tiles of the roof, throwing me over the curve of the roof peak.

Mom holds me.

"Fuck you, Katrina!" says Father, watching water carrying broken bits of cars, plastic, branches and, sometimes, swollen bodies.

Fuck you, Katrina.

Always, words to wake and shiver by.

I still shivered, inside this Church, where we hid against the giant dust cloud spewing from the south, hanging ever higher above the hundred-foot Super-State wall.

So, I sat and prayed, just like the others.

What do I seek? God? Or my lost family?

After the opening prayer I waited, with enduring patience, for the coming apocalypse.

Jesus won't be long to arrive on those Blessed Clouds of His. Signs and portents, while the sun flays our cancerous skins like cattle hide – and we implore Rain from an angry God, bringing on the ruin of the world.

Pastor Johns built his story with certitude, a tall, white, severely dressed man in black, his grey trimmed beard filling out his cracked and hollow face.

He warned us all to stay loving and welcoming to fellow Americans, even the *Dusties*, as Jesus Himself could be coming over the Wall, on the gathering storm.

The pastor skimped over his description of hell for transgressors; hell was all too evident outside.

Here, he taught us that the climate catastrophe was God-given, as it heralded the arrival of the Lord.

Every Sunday at ten at the Third Hydro-City Baptist Church, it's the same. Sameness is reassuring, my back starting to melt into the pew, even though this is only my fourth visit.

And, in my usual seat at the back corner, people didn't bother me any, seeming to know I wasn't the friendly, or effusive type.

It's so tiring, pretending to be normal. Whatever that is.

"And we will be raptured with Jesus on the winds of the storm, as the Earth dies beneath our feet," claimed the Pastor.

"Amen and hallelujah, Lord!" Someone in the pew ahead shouted, but with restraint.

Why would God want to destroy the planet? I've heard of blaming the devil to evade personal responsibility. Do we now blame God, to avoid collective guilt and complicity?

The last hymn was sung.

"Mine eyes have seen the glory of the coming of the Lord. He is trampling out the vintage, where the grapes of wrath are stored... Glory, glory..."

I readied myself to leave first, so no one could talk to me, but today the thick bearded Deacon – who usually handled the Tithe Plate – stopped me, with a firm but sticky palm on my wrist. "I'm sorry, brother, Pastor Johns wants a word with you."

I snatched a glance down the aisle, where everyone else was filing out, behind the Senior Pastor. *I'm dressed respectful and am clean and don't stink. I have not cussed at anyone. What you want, Man of God?*

The deacon steered me towards The Meeting Room.

I disliked being touched and pulled away.

The Deacon shrugged, stepping ahead to open the door and wave me in.

I entered, slowly and suspiciously.

The room was large and covered with pictures of natural spaces, mountains and rivers and natural stuff that's almost all gone now; but lit up by heavenly radiances.

Just like the radiance that was shrouding the heads of Jesus in four identical pictures at each corner, as if He were guarding the walls of the Church. Jesus was white and demure in a frilly kaftan, looking down at His

18

praying hands, as if there was a bulb lit inside Him.

In the background – behind the four Jesuses – were crosses in the distance, with ancient inscriptions no doubt saying 'This is the King of the Jews' – if my eyes had been devout enough to read such fine and distant print.

The Pastor stood in front of me, as if attempting to catch my gaze, so I looked up at the tall man's dog collar, wondering why in Heaven they called it that.

White plastic on black cloth.

"God has you on a leash?" I asked, without thinking.

Momentary silence. "Uh, thank you for coming in to have a talk with me, Mister uh, Green."

Silence spread for some nine seconds or so, before I realized the pastor expected a response. "What is it you want to tell me, Pastor Johns?"

"Take a seat, Mister Green, please," the Pastor waved behind me, so I stepped backwards, to sink into a red armchair.

Odd reply to my question.

He dropped his long frame into a swivel chair, pulling it closer, as if wanting to get all personal.

I grated my chair on the wooden floor, pushing it back hastily with my heels. *Too close, too close.*

"Um, we just wondered, Mr. Green, seeing as you have only been coming here a month now, firstly, do you want to become a member – have you been saved? Secondly, if not, have you considered another church?"

A man who numbers his statements. I like that.

"It's good to see you smiling, Mister Green," the Pastor said, his throat bobbling above his tight collar.

Just when I'd been starting to think I could handle this. What does it mean to be saved? And why should it influence whether I can attend here, or not?

"Is there any way I can continue attending *without* becoming a member, Pastor?" I asked.

Commitments hurt, and families disappear.

"I can understand your hesitation," Pastor Johns said, dipping his head, as if trying to catch my gaze, "What about considering The Fiery Baptists out in West Kern City?"

"Why? I've come from there. They're too noisy. I like quiet. I like order. Your church is both."

The Pastor's eyes were disconcertingly blue and piercing, so I looked away. "But surely you feel more at home, there? They are *your* people, after all – and at least there, you get to sing most of the time."

"I hate singing," I said, getting up, feeling confused, and even a little angry. *What is he getting at? Who are 'my people'? Why are conversations always so hard, with hidden meanings that fail to announce themselves with any certitude?*

Ahh, melanin, must be, singling out my 'people'.

Mom was white, both her and daddy long dead, long gone, in that gas-car accident. Since I was eighteen, I've felt alone, never comfortable in my own skin. I have no people. Still, I am pale enough to 'pass' often, so am lucky enough not to know what it means to be constantly black.

Dad had told me once, sternly, I must never hide in 'blinkered whiteness', though.

"It may be safer – but it's not right. The Tulsa Massacre happened *right here* in this town, m'boy."

It was after my fifteenth birthday, when only four boys – out of twelve invited – had arrived.

All white. I became ashamed I had only invited the white kids; and said nothing.

"The future will be post-racial," Mom had said.

Dad had just laughed.

But with this pastor, in front of me right now, I have obviously not passed.

"But I prefer *your* church, Pastor Johns," I said, getting ready to leave. "Although I don't understand why you have four identical pictures of Jesus up on your wall?"

The man wrung his hands, as if he thought he was the Saviour himself. *He does not have a bulb inside him, though, and his hands stay sweaty pale.*

"Each one to counteract the Four Horsemen, running loose right now," he said.

He's a numbers' man too?

I opened the door to leave. "I should imagine, though, with weather as it was in first century Palestine, Jesus had to be black."

I left, without looking back.

Facts are important.

Indeed, I might have been smiling again.

Thankfully, the rest of the congregation had all gone.

The sun glowed through the rising storm, so I goggled and masked up. The dust surged towards the apex of the sky, filaments turning the sun an increasingly bloody purple.

I was alone, and felt even more shrunken, than when I'd been sitting inside the Church.

How do you replace a family that is gone?

How can you have faith, when the world is on fire?

I rushed home, even though Gen, the Green Turtle screen-watch on my wrist, told me the storm would not strike until the definitive wind shift came from SouthCal later in the week; Thursday, most likely.

Four days' grace, until the apocalypse arrived.

Hallelujah.

Monday, Monday.

Work was all right – but it would be a *lot* better, if there weren't anyone else here with me. *Not sure by how many increments of magnitude better. No straight forward parameters to use to calculate.*

"Here's your coffee, Art," said Zeke, dropping the recyclable cup onto my desk – hot, black and no doubt two generous spoons of brown, sweet stuff in there.

"Thanks, Zeke," I said, reconsidering the need for such a calculation, after all.

I refocused on the latest water qual figures coming in from the new deep well testing up 'Frisco way, the Fresno Drill. *Gone down thirty miles before heat seizure on their drill equipment – not bad, but still only tickling the Earth's surface.*

Zeke always teased me this was 'Holy Grail' stuff – the race for the cheapest and first way to get down past the mantle zone; way, way below and into the fresh water Earth Ocean they say swilled some four hundred miles or so deep, or even deeper. *Ocean of the Phoenix, giving rise to new life and rebirth.*

That and/or looting the Antarctic for the last of its ice.

"Well, what do you say?" Zeke asked, waiting by my desk, but having a slurp of their own Latte *Affectionato*.

They're a Gender X *Neut*, wearing leather suspenders from grey coolant pants over a white cotton shirt, made with plenty of room to continue hiding their sex. Always trendy, and so hard to second guess what they might turn up to work in.

Me, I've never really been interested, but I have overheard others at the paid water-well, swapping illegal bets in advance on the topic.

Boy, girl, who cares.

Zeke is Zeke.

Me, I'm happy just to snatch small sips of water, say nothing, and mosey back to my desk. As for my sartorial elegance, I have five pairs of identical blue undies, pants and shirts, washed at 6pm on Friday every week; a routine which takes the sweat out of work clothes' choice.

No one takes any bets on my *clothes.*

"Thank you for the coffee, Zeke," I said, "Where are you going today?"

"New Fresno Lake near Millerton, Art, *meetin'* some FreeFlow hydro engineers and managers, to discuss the lake and aquifer pumping. Have you – uh – checked those figures for me yet?"

I have enough of my own work without checking on your Ivor the Avatar numbers. Avatars are so gloriously good nowadays; they even get to go to court. And I'm talking Supreme, not District. They don't make mistakes no more.

Well, not many… and I'm the senior here.

I'm the one who should be getting others to do things.

Still, Data Sweeper is one of my roles – double-checking the details and keeping in mind the bigger pictures. AIs are still new – the larger patterns and connections not yet their strongest suite.

"I'll have the numbers checked when you get there – around ten?"

Zeke nodded and moved off, tapping their left ear where Ivor sat. "Mail me if you get in early data that's contradictory. That scary bastard Watson may be there – and he doesn't like us."

No, why should he? We keep tabs on FreeFlow pushing the limits of law to turn a water profit, especially into the Hydro-City Golf Course, where he sits as Board Governor. In their eyes, what's to like?

"You've got eight now," I called after Zeke, having counted the sticking plasters on their smooth, sharp white face.

"All growths removed – and still benign," they shouted, starting a sprint up a flight of stairs, to ground level.

Guiltily, I kicked in the command to raise the table, standing and stretching my three spare mid-riff tires. They had dripped rings of sweat onto my shirt and I scowled.

Sweat stains are asymmetrical and clearly not part of the shirt's design. I can't afford the latest juice suits with my pay check – I sure would love to just be able to sit and sweat – and drink my own flavoured liquid discharges. Orange rum sweat, maybe?

"Hey, you day-dreaming again?" Something bounced off my right shoulder blade and, without looking around, I knew it was a crumpled piece of paper, thrown by *that* Suraya Khan.

Suraya was short and thin, with an oily complexion that served her well in the perpetual heat. She wore a discreet silk headscarf, blue and gold, and liked to work at the standing screens closest to the gender *neut* toilet – she clearly had some urinary problems, so it was a work place adjustment.

Mind you, when she's not taking a piss, she's doing some damn fine bio-chemical analyses of water and soil samples, from all over NorthCal.

Just then, though, she was pretending to spar like a boxer, jabbing at me with her short arms, dancing on her light feet near the Holo-Mat.

I could tell Suraya didn't like Mondays either.

I gave her a wide berth, heading to the restroom to give my shirt and arm pits a sprinkle of water.

Not too much.

I entered my pay-code, just enough to get the tap flowing.

"You managed to get the water condenser past security?" I shouted through the half-open toilet door, flicking myself wet from the tap. The water was cooling at least – aircon was minimal down here, given we're public service.

I stepped back through the door and Suraya was waiting for me, as if already bored to tears with her own work. "Nope, got confiscated, in case someone 'jury rigged it into a terrorist device'." She mimicked Bondi, the security guard's voice very well, and I smiled.

Suraya continued, "I'm a state registered Muslim, remember, even if I'm an employee who's passed all the security checks. Bullshit I say, FreeFlow just want to keep charging our water usage."

Suraya's gaze dropped, as if startled at the state of my shirt. "Hey man, why you such a drip?"

I looked at her blankly, before swerving past her, en route to my desk.

"That's a joke," Suraya said, hovering behind my left shoulder, "Don't you *geddit?* And why don't *you* try and smuggle the condenser in next time?"

"No," I said. "I *don't* get it. And I'm black, they would nail me too."

"You mean your daddy was black," she snickered, "You, you could pass."

Go away, I got work to do... Big Dee wants that data on the Fresno drill too.

"You want some help with that Ivor the *Avvie* data Zeke gave you?" Suraya asked.

Now you're talking. I wired her the data. *Sometimes it's not so bad to have others around, after all.* "Zeke calls the file J. Edgar," I said, "Have a look at the lake micro-chemistry reports. I've promised to check the extraction and seepage data. Zeke's on their way there, right now. Seems like they anticipate trouble."

And it's always like Zeke to rush in.

I concentrated on playing with the data from the Fresno Deep Water Drill – Big Boss Dee, aka Dr. Rosemary Carruthers, had told me to check the findings, and ensure that the drilling was safe.

In the end, it's all about respecting the hierarchies responsible for your pay check, at the end of the month, after all. Work, pay, work, pay, work – is this all there is to life?

Especially when home was so empty.

But Carruthers was *never* one to trifle with.

After an hour of modelling and remodelling the raw data, I wired my terse report up to Numero Uno, almost predictably on the first floor: 'FDW water drill parameters appear safe and water quality uncontaminated, but just NOT ENOUGH OF IT'.

Like my pay-check at the end of the month, I wanted to add, but resisted.

'Better be right. We don't want no Flint Michigans in NorthCal. Yours, RC.'

Boy, is she quick!

Rosemary Carruthers – no one dared call her 'Rose' – the Big Dee, Doctorate in Water Management from Cadillac Desert Department, UC Davis.

"I've wired you Zeke's report," said Suraya, "It doesn't look good."

I tapped the file open. "Thanks Suraya, I'm going to inspect it on the 'Mat."

Okay Zeke, time to get your back, you should be there in thirty minutes plus. Skates on...

"Three-Dee New Fresno Lake specs, numbers and kinetic diagrams." I made my way over to the Holo-Mat in readiness.

The aquifer, rock structure and pumped section of the Lake hovered, pulsing over the Mat. Numbers from a week ago and yesterday spliced off in shining yellow arrowed trails to crucial dimensions mapped in red and green; volume, flow, seepage, evaporation, *yadda yadda yadda* – all the crucial dimensions of water movement, usage and, most importantly, reported and remaining retention.

Except there is no green.

I whistled through my teeth. All the vectors were red, and the Lake was below twenty percent. I looked again, this time moving amongst the data projections, so that I could feel the buzz of numbers and shapes prickle across my hot skin.

Everything in the red?

No wonder Zeke had been so keen to get us to check the data. They were *not* going to be given an easy time at the Lake by FF officialdom. Water restrictions might be bumped up to maximum, and the most vocal high-band rate payers will start to complain about their browning golf courses.

Or their big fucking swimming pools.

"What do *you* think Suraya?"

No response, so I turned.

The toilet door was closed.

"Stuff 'em, I say. Open loop, to Zeke Klein."

The lake hologram dissipated with a fizz, replaced almost instantly with the fuzzy outline of a beefy looking middle-aged white man in yellow-green hazard suit and brown helmet.

The engineers had obviously called in their Big Gun for the meeting, PR Main-Man Birdie Watson, from the FreeFlow Corps.

By the aggressive tilt of his head, I guessed I may not be at the start of the conversation, being picked up by Zeke's Ivor optic cam.

Even I had a good few inches of height over Zeke, so they must be feeling rather intimidated, by the glowering and obviously angry bulk of the man from FreeFlow.

The Fresno Lake wall was behind Watson, but it was hard to see the water, it had dropped so damn low. There were several engineers standing behind, though, in the shadow of the wall, as if they'd stopped to enjoy the show, even in that indubitably hot and murky sunlight.

"Ivor tells me you're online, Art," said Zeke, "Please help."

"No way we're cranking restrictions up to Max," snarled Watson, "Our data tells us we're holding steady."

"Tell him he must have alternative facts, maybe they've whitewashed their figures for the state voters. We retain direct federal data access – and our independent analysis will contest this."

Zeke rattled off my last sentence from inside their left ear, verbatim.

Watson glared directly into Zeke's eyes.

"You got another smartass covering your butt in the office, have you? Who's your boss, shithead?"

Zeke coughed, "Dr. Rosemary Carruthers."

Watson's face fell and he stared Zeke down, as if to check the veracity of their words. "I'll get you for this, motherfucker – and what are you, a boy – or a confused fucking girl?"

Zeke said nothing.

Watson glared into Zeke's eyes, almost as if he could see along the optic nerve, into Ivor's neural camera, and straight at my face. "As for you in there, clever shit, I can track you down like a fucking dog if I wanted to."

Then, without another word, Watson turned on his heel and strode off.

"Phew," said Zeke, "Thanks Art."

"What a bastard," I whispered.

I had seen Watson's neck and face in bloated three-dee close-up, for some moments. "Looks like he has three potential carcinoma spots near the jugular on his neck. You want to warn him?"

"No fucking way," Zeke said, "He can find that out for himself. Out."

The Fresno Lake wall disappeared.

Red words hung momentarily in the air in front of me, like blood-rain:

I'VE MARKED YOU OUT, MOTHERFUCKER.

Breathe, Art, breathe…

'Gen, how'd he do that?'

<Must have the best Rig money can buy, the super-hacker C33>

A muffled flushing noise, from the nearby toilet, sent contents of the bowl down to their reclamation pond, in the bowels of the Earth.

Recycling water, like almost forgotten rain.

Chapter 4
Graham — On Ants and Water

There were no rains here at home, either.

One old man near the road home held out his pale palms to me – but I've always avoided paternalistic gifts and dependency; this was Africa.

I kept my windshields up, my doors locked.

The fields on the hill were brittle brown and eaten to dust by scraggly herds of cattle, watched by boys with sticks in hands, some with shoulder-strapped and cocked Chinese P.L.A. T-74s, that looked in danger of blowing off their skinny legs.

The bovine numbers were dwindling, owners hit by increasingly heavy carbon taxes and the need for both reforesting and agricultural spaces, to bolster food securities within these drought lands.

Red meat was *very* expensive.

As for the veg, yes to intercropping fields of sorghum, cassava and sweet potato, but Lizzie's beetroot will always be my favourite. Shit man, we're so lucky we have our secret well backup, a hedge against the soaring costs of privatised water.

My eyes blinked heavily in the alternating early morning sunlight, with the spidery-web shadows of overhead pirate cables, snaking down from Council Electric pylons into the makeshift shacks along the roadside. *The cables will be cut by officials come sunset tonight and will have sprung back magically by tomorrow morning. Crazy, man, absolutely bedonnered, holding an impoverished community to electric ransom, when there's so much sun for free.*

The car turned on auto, up the long and bumpy drive to our smallholding, 'Cope's Folly', an old disused farmhouse we'd bought at a financial stretch in search of a 'simpler' semi-rural lifestyle. *Hah. Be careful what you wish for.*

I closed my eyes sending yet another desperate message, almost a plea: *<I'm home, Lizette.>*

The red light under my left lid continued to ache for moments - and then flickered green: *<About bledy time, Mister Graham bledy Mason.>*

Relief flooded me. *She's still pissed off with me. That's something, at least.*

The black electrified gates swung open, to the car's emitted e-password.

Liz waited, arms crossed, gum-booted and dishevelled in loose and dirty clothes, glowering. There was a barrow of carrots next to her – a good looking bunch, so no doubt due to be sent to the neighbouring Imbali

Township Co-op, the ITC, as she's done ever since we moved here, and she started growing our own food.

We pecked cheeks warily, eye contact tentative, and I felt awkward with a complex mix of feelings.

Lizette was a shortish big-boned woman, dark of skin, with wild hair that she had shoved back with a red Alice band. Her black hair was greying quickly, which she flaunted with a twist of her band.

I gave her a furtive glance. Even angry, her brown eyes were lovely. But the anger seemed to have dimmed, she was almost... anxious?

It's not like her to be fearful – with her illness, she'd learned to put her fears into perspective. Nah, I must be wrong. She couldn't be nervous, not Lizzie.

She wheeled the barrow off, to pack the carrots away, in the front garden shed.

I stepped inside and through to the hot sunken lounge, with its big AG ('almost green') Aircon against the far wall.

My presence tripped the air-conditioner switch with a *click*; whirring on. *Ja, an indulgence I know, but I pay my bloody taxes.*

The web portal was tucked away discreetly in the corner as she'd insisted when I'd first installed it for her, but the controls were on red, as if constantly locked, unused.

But she'd sent me that response, just before I arrived.

Sparingly used.

A new decorative screensaver spiralled, a fuzzy grainy floating picture, which was hard to make out, as I walked through to the kitchen to make corn sandwiches for us, and to grab a drink of water.

Liz waited on the single chair when I came back, and she took the plate with thanks, putting it on the side table as if not hungry.

I sat on the couch opposite.

She looked at the floor.

Oh no man, was this going to be another rehash of the argument we'd had before I'd left? "Why can't you demand to stay on local assignments, you've never been able to stand up to Du Preez, blah, blah, blah."

"It looks like the garden's been productive, despite the lack of rain," I said, breaking the silence, but putting my sandwich down, suddenly not hungry myself.

She looked up at me and smiled. "Yes, our solar well-pump has helped."

I smiled back, relieved to see her relax. "A bloody godsend that was, you bringing in a surveyor – you've always had damn good intuition, Lizzie."

She grimaced and stood up, pacing restlessly over to the web portal.

What the hell did I say? Must be the swear words – she hated me swearing, never gets used to it, keen Churchgoer and all – 'bledy' was the worst of it from her, and even that had only arrived, these past few years, along with her illness.

Her dark eyes brimmed with tears when she turned to face me.

She leant against wall and touched the computer screen, the floating screensaver froze and sharpened, beneath the pressure of her fingers.

A little barefooted black girl in a broken yellow grimy dress, looking up at the screen, face taut with pain. And it looked like it had been snapped from the CCTV, on our outside gate.

"Her name's Thandi," Lizette said, "She came here yesterday morning after you left – her tongue was so thick she couldn't drink. She was dying of thirst, Graham. Dying, man, *vrek*, out on her little feet, *true's* God. I didn't know things were *this* bad! She's just seven years old, but I had to dribble the water down her throat; her tongue was almost *choking* her."

"So, you gave her tap water or water from the fridge," I said, standing up.

She shook her head: "*Nee*, Graham, I gave her water from our emergency well supply and called the village Traditional Leader to tell him about it, and to find her mom. There are others like her, just down the *bledy* road, man. I told the Chief's rep – and I said we might share some of our water."

"Ach shit man, Lizzie, you didn't, did you? That's *ours*! Why the hell didn't you ask me first? You've had free access to my head for three years now. And why didn't you return my calls, or let me know you were okay, at least?"

"It's hardly free," she snorted, "I can only hear what you *choose* to tell me. And what would *you* have done and said, Mister Graham Mason?"

She stood up, as tall as she could, as if suddenly sure of herself.

I rumbled on: "I'd have given her water from the fridge and told you to keep quiet about the well. You know we have to keep this a secret for our *own* safety, otherwise we'll be the target of every water bandit and *tsotsi* in KwaZulu-Natal!"

"See, I knew you'd say that, and I hate arguing when I can't see your face. I knew that calling you would end up in a fight again. I'm sorry I ended up saying nothing and worrying you, but I *had* to make this decision on my own. Dumisane is a good man, *hy sal niks se nie*... and there's no way I can live here, with children dying just down the road. No ffff –" She clamped her mouth with her hand and took a breath before releasing it and finishing, through clenched teeth: "No... way!"

Lizette *never* swore – and only reverted to Afrikaans when she was distraught. She crumpled slightly, clutching at herself, sobbing.

The little yellow-dressed girl spiralled randomly across the screen.

Of course... she'd always wanted a little girl too. Mark had never felt enough for her, which had made me feel, sometimes, as if I were not enough for her either.

Anger emptied into a desperate sense of helplessness. I hovered uncertainly, and then stepped forward to coax her to turn *towards* the screen. *Just show her comforting* emoticons *from Love&Peace Dotcom.*

Her eyes froze me, though – her dark, lovely, lined, but still frighteningly fierce eyes.

I knew, with certainty, that if I tried touching her, turning her to face the computer screen, she would scream, and hit and push me towards the outside door and gate.

Beyond that, I could see that there was no returning, in her eyes.

My arms hung in frigid confusion, as tears streamed down her cheeks.

Shit, what else was there to do?

I could only reach out to hold her, awkwardly wrapping my arms around her taut, trembling body.

Her arms were rigid, almost pushing at me for moments, but then she seemed to let go, and the sobs strangled in her throat; her hair was thick and tickly in my face, my own eyes stinging from a sudden bite of emotion.

I smelt the coconut fragrance in her hair and remembered it had been her favourite shampoo, when we'd first met, almost thirty years ago. *Hell man, it must be years since we'd last really held each other.*

Since Mark had left.

<*News of note in,*> said Cyril, switching on the screen behind us, <*I recognise the boy.*>

I let go of Liz and walked towards the screen.

A drone-cam spun downwards onto a human encampment, near a massive stretch of rock-face, dribbling water. *The fucking Vic Falls.*

Smoke obscured the scene for a moment and then it cleared, fire blazing in three of the prefab buildings, people being evacuated, fire-fighters in. *Thirteen dead; their faces scroll along the bottom of the screen.*

"Game-Boy Boy," I said and, for the first time in many years, I wept.

"Come, Graham" Liz said, taking my hand in hers, as I wiped my face with a shirt sleeve.

She pulled me towards the bedroom.

Oh… right, so she's not taking me out to see how the veggie patch has grown.

Dear God, I'd almost forgotten how much of a woman she was.

And, in the end – despite my constant thirst – I wasn't nearly as dry as I feared I might be, either.

I woke to the sound of voices outside. Liz was gone.

I rolled over quickly, pulling on trousers and shirt, making my way through to the front room. The outside door flickered and dallied while it de-armed, as I inserted a taser-rod into my belt, barking at Home Help Harry to tell me who was outside.

<*Your wife and a certified rep from the ITC*> Harry told me, tersely.

The door finally opened.

The mid-afternoon heat poured in, like hot water.

Lizzie leaned against the inside of the gate, back in grubby shorts and shirt; the electric charge obviously deactivated. She was talking to a tall, thin black woman in blue overalls, in rapid and fluent isiZulu.

Liz turned to me, "This is Graham, my husband."

The woman held out her hand through the gate, "I'm Busisiwe Mhlongo, a hydrogeologist for the FreeFlow Corporation. However, I reserve room for a little private freelance work in the services of my local community – strictly off the record, you understand."

"Oh," I said, with an African handshake of palm, thumbs grip, palm again: "Graham Mason, pleased to meet you. And, of course I understand." *Wow, strong grip.*

"Your wife has kindly invited me, through our Chief, to survey the underground water on your land. Of course, *before* the white man, all this land was *ours*, anyway."

"Oh," I said, "Is that a… veiled threat?"

She chuckled: "Don't be so paranoid, Mister Mason, we amaZulu don't veil our threats. It's just an historical observation. Your wife looks out for us, so we will look out for you, too. Are you willing to share your water with us, once I've ascertained how much you potentially have?"

Lizette looked at me. *It's been a while since I'd seen hope in her eyes.*

"This is Africa," I said.

Liz's eyes dropped.

"So yes, in the spirit of *ubuntu*, we will share."

I felt Liz's eyes on my back as I turned to instruct Harry to open the gate. *For you, Game-Boy Boy.*

And for you too, Liz.

The women swept past me, laughing and talking, Busi carried a shoulder bag of equipment. I could tell they were getting along like a shack on fire.

Hopefully not too well.

I wished Liz hadn't told me about that rebellious one-night stand with a woman she'd had many years ago, at Free State Varsity – I'd thought Afrikaners were all strait-laced conservatives.

But Lizzie's always been – different. That's why we're married – ne?

I waited for the gate to close again, as the Office light bleeped on, behind my right eyelid. *Sigh. I need some days off.*

<Hey, where the hell you been? You must upload your video clips from Vic Falls for the day!>

You bastard, Du Preez. I glanced at my watch; it was after four. "Work's over, I'll do it tomorrow."

<You'll do it now! Jeez man, I've heard of sleeping on the job, but you just took the bledy *cake on that one earlier, with your wife.>*

Shit, I must have forgotten to switch Cyril off, swept up in the day's events, and he, he had just... watched?

"Did you?" I asked.

No answer, but he must *know what I'm asking.* "Damn you, Du Preez, cut Office."

<No!> he said; the bastard had an emergency over-ride button. *<We have a problem. Bongani says we have had a sophisticated corporate hack on our files – specifically the ones you're leading on, about water. Someone's after the water data. Watch yourself, boet.>*

"I want danger pay," I growled, reluctantly, "Did you get a trace?"

<It all went back to No One; (gruff laugh); Mister – or Mizz – Fokin' No One. You had any recent contact with water officials from another company?>

No One – at the Falls. Stalin? Who the fuck is that Stalin stunt-double? Recent contact?

I looked at the open door.

The sound of women's laughter floated through.

Could it be Busi – she's about the right build and height – and I may have thought white, when I saw the facemask?

Mizz No One Busi?

Chapter 5
Liz — Carrots, Church and Kill-dozers

Busi laughed, as she closed the well lid, having taken a full reading with her machine sensors. "No, I don't get paid double for working for FreeFlow and ITC. My work for the ITC is pro bono, they are my community, so I pay back with my time and my expertise."

How do I pay back to mine? By going diligently to Church? Is that it? Is that all?

"The Chief tells me you send vegetables to us via volunteers at Maritzburg Town Hall," Busi stood over me, head tilted, as if she were listening elsewhere.

Ah, she must have a Rig too, like Graham.

"Yes," I say, "I try to help a bit."

Graham wandered through, but he looked distracted and irritable. *What's up with him? I'd never expected him to agree to share, but he seems a bit different lately, as if haunted by his job? He must leave that* Meneer *du Preez.*

"Well, it's a shallow aquifer you have here," said Busi, brightly, "Enough for both of you for a good while, but not enough to share further. Thank you both very much for your kind offer, but we will have to look elsewhere, to further supplement our water needs."

Graham put his hands together and bowed.

She's Zulu, not bledy Asian – what is up with him?

Busi looked down at me again, and I suddenly felt both short and dumpy. "Do you want to come with me Liz, to Imbali? It may be that you can help us more – if you have the time, that is?"

"No, she doesn't," said Graham, "She's ill, she can't do much any more."

"I'm sorry," Busi looked shocked.

"Don't be," I said, "Endometriosis. Pelvic pain. No cure, but it won't kill me. I'm not an invalid, Graham, and I've never stopped cooking your food. Yes, Busi, I *will* come with you."

Tired of the ever-shrinking circle of pain – I must push back against this isolation somehow… And no one tells *me what to do any more.*

"But it's a township," Graham protested.

"I will be home before dark," I said, "Or before I turn into a pumpkin. Please help me pack the carrots."

He did as he was told.

Good.

Busi stopped her small, red car near the top of a rise, overlooking Imbali Township.

Brick buildings and shining shanties sprawled for miles, fifteen kays from Maritzburg, pirate cables strutting skywards like giant spiders' webs, hanging over half a million people and rising. The infrastructure here was not just creaking, it had given up the ghost.

On the back seat were three boxes of vegetables, two of which were carrots.

Busi stepped out of the car, waving me out too. She had parked on a curve in the hill, and strutted up to the apex of the hill-road, before pointing around the bend.

I followed more slowly, puffing hard.

Dear God.

There was a line of massive bulldozers, at least thirty or so, electrified, chained and silent, like giant beasts, held on a massive leash. A laser-cordon surrounded the empty machines, their digger maws jagged, like rows of over-sized shark's teeth.

"There's a gentrification order," said Busi, "LeisureLand have been given permission to destroy several of the informal settlements to bring in *affordable* housing and a golf estate. Our view of the plans indicates that not even the Mayor of Msunduzi would be able to afford to live here."

Kill dozers, these, implicated in nine deaths in a slum clearance in the Eastern Cape last year. Their size and restrained power frighten me, lights blinking inside the machines, as if they were conscious.

Busi looked at me, "Land theft, in the name of capitalism. We could use all the help we can get, sister. If you really want to help us, how far would you go – would you step in front of one of these?"

Slowly, I shook my head.

"I thought not. Shall I take you home?"

Again, I shook my head. "No, please let me see the place first – and I want to deliver my vegetables."

Busi laughed. "Fine, carrots and sweet potatoes will do, instead. Let's go."

She headed back the way we had come, before turning onto Fj Sithole Road. The houses were a mixture of the good, the bad, and the even worse.

The community centre, Manaye Hall, had a large wooden cross like the X-men symbol, on a stone plinth outside. "*Madiba* Mandela gave his last speech as a free man here, before the *boere* arrested him near Howick in nineteen sixty-two. *Amandla!*" Busi said, as she parked.

I wanted to say '*awethu*', but I knew it was not my place to do so.

A young boy of about fourteen or fifteen came rushing from the front door, to help carry the boxes inside, swerving around informal market sellers within the parking lot, pedalling the latest interactive *Threedee* blockbusters, graft-phones and 'smileys', sheep-heads cooked to grimacing perfection.

Solar powered stand-brellas with hood fans whirred marginally cooler air across the bleeding tarmac surface. I waltzed behind Busi with a box, the young boy with two.

"We're going solar," said Busi, pointing at the roof, "But I think they fear our growing independence."

Inside, the aircon running from the solar roof tile array, was a refreshing fifteen C cooler; the large room and stage awash with people chatting, drinking, gaming or watching a giant screen football.

Red versus blue, I haven't a clue, as to who was playing who.

The boy followed my gaze, "Liverpool v Everton, Super Saturday game, a local derby in the British Premiership, Missus."

"Ah," I said, none the wiser.

The boy put the boxes down next to a door leading in to a large kitchen, so I put the sweet potatoes on top.

"Lizette!" Busi shouted, beckoning me, from across the busy hall.

I was becoming used to the curious, sometimes guarded glances I received, as I followed the boy pushing a path through the milling space.

Most people were standing, as seating space was limited and generally kept to the periphery of the hall. Fifty-four years past the first democratic elections to end apartheid and white visitors to the townships were still relatively rare – unless medical personnel or foreign tourists, bussed in with weaponised guards during central daylight hours.

Busi called me over to what looked like a reading and writing section; partly cordoned off by a barrier of discarded driftwood, graffitied with literary quotes from local readers and writers.

The biggest letters in blood red across the rough board: MAKING OUR OWN STORIES.

Plastic seats crowded around the round table, which was brimming with phones, tablets, scribbled pieces of paper and the odd yellow paged, dog eared book.

All the seats were full.

Twenty or so youngsters flicked novels and stories at each other across their devices, some also busy perhaps writing the next great African story. One was even painting a cover – or perhaps it was going to be a comic book or graphic novel? *A space rocket on Mars, by the look of it.*

"Pretty cool, huh?" asked Busi. "And this is what they want to bulldoze."

I nodded, feeling strangely frumpy in my loose, brandless white T-shirt – loose enough to hide my hip rolls – and my brown shorts. *Get a grip, Basson, since when were you worried about what you're wearing, for Heaven's sake?*

And what about this poor young thing?

A small girl in a wheelchair perched at the end of the table, unable to squeeze alongside her friends. But she was drawing, in wobbly but determined lines, with coloured pencil crayons.

I stood behind her.

Monster? Or beast?

"That's so beautiful," I said. "What is it?"

A massive snake, maybe, but with a large head and many legs, as if it lumbered on land too, like a hippo.

The girl laughed, but did not look up, tongue sticking out as she greyed in the monster's multiple legs. "Mamlambo," she said, "Goddess of our rivers."

"Very nice," I said, none the wiser.

Busi tapped my shoulder and pointed to a large tan tarpaulin sheet, screening off a section behind the creative desk.

"What's in there?" I asked.

"Come see." She didn't wait for my reply, ducking underneath the awning, to enter the booth.

I followed and gasped.

There were no desks, but the place was littered with wires, circuit boards, screens and a 3-di printer.

And one older man and five youngsters were all busy, dictating and tapping, a couple with old fashioned key boards.

"What games are they playing?" I asked.

An older looking girl, with afro puffs, glanced up at me.

She looked annoyed. "We're busy developing online machine intelligences for our community."

"Sorry," I said, with tingling cheeks, "That stuff looks expensive. Where did you get it from?"

"It's not stolen, if that's what you mean, aunty," said a young boy, busy servicing the printer. "Donations, recycling bins outside IT corporations, making shit ourselves."

Not what I meant. I kept quiet, my cheeks now burning.

Busi smiled, "Welcome to our budding 'Net engineers, Lizzie. And the software, guys?"

"Open source, donations, the Soft Commons," the older girl piped up again. "Now, we just have to build online sentience. Intelligence is surely going to be emergent from both simultaneously distributed and coalesced sources, within dynamic and evolving cognitive architectures. We just need to find the right identity, to draw out of the 'Net."

She paused, to look up at me. "But that's very much a lay explanation, for you, I'm afraid."

Busi chortled, as if trying to choke a laugh.

I left them to it, feeling *much* less intelligent. *Making stories is more within my comfort zone.*

"Now that went well," I said, when Busi joined me at the table, but she just laughed.

The table was noisy, the kids animated.

"*Wanna* go out back for a chat, where we can hear each other?" Busi asked. "The kids here don't need us oldies watching over them all the time."

She must have been almost twenty years younger than me, but who was I to correct her?

'Us' oldies?

'Out back' turned out to be the exterior garden area, straggly brown grass merging almost seamlessly into a small sandpit, and home also to two ramshackle swings, under a plastic awning. Busi sat on one swing and hauled a big cigarette out of her bag, lighting up and inhaling with a sigh. I could smell it was no ordinary tobacco.

"Take a seat, sister," said Busi, indicating the other swing, with the cascading ash from her *zol*.

I stood stiffly and Busi laughed. "Stop scolding me with your face. Our men used to smoke this for courage, before they faced British guns. I might as well scold you, for your sips of communion wine."

I sat tentatively on the neighbouring swing, wondering whether the creaking ropes would snap under my weight. "How do you know I go to Church?"

Busi was pushing herself with her feet and then lifting her legs up, as she swished past, leaving a trail of sweet-smelling smoke. "I thought (puff) all Afrikaners (puff) go to Church."

I dug my heels into the hot sand, refusing to move. "A… stereotype – many of our youngsters no longer go, no matter how hard their parents press and pray for them."

This morning, we were talking about the joys of home foods and cooking from our childhood, today…?

"I'm (puff) smoking a stereotype too – *cough, cough…*" Busi dragged her heels, bringing her swing to a sandy spray stop, having seemingly inhaled a burst of too much smoke. She stubbed out her *entjie* in the sand, leaning forward on the swing, back heaving.

I tried not to inhale or cough, but still felt light headed.

Busi turned to me, with a subdued smile, "So you *don't* go to Church, then?"

I looked down at my feet, I could feel sand gritting inside my shoes.

"Well, I go, because my community expects me to go."

Busi stood up and stretched, "But do you still *believe?*"

I laughed: "I'm too scared *not* to believe. Hedging my bets."

"You know what?" Busi stood in front of me, and I felt very small, on the swing.

"Uh – what?" I asked, in sudden trepidation.

Busi flicked the butt of her *zol* into a nearby Zibi-can and squared up, hands on hips. "Do you know why I decided to trust you, after you looked after Thandi?"

I looked up, unable to make out Busi's face with the sinking sun behind her, slightly reddening her black hair. "No, I don't. Most... white women, would have done the same."

"Ah –" said Busi, "Maybe, maybe not. But most white women would also have bathed her, probably with second hand water, to both clean her – and get rid of her smell. Why didn't *you?*"

I shrugged, "Water in her mouth was what the poor girl needed the most. Anything else would have felt an imposition – a sort of *invasion*, even."

"There you go," Busi held out her hand, "Other white women would have felt some ownership, but you didn't. I like that. I like you. Her *mamma* is very grateful. Come, it's getting late. How about we check on the youngsters – and why don't you stay for a meal and overnight? The roads are less safe with the coming dusk and darkness. And anyway, it's Sunday tomorrow. How are you feeling right now?"

Ah yes, she knew why I retired early from teaching.

The pain. Always the pain.

I've learned to keep it mostly quiet, a background ache in my pelvis that saps me, but I'm no longer going to let it stop me doing what I want to do. *Good old* bledy *endometriosis.*

I hesitated, before stretching my own arm out, towards Busi's grasp.

I was yanked to my feet with unexpected force, almost falling forwards. Laughing, Busi braced me with her left arm. "Not bad, hey? I work out when I can, you never know when you might need it."

Strong. I'm no laaitie. *Her skin is nice to... touch.*

"I'll have to speak to Graham first," I said, but Busi was already heading indoors, calling out the names of the children in the reading group.

It was less noisy inside than it had been earlier, and it sounded like the football on TV had finished.

I smiled to hear the groans of the youngsters, at the reappearance of Busi – sounded like they were doing just fine on their own.

I thumbed my phone on the doorstep, while I still had a signal: "Graham, love?"

He was obviously a lot less fine, being left on his own. He grumbled a bit – and then he told me, he thought Busi was a corporate water spy.

And he wanted me home to cook his supper.

I laughed and ended the call.

Ridiculous, being jealous of another woman. And why don't you get a little taste of what I go through? Often.

Why does he tire me so much?

Sometimes, I've caught myself almost wishing he would go on his trips again.

Busi, on the other hand… I hardly know.

I emptied my shoes of sand.

I'd never spent a night inside a township before.

Imbali – the name itself quickened my heart.

About to step inside to join the reading group, I noticed the graffiti over the doorframe, sprayed in Save Our Water colours: blue, green and gold: STOP LEISURELAND.

Huge predatory cartoon kill-dozers hovered on a black hill, with AMANDLA scrawled over them.

I shivered, despite the heat; unable to say '*awethu*,' even though alone.

Inside, Junior told me Liverpool had won 2-1.

Thandi walked past with what must have been her mother, hand in hand, her mother also carrying a baby, blanket strapped to her back.

Thandi waved shyly.

I smiled at her, but my eyes were seeking out Busi.

It was a strange night.

The sun had set by the time we parked outside a small house with a neat, green themed décor and a solid brick build.

"We don't all live in shacks, you know," Busi said, stepping out of the car.

The dull dry heat was fading fast, the sun gone.

I followed Busi inside. The stone floors were cool, the small lounge with brown chair and couch led seamlessly into an open plan kitchen and short corridor – probably harbouring one bed, one bath, I guessed.

Busi checked the monitor on the kitchen tap: "One point two litres of my daily water allocation left – fancy some tea?"

"Sure," I said, wondering if I could sit down on the couch.

It was a strange night.

The tea was green and fragrant and there were no sirens outside, just the occasional hoot of an owl.

We spoke about education and jobs.

I had been a primary school teacher in model-C schools in Maritzburg, before we'd moved out to a small holding and I took early retirement, exhausted by family, pain, politics and lack of school resources.

During that time, I'd taken up learning and speaking isiZulu, though, despite Graham being content to only learn the odd phrase or two.

"How did you get to be a water engineer, Busi?"

Busi had long since finished her tea, and shifted her weight in the chair. "*Umama* was a seamstress in a local clothing factory, my father was a migrant worker in the gold mines in *Jozi*…"

I waited, feeling the couch creak as it sucked me in, time itself slowing.

"I was a Born Free, though, so I worked like a dog at a Model-C to get into varsity, and to do a degree that I *knew* would most likely get me a job."

"Water is life." I sank further. *Nice. Most chairs just make my pain worse.*

Busi smiled, but in slow motion: "Indeed – and thank you for your offering to help, with sharing your own water."

"Uh –" I felt heavy, tired, struggling to locate my words. "No problem, although Graham took some persuading."

"I – uh – gathered," Busi hesitated, "How are things between you?"

I looked down at the floor for a moment – *Cape Oak wood laminate, mildly scratched.* "Not too bad, but it could be better."

I spoke, without raising my eyes.

"Is it that *shit*, huh?"

Laughter took me by surprise, sending my gaze straight back to Busi. "Well, you're a plain speaker, that's for sure, young woman."

Busi shrugged and took a sip from her *Brenda Fassie* mug, "I may be young, but life still feels too short, to beat around the bush."

Is she saying what I think she is saying? How can I act on a sudden flicker of feeling that seems to be dancing between us? The dominee would not approve. God does not approve. Yet, we are told to be honest.

And perhaps it's not me – could it, could it… be her too?

"Busi," I stuttered, "Um, h-have have you ever – you know, like fancied girls?"

The *Brenda Fassie* mug hovered for a moment – and was then placed firmly down on the table between us. Busi leaned forwards, as if for emphasis, "That's a dangerous question, in my community."

"I'm sorry," I said awkwardly, wishing I could crumple deeper into the couch. "Um – I guess I'll be sleeping right here, hey? Thank you, Busi – it's *so* cosy!"

Busi burst out laughing and picked up the mugs, making her way to the kitchen. "Who said anything about sleeping yet? *I* did consider sleeping there and giving you *my* bed, but I'm too tall for that. It's not even eight, though, and I'm *gonna* make us something to eat. You're not vegan, are you?"

"N-n-no," I said, struggling to get up. "I'm not. Can I give you a hand?"

"Next time *you* can make *me* something." Busi tossed the words over her shoulder, scouting in her fridge. "I know all the save the planet arguments for veganism. Just wish I didn't like meat so much, given it's expensive as shit, with all those carbon farming taxes. Changes made so far, will require continuing sacrifices from everyone, apart from those who have nothing at all…"

We ate together at the small table in the middle of the kitchen, and it was good; chicken and rice and salad, although the green leafy sauce was odd.

"What is it?" I asked.

"*Dagga* cream cheese," Busi said, "It might help you with your pain. Medicinal dagga costs a bomb – but you can try my home-made sauce, for free."

I laughed, in disbelief, but tried a little, nevertheless. *Tangy and granular on the tongue.* "It's – different," I said, ladling on a few more spoonfuls.

And, as the meal and evening wore on, I struggled increasingly to track our conversation, as time decelerated.

Words began to accrete whole universes of meaning.

"So," said Busi, raising a glass, "I see your husband is investigating the parlous state of the world's water."

Why so? What's parlous? "Did he tell you?"

"Not exactly, but there were some printouts on your dining room table, of a fire in Livingstone, and water shortages on the Zambezi."

"His latest trip."

"Did he tell you about it?"

"Not really…" *Giggle. Not funny, surely?* "Why do you ask?"

"I work for a water company. Water is my business. Who holds the water; holds life."

Graham's words came back to me. *Spy?* The word floated away.

"What are you holding right now?" I asked. *It's not a glass any more.*

It looked like me.

"Bedtime, Mizz Basson, you're not able to talk properly. Just moving you, to get a pillow under you."

So soft.

I slept, eventually, on the couch as agreed, but the night stayed long, and filled with peculiar dreams.

It was indeed a strange night.

I remembered owl hoots and the Moon, and drifting between rooms and beams of moonlight, as if a ghost.

The sun woke me, and, for panicky moments, I could not remember where I was.

I smelt coffee.

Coffee with a question.

My bleary gaze took in Busi, busy in the kitchen.

"Morning, sleepyhead," she said. "Did you sleep well?"

"Hello," I smiled, "Um – I had a few funny dreams. They, er – were dreams, weren't they?"

Busi brought me the coffee in an *Yvonne Chaka Chaka* mug. "Have you always walked in your sleep? Twice, I had to take you back to your couch. It's easy to get confused, as to where you are, in a strange house."

"Of course," I said, "That must have been it."

"Your turn to make me a meal," said Busi, "Don't worry – breakfast is easy. I'll show you where everything is."

I enjoyed that.

There were a few bantam hens, in a coop at the back of Busi's garden, from which we retrieved two eggs.

Busi pointed out a large leaved bush, flourishing under her kitchen window. "*Umthunzi wezinkukhu,*" she said, "How is your pain this morning?"

"Better. But I don't know *those* Zulu words."

"It's translated as 'shade of the chickens,' as chickens used to sleep under this bush in many of our households – it's called cannabis in the west, but here it's more colloquially known as *dagga.*"

"Oh!" I said, scrambling eggs with a fork. "But it's harmful, even if legal."

Busi snorted, "Whose laws, huh? Alcohol is much more harmful, but that's okay, it's a western drug. Plants from the east – and the global south – are feared and vilified. The persistence of colonial narratives."

I was annoyed, it felt as if I'd been lectured.

Graham had done that a lot, increasingly, over the years. *Shall I say something to Busi? Just in case this is the start of a pattern? Or am I just sensitised to this, because of Graham?*

"Fried – or scrambled?" I asked. *Too early to say anything more, cultural bridges need understanding first, before one puts any weight on crossing them.*

After scrambled eggs on slightly burned toast, we had some *rooibos* and Five Roses tea.

"Strong, without milk?" checked Busi.

I nodded, counting five missed calls from Graham on my silenced phone. "What do you want out of life, Busi?" I asked, slipping my phone into my tracksuit pocket.

The young woman looked at me, sipping her own tea slowly, with the quirk of a smile on her face. "*Woahhhh*, now that's a *big* question, early on a Sunday morning. What do I want? Sounds like you need to join our Philosophy groups, on Tuesday mornings."

"Yes," I said, inhaling the pungent fumes of my hot rooibos, but fixing my eyes on Busi's face. "What *do* you want out of life?"

"I want our new, first ever woman President, to succeed in her struggle to destroy patriarchy and gender violence. A small ask," Busi smiled, "and I also want it to rain and rain."

"Men – and water – must fall," I said, taking a cautious sip. *Good tea.*

"Amen to that, sister," said Busi.

Amen. Oh nooooo, it's Church again today.

The Church puts a straitjacket on everything – but, it's a straitjacket comfortable in its familiarity. Dare I ask the… question? The one that I had woken to.

And does Busi go to Church?

I hesitated, and, as Busi glanced away, I blurted, "I don't suppose people can like both men *and* women, can they?"

Busi gave me an amused smile, and I looked down, hurriedly. "Why not, *sisi*? At least, then, you're spoiled for choice… So, what do *you* want out of life?"

Phewwww… but what do I want? "To love – and be loved. To live in a fair and just space."

Busi laughed, "You and me both, sister. Not much to ask for, but it's a seriously fucked up world right now, isn't it?"

The small digi-mat on the coffee-table blinked green several times, before the head of an old woman, grey hair cropped close to her dark scalp, mushroomed electronically onto the table.

"Hello, Lizette, I'm Winnie."

I put down my empty cup, "Hello, Winnie. I'm sorry, but I don't think I know you."

Winnie smiled, "I'm Busi's neural Rig. She thought I'd best introduce myself, before you start suspecting her of hearing voices."

How… quaint? Graham had never bothered to introduce me to Cyril.

My phone buzzed again. I glanced down.

Not Graham.

Suzanne, an old friend, texting me about meeting up at Church later.

"I have to start getting ready for Church," I apologised. "Got to rush home to get changed."

"The Gods are coming back," said Winnie, before winking – and vanishing.

"There is only one God," I said, looking at Busi.

"Of course, there is," smiled Busi.

Ever since I could remember – and my parents had started taking me from the age of five – the *Nederduitse Gereformeerde Kerk*, or NGK, had been a dark, austere and intimidating place.

It was still the same, even though I was close to fifty, and this was a new Church, built suitably just ten years or so past, on the outskirts of Maritzburg, not so far from us.

It had felt, at the time like, both Divine Providence and Insistence, given the low numbers of Afrikaners living within KZN.

Graham would never come of course – but then, he didn't even bother to go to an English church either. He always said he preferred praying at home, but there were fewer beers in the fridge whenever I got back, so I believed him less and less.

Suzanne Kleynhans, on the other hand, was both an old teacher colleague, friend *and* someone who remained unstintingly devout to God.

I wish I knew how she did it.

I glanced at her sideways in the pew, all demure in navy blue, greying hair curdled pink – but she was praying, eyes screwed shut, as if afraid to see anything.

The whole congregation stood, as the dark-frocked *dominee* walked down the aisle, his pale hands heavy with The Book.

I had dressed demurely in high buttoned white blouse, grey waistcoat and long grey skirt tapering to flat black boots.

I stood too, with as much holy dread as anyone else in that room, I'm sure, underneath those dark timbers and scolding organ. I felt close to five years old again, when Dominee van der Heever reminded us all to sit, from the dizzying height of his pulpit.

I smiled at the young teenager in starched red dress next to me, on the other side from Susanne.

The young girl leaned forwards to hide the thumbing of her 3 Di cellphone. *Flashing pictures of young men – how times* had *changed, come to think of it.*

The Dominee himself was a young man, with severely clipped black beard and hair, just three months into his appointment. He was opening the Bible with due reverence, yet also slowly enough to ratchet up the anticipatory tension, amongst the craning heads below him.

What's he focusing on today? Romans 1, versus 26 and 27, I don't remember that.

The *dominee's* high pitched voice slightly belied the solemnity of his reading, but each of his words dropped like a cold stone into my stomach.

Not real. Not possible. Misheard him?

But, as the sermon proceeded, I realised I had *not* misheard.

Hard to breathe. The dominee's *vitriolic passion was suffocating me. Even though I didn't want to hear his words, his sentences started to slug me.*

"The sin of a woman lying with another woman will earn the wages of sin… Death… They are an aberration and an abhorrence before the Gaze of God…"

Shit, no. Why is that youngster looking at me through the corner of her eyes? Does she know that I have… feelings stirring? Do they all know? Was this planned for me? Or is this straight from – from, Him?

The words rolled on, but I found my hearing had gone, I could only make out a strained and panting sound. The girl next to me had forgotten her phone and was staring at me full on – I realised it was myself making the noise.

"Lizzie, what's wrong?" whispered Suzanne, on my right.

"And Satan shall both mock and punish them!"

"Enough!" I shouted, the word thrusting me to my feet. "That's, that's fucking enough!"

My words were like a gunshot in the room, echoing outwards.

The *dominee* stopped, startled, raising his head to peer down at me – and I suddenly realised he had been reading a script, all along.

Scripted, rehearsed, cold.

"Enough," I said, aware that all were turning to look at me. *Oh dear, no! There's* Mevrou *Jantjies, Mark's old school teacher, and* Meneer *Bruintjies, IT fixer at Scottsville Mall…*

Susanne took my right elbow, "Lizzie…" she hissed, as if in warning.

But I could not stop.

"Enough hate!" I said, my words struggling through sudden sobs, "And why's it still so *white* in here? What about the dying children on our own fucking doorsteps?"

There was another loud gasp. *No, stupid, stop gabbling, you've said too much. Go. Gotta go, can't handle this. Stop staring, stop looking at me.*

I pushed past Suzanne, rushing down the aisle to the main doors leading out, wondering why it was in agonisingly slow motion – a*nd what would that bloody youngster do, with the phone video she was making of me, right now?*

I exited fast and face first, into the dulling evening heat of a sinking sun – but it felt like my back was burning up, with the full weight of social disapproval.

Suzanne did not follow me out.

I drove home, alone.

Graham was ostensibly waiting for me, but he was busy watching a *skop, skiet* and *donder* movie. I caught a glimpse of the screen and shards of flying glass as I came in through the door – probably 'Die Hard' – 23 or 24? The lead was played by the Nigerian Nollywood version of Bruce Willis, Tom Ekubo.

Graham put the *fliek* on pause and looked up, "How was Church?"

I sighed. *A routine weekly question, spoken without thought, or much interest. Still, asked, at least.*

I put my taser on the rack and turned to him. "I told the *dominee* to fuck off."

Graham switched his favourite movie series off.

So, it begins…

Chapter 6
Art – Lead Babies and Storm-Flying

Tuesday, Tuesday.
A call from Rosemary Carruthers, our Director – and when she calls, you go running.
Up two flights of stairs.

The door of the office slid open, revealing the Director's huge window view, always cool and green, overlooking a well-hosed nearby golf course.

The air was dark and hazy, though, due not so much to the heat as to imago-cloaks: airborne nanobots that coalesced to create a screen, as if protecting the golfing estate from external scrutiny.

The Director stood with her back to me, her gaze firmly fixed at a point beyond the wall surrounding the golf course, as if she could see past its screen of microscopic, airborne robots.

"Come in, Green," she snapped, without turning around. "Tardy as usual. Get your big ass over here."

"I've lost three pounds since I was last here," I gasped, making my way towards her. Normally, for the sake of my health, I climbed the two flights to her office, usually arriving sweating and out of breath.

She never seemed to notice, however.

The EPA Director, or Big Dee, as Carruthers was also known, was a tall, thin woman, with square shoulders, as if she'd been a swimmer, or a man, at some point.

My money – had I been a gambling man – would have been on swimming.
Swimming scares me.

"Come in, Green," she snapped, without turning around. "Stand next to me. I don't bite."

I made my way around and past the Director's big oak table.

Carruthers was an inch or so taller than me, in flat no-name trainers and a white, smart-silk suit that regulated her external skin temperature.

Cool if you had the bucks for it. *Only way I'd get that sort of money is by some freakishly lucky gambling, or by finding that Deep Ocean seepage, with its huge prize. Too bad I don't believe in luck. It's sweat of my brow; till the day I die. Unless the Good Lord decides otherwise.*

As I stood by the Director, I saw why she hadn't turned around.

She had a digi-scope clipped to her nose, and was staring through it, to the landscape beyond. The walls of a rich golf estate, abutted to the left and centre of the open Communal Space, before the massive Central Gate in the wall between North and South.

The Wall Gate was shut, so I assumed she was trying to peer into the golfing estate, *through* the nano-cloud.

She muttered instructions to the device under her breath. In response, a green light flashed on the crook of her nose, indicating that the scope had adjusted its range, or material penetration.

"For fuck's sake, Theia," the Director said, more loudly, "that's worse. I need higher rez and decreased magnification, not the other way around."

Theia was the Director's Rig, named after her partner of many years standing. Or so Suraya had told me.

I had never seen Carruthers's smile. Her face was lined and sharp, etched with sixty-plus years of permanent annoyance, except when she was reciting poetry. Finally, she turned and looked at me.

Sort of.

"Is that you, Green? I can't see for fuck, with this so-called Sight Goddess on the end of my frigging nose."

"It is me, Director," I affirmed, peering at hazy movements on the golf course. *What* was *she trying to see?*

The rich Wallites had put in yet another planning application to raise the internal community walls higher, for large private estates, but so far, the municipality had resisted, citing the need to keep the city socially integrated. The Community Planning Act of 2031, that was – designed to minimise inequity and inter-factional urban disintegration.

"Have a seat, Green." She unclipped her scope and placed it in her desk drawer, sighing. *"something there is, that doesn't love a wall[1]."*

"Pardon?" I asked.

"Never mind – you and your little team have caused quite the stir up at the Fresno Water Centre. Got me an irate call from the FreeFlow Director – he happens to be two stories *above* me, if you get my fucking drift?"

I nodded – I understood hierarchies all too well – and that I was clearly the bottom feeder, skulking in the basement of the massive twelve story NorthCal Water Conglomerate.

"We got the Agrics over us, the water companies above them – and you know what's all the way up on the top goddamn floor, don't you?" The Director skewered me with her green-eyed stare, from across the desk.

I nodded, miserably. She'd sent me up to the top once, three years ago, when I'd challenged the legality of a water siphoning activity I'd picked up

---

[1] Robert Frost (1914), 'Mending Wall' in *North of Boston*. David Nutt

from the largest of the WC's, FreeFlow. The entire top floor was devoted to computing, 1st Gen. AI's, and lawyers, all arguing loudly over Californian water rights, both ancient and modern.

It had been like entering the Tower of Babel.

I'd had my five minutes back then, with a State lawyer called Jenny Johnson who worked on the top floor, a middle-aged, tired and pale woman with prematurely greying hair, who took it upon herself to explain exactly how hard litigating against FreeFlow would be.

"Leave it with me," Johnson had finally told me, "and come back in ten years and see if I've gotten anywhere. Assuming this job hasn't killed me by then."

At first, I'd smiled, thinking she was joking, but she had stared back at me, with a poker face.

I'd left in a hurry.

"It's a fucking legal black hole up there," the Director said, "Let's not sweat the small stuff, huh? In these shitty times, *everyone's* a bit dirty. So, they're massaging the figures a bit – let's give them a five percent leeway before insisting we trigger Level 5 restrictions, okay? Some of our rich patrons – whom shall remain unnamed – are partial to a game of golf, so, unless you catch someone taking a massive dump into our main water supply, we're cool, you get it?"

I got it. Golf was special. Why?

The world is full of weird shit.

The Director looked at me and sighed, "Sorry I called you a big ass, Art. You do realise we live in a fragile place, where I'm doing my best to herd cats, to look after what little is left of our natural world – and there's some big frigging tigers out there – and you *do* know I'm not talking about the extinct animals from India, here."

I nodded. "Tigers who play golf."

The Big Dee laughed. "Smart man. Oligarchs are not just Russian. Do you know the demographics of the remaining few climate denialists in America?"

I shook my head. Generally, I preferred numbers over people.

"White conservative men – the richer they are, the more they deny. Blowing off hot air, all to make it seem as if it's still a debate, and to fug the atmosphere and obscure reality. Sartre would have said they live in bad faith. They have grown fat on killing the world – mind you, hashtag not *all* white conservative men."

I smiled and quoted a relevant senator, "It's all just an extended run of bad weather."

She smiled back, a real to God smile, but shifted the topic. "What do you know about Game Theory, Green?"

I shrugged, peering over the Director's shoulder, as glistening drops in the air over the golf estate wall began to shine, turning into a glinting mass of nanoparticles.

The Director smiled, "It's on the hour, isn't it? I can feel by the heat on my back, the other side of the wall are giving me the finger again. Watson and Co."

I stood, as the particles from the golf course congealed into a floating mirror, bouncing a beam of blazing sunlight into the Director's office.

The Director lifted her right fist, middle finger extended, high above her head. "Let your cam-bots take a picture of that," she said. "A bird for Birdy!"

The mirror dissolved.

"Look up the Prisoner's Dilemma in Game Theory, Green, and tell me how we can get people – on opposite sides of a wall – to make sacrifices and co-operate for a better, but perhaps more equally frugal, deal together. We need to keep reeling in the carbon and water, but also bring the richest with us too."

I nodded and left the office; but this time, I took the elevator downstairs, welcoming the malodorous whiff of heat and the body odour of my two colleagues, as the door opened at the bottom.

"Well?" asked Zeke, looking up from water quality graphs.

Suraya had just come out of the toilet.

"We got a rap on our knuckles for doing our job," I said.

Zeke turned back to their screen, "All's well with the world, then."

"And I've been asked to figure out how to stop walls getting bigger."

"Now *that's* one hell of a task," said Suraya, "I'll stick to analysing bio-chemical composites of the San Joaquin delta flow, thank you very much."

Coming home is a long and lonely business.

I'd learned to avoid Hope Street and the ICE centre, for processing SouthCal immigrants. There had been several brutal beatings of non-white passers-by, but no one had ever been caught, despite the sensors on display. An extra half-hour to my walk, but the lack of bruises and broken bones was worth it.

Here we are.

Home.

Open door with thumb print on plate.

Step inside and look down narrow corridor into kitchen, still reeking of Hop-Tarts Kwik-Kook Breakfast. (Usually blueberry and lime cheesecake.)

Glance into empty double-bed room with cot (to be dismantled coming weekend.)

Enter kitchen and sigh at grime on two plates in sink, soaking in minimal water and detergent.

Make weak coffee and stand, cup in hand, staring out window over rooftops – tenth floor single room apartment – towards dust storms looming ever larger south of the Water Wall, as dusk deepens.

Realise solitary silence smells like stagnant water on dirty plates.

I jumped, as the screen jangled from the bedroom, a latest Grit-Funk tune Gen had loaded for me, by The Empty Assholes, 'Seeking Solace'.

My heart crunched, as Gen blinked Michelle's name.

Long time, wife.

Scary long.

"Three years, Art, almost three years since we last talked." Michelle's dark face had hardly altered in those three years, I noted, more crow's feet around her brown eyes perhaps… but I knew better, than to mention those.

Keep it straight. Simple. Civil.

"Why didn't *you* call me?" I asked, peering behind Michelle's looming visage, to see if Sally was there. All I could see was an empty couch, strewn with clothes and a small soccer ball.

Is Sally of an age to play now? What is she like?

Michelle's snarling face brought me back to the conversation. "Because I told *you* to call *me*, I've *always* called you first – or did you forget… *again*? Three fucking years, Arthur!"

Simple failed; try diversion.

"How's Sally?"

Michelle stopped mid snarl, and her face softened, momentarily. "She's growing quickly, she asks about you. Too much, given you're not here and never call. Not even on her birthday, you creep."

How old is Sally again? How can I hide the fact I don't remember my own daughter's age? "She's playing soccer, I see – which team does she play for – or is she with the older girls?"

Michelle sighed and flicked beaded plaits out of her face. "You've forgotten how old she is, haven't you? Jesus, Art, for a smart man you sure can be dumb. She was three when you left and four when you last spoke to her. Do the maths, Einstein."

"Don't take the Lord's name in vain."

"Is that all you can say – after three fucking years?"

I hesitated, aware where some of her anger, at least, might be coming from. It was always there – well, since Sally had been born, an event that had brought a cloud of fear, rage and anger over *that* trauma, the obstetrician dangling a blue, momentarily limp body – a cloud that had never fully dissipated.

"How – how is she? How's school been? And, where is she?"

Michelle grimaced, "She's okay. Settling in, she's turned out not as bad as I feared, managing the work, mostly, which is a relief. The lead in her body seems to have damaged her gross motor functioning, mostly, so they tell me. She's certainly not going to be in any soccer *team*, at least, not anytime soon. School also tires the shit out of her, though, so she's already asleep for the night."

Water, bringer of life, if you looked after her, and treated her properly. *Otherwise, things like Flint (IV) in Newest Orleans happens. Forty-five thousand children, all from mid to lower socio-economic status. You get what you can afford to pay for. Bronze level water supply; laced with lead.*

Even alone, I had been unable to afford a move up to a Silver supply, here in NorthCal.

"I'll send a vid to her – please send me a recent picture of her. Alimony's still going through, isn't it?"

"Yes," Michelle said, "I need a raise, it's been three fucking years, Art."

"I know, you've told me that more than once." I put my cold coffee down, on the bedside table. "So, Sally turns eight in two months and twenty days' time."

Michelle's strong jaw sagged briefly – the cam was catching her from the neck up. She flicked beads from her dangling braids out of her face again; blue, white and gold. "You remembered her birthday, but sent her nothing?"

I hesitated, afraid of saying it.

The res on my new screen was almost holo-perfect, I saw her sharp eyes narrow. I missed her fierce, uncompromising gaze, almost as much as I feared it, too.

"Art…?" She stared hard as she spoke, drawing my name out, as if trying to suck out my unspoken words.

She knows how much I struggle with stares.

I dropped my gaze, peering momentarily at the brown wooden floor, then flashing my visual focus across to an old e-photo, hanging half-obscured behind my cupboard. It was a picture of me holding my daughter on my hip, aged two, the small girl's eyelids drooping, as if hiding unseen, internal damage.

Sally had not said a word by then, just drooled and babbled, with poor and painful control.

Say it. Break the spell.

"I have nightmares," I said, "The week before, and the week after, her birthday. On the day itself, I'm allowed off work, when I stay in bed, doped up with PTSD meds, while Gen counsels me." *And crazy images circle of the obstetrician hanging the dead baby from a machine, while leaded saliva drips from our girl's flaccid blue tongue, in her silent gaping mouth.*

I could not look at the screen; Michelle's face was a vague and brown smear. "Why have you never said anything…?"

Always afraid giving voice to this would makes it even stronger – and for me to be weaker. "I'll call you on the weekend after Church. I want to say hello to Sally. And why have you called me now, Michelle?"

"You used to remember today, at least. When we were together, anyway."

November the 8th.

"I'm sorry," I said, "Happy fortieth birthday, Michelle."

She did not smile; but peered closely at me. "Just talk, Art, that's all I ever wanted – just tell me stuff, even if we're not together any more. Let your walls down a bit."

The screen went blank.

I stumbled through to the washroom, finding toilet paper to dab onto my stinging eyes, involuntarily holding my breath. In the kitchen, I washed the plates and coffee cup in a shallow bowl of water, a bowl just deep enough to remove the morning's shit, when I tossed it down the toilet.

Damn the expense and shortage of water.

I rinsed my closed eyes under a running tap, if only for five seconds.

Running water smelt like being noticed, like caring and being cared for.

Five minutes later, after sending my video for Sally through, I needed another dose of tap water.

Is this letting 'walls' down even more? What are my walls here for – protection – and pride?

This time, though, it took a full minute of eye washing, catching three bowls and a jug, as a by-product. Two days' worth of toilet flushing were stored under the kitchen table.

Letting walls down is sore and costly. What's the gain?

Sleep took a long time coming; my bed felt too big, too empty.

Even now, four years after leaving Louisiana.

Wednesday, Wednesday, the scheduled day before Dust-Strike.

During my lunch hour, I walked from the Water Tower to the Wall – *time to view the brewing storm, before it struck the city, sometime tomorrow.*

I'd always believed in the need to face your problems, even if you could only manage to do so, on occasions.

I'd walked the route onto the Top of the Wall several times before. I'd even taking youngster Sally on my back-buggy one weekend, to show her the Valley view, still some months before the Big Fight and their leaving me alone here, to return to their Newest Orleans apartment.

The streets were busy with bikes, cars and trucks, mostly electric, driverless, ferrying goods across to the High Street and 'burbs of Hydro-City, readying the town to batten down.

The roads and sidewalks were gritty with ill swept dust, the cleaner bots struggling with the growing storm load brewing from the South. The occasional petrol fart from an illegal gas-guzzler burned my nose with acrid fumes, and I readied my mask and goggles.

The Wall loomed above me, as I walked down Boundary Avenue. One hundred feet of Smart-stuff, rock hard but impregnated with sensors that scanned your ID implants within twenty feet of approach, electrified on the south side to halt *Dusty* refugees.

I was always relieved when Gen blinked safe green on my wrist, I'd heard the stories of illegals from 'Angeles being charred, for failing to stop on the other side and carrying no protective tags, to indicate due authority.

The road came to a stop at Viewing Elevator Three – one of only two elevators with an unsealed viewing dock – Boundary Avenue turning right along the Wall, to the busier Central Gate of the town, one of the few official entry points between north and south Cal.

The solar elevators were used sparingly now – most people had tired of the view south; so much could be seen digitally, and without even moving a muscle.

Someone had painted MAW in red, on the silver lift door – Make America White again.

I sighed, as Gen called the lift.

I always preferred to see things myself, however awful the view.

I strapped on mask and goggles in preparation. The elevator door opened, revealing just one old woman of medium height, but stooped in her dust-brown overall, thick greying hair bunched into a *scrunchie* behind her head.

I stepped aside to let her pass, but she beckoned me in, her voice filter strangely deep and masculine. "Thank you, sonny, but I think I'm going to take another look. The view might be different with someone to share it with, know what I mean?"

I groaned, fighting to stop it leaking into my voice filter, "Sure, ma'am." *I prefer alone. Please just keep quiet, okay. I want to look and not feel the pressure to talk. Least of all, to a weird old woman.*

The short ride to the top was silent; I glanced at the legal disclaimer against any injuries or illnesses incurred at the top.

The woman had turned her back, so that she was facing the exit door, ready to leave first. I stood at a respectful distance behind her, twiddling with the air nozzles on my cheek flaps, leads clipped to a small oxygen canister strapped to the crook of my neck.

Glancing across to the woman's neck, I noticed that tying her hair back had caused the leads to her canister to hang loose, disconnected.

The elevator door opened, and I placed my hand on her left shoulder before she could step out. The wind whipped in momentarily, carrying a stinging blast of dust. "Seal door," I said.

The woman turned to me. It was hard to see her eyes through refracted goggles. "What's up, sonny boy?"

"You're disconnected at the back," I said, "Don't know how long you were planning on staying up there, but you'd have some difficulty breathing."

Without a word, she turned around and I clipped the leads together, with some struggle. I'd never been great with motor-co-ordination myself, either, getting jokes from the jocks at high school about my lack of sporting prowess, *despite* being brown of skin.

I'd handed them their asses in school work though.

"Thank you," said the old lady, "Open door."

The wind and sand whipped in again, despite the gauze filters erected at the front of the viewing dock.

We stepped onto the secured section at the top of the wall, large enough for ten, with hand rails to cling to, the filters sifting the worst of the dust from the wind.

I shivered.

It got me every time.

Over three hundred massive miles of Super-State Wall, stretched east to west and ripping the state in two, above the counties of San Bernadino, Kern and San Luis Obispo.

The Central Valley and the long-contested Kern Water Banks were below, but hidden in a dark and twisting cloud of dust, scouring the valley floor of soil, leached dry of any binding moisture.

I was strangely relieved not to see the parched and empty earth, a former green and lush valley, burned in cascading wildfires that had left it bereft and dead, empty of almond trees and grape vineyards – this dark cloud *moved* at least, showing signs of life and energy.

"Do you know what this reminds me of?" The old woman croaked.

No. I don't care either. Just look at what is here, stop distracting yourself with words. Words just hide the moment.

"Black Sunday – The Oklahoma Dust Bowl, and the Grapes of Wrath."

"No grapes here – even the Almond King has gone – but it looks like plenty of wrath," I said, for want of anything better to say.

"Mine eyes have seen the glory of the coming of the Lord. He is trampling out the vintage, where the grapes of wrath are stored," said the old woman.

Am I back in Church? A vast church indeed. The circling storm is itself a wall, but far, far higher than the one we stood on, rearing up into the height of the sky, slowly moving across to blot the sun.

Gen burned a red warning into my wrist, but I failed to respond.

I watched four or five human shapes further along the wall, sticky boots enabling them to stand on the jagged shards spiking the apex of the wall, on the other side of the safety fence.

They shifted from boot to boot, flapping their arms excitedly, to reveal winged flying fox suits of various designs and colours.

Storm-chasers prefer broadcasting live, from within and above, nowadays.

A sixty percent eventual death rate, though, for storm flying. Semi-legal, but hard to enforce. FDT (Flying Death Hits) was a popular online site…

Not for me, though.

The wind was buffeting, turning into a painful sand blaster.

Surely the Storm hasn't arrived already? It's not due to strike until around nine tomorrow morning.

"People are dying in the refugee camps we can't see down there," said the woman. "They could have been offered shelter, this side of the wall."

Yes, but people die this side of the wall too. Owww, the wind is becoming wicked.

I turned to look at the old woman, goggles scoured by sand, both of us clinging tenaciously to the safety rail.

"Shit!" said the old lady, "Elevator – open."

We were flung inside, by the first blast of the breaking storm.

"Yeeee – haaaaaa!" came screams from outside, as the sky-riders took off.

The door sealed, heading rapidly down.

I lay, groaning, winded.

The old woman was sitting up, having unclipped her mask. She started laughing. "Now that was fun – shall we do it again?"

The woman was clearly psycho.

The elevator opened, and she was gone.

But, before I could step out, a face hung before me – a seamed middle-

aged male face, three carcinoma spots on his thick neck. <*Accidents happen,
Green. Ease up; or watch your back.*>

Wind whipped inside, blasting through the fading face.

Hologram hacked into elevator projectors?

I stumbled out quickly, as Gen hailed a Robo-Cab to get me home.

As the cab pulled up, I glimpsed the woman's shape, disappearing into
the dust storm furiously funnelling down Boundary Avenue.

"Get me home," I said, stepping inside, "but follow that old woman,
and pick her up first."

"What old woman?" asked Cab-Bot #449, "There's nothing on
sensors?"

Above me darkness raced, howling.

I shivered.

For a briefest flash, I could have sworn the bot's steel face was Birdie
Watson.

I coughed, and sneezed grit out of my nose.

The storm was here, earlier than the numbers had said.

Numbers alone are not enough.

Above and behind me, there was only dust and darkness.

Chapter 7
Graham – Water Jockey

Darkness had long descended by the time Liz got home from Church and told me what she had shouted at the pastor.

"You said *what* to the *dominee?" Has she lost her fucking mind? Stay calm,* boet, *it's more than* that *time of the month, for sure.*

Liz looked calm enough. Standing at the top of the steps before the short drop into the lounge, all smartly suited in severe grey, with a skirt long enough to hide her knees and black boots, clothes at least respectful of where she had just been.

Her wild hair was corkscrewed back into a tight bun and her face was serene.

Must have heard her wrong?

More slowly this time, less heated. "What – did – you – say – to – Dominee – Van – Der – Heever?"

"Well, it was for everything that was being said, truly. Fuck – off!" She dragged the two words out, as if in calm mockery of my own question?

I don't remember her swearing like this before.

I sighed, wondering if I should just put 'Die Hard 33' back on again. No pressure watching a screen, just people being killed, in diverse ways. Listening to what lay behind Liz's outburst would be hard and long – and messily *ingewikkeld.*

I was tired of complicated.

Liz turned, as if heading up to bed.

I knew that turn. *No chance of sex, probably for another long, long time – she looks calm, but still probably deeply pissed inside. What's set her off so?*

"Make you some *rooibos?*" I walked across to the kettle, without waiting for a reply.

Slowly, she stepped down the three steps.

I stirred the tea bag hard.

Liz always liked it strong, without milk.

I walked back into the lounge, to find her sitting in the chair opposite my couch, where I had sprawled out, with crisps having spilled from my stomach onto the floor.

I gave her the mug and swiftly scooped up most of the crisps.

She glared at me – the nearest bin was back in the kitchen, so I shoved the crisps into my right shorts pocket.

They gave off a crunching sound, as I sat down on the couch.

"I do your washing too," she said sweetly, taking a cautious sip of the still hot tea. "Despite my illness, I clean your shorts."

"Thank you, dear," I said, "But what on earth made you swear at the *dominee?*"

She took another sip, as if unsure how to answer.

"What happened? What did he do – or say?"

"He was – he was – angry and abusive towards gay people."

What? What the fuck? "Uh – nothing new in the Church, most of the Churches are still backward on gay rights, the NGK are never going to be any different. They supported *apartheid* with Biblical texts, for Christ's Sake. But you already *know* this, Lizzie."

"Yes," she said, "The English churches too, you know. But it was worse hearing it today – there's so much real badness and pain in the world to be concerned about, so why are they adding to it?"

"Churches, smurches. That's another reason I don't go to Church," I grinned, trying to lift the mood, "We can always do something together instead? I've caught you watching Tom Ekubo out of the corner of your eye, pretending to be on your phone."

I laughed, showing her it was a good-natured joke, even about her interest in another man, *and* I was not jealous.

Slowly, she put her half-finished tea down, and stood up, kicking off her shoes. "That's all in *your* head, not mine, mister. I think it's *you* who fancies Tom, actually. Me, I prefer girls."

She turned and stalked up the stairs.

I heard the grind of the bedroom door as it locked.

What. Did. She. Say.

Seriously? Seriously?

Was she a… lesbian? Couldn't be, we'd had sex a gazillion times, and even had an adult son to prove it. What the fuck had happened to her?

I got another beer out of the fridge, hands shaking.

Fluffing a pillow, I stretched back out onto the couch. *Gonna be a long night. Might as well watch* Die Hards…

But when Tom Ekubo burst into the scene, biceps rippling through his tight T-shirt, I had to switch the television off, feeling strangely uncomfortable.

"Lights out," I growled.

In the dark, I seethed. *She's fucking ruined* Die Hard *for me. How can I watch it now, after what she's said? What's up with her? Is this just a fucking Mid-Life Crisis?*

I emptied the beer, suddenly exhausted.

I placed the bottle carefully under the couch, where I would not trip over it, if I needed to go for a piss in the night.

Lie back, get some sleep. Du Preez has called you in to the office tomorrow. What did that little shit want with me? 'Play me some light noughties pop, Cyril.'

Sleep drifted in slowly, through the fog of beer, Minogue, and marital fear.

Growing dimly uncomfortable on my left, I rolled onto my right side.

A loud crackling noise jolted me awake.

"Fucking... fucking crisps!" I shouted at the dark, and the locked bedroom door nearby.

No one answered me.

"Hell, *boet*, you look like shit – what the *fokin'* cat drag in, man?"

Du Preez in the flesh was a small, sallow man with a foul mouth, and an even fouler temper. I was used to tiptoeing on the egg shells that the man seemed to unconsciously sweat out of his pores, with his miserly office Air-Con, barely keeping below thirty Celsius.

"Nice view," I said, looking down onto the Durban Beach-Front, from six stories of the Net-Zone Building.

The beach area and water were packed as usual – whatever day of the week, or time of year – with police drones whirring above the heaving crowds, keeping vigilant, like so many shiny dragonflies.

I couldn't see the 'whitening' of the crowds that some local black people had complained about – sure, water in this area of the city was super-expensive, but it still looked like a good number of blacks could afford these rates too. The bot police on the ground were taking no chances on trouble, though.

"*Ja*, I know it's a nice view, you say the same *fokin'* thing every time." Du Preez stretched behind his desk, obscured by upwards of twenty screens of various sizes; tracker pigeons, raking in digital money.

He's old fashioned, a 2-di man.

"Would you believe it, still no rain at the Vic Falls, hey, some *fokin' dief* has stolen the rains."

"It's called Global Boiling," I sighed, standing and straddling my legs apart on the other side of the desk. I always tried to make use of my larger size, I felt so disempowered in all other areas.

"Got a new job for you – your Big Brrreak, sets you up good for another decade, *ek se*. Your *lieflike vrou* will be super-chuffed for you, man."

"Leave Lizzie out of this – and no more watching us, okay?" I flexed my feet, as if this time I were seeking egg shells, on which to stomp.

Du Preez looked away, "Okay, man, I promise – hah, that'll save me five *fokin'* seconds of my own life, tops."

I sighed, "So tell me – what is it?"

Du Preez's scraggly black hair was greying and untidy, but there was nothing untidy in the smooth way he leaned forwards on his chair, clasping his hands in front of his screens. I could see the sharp man's eyes scanning the screens, storing information, keeping tabs on his workers. I knew the man was not distracted, not one little bit.

"First, you sit."

"I'm not your dog," I said, sweating, "What's the job?"

"Sit." Du Preez refused to look up, but the knuckles on his interlocking hands whitened.

I sat.

Du Preez smiled, but I also knew there was nothing happy or funny in his expression. "Right – your job is to catch me that thief."

"What thief?"

"The one who's stealing the water, man. You ride the water where it takes you, as long as you catch me that *fokin'* thief who's stealing it. You're the *fokin'* water jockey. Must be that hacking bastard No One."

"I told you. It's just climate change," I said, "I can't interview the climate."

Du Preez shook his head and took a box of his favourite mini mints from his top drawer. He put three in his mouth and flicked the tin between the screens towards me.

I caught it.

The imperial *mints. Okay, so now we're getting down to it.*

"The Syrian War in the late teens – water shortages and farmers with nothing left, joining the resistance to Assad. ISIS captured a dam for *fokin'* water terrorism, and to taunt their enemies with thirst. Rio, then Cape Town Day Zero. That was just the start – the World is full of small water wars, *boet*, and I want you to get me those stories, before they escalate and *fokin'* leave us a planet dead of thirst. Who's winning these wars, who's taking our water, and who's leaving shit for the rest of us, hey?"

Du Preez rarely gave speeches, but when he did, they were always with full passion, conviction and invective.

He separated his hands and snapped his fingers, inviting me to flick his box of mints back to him, through the sprawl of screens.

I stood up and walked around the desk to hand him the box, defeated.

"And if, behind it all, it's just an act of God?"

"Then you *fokin'* interview God Himself, get me?"

I did. "What's my pay?"

"Add a nought onto usual rates," Du Preez fished another three mints out of the tin. "Officially five times, unofficially ten."

Ten times my usual fee, half of it undeclared and untaxed – that could set us up very nicely for a good, long while… well, as long as Liz and I were still an 'us'?

"Travel?"

"Fully paid, of course, there's *gonna* be a shitload of it."

"Lizzie won't like that," I said, backing away.

This time Du Preez glanced up at me, chewing hard. "Jesus, *boet*, who's wearing the trousers, who's bringing home the *fokin'* bacon here, hey?"

"She still won't like it," I frowned.

"Don't worry none about your missus. We will keep a safe eye on her. As for you, you can always go back to accountancy."

I grimaced. The bots and software had displaced me. Du Preez was just taunting me, a gloating comment, revealing the grip he had on my short and curlies.

A hum in my right ear and a flicker of movement, spun me around to the window. A small drone hovered, camera flashing, 'Du Preez Industries' painted on its carapace.

"Start in the divided states of America – the Yanks are always a good place to begin. And remember, Little Brother is watching you all the *fokin'* time, okay?" And with that, Du Preez laughed and laughed, as if unable to stop.

Choke on your fucking mints. I left the room, wishing for fresh air.

On my way out, I nodded at the PA and gave Bongani a wave, through his open door.

Bongani Dlamini, Chief Technical Officer, had a small room off the Du Preez Industries main reception, a room scattered chaotically with electronic material, holo-pads and 3 Di mats.

Bongani caught my wave from the corner of his eye, swivelled on his chair and gestured me to stop, and come in.

I leaned against the open door, watching him fiddle with a small holographic display. "Did you get much joy with my Vic Falls footage, Bongani?"

The snappily dressed man – he always wore a long navy-blue apron to protect his collared suits and trousers – looked up at me with a terse smile. "Transposed some footage from the Zambian floods a decade ago and managed to engineer convincing and compatible res – Stanley did eventually buy it. In the end, *everything's* fake, isn't it?"

"Uh – good job," I said, suddenly depressed. *Like that tourist pretending to see those elephants,* ja – *but does that principle apply to relationships too? Was I really married?*

Bongani was obviously brilliant, though, he always made me feel even more inadequate, watching him work his technical wizardry. Du Preez had grudgingly mentioned to me, on several occasions, how lucky he was to have enticed the smart software engineer from a rival *Jo'burg* firm.

"That's the easy stuff," he went on, "Now, the *really* interesting stuff, is working on identifying AI's emerging from the nodes and soup of the 'Net – a few even seem to be Zulu, as if also being fed by the shades of our ancestors. Who are they? What do they want? How much are we humans behind them?"

I said nothing. *Okay, no need to show off.*

But he was obviously on a passionate roll. "I've been checking most likely emergent AI sites. Not from corporate or University centres – but the streets. And not just any streets, but *township* streets. How amazing is that?"

"Woohoo," I said.

He glanced at me sidewise, hesitated, but then asked, as if taking a plunge. "I was wondering where Du Preez is sending you next, Graham?"

"First stop, the Federated States of America," I said, "And it's Mister Mason to you, not Graham."

Bongani looked up, as if astonished for a moment, but then flashed his teeth, "Well then it is *Doctor* Dlamini to you, PhD Wits… not Bongani. So, you'd best skedaddle right on out of here, *pardner*. Yee-haaa!"

He bent his head, to resume his tinkering.

Too smart by half.

But, as I was about to leave the room, he piped up behind me. "By the way, new software for Cyril and others, means employers get to watch you, without your knowledge."

I turned.

Slowly.

"What do you mean?"

He did not even look up. "Check the small print in your new contract. They pay us, they own us, the bastards. Office off, may only *look* like office off."

I scowled at Du Preez's PA as I left the room, a young black woman dictating with a barely concealed smile, no doubt having overheard our brief, verbal interchange.

The lift, at least, was quick and servile.

As I stepped onto the busy beach-front promenade, dodging tourists and Zulu rickshaw riders, my sense of depression began to coalesce heavily into my churning gut.

Liz had agreed to meet to talk and I'd booked a lunch table at her favourite spot. I liked eating there too, but I'd lost my appetite, and had never been great at talking. Add in the potential topic of gay sexuality, and I was looking forward to this conversation, like a hole in the head.

<Don't be late!> Cyril relayed a message in my ear.

I did not need to ask whom it was from.

It was a long, long drive to Midmar Dam.

Security was even tighter, getting into the Dam, than it had been last time I'd brought Liz here – uh, on our tenth anniversary, or was it the eleventh?

Liz will know for sure, so avoid the topic.

No avoiding this 'bot, shoving its metallic finger towards me in order to scan my iris from inside the barrier box. "Welcome, Member Mason, drive carefully and avoid the wildlife."

The booms lifted, and my car drifted into gear – no speeding possible here, the car had been lassoed by the automatic Drive Cloud that floated within the park's E-Mobility system.

My car trundled along the manicured path, alongside yellowed grass and thirsty, thorny acacia trees, wilting in the sun.

"Shaka Hut," I told the car at the T-junction, and it dutifully rolled left and down the embankment towards the picnic and public eating area. There were a few parking places left, given it was a weekday, but nothing in the shade.

The patio of the restaurant would be well shaded with plastic trees at least, and cool fans pumped air over the woodwork and down towards the Dam. A slight breeze was tainting the air with stale mud and rotting vegetation, from the edge of the retreating water.

I gulped.

The Dam had shrunk even further and was starting to resemble little more than a glorified muddy water hole, albeit still an unusually large one. The old Midmar Mile annual swim had long been discontinued – it had been moved, a decade or so back, into the rising Indian Ocean instead, and had been renamed the Umhlanga Mile.

I was five minutes early, but Lizette was already waiting for me. I spotted her instantly, even though Shaka's was almost full, families with young kids moving uncertainly between inside Air-Cons and outside scorching al fresco.

Lizzie always liked the outdoors, however hot.

I joined her at our favourite table, furthest away from the restaurant and closest to the Dam.

She kept swatting at mud midges with a sheaf of papers, most of her head and face hidden by a large, wide brimmed soft cloth hat. She was wearing a light, white summer dress, dripping with painted *proteas*.

She still looked good. *Can I tell her that?*

I sat and gave her an awkward smile. "Those aren't my divorce papers, are they?"

Liz slapped the papers down onto the wooden table, rocking it slightly. "Was that meant to be funny?"

"That's a no then?" I grinned, wondering if my smile might freeze into place, should the wind shift direction.

Liz sighed. "So how was your meeting then? Did you give Du Preez hell?"

I signalled a waiter, feeling sweat trickle into my armpit, underneath my rolled up, long sleeved shirt. Light blue tended to get the best out of a bellicose Du Preez, generally.

Not today.

"He's increased my salary ten-fold, with a new project."

Despite herself, I could tell Liz was impressed. She always glanced away, when wanting to avoid showing me, just *how* impressed she was.

The waiter, a young umZulu man badged as 'Anele' arrived, e-pads in hand.

"The cheapest tap water you have," said Liz, "with ice."

"A pint of your best Lager for me," I said, "preferably iced for at least a day."

The young man nodded and left two digi-pads for our remote food order. Neither of us glanced at the menus. I leaned back, forcing my body to appear relaxed.

"I'll be able to get that new greenhouse you've always wanted, dear."

Liz took off her hat, hair spilling forward and dropping her sunglasses across her eyes. I could see the beads of sweat line her cheeks, even in the shade. "And what has the devil asked of you in return?"

I grimaced, "He's not that bad, you know. He wants me to travel and obtain news about the vanishing water in drought areas worldwide, starting with the FSA."

"That's a big job – you're going to be away a long time."

I nodded, reluctantly, picking up a digi-pad and keying in our usual main orders. *Tuna salad for her, the Thousand Rand T-bone steak for me, with greens not fries, to halt the flabby spread of my stomach.*

"And have you told the officials about our water well yet?"

I shook my head, "It's on our land, and it's our property."

"It's not that simple. Now that others know of it – if *SARS* find out, it might get nasty. If a find increases the value of the property, it may need to be declared, as our property rates may need to be adjusted accordingly."

I shook my head again, "I'm the accountant. I fill my forms and pay our taxes. Bad enough we're already giving such a lot of it away."

"Bad enough?" Liz raised her shades onto her unruly hair and wiped her cheeks with a napkin. "We have a duty to help those, without any water."

"My taxes do that," I said, aware that the elephant metaphorically hovering in the air between us, was yet to be broached. *How the hell do I raise last night and her sudden stated change in sexuality – especially with families and children nearby?*

"I wasn't that bad, was I?" I asked, "Last time we, uh, you know, did it?"

Liz looked at me, momentarily bemused.

Anele brought our food and placed it expertly in front of us.

Liz burst out laughing and Anele scuttled away, as if sensing something was about to kick off.

I sensed it too.

"Who is she?" I asked, but deep down, I already knew.

Liz swigged some water and stood up, "I went off tuna seven months back – or hadn't you noticed? Enjoy your trip, but I don't know if I'll be home, *when* you finally come back."

She put down a fifty rand note as a tip for her water, rammed the hat back onto her head, and stalked off to the car park.

I sighed, feeling hot and ill.

I eyed the plates but was certainly not feeling *that* hungry.

Maybe just a waffle, cream and cake?

Then I noticed the sheaf of papers Liz had left, wedged under a side plate.

I reached forward and pulled them free, flicking through the pages in a way that acted like a mini fan too, spraying a small breeze onto my sweating nose and brow.

Poetry – and African political philosophy?

What the fuck is happening to you, Lizzie?

Chapter 8
Liz — Of Frogs and Magistrates

Resting one hand on a mulched spade, I watched well water slowly circulate into my closely spaced parallel rows of carrots, beet, radish and turnips. My horticultural circle of soil sanctuary, mostly permaculture modelled.

I could tell they were not long off maturity, but could not stop wondering about *what next? They get harvested — we eat some, I sell some — and donate the others, to Imbali again?*

Then, what next? I grow again, we eat some, I sell some... but this time and next time, it is almost certainly I, not we, as Graham will go again, roaming the world, while I toil alone here, keeping things running, as the earth continues to crack and fracture, gasping for rains that are ever later to arrive, ever stingier in their fall.

The well seeps dry, as the aquifer empties.

And, as for Imbali, can I face down a mountain of Kill-dozers? No, I don't think so; this constant pelvic burn has robbed me of courage.

I patted at a small mound of sand sprouting out of the yellowed *kikuyu* grass near the water tank hole, fuelled by the underwater aquifer. *Ants — Matabele no doubt — bad ants. Got to blitz that mound. Ants will end up ruling this world, long after we humans have all cooked ourselves alive.*

They, at least, know how to co-operate.

I moved to the shade of a giant aloe, fanning myself with my free hand, holding a black and red Spanish fan that Graham had brought back for me, on one of his travels into Europe. I'd asked to go along, but that bastard Du Preez had apparently said there was no spare cash in these austere times.

Well, not for me, at least.

The phone buzzed in my overall pocket.

Almost certainly Graham, stuffed full of two meals from Midmar Dam, coming home, tanked up on beer, in his driverless car?

I dropped the spade and thumbed the phone on.

Number unknown?

Du Preez looked up at me, *"Goeie dag, mevrou, is jou man hier?"*

I scowled, "No, he's not home yet — why are you calling *my* phone, though?"

Wasps started buzzing around my head, so I swatted at them with my fan. Still seemed to be a lot of insects around, despite the decline over the years from toxic pesticides and giant food monocultures. *More concentrated maybe? What about spraying this* bledy *pest on my phone?*

"Just thought I'd let you know your man will be away for a few months *and* getting very well paid by me. So, if at any time you feel a bit lonely, just like give me a call, okay?"

I dropped my fan and took my phone into both hands, pulling it upwards to my face. "*Errrggghhh – What* did you just say?"

"I just wanted you to know that my screen saver is your face, and it's a great shot, taken the last time your man pleasured you, when you came. I'll have you know I can do a lot better than him. A small man has an even bigger you know what, missus, *hahaha*, just, *ja*, like give me a chance, *ne?*"

I was bitterly cold, in the sweaty heat, "I wouldn't touch you, if you were the last *fokin'* man alive. Don't you ever, ever, call me again, got that?"

I snapped my phone shut and dropped it onto the earth.

And then I killed some wasps.

Lots of them.

Graham found me inside shaking and crying when he returned ten minutes later.

He stood at the open front door, keys and a taser in hand, looking helpless, "*What'sh* wrongs, love?"

"You're drunk," I said, heading into the bedroom and locking the door.

I lay on the bed with a sigh. *This is starting to become a recurring theme. I need to find a way to break out of this. I'm tired of locking doors.*

"I loves you," crooned Graham, through the bedroom door.

"Then tell your fucking creepy boss that!" I shouted.

Silence.

I unlocked and opened the door, just as Graham slid down it.

I was prepared, having a boot wedged against the door, just in case. I eased it open slowly, bracing and stepping back gradually… tempting though it had been to spring it open, suddenly, and let him fall hard, like a sack of rotten potatoes.

Graham lay on his back, dishevelled, sweaty, and smelling of beer and brandy. His eyes were open slightly, but I knew they saw nothing. I'd found that a bit freaky, when I'd first noticed it, more than a quarter of a century ago, after our first time.

Looking down at him, I thought. Genoeg *is* genoeg; *enough is enough.*

Graham started a slow, throaty snore.

There's no way I can pick his fat arse up.

I went outside to fetch my fan and phone, blocking the last call number. I washed my hands and face in grey water and prepared supper for us both;

home grown vegetables and rice, sequentially cooked in recycled water.

Graham woke up to the smell of me spicing the beetroot, a favourite of his since we had first met, in a Cape Town bar, when I'd been young and just a little bit daring for my conservative background.

Supper tonight, though, was a quiet and subdued affair, with only one question asked.

"You know that metaphor you used for global warming all those years ago – about a frog eventually suffocating in boiling water, because of getting used to – and failing to jump from – a gradually increasing water temperature?"

Graham looked at me blankly, over his hovering spoon of beetroot. "Uh... huh."

"What was the hottest temperature, when the frog could still have managed to jump?"

"Fuck knows," he put the beetroot in his mouth, as if in the hope he would not be expected to say anything more.

I locked the bedroom door again that night, but this time without the slightest compunction, or hesitation.

Graham slept on the couch again, although I noticed that, for some reason, he appeared to have gone off his 'Die Hard' movies.

Me, I'm ready to jump.

Strange, heading out to Imbali, this time on my own. Echoes how I feel inside. Empty. Unsure of where I'm going. Or what I want. So grateful to the car's automated satnav, cued in with co-ordinates from Busi. Just wish someone could give me some directions, as to how I should live, what I should do.

Manaye, the Imbali Community Centre, was cooler, as I arrived just before ten. Junior was hanging outside, as the stalls were setting up, the fans starting to hum.

"Nothing to unpack, missus?" he asked me.

"No, Junior," I shook my head, somehow knowing better than to ask him why he wasn't in school. *No need to keep bringing stuff, as if attempting to counterweight the burden of my white guilt.*

Junior did not follow me inside.

Within, a young band was rehearsing on the stage, about twenty or so of recent school leaving age, with a mixture of brass, string and electric instruments, of varying condition and provenance. They were rattling through an instrumental, led by a vigorous older conductor, as an accompaniment to digital images above them, of a woman running along the Msunduzi River. She was leaping the ragged, shallow stream in various places, as if to highlight the lack of water that had led to the abandonment of the traditional canoe marathons. *All kindly sponsored by your conserver of water, FreeFlow, Limited.*

A small community crèche ran in one of the corners, fenced off with plastic green markers, inhabited by crawling and squalling babies and toddlers, in a pen of limited toys and a few chewed cardboard books. Two women and a man moved amongst the youngsters; responding by feeding, talking, checking, trying to keep the children happy, and the noise level down.

It's been too long since I spoke to Mark in New Zealand. Last I'd heard, he'd met a new young woman of interest. When will I become a – grandmother? What about my own mother – and father – in Cape Town?

The bar in the corner had yet to open, but I stalked over stiffly to the small group, gathering where the young reading group had met previously, broken driftwood board signed: 'MAKING OUR OWN STORIES.'

The covering where the 'Net engineers had been working was gone, but the space was still littered with data mats, screens and printers.

There were only four persons, including both me and Busi; so, three women in total, and one man.

"Saartjie Baartman," Busi introduced the old woman first, with a touch of reverence and respect, "Formerly of the Trans Collective, who challenged the intersectionality of Rhodes Must Fall from within, in 2016."

Not her real name, surely? I gave the tall, old woman a respectful African handshake; clasp, thumb, clasp, slight bow.

She was lined and grey, but still stout and strong, wrapped in light white cloth etched with minimalistic green and blue beadwork.

I smiled at a glimpse of the woman's purple trainers.

"We've met," said Saartjie, "I collected young Thandi from your property."

I nodded.

The man, Busi introduced with a cursory wave: "Andile Goodwill." A tall thirty something man, neatly dressed in knee-trousers and cotton coloured Madiba shirt; wearing circular smart specs and a graft-phone on his right forearm – left-handed?

The Reading group wall was now marked ETHNO-PHILOSOPHY. We sat across the table. I was surprised to find myself feeling a little isolated, sitting next to Andile, and over the table from the other women.

"What's happened to the covering, that was sealing off work space for the 'Net engineers you showed me last time, Busi?" I asked.

She chuckled. "Removed by mutual consent. Both groups were over hearing each other and decided sharing their stories and endeavours was a much better idea."

I nodded.

It looked like they were expecting something more from me, so I spoke again. "What's 'ethno-philosophy' mean?" I asked.

"Good opening question, but wrong language," said Andile, switching into isiZulu. "It means we got no philosophy of our own – and it's *gotta* be because we're 'ethnic'."

"Code switch for dumb," said Saartjie.

"Dumb... and black." It was Busi this time, obviously enjoying the opening riffs of the meeting.

I watched warily, wondering how much my relative lack of fluency in isiZulu was going to hamper me. *And, even more so, my whiteness.*

"So, Liz," Busi faced me squarely, "Would you face down a Kill-dozer here?"

I hesitated, I'd thought long and hard about this, since she'd last asked me. "Maybe – if there were others with me too."

Busi smiled and gave me a brief clap. "I think you're getting it. Our power comes from standing shoulder to shoulder. Alone, we are nothing. In togetherness, lies our collective strength."

"Your turn to make a statement," said Andile, turning to me on his left.

I'm even warier. "Are we taking turns making a statement – but *you* haven't been, as yet?"

"Ladies first," said Andile, primly.

"Uh, uh, uh," said Saartjie, "no sexist bullshit, that's not philosophy. Patriarchy is an ideology, that must be both acknowledged and challenged."

I watched the old woman curiously – she spoke with a low, firm voice, as if used to being heard. A young man – not Junior – brought us a tray of teas and coffees, milk and sugar on the side.

Andile took a plain tea, "I'm asserting my philosophical right, as a man, to dictate the agenda and order."

He smiled as the two women jeered.

I watched on, nonplussed.

The automatic fans kicked on, as the temperature rose above 25C. We huddled closer over the table, as if to better hear each other.

"We want a more profound philosophical contribution than that, Andile," said Busi.

"How about me pointing out your royal 'we' is an assumption, not predicated on obtaining confirmatory evidence from your colleagues first?"

"Smart arse," said Busi.

"*Argumentum ad hominem* is also ruled out," smiled the man.

He's smug, but he knows it, at least.

"Talking about arguments against people," said Saartjie, fixing me with intense brown eyes. "You're not a TERF are you, Missus Mason?"

I looked at her blankly. "What's a TERF?"

"Trans Exclusionary Radical Feminist," said Busi. "They want gender diluted, but not sex. You can't have your cake…"

"Help," I said, "Just call me Liz. I *still* don't know what any of that means. I'm not sure I even qualify as a feminist, let alone any of that other stuff."

"She's cool, Sara," said Busi.

Andile turned to me, "As our guest, Liz, I'm curious about what you know of black, or African philosophy?"

Done some reading on this, at least. "*Ubuntu*? Sharing and celebrating the universal bond of all humans?"

Andile smiled, but his lips were tight. "What most whiteys know; anything – or anyone – else?"

"Guys, go easy, she's cool," I could hear Busi's exasperation.

"I've started reading '*The Wretched of the Earth*'," I offered.

Andile smiled, but more broadly this time. "Fanon. A good start."

Saartjie gave a grudging nod. "So… Liz, as our guest, what do you think is the most pressing question of philosophy, that we should discuss this week?"

I hesitated, trying to second guess what they might want from me.

"Of course," interrupted Andile, "Our Algerian brother Camus felt the most important question was – how do we best live? And, given the state of the world, what stops us from opting just to die, instead?"

I decided to stick with my most pressing recent question; the one Graham had effectively ignored.

"Well, this is nothing as profound as Camus, but it's been on my mind recently. A frog is put in a pot with tepid but comfortable water, so she doesn't jump out. Slowly, slowly the temperature is increased, so the frog acclimatises, until it's too late to jump out. She has been cooked. When should – or could – she have jumped?"

"Who's doing the cooking?" asked Andile, "and who owns the water?"

"Is it a poisonous frog?" asked Saartjie, "is one killing going to lead to another?"

"No real frog would sit still like that, in any water. It would have jumped out right away," said Busi.

"If it's a *stupid* frog," I asked, "when's the latest it can jump?"

"Now that's a stupid *question*," said Busi, "there is only right now. Any delay is only going to be cooking time."

So, am I cooking – or ready to jump? There is indeed only now.

"Let's agree that no question is stupid," said Saartjie. "We all have differing vantage points for living. All questions are valid."

There were mutual nods, and I felt less stifled and exposed.

Even white questions?

"Have you taken her to Marikana?" Saartjie turned to Busi, who shook her head, slowly.

The large, old woman looked across at me. "That child you found? We have hundreds more like her, in the poorest and nearby Marikana township – we share what we can, but there is not enough affordable water. Three have died, more will die soon, unless we can find a place, with water freely available."

"What can I do?" I asked. "We're not that rich, but maybe we can help a bit."

Me, not we.

"But who *are* you?" asked Saartjie.

"Uh," I looked across at Busi, "I'm a..."

Saartjie shook her head. "That's where you *whities* have got it wrong. You shouldn't think of yourselves as 'I's,' in your little isolated bubbles. You're easy pickings, on your own, for the people in power. For us, we are always we. *Our* identities are always relational. I'm a grandmother, a community activist, a lover. On my own, I am nothing."

"But, more than that," said Andile, reaching across to the rough driftwood sign, nailed to the outside of the table. He dragged his right forearm, below his phone implant, along the jagged wood – and then hung his arm over the table.

Blood dripped; thick, slow, deep red drops.

The blood curdled into a small, almost purplish pool, on the light brown table top.

"Now, is *this* statement profound enough?" he said, "My question is, at the end of the day, *are* we alone? Do we die alone, given no one can die with us? Where is God hiding? And why is the world so rough for black skin, if God truly exists? Why is He so shit at Health and Safety Planning, especially if you happen to be black?"

"*Tchacchhh!*" Busi let rip, but I could tell her exasperation was familiar.

Andile tilted his head to look at me. "No answers. Okay then, my next question – are you willing to really *be* with us, and to bleed with us, white woman?"

I held his gaze, my lower stomach grinding in heightened pain.

I gave one, slow nod.

He smiled, "We shall see."

Busi gave him a large translucent *Steristrip* to seal his wound. *Scarred left arm too. Not the first time?*

The band had finished their practice and were packing up. Above us, the woman had finished her river run, and a long credit roll of endangered animals in the 'Dusi was scrolling, several species of frog amongst them.

The young man came with the tray and bill.

"Mandla," said Busi, "Where's Junior?"

The young man shrugged, "He went off with Imantshi."

Busi's face dropped, as if with both shock and anger.

She flicked out her phone, but Andile was already talking into a mike grill wired into his forearm, watching a screen dance on his skin.

"What's that? Where the fuck are you?" asked Andile.

Junior's voice was tiny and tinny. I could not hear what he was saying.

"Tell him to bring you back, sharp sharp…"

Brmmble, britzzz, plshhhh…

"What's he saying?" demanded Busi, obviously unable to hear clearly either.

Andile looked up glumly, as the screen went black. "He says Imantshi told him he's not our bitch."

I had never seen Busi look so calm and cold.

She stood up, waving everyone to their feet. "You got a tag on Junior's phone. I say we go get him."

Andile looked hesitant, "That's a big thing, Bus', crossing the Magistrate."

I asked, "He's not a real Magistrate, is he?"

Andile shrugged, "Near as fuck, in this neck of Imbali."

The room was emptying.

"Where's Busi?" asked Saartjie.

There were only three of us in the room, the band had all packed up and left.

Despite the heat, we rushed outside.

Busi was in her red car, revving and ready to go. Andile waved her down, gesturing at his forearm.

"I have a track on Junior's phone – Imantshi's bringing Junior back."

The stalls were getting busier, but people scattered, as a convoy of three armoured cars squealed around the corner and into the parking lot, the leading car plated like a tank, with stolen sirens flashing.

The vehicles screeched to a halt near Busi's car – she was standing tensely behind an open door on the driver's side.

Saartjie marched to her one side, Andile flanking slightly behind her.

I hung back with the crowd who had scattered from the stalls, hovering near the entrance to the Community centre, preparing to take refuge inside. We were about thirty or forty people, nervously flashing phones and milling behind each other, as if afraid to be exposed.

The tarmac on the parking lot began to shimmer, as the tank-door opened, and a youngish man stepped out, smiling and waving.

He wore a one-piece light grey, smart wet suit – tailored to look like an expensive lounge suit, but glittering with talking tech, that kept him both cool and informed. "My people," he said, "Come to me, all you who are thirsty, and I will bring you drink."

"Where's Junior?" asked Busi, sharply.

Although standing about twenty yards away, I picked up a faint tremor in her loud voice.

The man smiled, "No need to go solar, sister, I have our young brother with us, teaching him the tools of the trade."

Biological brother? Or township talk?

I shuffled to the front of the small crowd, sensing Busi's fear.

A young boy got out of the second car and ran over to Busi's small group. "Aunty, I'm fine, been learning good stuff…"

"Go inside," said Busi, without taking her eyes off the smart suited, smiling man.

Junior stopped and loitered, looking momentarily confused. "Aunty?"

"Go inside," she said.

Junior pushed past us to go inside, but I caught the look of fury on the young man's face.

"*Sisi, sisi,*" Imantshi shook his head, "No need to be so hard on the young man. Just teaching him how to survive, in this cruel world."

There was a collective gasp, as Busi stepped out from behind her car door, stiffly stepping towards Imantshi, and thumbing him in the chest.

There was a clatter of men and two women leaving the tank, car and black *bakkie* at the back – all armed to the teeth, mainly with automatic rifles, but also with the odd gleam of a long blade.

Busi stood her ground, hands on hips. "He needs to go back to proper school. Stay away from him. Stay away from me."

I crept closer, moving behind Andile and Saartjie Baartman, who were quivering, coiled as tight as wire from a jacked Telkom box.

Busi's hands were squeezing the tiny roll of fat on her own hips, tighter and tighter.

Imantshi gave a big and theatrical sigh, turning away and waving weapons back into vehicles, holsters and various parts of the grey smart suits of his coterie; five men and two women of varying size and stature, but all with faces betraying no fear of aggression.

"*Sisi, sisi*, no need for dramatics, just giving the boy a career opportunity to stop him becoming a loser... LOSER!" Imantshi shouted, as he stepped into the back seat of the tank, opened by one of his woman guards.

The last word was a shout, as if meant to carry into the inner chamber of the Community Centre. I turned and saw that Junior had not gone inside, but was lounging by the outside door, dragging at a cigarette as if he meant to inhale the entire object, ashes and all, in one huge and angry suck.

Imantshi hovered half inside the tank, hanging on the still open door, the vehicle thrumming with heavy aircon. "For the people of Imbali, from your very own Robin Hood, Imantshi, I give you... water!"

As the door slammed shut, two men started offloading from the back of the *bakkie*. Bottles of water – *huge* bottles.

A roar of approval went up and people swarmed forward, to the point of offload, near Bra' Beard's Net-Hacking stall.

I stepped forward to join Busi and the others near her car, but Busi whispered fiercely, "Stay back."

Imantshi had partly rolled down his tinted window and was cocking his finger at Busi, as if pulling the trigger of a gun. Then, with his laugh fluttering behind from the open window, the tank pulled off, screeching in a semi-circle to leave the parking lot, an old lady jumping to avoid being hit.

"What an idiot," said Saartjie.

"Hmm," said Busi, "but a dangerous one. We best check that the water distribution going on is being handled fairly, before it turns into a riot. As the English say, beggars can't be..."

We had to fight our way through the scrum of people, as the *bakkie* and second vehicle raced off.

By the deposited array of giant water bottles, a lanky old man in a wheel chair and a younger man and woman – who looked cannily like younger versions of him – were busy trying to organise people into an orderly queue.

Busi held her phone level to her mouth, "I'm jacked into the Com-Centre's speakers. On..."

There was a squawk of feedback noise from large speakers within the hall, the sound spilling out in hot waves onto steaming tarmac. The noise partly stilled the hubbub of people arguing for their place within an unseen queue.

"People, quiet! No timewasting in this hot sun. Our *induna* Baba

Dumisani and his children want a queue, so we must queue. There will be enough for all. First the jobless, the children and the elderly, then all the others. We will give you a fair ration, according to your means and resources, which we have on tap on Com-Net."

Slowly, messily, a rough and crooked line started to form.

Busi was sweating heavily by now, as were we all, and she wiped sprinkles of sweat from her phone, before speaking again.

"We know the volume of water here, so we need a very clever person to do some calculations for us – Junior, please come up to the head of the queue."

Silence.

No one stepped forward.

"Junior, we need your smart brain," called Busi, "Please."

Still no one stepped forward, and several people started to shout, tempers fraying, alongside the mercury in the roof display.

35C, flickering higher...

Saartjie leaned forward and snarled into Busi's phone, "Get your young ass over here, Mister Junior Motholo, sharp, sharp!"

Junior came stalking through the broken line, face still glowering.

Busi put her phone down and sighed, exasperated, "At least the little shit is coming."

Junior stopped.

Busi's phone was still jacked in, to the very sensitive public speakers. Her whisper had been broadcast to all – and very clearly.

"*Hayi*, no..." she said.

But Junior had gone.

"The frog's jumped," said Andile.

Chapter 9
Art — The Four Horsemen

Fuck you, Katrina.
From the top of our roof, we watch bodies float by, and the government don't come.
"It's because we're black," says Dad, "Never forget you're black, son."
Mom says nothing.
I perch on the extreme left of the roof apex, ass hurting, readying myself to jump and drift with dead bodies and broken pieces of shit.
Daddy holds me.

Sunday, Sunday

I tried another Church; but sitting, as usual, back left pew, far corner, and feeling very alone.

My ass hurts, even before I sit down. as far away as possible from the eagle eye of this new pastor, in this new Church. Here, will I feel more human, more accepted? Why did I come, though? End seat means there's still time to bolt. Or jump? Family filing in look as if they want to join me. No, please don't, there are still seats up ahead. Why is this Church filling up, and so quickly?

I grimaced a smile at the young man of mid-twenties or so next to me, blue-suited and in shiny shoes that reflected the back of the pew in front.

He looked grumpy at least, as if not entirely here of his own free will – getting too old for his parents, even as a probable generational Boomeranger?

Give them a break, young man, we parents, we do our best.

The parents looked like solid folk, smartly dressed, the younger sister on the other side of them pouting and wiping off sand from her white dress, as if the sibs were physically estranged, separated by parental presence.

I felt strangely pale here, exposed – *but why are the Churches still so visibly segregated, almost two centuries after slavery has gone?*

After Katrina, Church had stopped.

Even after leaving drowned Orleans, my parents had lived in this strange limbo of isolated endeavour, away from their disapproving families, recycling used laptops and cleaning offices in Tulsa, OK, to bring home food – and then just to fall into bed.

I only started going to Church after losing my second family – an angry wife and a damaged daughter; looking for reasons, looking for God.

The Fiery Baptist lights were burning brightly, even though it was the eleven am service. The sun was a vague, fragmented ball this past half-week – holding little power against the black roar of the ongoing dust storm, now dissipating slowly, at long last.

The Church was full, the choir filing in to take their place at the front, benches lined alongside the pulpit.

People stood, and there was a frightening cheer, as the pastor bounded in, a large man, beneath his voluminous black robes.

Pastor White was black.

I smiled and relaxed, I loved old time twentieth century music. The man reminded me of a thin version of one of my long dead, soul favourites, Barry White.

"Praise Je-sus!" the pastor shouted, and the congregation echoed a response.

Not from me, nor the young man next to me, though.

The youngster had surreptitiously popped on a pair of smart glasses, screen darkening, having inserted an ear worm into his left ear, all out of sight from parental view.

"Hallelu-jah! Praise the Lord! Je-sus!!"

I was disappointed; the pastor had a thin, febrile voice, leveraged by his robe mike, sounding absolutely nothing like Barry White.

I could sing or sound better.

"Praise Jesus," I whispered, unable to hear myself amongst the congregation's roared and repeated responses.

Pastor White bounded behind his e-pulpit, as if he was preparing himself for a World Wrestling Association bout.

Your beard is greying, you've earned the right to walk, not fight, sir.

A small screen flashed on behind the pulpit, backlighting the pastor's head.

Alongside him, behind the two choir lines, dropped large bilateral 2-Di screens, with a hiss of flaming inscriptions: *We Are the Fiery Baptists.*

The Congregation cheered, shouting a babbled mixture of praises; a swelling, incoherent cacophony of excitement.

I groaned, wondering whether the young man on my right might have spare ear worms on him, and whether I dared ask him.

Surely too noisy for answers, too noisy even for God?

"Await the Lord on the Fiery Clouds of Storm," shouted Pastor White, gesticulating at the screens.

A dual image rose up before us.

I grunted, recognising it instantly.

A video clip from the Wall Elevator, surely? Wednesday, just past noon. There's the back of us – the smaller old woman, the larger me – since when did I get so large? There we are, tiny masked meat sacks, facing this huge rising cloud of glowing dust, the tinny hiss of sand starting to pound against the elevator sensors.

The camera panned along the wall and the congregation gasped, as four Storm-Fliers hove into view, arms flapping and legs dancing in nervous anticipation.

I noticed the young man's taller head next to me, bobbing with restraint, as if to a different, internal beat.

"Rise!" Commanded the Pastor, doing his best to coax his voice towards thunder, rather than light breeze. "Rise and witness the Four Horsemen take flight, winging their way to the Heavens, as they herald the final Apocalypse of the Lord!"

The dust cloud exploded, and I held my breath, as everyone leaped to their feet.

The two bodies were gone, hurled into the elevator, I knew, rubbing my ribs in bruised memory and staring in terrified horror, as the thermal camera swung and followed the flight of the four.

"Disease!" Screamed the pastor.

"Praise God!" Call and response kicked in again, but I could only watch in silence, as four bodies swirled higher and higher in the storm vortex, as if seeking transmutation into dust.

"Famine!"

"Hallelujah!" I could only make out two bodies now.

"War!"

"Praise Be!" One?

"Death!"

All is dust.

I recognised the opening bars from the Church organ; an old twentieth century rock anthem; *The Doors,* and *Riders on the Storm.*

Devil's music, fading quickly, but enough to provide just a hint of demonic menace. Never got that, never will, music is glorious, not evil.

Some of it is just closer to God than others.

A tiny, tinny, hip-hop beat next to me, a sound of street heaven?

"Let us sing – He Has the Whole World, in His Hands!"

"Hallelu-jah, Jesus!" rose the returning roar.

The choir stood with the congregation, some leaving their pews, as if anticipating a dance at the front too. But I focused on the whisper of sound leaking from my neighbour's ear worm.

I took a deep breath. *Shall I, shan't I?*

"He Has the Whole World –"
No father left to hold me any more.

I squeezed the young man's shoulder and was rewarded with a sidewise glance beneath the shades. The youngster bent his head down and leaned his left ear towards me, popping his ear worm out, muttering "Hey, *wassap*, Mister?"

"Breaking Good; by The Empty Assholes, that's one of my favourites," I whispered.

"– in His hands."

Without a word, the young man fished another 'worm out of his pocket and popped it into my hand. "No sweat, Mister, there you go – name's Brad, by the way."

"He's got –"

"Thank you Brad, I'm…" *That's the way it's done, isn't it, name exchanges at introduction? Forgot that.*

But Brad was already back in his head, bobbing to –?

Seriously? How old is this kid?

Fight the Power!?

"A-Men!" I shouted, raising my hands up, channelling Chuck D. "Fight the Power!"

Brad bumped his hip against my side and grinned, finger to lips.

Does that mean… friends?

Outside, through the Church bay windows, the sun glowed brighter, as dust started to fall, like dirty snow.

Brad had switched to a news site, on his specs and ear bud feed.

"…We have news that all four bodies who launched themselves into Tornado Trump have now been found and identified."

Here, at the Fiery Baptist Church, we'd renamed them, immortalised them. *What's in a name, after all?*

A tug on my right sleeve from Brad, and I realised abruptly, I was the only one standing in our pew.

I sat hurriedly, feeling a surge of panic, as the pastor fired a penetrating stare at me, before launching into the Book of Revelations.

"Didn't catch your name, Mister, what is it?" whispered Brad, out of the corner of his mouth.

"Art. Art Green."

"Cool name."

Yes, friends.

Afterwards, outside Church, we spoke and shared ideas, swapping numbers and digital tags, before Brad introduced me to his family and we both eventually headed off to our respective homes.

Friends.

This time, home did not feel *quite* so empty.

Although I watched repeating videos of my parents, ghosting across the walls in my living room, as they spun through an immersive 3-di projector. Their voices muted, I watched only, listening instead to a play-track of the Dark Soul Beats.

I was thirteen years old, in one scene loop, filming our holiday at Camp Loughridge for a school project, and dad was laughing and coaxing me to get into the crowded, Aquatics Centre pool.

In my head, I heard my high-pitched voice, over and over, again.

No. I can't swim.

Monday, Monday… place looks like hell.

Zeke and I stood in the Basement Courtyard at the back of the Office, rear entrance, surveying the thick accumulation of dust.

Zeke sneezed every time one of us moved. The sun was trapped in circling concentric glints of gold, as dust continued to settle on a clear, quiet and windless morning.

The cacti in the open-aired courtyard poked through a silt layer, almost an inch thick.

"Jesus," said Zeke, after their sixth sneeze.

"Sorry," they said, wiping their nose, having caught my angry glare.

"They say almost forty percent of the cleaner bots failed to work this morning," I said. "Dust damaged systems."

"Gets in everywhere," agreed Zeke, shaking their head and hair, as if attempting to stop their next sneeze, "It was like walking through a buried city, a dead city, this morning."

"Hmm," I said, turning to thumb the door open. "Technically, cities *are* dead, it's just we inhabitants who live."

"But for how much longer?" mused Zeke.

The door slid open and I bumped into the tall figure of Director Carruthers.

"You're both three minutes late," she said.

"We were planning the day's work," said Zeke, walking around her.

I stood, shocked, unable to move, or say anything. *What's brought her down here? She never slums it.*

The director ushered me in, propelling me physically with a forceful hand between my shoulder blades. The door sealed. *Must be something* very *important.*

"*Theia*, data dampers on," she commanded.

Zeke turned in alarm, hearing the bite in the Director's voice, and waited. Dr. Carruthers cocked her head, as if waiting for internal reassurance, and then waved us to sit.

"Smelt," she said.

"What?" Zeke looked at her as if she'd gone mad, but I sensed the emotive resonance of the word.

"*Delta* smelt?" I asked, just in case she was referring to my personal hygiene.

"I didn't deal any smell," said Zeke, "I've been sneezing, not farting... Okay, maybe just a little one... but that's not a crime."

The Director looked at Zeke, as if they were an idiot. "The fish, it may well be back. One of our bots spotted a likely one, near Suisun Bay and the drainage basin of the Joaquin – Sacramento delta. The Greenies picked this up off a FOI injunction they have on our sensitive feeds. They're climbing all over me this morning, seeking emergency protection measures."

"Oh," said Zeke, "you mean the fucking fish? But it's been extinct for years."

"Not any more, it seems," said Carruthers, "I need you both to go up there and check data veracity. Images have distorted from the distance amid water interference. I need you up close, scoping the sighting spot and checking the original data – and fucking *now*, before the Agrics get wind of this, and start wrapping us in red-tape, to protect their own water supply!"

Outside the external door, a small wind was whipping up again, rattling courtyard sand against the window.

"It's going to take a while to get up there, the roads are a mess," I said.

Zeke was gawping through the window, as the roaring sound grew louder, small stones and plant debris thrumming and thudding against the reinforced window and door. "Jesus," they said again.

"No, it's not Jesus," said Carruthers, walking across to open the door.

Zeke sneezed as dust and debris swirled in, blown by the dying rotors of the tiny Nova-Lite; a two-seater copter with sealed glass bowl, solar engine, and the barest of skeleton and moving parts.

"Tornado Trump has headed up the coast and is dying out. You'll be fine, as long as you take the inland route, the co-ordinates and safe flight path have been set."

Zeke was already opening the 'copter door with one hand, holding their dripping nose with the other.

"What about Suraya?"

"She's late, she can hold the office fort while you're gone. *And the fish worship the source, bowed and fervent, but their hearts are water[2]."*

The Big Dee sure loves to end conversations with obscure poetry. "What about additional insurance?" I asked, "This machine looks unsafe."

"*That* insurance," said Carruthers, "You can ask of Jesus. Keep me looped in – and tell no one."

Carruthers ducked her head to step inside, with the faintest hint of a wave.

Zeke bounced up and down inside their seat, already strapped in, "Get your ass in here, sir. Let's see what this baby has."

I hesitated, as dread sapped into my bones.

Not *a fan of heights.*

"Delta smelt," grinned Zeke, palms apart to indicate a large fish.

They knew what made me tick. Reluctantly, with shaking legs and hands, I climbed into the other 'copter seat. "The smelt's a *small* fish, not nearly as big as your hand gestures, Zeke."

"So, sue me," they smiled, "We've got some fish to fry."

<*My name is Kelly,*> said the 'copter, <*Let's rock and roll.*>

I screamed.

Gen injected me.

The journey was a jumble of brown earth and thin strips of meandering green, framed by a hot yellow glare, even through the darkened glass. I could feel the jolting swing of Kelly's elliptical path, but registered little of what drifted beneath.

Zeke kept up a cheerful conversation, of which I remembered very little, apart from several eulogies about their helpful Uncle Simon.

Finally, the jolting stopped, and air ripe with a smell like eggs rotting in vinegar pinched my nose.

Hydrogen sulphide?

Kelly had opened my door and a sharp burn in my left arm alerted me that Gen had injected me with a sedative antidote. "Where, where are we?" I asked, but the seat next to me was empty.

<*Near Suisun Bay, the Sacramento delta, last sighting of a delta smelt two days and two hours ago, the sighting bot is nearby on beacon alert.*> Kelly's voice sounded soothing and helpful.

More so than Zeke – where'd they gone?

I stepped out and swayed, on muddy wetlands ring-fenced by bushes and fizzing fences, with the trickle of water underfoot, through tussocks of

---

[2] Ted Hughes (1983): 'Torridge' in *River*. London: Faber & Faber.

soggy ground. *Ah, there they are, bending by that small tributary stream, fishing something out of the water.*

"Zeke! What you got there?"

Zeke trudged over towards me, and I could see they'd put on blue plastic over-shoes to protect their footwear.

They were carrying an oddly shaped metallic container, shaped like a cross between a soccer ball and a bloated fish. Mechanical tail and fins still wiggled, but there was no face. I could see pockmarks on the shiny, dripping surface, no doubt camera openings.

"Meet Fish Bot 358," Zeke said, "with purported unique sighting of a delta smelt."

I crinkled my nose, "We'll need to recheck water quality data as well – you get that stink too? No one's been to check up here in years, the bots have been pretty reliable so far."

Zeke nodded. "Kelly," they said, "Can you tap the relevant footage from FB358 onto your screen?"

We both clambered in and the doors closed, the glass in front of us transmuting into a screen, darkening against the bright early afternoon sun.

Images flashed, rolling stones, plastic cups, water weed, a fish...

"That it?" asked Zeke.

"No," I said, "Sturgeon, keep rolling – I told you it was a small fish – freeze!"

The upper half of a tiny thin fish had splashed into view.

"Jesus!" I said.

"What's sauce for the goose?" frowned Zeke.

"I meant *praise* Jesus – it's, it's a delta smelt, I'm pretty sure. *Hallelujah!*"

"What about that?" Zeke was pointing across me and up into the air, "What's that? Is that also a miracle?"

The sun had dimmed, as if a light cloud fog had descended.

A thin whine filled the air, and something momentarily blotted the sun. "Open my door, Kelly," I said.

A drone hovered nearby, four mini blades rotating furiously on its sides, the body casing scrubbed clean of any identifiable markings.

"Fuck off!" shouted Zeke, "This is federal land."

Almost as if it had heard, the drone lurched and whizzed off sideways, heading out eastwards, flashing momentarily between trees and across a particularly tall, buzzing fence.

"Who owns that land, Kelly? Where has the drone has gone?"

<FreeFlow.>

"The Corporation have a free license to salvage some water to sell," said

Zeke, "Given they provide employment to so many."

"Yes, I've heard," I said, "but they also have extraction *limits*."

<All records indicate they operate within legal parameters here,> said Kelly.

"But can you trust records?" I muttered, "We have a blurred image of a fish – I'd much rather have seen that fish for myself. Next to a live green turtle, there'd be nothing better to see, in this world of the Sixth Extinction"

"Come, then," Zeke jumped out of Kelly, and strode off.

"Wait," I pulled on plastic over-shoes from the supplies bag behind my seat. I picked up the surprisingly heavy, and still damp fishy bot 358 – whose fins at least had stopped moving – and followed Zeke's rush, across boggy ground.

They had reached the river spreading towards the gleaming Suisun Bay, on the north western horizon curve.

I paced my way to the water more carefully, watching my feet to avoid any missteps, in the potentially treacherous domain. The stinky smell had disappeared. "Gen," I said, "activate your gaseous sensors."

The turtle on my wrist glowed green.

A trusty companion, not fully AI, but not inserted into my brain at least. I had always baulked at the thought of neural implants.

I reached the river and swore.

Sorry, Jesus.

Zeke had taken their cream shirt off, stained with sweat along the back, leaving only billowing camouflage trousers. They had pulled their shoes and over-shoes off too, all rolled up and left on top of a riverside rock.

"Uhhh –" I said, trying not to stare, "Are those –?"

"Maybe," smiled Zeke, "Or just maybe they might be *moobs* instead. I know *you* can keep a secret, Art!"

With that, they jumped in, splashing around excitedly, "Oooh, it's fucking cold – and deep, I can't even stand."

I bent down and held the bot underwater for a few seconds, waiting for its neural circuitry to kick in.

With a jerk, FB358 lurched out of my hands, and sank out of sight in the murky grey-brown water.

"We're federal employees' boss," shouted Zeke, "this is fed water. Come on in and have a look for the smelt fishes. The water's a shade on the cold side, but it's still lovely."

"No, I don't swim," I said, trying hard not to look at the half-naked Zeke.

Zeke laughed and spun in the water, a happy, confident swimmer, "Is that a black thing then, not swimming?"

"No," I said, bending down at the stream edge, to take a sample of water with a bio-capsule from my trouser pocket. "It's an Arthur Green thing."

'Fuck Katrina!' Father's voice, in my head. Again.

I coughed in shock, at the cold splash of water across my face, and on my throat and chest.

Zeke peeled off a chain of laughter, having obviously just splashed me, "Got you! Come on in to the shallows then, we'll dry off in no time, in this crazy heat."

I wiped my face, with a sweaty sleeve. "I. Don't. Swim."

I turned away, as Gen blinked on my wrist.

<Picking up a faint trail of hydrogen sulphide,> said the turtle.

"Take me along it," I said, watching direction arrows light up on my wrist.

Slowly, I stepped across spongy ground, following the shifting arrow on my wrist.

"Boss, where are you going?" shouted Zeke, but I kept moving, focusing on following the arrow – and concentrating on avoiding twisting an ankle, at the same time.

Some three hundred yards further and I found myself up against the electric fence and the screen of trees, that the drone had flown over earlier.

"Who owns the land on the other side?" I asked Gen, already knowing the answer, but wanting confirmation.

Gen was quiet and cold on my wrist. "Gen?"

"Hey, what are you doing?"

I turned, to see two men standing behind me, watching me, with one hand on army fatigued hips, like GI Joe clones.

The one who looked as if he had just spoken, was armed, and holding out a data dampener.

"Are you military?" I asked, "What are *you* doing, on Hydro and Fish-Wildlife Service land?"

A whine overhead and a weight dropped on me, pulling me down onto my knees. *Vision criss-crossed – I've been… netted?*

"Got the mother-fucker," said the man, levelling his gun.

Gen burnt my wrist.

Then, a thud in my chest.

Chapter 10
Graham – Looking For America

Chest heavy, head sore – Shit man, how can so much pain lodge inside one head?
I struggled to sit upright, feeling both nauseous and angry, with the solar glare lancing through the sitting room slats. *How the hell did I end up on the floor?*
Oh…
Jurre, *I made an arse of myself with Liz.*
I pulled myself onto the couch and sat, head between knees, groaning and massaging my temples. Long time since I went on such a bender; they may feel good at the time, but I always ended up with a sore head – *and being even deeper in the kak. What did I say to her? Mmm, nope, all I can remember is some damn fine spiced beetroot; man, can she cook that stuff.*
Puffing out breath from a heavy chest, I stood up, slowly and carefully. *Good.* The nausea stayed settled deep in the pit of my stomach.
I shuffled towards the window, that looked over the rear vegetable garden and twitched the blinds gingerly, to look out.
Veg garden empty. Where is she?
<Incoming call, Office> said Cyril.
Bugger Du Preez, I want my wife.
I went back to sit on the couch, gathering my strength and slowing my breath, "Mason here."
<Hey, boet, I got your flights to America.>
"Oh," my heart sank, "When's that?"
<Leaves Durban Airport, eight pm tonight.>
"You are fucking kidding me, right?"
<Hey, nooit so. I'm pinging your tickets to Cyril now, now, okay?>
Is this even possible? How can my headache get even fucking worse? I burst out into a torrent of frustrated invective, as if a dam had burst, of all the swearing I'd wanted to do, but never could, when Liz had been around.
Finally, I stopped for breath.
There was a brief silence.
<Hey feel better now, my man? Did you hit the bottle again last night? Are you babalas?>
Spent, I only managed a thin smile. *We go back a good few years, the bastard knows me well. I will give him that.*
I sighed. "*Ja*, all right then, I've got to say goodbye to Lizzie of course,

once I find her."

<Careless to lose a wife, hey – was she, uh, was she okay, last night?>

Odd question. I thought for a moment, trying to remember.

"Dunno," I said," I'm gonna go find her. Out."

Mouth sticky, I went across to the fridge for a glass of premium bottled water, prising it open with some difficulty. I could almost count the Rands, with every gulping swallow.

"Ahhh – Cyril, where's Lizzy keeping the *panado*? And have you got a link to her phone? Where is she now?"

<Under the sink, in Imbali>

"What?" *Why is she under the sink? Or why did she take the medication to Imbali? Oh, no, split the sentence, the tablets are down here.* Bending low to get the tablets out, was *not* a good move. *Shit. At least the sink is right here…*

Once I'd stopped heaving, my thoughts started to cling like flies again. *Why's my opgooi so red? Am I bleeding inside? Am I dying? This shit stinks, hey, wash it down the plug hole with silver water. Oh ja, not blood, it must be the pickled beetroot last night, surely?*

<Shall I get the car ready?>

"Can't we just call her?"

<Her phone is off.>

How could she have switched her phone off, in such a dangerous place? *Imbali? Never been there, nor any other township, before. Don't know how Lizzie does it. Scary place, man, for whities like us.*

<Car sir – Lizette has the electric, but the old programmable gas guzzler is available. Two more legal years on that one.>

"Don't try and be a fucking butler, Cyril." *Let us finish that hundred Rand bottle of water.*

I put the empty bottle down on the kitchen table and closed the fridge. *So easy just to leave and go. Imbali is wild-west, man. Hah, speaking of wild-west… if I'm going to America, maybe I get to be a proper cowboy?*

But I couldn't leave, not without saying… goodbye, to Lizzy.

I love her, even though I can't remember when I last told her that.

I chose the biggest gun from the front door rack and packed a bag.

I'm gonna need to check the gun in at the airport on the other side. So, here the journey begins. With an R-1 rifle, and an old banger car – rigged, at least, for self-driving.

As we set off, my head was *still* fucking sore.

This sure as hell's not going to be a holiday.

The car headed into Imbali via the Edendale Road.

I tightened the grip on my R1. It was a relic handed down from my father – who'd forgotten to hand it back, after being demobbed from the SADF, the South African Defence Force – during those chaotic transition days to a new democracy.

Twenty cartridges, still unused after many years, locked in the chamber, safety on.

Dad had been a careful man, give him that, at least. "Good bloody rifle in the bush war my boy, much better than that commie AK shit!"

Whether it had killed anyone, he'd always refused to say. *Dead to cardiac arrest a decade past – now, no one would ever know.*

The car stopped, alongside a wall and a large sign that said: WELCOME TO IMBALI.

I readied a sweaty finger on the safety catch, keeping the rifle low and out of sight, peering hard through the windscreen ahead. Cars were coming down the main street, usual township bangers, a few electrics and one black souped-up bling item – with a BLACKDEATH plate – roared its frustrated petrol power into the air.

"What's the problem, Cyril?"

Then I saw it. The road was being cleared to make way for a mini-convoy, of three armoured cars heading towards me, the huge tank-like vehicle in front spinning a siren that cut through the hot smog, with its bright blue scream.

The car pulled over, and I sunk deeper into my seat.

The tank-car moved past – but stopped, and reversed, until it was level. The car behind reversed too, the driver not sounding their horn.

Trouble fucking central. The kingpin must be in the tank. No one dares bark at the master. Or mistress? You never know, in this new world. Could even be both – or neither. Shit! Rifle doesn't squeeze under the front seat. Can't hide this baby.

'Cyril, 999 to local police,' I whispered, keep it sub-vocal.

The tank door passenger seat opened, almost simultaneously with the other three doors, releasing two armed men and a woman, as if sprung from a jack-in-the-box.

The passenger was more languid to step out, as if aware *they* were the one to be watched.

An average sized, slim black man, of shaved head and indeterminate age, but in a clearly expensive grey, smart suit. Slowly, he walked up to the back-seat window and waved my window down.

I could see this was a man *not* to be crossed.

<Emergency Services. Say 'One', if you are in extreme and imminent danger; 'Two', if danger is close but not yet realised; 'Three'...>

"Roll down the window, car," I whispered, words sticking in my throat.

The smart man smiled and put his hands on the window sill. "What's an *umlungu* doing here?"

<Sir, what option do you want?>

"One," I croaked, "It's a free country."

The man threw back his head and laughed. "Nothing in life is free any more, my friend, or have you not noticed? And one what? Or is this the start of a list, to try and convince my clever black brain, that you have a special right to be here?"

<We are now going to list Dire Emergency options in all eleven official languages, starting off with the most widely used, isiZulu...>

"For fuck's sake," I said.

The man narrowed his eyes and leaned forward. "You seem to have a piece of dangerous museum shit at your feet, *umlungu*."

He nodded over his left shoulder. "Search him. *Kahle kakhulu*."

<...isibhamu...> 'Shit. Cut link, Cyril.'

My door was opened by a man carrying a rifle straight out of Star Wars XX. I staggered out, my legs jellied and my bladder suddenly full. The man levelled his rifle and I raised my arms. *Shit, I'm harmless, man.*

The man kicked the door shut. "Up against the car, facing away from me."

Four armed men and a woman – and is that a young teenaged boy, standing behind the rear door, in the last armoured car?

One of the men searched my car thoroughly, while I bent my head over the roof of the car, burning my fingers. *What I do for you, Lizzie.*

"Just lots of cake and sweet wrappings and shit," said the man eventually, with a muffled laugh, from inside the vehicle.

Movement behind me, I turned. The smart, shaved man was standing in front of me, but with dad's R1 rifle swinging from his shoulder. "This is *my* town. I'm the one with the guns here. Let me guess – that white woman, I saw helping out at the Community Centre – she's your wife, *ne*?"

I nodded, throat locked with anger and dread.

"One. A word of advice. Keep her on a tight leash."

I opened my mouth, but nothing came out.

"Two. Go home. You don't belong here."

The smart man turned and stalked off.

"That's mine!" I shouted.

He stopped, laughed, and swivelled around, the rifle clattering against his hip. "I *might* let you have it back – if you can tell me – how many of my people did this shit-stick kill?"

Slowly, I shook my head. "I don't know."

"I thought not," the man turned and shouted across to the teenager, "Junior, you got a position lock of them on your phone?"

The boy nodded and got into the last car.

The smartly dressed man barked commands in isiZulu and the cars reloaded their *four jacks and a jill,* storming off, tyres screeching and sirens racing. Behind them, BLACK DEATH roared past, in gleeful slipstream.

"Where to now?" queried the car. *Dumb stimulus-response computerised shit, there's no AI interface inside* this *old* tjorrie.

I closed the door.

A small crowd had gathered at a discreet distance down the road, but they were melting away, the road up ahead clearing.

"Call Liz, Cyril."

<Phone disengaged>

"Durban airport," I said.

The car completed a three-point turn, while I wiped my face dry.

Out of Africa – and into the Federated States of America. A country broken years ago, by one some there called 'The President Who Shall Not Be Named'.

The car slowed, as we approached the San Ysidro point of entry, from America into Mexico – the cars and trucks starting to pile up around us. I caught the glance from Pedro, my driver, through the rear-view mirror.

"I show you the FSA-Mexican border wall further along, we not cross into my motherland, senor."

"Yes, yes," I said, impatiently, "And why don't you call me *gringo?* Are you really an illegal immigrant?"

The driver swung off along a slip road and headed towards the coastal wall.

The mirrored glance from the swarthy man was a little more intense. "I have the papers to prove it, *gringo,* stamped by the FS government. But you yourself, you do not sound American?"

"No," I said, "I'm South African."

The man guffawed, as he pulled over into a parking lot. "Now I know you joke with me – since when are Africans white?"

The Pacific Ocean was a green broken blur on the horizon, screened by an array of buildings that swarmed along a wall of majestic height, laced with buzz-wire on top.

I placed my floppy blue and white Cape Cobra cricket hat on my head – and braced myself for the heat, as I stepped outside, away from the car's aircon.

Hah. It was surprisingly cool, an overcast day, with a sea breeze fanning in faintly over the parked cars.

"Denialists love days like today," said Pedro, "for them, exceptions are the real rules."

"You still have them here?" I asked, sauntering over to the MAG wall, greyed in anti-climb paint. I whistled, "Twenty feet tall, give or take?"

<*Twenty-one,*> said Cyril.

"There are a few loud and dissident voices still left – but mostly not here, where the water is gone," said Pedro. He was a large and round-bellied man, who made me feel less ill at ease in my own body. "Come, I show you the real majesty of the wall, not many people know this section."

Pedro walked behind a busy Taco Bell, where a few richer people were congregating for lunch, and headed along a broken stone path, the Pacific at our back. He walked quickly, for such a large man and, after a while, as the buildings were left far behind us, I started to pant.

"Couldn't we have parked closer?"

"No *gringo*," said the man ahead, pushing through a bush, "That was the closest you can get. They do not like people to know about this."

"Any ideas where we're heading, Cyril?"

<*Based on our position and trajectory, I think we may be approaching a new tourist feature on the Rugged Guide to the FS, although the FS are demanding they remove the reference...*>

Pedro stopped, as we hit a blank wall perpendicular to the great border wall, which ran across our path, as far as I could see. Here, the wall was black and about eight feet, but sternly sprayed with anti-graffiti paint.

"So?" I asked, underwhelmed, "What's the point of this stupid wall, it's just stopping us going further along the border wall?"

Pedro grinned, his face shiny with sweat, and pushed aside a large dry bush, which seemed to be flowering broken plastic water bottles. A small irregular hole was smashed into the black wall and Pedro climbed down onto his knees.

"I fit through, you fit through," he said, as he started to crawl.

I followed, hesitating a moment, as I ducked to get under broken bricks. *Great place to get mugged.*

But Pedro's large hand was there, pulling me helpfully through. I stretched tall again, knees aching from broken stones.

I gasped.

Here, the wall was only about four feet tall. At various points along, torn and rotten blankets were hanging over the dead buzz-wire. A purple graffiti – smeared in irregular comic sans – spelt out NO PASARAN!

Flies buzzed around a drying pile of human excrement.

"FYI, that graffiti is blood, not paint," said Pedro. "Here, the Make America Great wall ran out of money, as well as cheap and illegal Mexican labour."

I laughed, "I didn't know that."

"It's an alternative fact."

"Of course," I said. "Cyril, get a shot of this."

"You do know this place is barred. They will scan your Rig before you leave. We will be on their MAG wall CCTV's. For this, I expect the price of bail three times over, should they arrest me."

I nodded. "My boss – uh, can *sometimes* be a generous man. I'll have deleted it all, before I leave. The electronic djinns have long fled the bottle."

Pedro smiled, "Just doing my legal duty as an illegal immigrant. Wanting you to stay mostly on the right side of the law, in the land of the free."

"After you, *senor*," I waved Pedro through first, "Did *you* climb this wall?"

The man hesitated, before getting down on his knees. "No, sorry buddy, I'm a legit FS citizen. I've just long figured most tourists want the street spice of the illegal."

I barked a cynical laugh as I crawled after the large man, wincing at what felt like further bruising of my knees, even with my tough clime-trousers. I let Pedro pull me to my feet.

"So, the name's not Pedro?" I asked, starting to sweat again. I pulled my hat from my belt and hunkered down, underneath the floppy brim.

"Pete," the man smiled, "Pete Gonzalez, I do have Hispanic roots. The best lies are half-truths."

"Well Pete," I said, alternating my gaze along the right-angled walls of grey and black, "I'm not sure *what* to believe. But you've been worth every penny so far. Still, I prefer Pedro. So, they built a wall, just to hide another wall. Why not just stack it on top of the shortened MAG wall section?"

"New Pence administration, new voters to please – and Mexico had had enough, trade was being renegotiated, as the States started to fracture. Red and blue lines – and all the colours in between. So now they keep hiding the worst of it, with that fucking Wall-Of-No-Name. And then the Union got suspended, whilst they've been sorting out Congressional impasses and central government failures. Individual states rule, at least for now."

Hmmmm, faux Mexican peasant accent gone too. Who is this guy, really?

"People can still get around the wall to have a look, surely?"

"Hah, *you* go, but you can leave *me* out of it. The place has been eco-mined with new thorn bushes, able to puncture the hide of a buffalo, let alone off-road tyres. And try walking in this heat. You just need to read a VanderMeer field guide, to know there's some weird shit going on out there. Come." Pedro began to head back in the direction of the Ocean, "All walls are stupid. But, at least with MAG on our left, we won't get lost."

The sun began burning aside the clouds, and I groaned.

It would be a long walk back.

I wished the denialists *had* been right. *Sweat is fucking itchy. And why do flies like it so much?*

"Here, *gringo*," said Pedro, stopping to turn and hand me a bottle of water, "FreeFlow Pure. Only the best, for such a well-paying tourist. Where you go to next?"

I took a big swig and flailed at flies homing in on my dripping neck.

"I have one day's grace before work begins," I said, "Hollywood, and the John Wayne museum, *pardner.*"

Pedro crossed his arms, "Legit. I have some Osage Indian in me too. I'm a fucking Mexican – American mongrel. So, no – I'm not your *pardner.* I'm no Tonto."

Oh.

Blunt man, but knows his shit. What's real here, though? Change tack. "How well do you know Hydro-City?"

Pedro finished off the bottle and put it in his recycling kit. "Now *that's* a proper fucking wall! Chops off San Luis, 'Dino and Kern from the north. I know it medium well, I spent five years there representing Southern Hispanic refugees, whose grasp of English was poor. That's until the Babel bots replaced us. Now they only call us, if there's a *cultural* issue to negotiate."

"Let me see what my boss says," I glanced ahead, looking longingly for a dash of cool green on the horizon. "Mongrels can be useful."

"*Gringo*, if the money's right, I can be anything," said Pedro Pete, heading off again, on the loping fast walk of his, with an ease that belied his bulk. "And mind them low down, nasty, rattle snakes."

I followed, feeling hot and fat, but staying alert to watch the ground closely, stepping gingerly.

"Any reply from Liz, Cyril?"

<Nada> said Cyril.

Fucking smart ass Rig.

This is America? Hot as hell here too.

Maybe more flies, even?

Chapter 11
Liz — When Home Calls

I slapped at the flies on my legs. *It's hot, I'm tired, and I need to go home. Where, though, is home?*

I've sat myself on a pile of leaves, in the shade of a tree in the corner of the rear garden of the Manaye Centre. I watched two children swinging, while another three played in the nearby sandpit, one having been lifted from a wheel chair. It was mid-afternoon, and the schools were out, and it had finally dropped into the low 30s.

The water queues had gone, taking their precious bounty — a few community police constables had tailed the older women home, to ensure there were no water hijackings.

Hard life for so many, we're blessed, we're lucky, are me and Graham.
We?

I checked my phone.
Missed calls. Graham. Message.

His face came up on the screen, looking tired and old, fleshy folds starting to hang around his jawline. It was a message from an airport digi-mat. I shielded the screen with a hand, to reduce the glare. "Tried to come out and see you there, in Imbali. Got waylaid by some serious bastards. I've had to go at short notice to the FSA; and wanted to say goodbye."

He looked down, and the video paused.
Restart.

This time, he looked even older.

"Met a… really nasty man, shall we say, in a tank-car, who stole dad's R1 and sent me packing. You're not answering… so goodbye, Liz. Speak later?" Graham looked away from the screen, as the clip spiralled into darkness.

"Hello, *sisi*," Busi had brought me some chicken and *pap* on a tray, with a mug of water. She put the tray down in front of me and sat down next to me, cross-legged, "Have the kids been behaving?"

"Lindiwe was a bit lippy, when I told her not to swing so high, otherwise all well."

"*Hayi*, Lindi's always lippy. And you, I see, are *not* well."

I thanked her, then picked up a chicken leg and started to gnaw on it.

"Graham? Or the endometriosis?"

"Graham," I swallowed, "Gone to America. Looks like he bumped into Imantshi, trying to come and say goodbye to me."

Busi tutted, shaking her head.

A small boy wanted a turn on the swing, but the larger girl ignored him, as he stood at a safe distance in front of her, waiting patiently. The smaller girl next to her slowed her swing with resignation, as if anticipating she would be asked to give it up.

I washed down some pap with water – I was starting to like it, having found it a bit stodgy initially. *Sometimes perseverance pays off – and opening yourself to new things.*

"Whose turn is it, to hand over the swing?" asked Busi.

"One guess."

"Lindiwe Makuba!" bellowed Busi, "Get off that swing right now."

The bigger girl kicked her heels into the sand to bring her swing to a sudden jolting halt and got off abruptly, scowling. The boy gave her a wide berth, before climbing on.

"Her parents were Burundian refugees," said Busi, "They're wanting to go back, saying life is much better there, now, and has been so for a long while."

The girl had stormed inside, as if to fetch her father.

"Have you spoken to Graham, since he left?"

"No," I finished the water and wiped my nose with the back of my hand. "I'll call him from home, he'll be in the air by now. I want to go home, please."

Busi stood up, with an ease and grace, which I wished I could emulate.

I got to my feet more slowly, with a grunt of pain; no, it seems like the 'metriosis *is* also working overtime today.

"Here comes *uyise*, Lindiwe's father," Busi whispered, as I bent and picked up the tray, with some difficulty.

Lindiwe's father was a small man, neatly dressed in brown cords and a blue collared shirt. He gestured his surly daughter towards Busi. "So, what must you say?"

"I'm... sorry."

He crossed his arms and said nothing.

The young girl turned to look up at him, scowling.

Puffing her breath out from cheeks full of exasperation, she glanced across to both Busi and I, "I'm sorry if I was rude, Aunties."

Busi smiled, "Thank you Lindiwe. We just need all children to accept that everyone should have their turn... Mister Makuba..."

The man had uncrossed his arms and was holding Lindiwe's hand.

"Could you and Lindiwe please look after the children for the next hour? I'll let the bar know water is on the house for both of you – and Lindiwe, you show them what being fair means, okay?"

The man hesitated and then nodded, looking across to the children playing in the sand.

"Yolanda's strong," I said, "If she wants to get back into her wheelchair, she doesn't need too much help, just got to be careful, as her shoulders dislocate easily."

A burst of five more youngsters arrived, an old woman, probably someone's *gogo*, in tow.

The man gave an ironic chuckle, as Busi and I left the playground.

"We're running low on water again," said Busi, "eThekwini have limited free water for the poor, but FreeFlow are charging fucking *everyone* for *everything*, since they have taken over running uMgungundlovu water. They insist water is a commodity, not a right. FreeFlow are hand in glove with LeisureLand. Those rich bastards are sucking us dry. We must find another way forward, if we're going to survive."

I heard her words, but did not respond. I was more concerned about Graham's last message. He looked so old. You can't just let almost thirty years of relationship go, either, just like that.

"Imantshi took Graham's rifle," I said.

Busi's walk stiffened, as we made our way through to the car park.

I clicked the car open and climbed in.

Busi hung on the driver's door, chewing her lip.

"What's wrong?"

"Imantshi's a man with a very thin skin, and a very large ego," she said, "He was not happy this morning. I want you to follow me. I know a less travelled way back to your house – a bit longer, but safer."

Busi closed my door, with a firm bang, that brooked no argument.

Dutifully, I followed.

They were waiting at the off ramp, and accelerated one armoured car in front of Busi, the other car behind me. The tank moved into the middle of the road.

Boxing us off.

An armed man and woman leaped out of both front and rear armoured cars, placing ROAD CLOSED signs up on either side.

The tank remained resolutely shut; as if waiting.

"Oh, dear God!" I shouted.

"Keep your doors locked," Busi radioed in to my e-deck, "I have you patched through, Liz. Stay calm, the bastard is sitting tight, wanting us to stew."

Frozen in terror, I was unable to move. Locks would be useless, I knew. Even my flame throwing key holes would not be enough.

The tank stayed shut, an enigmatic show of threatening power.

The man and woman stood, in military fatigues and white T-shirts, on either side of the tank, rifles readied, faces stone hard.

"Stay calm," said Busi again, "It may just be a threat. If not, it'll just be me they're after. They know white skins are still powerful in police stations. I've radioed in urgently to the police, although their fucking automated interface is due an overhaul."

I gripped the steering wheel with one hand, fishing out my taser with the other. I thumbed it on, as the tank door opened slowly. *God, I'm sorry I swore at the dominee. I will beg forgiveness from him and never stop going to Church again. Please, please help us.*

Imantshi got out slowly, naked, showing a large erection.

"Oh shit," I sobbed.

"I have a clear line of sight on your cock and balls," said Busi, through her car-speaker, "what's stopping me pulling the trigger?"

Imantshi's penis dropped like a flaccid flag, but his face turned thunderous.

He flashed both hands, signalling guards to train their weapons, one rifle on each car. A third man had stepped out of the rear door of the tank, perching his rifle against his right shoulder, eyes squinting along the sight.

I hovered my finger over the flame-thrower button.

So far, some three years ago, it had given third degree burns to a young man, who had only – it emerged from a subsequent investigation – been begging for money.

Now, only an extreme event would trip my finger.

This could well be it.

Come on, God, please *Jesus.*

Junior stepped out of the car behind Imantshi and gave him a *kikoi* to wrap around his waist.

"Junior?" shouted Busi, "I'm your aunty. Come here!"

"I am not Junior," the young man said, waving a large shiny *panga* he'd plucked from behind him. "I am Sharp Sharp Boy."

"Come, open your door and get in my car, Busi Baby," called Imantshi, "Or I will ask my guards to open fire. I will teach you how to show respect."

Busi got out slowly, stood behind her door, and levelled her gun.

What are you doing? Don't be crazy.

Imantshi laughed, flashing his hands towards his chest, as if inviting her. "Come on, bitch. I will give you such a good time in my car, you will never look at another woman again."

Crack.

Imantshi walked backwards and leant against the open door of the tank, held up for several surging heartbeats by the angled metal at his back. His nose and mouth spouted blood.

He looked confused, almost dismayed, before crumpling slowly forward onto the road. The guards and young man watched him fall, in horrified disbelief.

Busi kept her pistol levelled. "Police are on their way. I advise you to drop your weapons. Now!"

Guns and a large knife clattered onto the hot tarmac.

"I *will* get you home, Liz," said Busi, "But there's going to be another detour, I'm afraid. At least a police charge office should be fractionally safer."

I wept.

Terse texts bleeped on my phone. *Goodbye. On Plane. Will call from FSA. Love G.*

Busi scolded Junior. "Get in the car right *now*, mister!"

He got in.

Quickly.

Sirens…

Slowly, I took my finger off the flame-thrower button.

And sobbed some more.

"Who pulled the trigger?"

The detective was a sharp-looking middle-aged woman in a neat brown suit, her dreads coiled into a tight pile on top of her head, as if in reluctant submission to a strict police dress code. She had a square, tough face, and sat in the softest chair, which was also distractingly mobile. Her body swivelled from left to right and back again repeatedly, as she seemed to push off from one foot – and then the other, as she talked.

Busi and Junior, were sitting on hard chairs, on the wrong side of Detective Makholwa's large desk.

I stood, wrong side of the desk too, my pelvic pain having kicked in hard.

A scribe bot eagerly readied itself to take notes, digital ears flapping – but standing respectfully in the background, as if hoping to learn enough to become a detective one day.

I watched it all unfold, in tiny details, as if I were standing outside my body.

But this detective was watching all of us, as if she were an African Goshawk, swivelling in its nest.

"I did," said Busi, "I have a licensed pistol – and I was acting out of defence to a rape threat."

"What was the actual content of the threat made? Did they say they were going to rape you? And is murder better, or worse, than rape?"

Busi flashed a glance across to me. "Which question shall I answer first? And you're a woman, what are *your* views on rape?"

The detective did not bat her eyes. "Start with my first question. What did the deceased say to you, word for word? And remember, we have witnesses from the other party."

"Other party? They're a fucking murdering criminal gang!" shouted Busi.

"Calm down, and mind your language," the detective stopped micro-swivelling her chair. "Until proven otherwise, we are all equal in the eyes of the law. What did the deceased say, word for word?"

Detective Makholwa placed her clasped hands on the desk between us, and her suit rode up her arms almost to her elbows, but could go no further – it was held up by her rippling forearm muscles.

No movement. Her feet must be squarely on the ground by now, her gaze on Busi steady.

The bot in the background leaned forward, learning.

"I want a lawyer," said Busi.

The detective clucked her lips and tongue in annoyance. "There I was, thinking we were starting to get along so well."

She swung her gaze up to me, "And what were you doing there, *Mevrou* Mason? You're not a township tourist, surely?"

I licked my lips, to open my mouth, "I'm a voluntary worker there…" My words ran out, dried up by the searing gaze across the desk.

"And you, young mister?" Makholwa swung across to look at Junior, who had slumped in his chair, having pulled it a little further away, before sitting down.

Busi stood up, "I was taking him back to school where he belongs. Are we done, until I contact my lawyer? Am I free to go, for now?"

The detective looked up at her and chuckled, "You've not stolen a car, Ms. Mhlongo. You've murdered someone. You can go – for now – but Asimov here is going to have to put a data chain on your ankle. You get me?"

Busi nodded, ushering a truculent Junior towards the door.

I followed.

Asimov the bot had opened the door and was leading the way in to the charge office.

"*Mevrou* Mason?"

I stopped by the door and turned, reluctantly.

The detective had started her mesmerising swivel again. "The other party were in possession of an unlicensed automatic weapon of unknown provenance. Extensive fingerprints suggest your husband may have been in ownership, until very recently. I've pinged you my contact details, should you decide to talk. I would *strongly* advise you to do so."

I opened my mouth, but a shout came from behind me. "I told you that we want a fucking lawyer!"

Someone grabbed me by my shoulder, pulling me out of the room, and into the corridor of the police station.

It was Busi.

"Let me put on their fucking shackle, and then let's get the hell out of here," said Busi.

"Home," I sobbed.

"Home."

Home was empty.

And hot, very hot, having stored up the day's heat.

I had wanted to be alone, so Busi and Junior left, after the briefest of stays for a refuelling drink of well water. At least the aunt and nephew had started talking to each other again, even if only in terse, bitten words.

Not many words for me. What am I doing? Am I indeed playing a pitying tourist in the country of my birth, and the country of my foremothers, and their mothers before them?

What is my own mother doing now? I should give her a call.

I peered through the patio window – the farmyard garden looked bigger. And emptier.

Empty scares me, but aloneness terrifies me even more. To love and be loved.

I tucked a tiny taser into my pocket and walked into the garden, seeking out late afternoon shade from a large, orange aloe bush.

All I could hear was the repeating 'crack' sound – *and watch the slow crumple, of a naked human body.*

So, so dead, but so little blood from the young man's body to show for it.

'Bullet through the heart's a bastard,' Busi had said, revealing a decade of quietly diligent marksmanship practice, behind her eyes, hands and finger. *'Hashtag MeToo.* Many times, but no more.'

My phone rang, and my chest tightened. *Graham? No, he's still* en route *to America.*

As for me, where do I belong? Where do we belong?

"What is it, Busi? How are you? How's Junior?"

"Well, you know the feeling, after shooting someone..."

Silence.

No, not really.

"You could humour me with a chuckle at least, sister. Junior's warming up to me again, but maybe not in a good way."

"What do you mean?"

"He's called me a 'kick ass' woman, for 'taking down' the local water-king *tsotsi.*"

"Well, *you,* at least, handled it all so well."

"Not so –"

Was Busi – crying? Why did she have her video off?

"I, I...j-just wish we had libraries again, and I could be a librarian. Full stop. Paid enough, living safe, and reading all the shit I wanted."

"I'm sorry, Busi." *She is crying.*

I went to sit on the bench, by the wooden sculpture of a Burchell's Coucal, my favourite bird. I longed to hear its liquid call again, a flowing sequence of notes, like pouring water, summoning the rain.

Rain Bird.

Water is falling, but I can't see it, I can just hear it in the sniff and struggle of Busi's voice.

"I'm s-s-sorry," Busi said.

"You had no choice," I cursed and slapped a biting ant off my ankle, "Bloody *Matabele.*"

"Hey, the *Matabele* are my tribal cousins. It was you whities who named your fucking pests after us."

I chuckled.

"That's better, let's try and focus on smiling instead." Busi's face flickered onto the screen, her eyes puffed and pink. "My company have just summoned me to their HQ in America."

"Do you know why?" I lifted my feet off the ground. *Going to get the ant killer powder out. Pronto.*

"That detective moves quickly. She's too efficient for her own good. She's looking for intel, and I'm thinking she's let on to my employers. My hunch is, they're calling me in for a severance talk."

"Dear God, no, I'm sorry, Busi – whatever happened to innocent until proven guilty?"

"*Ja well*, you know the saying, it never rains, but it pours? Except it *does* never rain."

I chuckled again. *She keeps smiling, even through the worst of shit – how does she do it?*

"You – uh – do you want to come with me? They won't pay for you, but I've got a bit of money tucked away. We can maybe take a week, even see the place a bit?"

This space was too empty, too quiet.

Even the garden was turning against me.

But this place, at least, I knew. "I've got some early retirement money, from my past teaching jobs," I said, "I'll think about it."

"Thank you, *ngi'yabonga, sisi.*" The line went dead.

The sun was disappearing; the growing coolness chilled my skin, in the early summer evening.

I jumped over the line of ants, to go indoors.

Where do I belong?

Home is a hard word.

"Hello, my dear," said Du Preez, stepping through the patio door, "What a pretty garden you've made here."

I stopped.

Shocked, I stood frozen, near the tank-well, where the man hole was secured shut to prevent anyone falling in, and my throat crunched tight.

He was a small man, with a swarthy complexion, that may have tested the racial classifiers in long gone apartheid years. He was dressed in a casual, creamy khaki smart-suit, seamed with health apps to ensure he stayed in the best of shape, despite the adversity of our climate. His face was sequinned with pasty pink powder to keep the cancers at bay, his black hair combed over neatly, to hide the bald spot peering through near the top of his crown.

He carried a red rose. *I am watching it all, in fine, horrifying detail, as if I were hovering above my body again.*

"I got your pass code from watching your *hubbie* key in his home entry, he doesn't always switch his Rig off, as I'm sure you, ha, ha, know?"

"What. Are. You. Doing. Here?"

Du Preez bowed, holding out the rose, his gaze averted, "Wooing a wonderful madam. For you, my dear."

I avoided the rose.

Instead, I applied my favourite taser to Du Preez's outstretched hand.

The rose fluttered to the ground.

"*Shit…!*" was all he managed, before crashing to the ground, limbs jerking, face snarling.

He twitched and groaned for several long seconds, before closing his eyes and relaxing, lying on his side on the pavement, as if quietly asleep.

Some white mini mints had spilled out of his top pocket.

"Stings like hell, doesn't' she?" I said, looking down on him, but busy with my phone. "I call this taser my Button Spider. South Africa's smallest, but deadliest, widow. Hello –?"

"Hello, this voice is familiar. *Mevrou* Mason, isn't it? Are you calling to say it was really *you* who shot the deceased? Or have you shot another someone else, in the meantime?"

"Well, actually, I may have tasered someone, but…"

Detective Makholwa's sigh was a resounding one. "*Mevrou*, I will send a sergeant over there to investigate, sharp, sharp. Your husband must be a terrified man indeed, whenever you are nearby. Or is *he* the victim?"

The phone clicked off and I looked down again.

Du Preez was still unconscious, drooling down the left side of his crumpled face.

Matabele ants, drawn in by the sweets scattered around, were crawling over his body, a line filtering inside the front of his health-suit.

I winced. *Perhaps I'll hold off killing those ants just yet.*

I thumbed a text on my phone: *Busi? Yes, I will come to America with you.*

I knew Graham's itinerary – *perhaps we two can also be different, together, in a different place? How much are we shaped, by the spaces we inhabit?*

Reluctantly, I called the paramedics, just in case.

I waited, taser ready, for the police and medics to arrive.

The man groaned, stirring nearby.

My phone rang. *Busi? Graham?*

"*Ma*! What are you calling me for?"

Ma was on Vid-Kontak from Cape Town, her ice white curls framed a cheerful and age-creased face. "Just seen an online video of you going ballistic, swearing and storming out of Church, dearie – my goodness, what on Earth have you been up to?"

I readied the taser again, as Du Preez struggled to get to his feet. "You're not going to believe me, Ma."

The Button Spider bit again.

Chapter 12
Art — A Chinatown Meal

Chest hurts, as if bitten, or punched.

Dark. Cold.

And what's wrong with my arms? My legs?

Nothing moves. Am I broken… or dead? Is this hell – why's it so cold? I thought hell was fire and brimstone, whatever that is. This can't be heaven, surely. Heaven would not be so cold, so painful, so bloody dark.

A light? Getting bigger – it's an angel – no, it's a human face, it's…

…Jack Nicholson?

A light flickered on above me.

An eco-light, with just enough juice to reveal I was strapped in a chair, arms and thighs bound.

A bulky white man stood, across from a small and empty table, the masked face flickering under internal illumination.

A devilish, young Jack Nicholson e-mask.

No angels here.

"I trust you're feeling better?"

Jack Nicholson's voice too, seemingly resurrected from the grave?

Those masks cost a fortune. Someone wishes to remain anonymous.

Someone with money.

"Assault and trespass on federal land, you've already committed enough crimes. Let me go, right now." *Keep it factual, get them on the defensive. What do they want with me?*

"Yes, I'll let you go," said Nicholson, "First, you tell *me*, why were you snooping?"

Where's Gen? My wrist is empty, hollow without him, so fragile.

The man noticed my glance down to my wrist and smiled – a slow, devilish e-smile; the mask responding to its facial cues below. "We've had a go at opening up your smart watch, but it's gone back to factory settings, I'm afraid. You're a smart man, so no easy password for you, hey? What *were* you looking for?"

"Who's we?" I asked. "You've broken the law, so let me go, before the shit you're in, gets even deeper."

"Ooh, a naughty word, coming from a religious man. You tell us what we want to know, we let you go. Simple. And from where I'm standing, your seat is the place that stinks."

How does he know that I'm a man of faith? Creepy. And what is he saying – have I shat myself?

I sniffed, but the space – large room, warehouse maybe, our voices were echoing – was numbingly cold and empty to my nose.

Nicholson laughed.

Is he gaslighting me? Give him something. Anything. Something small. "We were looking for fish."

"Well, if you're hungry, why didn't you just say so?"

Another light bobbed, from afar, a pinprick, getting larger and larger, turning into…

"Faye Dunaway?" I asked, stunned.

"Very good," said Faye, placing a tray down on the table, "You're an old movie-head, I can see."

The plate was decorated with four thin, grilled fish, reeking slightly of cucumber.

"Bon appetite," said Faye.

"You caught and roasted the fucking smelts?" I shouted. "That's a highly protected fish!"

"Extinct, last I heard," said Faye.

"Ooh be careful," said Nicholson, "The Lord does not like a foul mouth. If this is the last of the smelts – which we sincerely hope so – we are offering you an extremely valuable gourmet meal, The Explorer's Club style, which many would pay *millions* for. Remember, every moving thing that liveth, shall be meat for you. Or fish. Genesis nine, verse three."

Nicholson threw his head back, to laugh uproariously.

So heartily, I caught a glimpse of his exposed throat and neck.

"I'm not hungry," I said, miserably.

Dunaway spoke, coldly and sharply. "You do know there's no fish on the land where you were looking, don't you? We're not dumbass jerks. So, what *were* you looking for, on solid land, by our fence?"

"Don't know," I said, "Bastards. Rot in hell bastards. Are you from FreeFlow?"

"We're the Men behind the Gold Curtain. We have paid for – and run – this fucking world. We fill it with trash news, for common herd brains, that keeps us hidden. You, small fry paupers, are like smelts – we eat you for breakfast – or lunch, depends on our fucking mood." Nicholson turned away, as if starting to lose patience.

Dunaway smiled. "And women," she said, "Never forget the women behind the curtain too, Jack. What *were* you looking for, dear?" She reached out to stroke my thigh, with a long pale finger and pink fingernail, but keeping a careful physical distance. *Why?*

Now I could smell it. I have shat myself. Why am I ashamed, even though it is they *who are the criminals here?*

"Nothing." Behind my tears, my voice sounded small. *Keep a grip, Art. We don't let them see they're getting to us, do we? Dad's voice.*

Nicholson turned back, as if excited by the drop in my voice. "You, at least, have properly disappeared behind the curtain, Faye. Me, I'm still pulling at it, waiting to be let in."

"Don't be jealous, dear. You will be disappeared in turn soon, I'm sure." She stepped away from me, as if abandoning any attempt at pseudo-seduction, "We've deleted Fish Bot 358's records. Bots are *so* prone to internal glitches. If you *have* found anything, know this. We know where you live – and where your ex-partner and your mentally retarded daughter live. So, you *bury it*. Whatever it is you were looking for, you say nothing – you shove it as deep as fucking hell itself!"

Nicholson moved in, clearly excited by the bite in Dunaway's voice.

"As for Zeke," said Jack, "you'd best get back to her. Very remiss of you to leave her swimming all alone. You never know what might happen. She is, by the way, very definitely a woman."

Nicholson laughed at his last line, an ugly braying bark, which froze my veins.

Faye nodded, and a man stepped from behind me, the man who had darted me.

He fastened a lifeless Gen back onto my left wrist.

"We're not thieves, dear," said Faye, "We just need to protect our investments."

"Well, if you're not hungry, Faye and I will enjoy this fish," said Jack. "It's time we let *this* other small fish go, hey Faye?"

"Wait for me," a voice called from the darkness, "Next to elephant or hippo meat, extinct fish is my favourite."

A tall man appeared, suited in white, with a strangely familiar e-face.

I blinked, "Lenin?"

He laughed, "A fucking dead Beatle? What on earth do they teach them in history classes nowadays? Don't you know who I am – who *we* are? As Adam Smith put it so aptly, in the glorious year of 1776, we are the Masters of Mankind. Oh, and I'm so very sorry about the accident your colleague Zeke had – you saw her drowning and rushed to help, but fell on the rock with the clothes, breaking your smartwatch, and knocking yourself cold."

The man next to me had a lead cosh in his hand and stepped in to smack my wrist.

Crack – crunch.
I screamed, as pain shot up my arm.
"Sorry, but we have bigger fish to fry," said – Stalin?
The cosh swung at my head.

This place was light and hot.
Wrist stings and throbs, head throbs, focus eyes and head. Bad stuff going down, deep bad stuff, devil bad. Remember. Wrist?
I wept. Gen, green turtle watch, crushed into splinters on my bleeding wrist.
Zeke? Surely not.
Where is Zeke? Get up, lying on hard rock, and wet.
Blood on rock, head very wet and hard to see, only one eye working. There, 'copter sits, lifeless. Here, stream flows, sun heading down into derelict buildings across the water. No one moving. Fed land, protected. Safe?
Where is Zeke?
"Zeke!" I shouted hoarsely, "Zeke!" I staggered along the stream, where I'd seen them last...
There.
Clothed, but dishevelled and on their back, mouth and eyes open, face blue. Lying, legs in water, as if they'd been drowning, and had tried to pull themselves out.
Dead.
No doubt.
Behind me, I heard the whirr of a drone.
I screamed, staggering around to see it.
It was marked with our blue water agency crest. The drone touched down, with a lurch, on the grassy bank.
"Art, what's happening?" *Suraya's voice.* "You've been incommunicado for almost three hours. Where's Zeke?"
"Zeke's dead!" I screamed, "Zeke's... drowned."
I collapsed next to Zeke's body, seeing their – her mouth, frozen open, as if hauling in a last and desperate gasp.
I could not touch... her.
I could only rock and keen, as Sally lay alongside me, a blue and dying baby. *Zeke, my baby, Zeke, my baby...*
"Emergency medical forensic team on their way, Art. Stay with me."
Suraya?
Zeke, baby Sally, Zeke, baby Sally... They... She... died... alone.
Weeping, I crawled forward and cradled Zeke's damp head in my lap.

Their tongue was stiff and half-bitten. *I'm so sorry, so, so sorry…*

So cold, as darkness crept in and chopper noises blew hard from above and behind.

Music bled from the drone.

Suraya?

She was feeding through my all-time favourite song, from The Dead Earth Brigade, "Voices of the Dead Live On."

People around me, they are strangers.

The music started to penetrate my bones, so I yelled along with the chorus, keeping the strangers at bay.

"The Dead Stay with Us,

Voices within Us,

And We Go On

Dead Beasts All,

(drums)… Arise, the Earth.

It's not over…"

"Till it's over." A woman bent down to take my right hand, "Come, Mister Green. I'm Doctor Sadiqa Haseem, my forensic team will deal with this. You need some cleaning up, and some rest."

No, I need to stay with her.

I should have stayed with her.

This is my fault.

Zeke.

So, so sorry.

"Come." The doctor was not to be dissuaded, her pull on my hand strong and insistent.

I stood, sobbing.

I knew, somehow, the delta smelts were truly dead and gone, too.

"Come," the doctor pulled me away and I followed, because her voice was kind.

And she knew good music.

Zeke was being stretchered behind us.

It was a big chopper, this one, but that's all I remembered.

Wednesday, Wednesday

Tuesday gone, buried in flights and medication, a sutured and strapped wrist, a bruise over my left eye, a police interview and DNA sampling, of which I remembered very little too.

Apart from their irritation at how little I said.

Each step down into work basement then, was a step of relief, a step further into a solid and safe familiar space. Gender neut toilet, 3-di Holo-Mat, three retractable desks with 2-di holo-screens, one empty.

Very empty.

"How are you doing buddy?" Suraya asked, eyeing me sympathetically from her desk. On my desk sat a black coffee, still cooling off, as if Zeke themselves had just dropped it off.

I looked across tearfully at Suraya, "Two brown sugars?"

She smiled and nodded.

Where to begin? What to do? A meeting with RC in an hour, a meeting with the state shrink in two. And I can say nothing of what happened...

Even though it had infiltrated my dreams, and stopped me from sleeping.

Alone, trapped, unable to say anything.

I scanned the all too familiar room again. *Have those two cameras always been there? One over the stairs, one over the Holo-Mat? Why have I never noticed them before?*

I sipped my coffee and gave a tentative thumbs up to Suraya.

How do I work? Gen is gone, my wrist strapped in stiff pain.

"Come up to my office, Green."

No mistaking the curt voice of Director Carruthers.

This time, I took the elevator, carrying my cup of coffee – which only seemed to be making the ache above my left eye worse.

I felt fragile, unable to deal with anything, and wondered if I should just go home – and call in sick. *But alone is the worst, when memories swarm in, like ill ghosts.*

The elevator opened, and I stepped out.

Turn right along the corridor and down one flight of steps, and I could leave the building, at ground floor reception.

'Don't run from nothing. Unless it's the winds of hell, boy.'

Twenty-five years dead, but still haunted by dad.

I steeled myself and turned left, taking a sip of hot coffee to wet my dry throat, as I approached Dr. Carruthers' door.

It dilated open, as if sensing me, and I stepped inside, almost spilling the last of my coffee.

The Director was in conversation with a stern white, grey-bearded man wearing a green suit, shimmering with tech.

The man stood up, as the director waved an introduction.

"This is the DA for NorthCal, John Shottens; John, my Data Sweeper, Arthur Green."

The law.

111

The man was of under medium height, eye gaze level with me, but with a grip on my good hand, that threatened to crush any resistance.

I swallowed, as I took a seat. They were turning up the heat. *What are they suspecting? Are they going to charge me with neglect, or even manslaughter?*

"Uh – do I n, n, need a lawyer, sir?" I put my coffee down on the Director's desk, making sure it was on a coaster, but my shaking hand missed, and it spilled.

Coffee dripped onto the desk, and off onto the carpet.

The Director waved at me, indicating I stay sitting and leave it.

"Depends," said DA Shottens, "if you're guilty."

"Of, of what?"

"Rape," said the DA, watching me closely.

I jerked. Shocked, mouth frozen. *Rape?*

The Big Dee responded, "Dr. Haseem is a forensic pathologist, with particular expertise at retrieving sexual violence evidence. Whoever raped Mx. Klein was under the misapprehension that running water would wash away all traces of crime. But... a woman's body, it is *not* a simple thing. It seldom just *lets go,* of the shit it's constantly dealt."

"But, but why are you telling me all of this?"

"Well," said the DA, leaning back, "There's been no DNA match with you, we've already tested for that – but maybe you were working with someone else, perhaps?"

I looked at them both, swinging my head in horror. *Can't say. What about Michelle and Sally? Will they be hurt? Can't say nothing. Trapped, like smelt on a plate, gasping for breath, dying.*

"This room is secure, Art," said the Director, "You're safe here – as are your family. We have them in a witness protection programme, just in case."

Relief. Big relief. "How, how did you know?"

"The police are not stupid – and you're a bullshit liar. They said you were terrified to say anything, as if you'd been threatened. Easy for us to think who we might need to protect, if we wanted you to feel free, and able to talk."

The Director must have given a sub-vocal to *Theia* – a holographic image of Michelle and Sally (with dino-fairy) flashed briefly onto her desk, and was gone.

"So, what do you say, Mister Green?" The DA flicked an organic straw from his sleeve and started to suck on his sweetened sweat. "We need to know if you have any idea as to who might have done this – we can't sweep the entire Non-Crim population in NorthCal. We just know the culprit is largely of Caucasian origin."

I hesitated.

"There may be other Zekes," said the Director.

I wept.

Only one Zeke. "Wat – it was Watson of FreeFlow – I was captured and interrogated by them, when I approached their land."

They both looked incredulous.

"Seriously?" said the DA, "We're going to need some pretty strong justification to test *him*. They have a hornet's nest of lawyers at their disposal."

"He was wearing a digital disguise, but, but I recognised the three potential carcinoma spots on his neck, near his jugular, forming an almost unholy triangle, about an inch apart."

The DA looked across at the Director, who nodded. "My man has the eyes and mind of an AI – and more. I'd lay a million down on him."

The DA smiled, tightly, "But we're talking over a thousand *trillion* business here."

The desk glowed.

"Is that you Suraya?" said the Director, "You were only supposed to call in an emergency."

A voice came from the air. *Suraya indeed.* "They've managed to patch some repaired information from Kelly the 'copter, Director. Seems like Kelly caught a data burst from Gen, before Art's smart watch went dead. Location was right against the fence of FreeFlow property, in the delta."

The memory hit me like Zeke's splash of water, their laughter still echoed inside my painful head. *Ahh, the burn on my left wrist, as the net dropped over my head. Intense data discharge?*

"They will claim coincidence," said the DA, standing up, "thank you both for your time. That's probably not enough I'm afraid, but we will see. I am offering you and your family witness protection throughout the investigation. You will need to disappear for now. But, in this day and age, that's one *helluva* thing to organise."

Safety. They will keep me close, though, too. Am I still a suspect?

"Let us know if we can be of further help?" said the Director. "Justice delayed, is justice denied." She nodded at the man leaving the room, and then reached inside her bag to take out some tissues. "Here you go, Art – the least you can do is clean up your coffee mess."

I wiped the desk clean and threw my cup into recycling. *Why is she watching me, and not getting on with her work?*

"Goodbye, Director," I turned to the door, but she placed a gentle hand on my good arm.

"Families are indeed our secret jewels," she said, "When they work well, they give us a glimpse of heaven."

Was that another poem?

"We look after those we love, don't we Art?"

"Yes, Director," I said.

"A bit of tough love is needed right now, I'm afraid," she said, "I'm sending you up to the top floor."

Not the black hole.

Why? "What about my family?"

"They will be at the airport at three, you have permission to leave early, after you've spoken to our shrink. But we *do* need to build a stronger case – so speak to Jenny – she's the best lawyer we have. The police will provide an escort for you and your family. Keep safe those whom you love – and that one's mine. Trite, but true."

My truth is:

Leave room and...

Go to the top floor. There, at least, lies safety. It's the most protected place in the State.

I sighed.

Up into the black hole, again.

My head throbbed even harder, as if in dreaded anticipation.

Chapter 13

Graham – From Hollywood to Hydro-City

Los (New) Angeles, Home of Hollywood.

John Wayne got nuthin' on me.

"What do you think, Pedro?" I posed, having strapped on holsters and shoved a wide brimmed, white hat on my head. Fifty FSD was a steep price for the holographic 'to order' stage set, a Comanche Indian camp, but I had always had an early childhood love of old cowboy movies. *The original* Die Hards.

As always, I blamed my dad. *Long dead and gone, but always loved.*

Pedro lounged at the open-door green café opposite the stage booth, spooning back some cannabis cake and washing it down with coffee, strong and pungently black. He ignored me, or else he was lost in cake and coffee.

People swarmed across my vision, blocking my view of the large man. We'd been ranging through VR exhibits of the Californian west, including many animals, some now long gone from the world, some perhaps barely hanging on, like those delta smelt fish, from the 'Frisco river region, other side of the Super-State Wall.

I spotted a small queue of three youngsters waiting for my holo-cubicle, chuckling amongst themselves. *Bloody boys.*

Pedro finally shouted, from across the corridor. "John Wayne, The Searchers? Have you checked the RCL, that is, the racism classification level of that clip – it's barely legal, no wonder you're paying over the odds, you goofy looking shit."

How dare he speak to me like that? But I *had* wondered what the blinking red seven had meant, underneath the 'tap in $50.00' command, when it had uploaded my requested scene.

"You *do* look like an asshole," said one of the boys, with no hair and a scalp full of electrodes, blinking like Christmas lights. "Get off, it's our turn."

Stupid *bloody kids.*

I didn't even bother to get a holo-photo. I stormed off, to perch opposite Pedro, who licked cream off a spoon, slowly.

The large man watched me over his raised cup, lifting his right eyebrow. "I did some research last night," he said, "Some South African whites are still worried or ashamed about the country's last century legacy of racism. Are you?"

"No. That's so *last century*. I do my bit to make things better," I growled, "and I'm not paying *you* for that sort of research, either."

I turned to glance across at the Holo-Cubicle, and watched with bemusement, as two Saturnian astronauts and a Plutonian Dragon engaged in open warfare, with lasers and fire. *Weird, stupid, bloody kids. What's with the new generation?*

"You look like crap," said Pedro, "What's eating you?"

I looked at him, surprised.

The man sat squarely, hands folded neatly, watching me closely.

"No call from home – and bad dreams," I said curtly.

"Ooh," said Pedro excitedly, "I dig dreams. Tell me."

"Nothing to tell," I said, reaching out to grab and finish off Pedro's coffee. I put the cup down between us. "I am being threatened by a man, holding my father's gun."

"Very oedipal," said Pedro, leaning across to snatch my shirt, before he yanked me over the table.

I could smell a sharp mixture of coffee and weed, as Pedro opened his mouth to talk.

Slowly.

"No... one... touches... my... *tinto*... without... asking... me... got that, white African?"

"What's a *tinto*?" I asked, alarmed.

"You *are* kidding me?" Pedro let me go, with a look of disgust. "Don't you speak English in Africa? Coffee – black coffee. The only kind."

I smoothed my shirt out. "I'm sorry, that was very rude of me."

"Don't even *think* of doing it again," said Pedro, as he turned to watch the dragon's flames be extinguished by incessant laser fire. "You drink my *tinto* again, I'm gone."

<*Call coming in. LB, Lizette Basson.*>

'Connect,' I muttered.

<*Graham, are you alone?*>

"No," I was both relieved and surprised, at Liz's sharp opener. *She's – okay? But what the hell has been going on?*

Pedro stepped away, to speak to the kids who'd finished their VR play. *Now that is polite*, I thought, with a brief pang of shame at my own rudeness.

"Yes, now, I *am* alone, what's up – are you safe?"

<*...Yes.*>

Why the delay? What's she hiding? "What's going on? Where have you been, Lizzie?'

<*Lots of shit going down, but it's not the right time or place to talk. Yes, I'm okay.*

I just wanted you to know I'm coming to America. I'll be in Hydro-City in two days' time. I'm accompanying Busi, who needs to report to her company there, FreeFlow. We can talk properly then. It is on your schedule, I see.>

"Yes, yes, it is." *Stunned.*

<See you then. I'm okay, but lots – and I'm telling you, lots to talk about. Ons gaan maar aan, ne?>

"Connection cut."

We go on, yes? What does she mean?

I stood up and Pedro wandered back to me, from across the small corridor, the place starting to empty out.

"Nice kids," said Pedro.

Ja, right... How is Mark doing, in New Zealand? Gotta contact him and find out soon.

But first, lots to do.

"I don't want to be a cowboy no more," I said, tossing my white hat into the empty cubicle. *Tired of feeling shamed. Claim that on office expenses.* "It's time to get to work. So, we're meeting your water contact, in the hotel lobby, in an hour?"

"*Sí,*" said Pedro, retrieving the hat, "It may look like shit, but it'll keep the sun off. Thank you."

He shoved the hat down on his large head, as I braced myself for the over one-hundred-degree Fahrenheit early evening heat outside.

"You're welcome," I said, dryly. *Got to remember, this is Fahrenheit, not Centigrade, and it's not really the temperature of boiling water, even though it sure feels like it.*

"A word of advice, senor," said Pedro, stepping outside ahead of me, "When we meet Luka, drop the phony American accent. You sound like a constipated Australian."

"How many of *those* have you met, then?" I shot back. *Outside. Shit, and I thought Africa was hot?*

Pedro stalked ahead at a rapid pace, for the three blocks west, from the Hollywood Wild West centre to our hotel, as if to stop me catching him up.

I contented himself with phantom quick Colt 45 draws and silent shots into his back, before I became too breathless and sweaty to continue.

Still, my spirits stayed lifted, as the sweat began to pour down my neck.

'Ons gaan maar aan' – yes, Lizzie, we do *go on.*

Luka was a *Neut* of indeterminate age as well as gender, with a tan onesie coolant suit, elasticised to support their large girth. I could swear their face and flesh-folds were tanned to match; their hair extended with black dreadlocks. They did not get up to say hello, instead they slouched heavily on a couch in the corner of the quiet hotel bar, the sun having only just set.

I sat on a stiff stool to keep jetlag at bay, while Pedro went to fetch three drinks.

"Record, Cyril… As Pedro told you, I'm doing a doc on the local water wars. Tell me who you are, and what it's like, living with the water crisis, here in LA, at this moment."

Luka smiled, showing off perfect white teeth, "We're cool, but also fucking hot, know what I mean? I'm Luka, and I'm a data designer for FreeFlow. What I really want to be, though, is a Water-Knife."

"What's that?" I asked, baffled, wondering whether I would need a cultural interpreter for my entire trip, too, despite the common language.

Pedro dropped three *mojitos* onto the table. "From an old *Bacigalupi* book – a decent film came from it too – describing a bad-ass dude who cuts water deals on the depleted Colorado River, in an arid South-West. *Kinda* like now – just cooler." Pedro was looking increasingly to be value for money, as a cultural interpreter.

"The first and best water-knife was Bill Mulholland," said Luka, sipping their *mojito* as if it were water, "LA was running out of water in the 1920s, so he cut secret deals on the Owens River and piped that precious shit, back over two hundred miles. Local farmers bombed the pipeline when they found out, but Big Bill nailed the law behind him. Genius Water-Knife. The St. Francis Dam failure was *not* his fault."

"They made a movie of that, too," said Pedro, "Chinatown, with Jack Nicholson and Faye Dunaway."

"LA always wins in the end. Fucking SF Forty-niners… Are you going north of the wall?"

Given that Luka's monologue and eyes were aimed at their drink, I wasn't sure who the question was meant for, but assumed it must be for me.

"Yes," I said, "There's always two sides to every story."

"Fuck no!" said Luka, "We *gotta* get rid of those lazy bullshit ideas. There *ain't* two anything. No two genders, no two sides to any fucking stories, no two races, no black or white…"

"Tan is the colour of the FS Post-Racial movement," Pedro said, having finished his drink. "Expense tab stretch to another round?" he looked hopefully at me. "Makes the interviewees talk easier."

"No," I said, "Their tongue is loose enough already." Hadn't meant to say that so loudly. But it looked like they hadn't noticed? *I'm not used to drinking on an empty stomach. Get them back on topic.*

"So how does LA survive, with enforced Northern water restrictions?"

"SouthCal ingenuity, that's how, TAD turns our shit into water, like they first did in Africa…"

"Namibia," I offered. "What's TAD?"

"That's what I said, Africa. TAD is the 'Angeles Desalination plant – and some mobile bots hoover up saline contaminated areas from sea rise, but that shit's expensive and they've had to keep raising the fucking taxes…"

"Meaning?" I prompted.

"The cities are shrinking, man. Hollywood's dying. Those bastard Nigerians and Indians have hi-jacked our movie business too. Although Tom Ekubo, at least, has come over here."

"He has?" I said, "Since when?"

"Since he's moved in with his boyfriend from Die Hard 22 – you know, the white villain."

"No," I said, appalled, "Not Jake Small? Seriously?"

"I know," Luka let out a shrill giggle, "What the fuck's he see in that shaven headed bozo, right?"

"Let me guess," said Pedro – I noticed him quickly knocking back the remainder of my *mojito* too – "Underneath that fucking face paint, Luka, you're white."

Luka put their empty glass down and glowered across at Pedro for a second or less, then looked away. "No such thing as white any more, mister, we're all shades of brown. And F-Y-I, it's melanin shifting. Face paint is fucking superficial, man. Cheap, but you get what you pay for."

Shit, I'm losing the thread of this. And Tom is… gay? Focus, Mason, get back to the job at hand.

"You got some clips we can use, on the local water scene?"

I glanced across warningly to Pedro. *Come on, let's keep Luka on topic, they're charging us by the minute and Du Preez could be watching, without me knowing, the bastard. God, I wish they had some good African beer here – even a Lion lager or three, would do me right now.*

"Sure," said Luka, leaning forward and flicking his e-pod. A building on giant tracks mushroomed onto the table, hoses gurgling, winches, cranes and pipes spinning. "The new DeSal 100, only the best from ElektraEng Mobile Corps, sucking the sea to secure water with sweet certainty. No more ice caps, lot more sea. Only the salacious best with sexy FreeFlow Pure." The machine morphed into flowing water in the shape of a naked, young and genderless human body, seemingly squirming with pleasure.

"Well?" asked Luka, sitting back and throwing a glance at Graham, "Cheap at 30 grands; for your documentary."

"You're talking *Rands*, aren't you?" I asked. That bastard Pedro had finished off Luka's drink too, but the Neut didn't seem to have noticed, he seemed to be swigging on air. *Who's being rude now?*

"What's a *Rand?*" asked Luka blankly.

"Never mind," I said, "We're not interested in paying for product placement. We want facts, presented in a fun way, which will engage people on the Stream-Webs."

Luka opened his mouth and arms, gesturing above his e-pad bemusedly, as if that was exactly what he *had* offered.

"What's the plans of LA to survive – you got any inside info, Luka?" Pedro leaned forward, breath smelling of fermented lemon mint.

Luka slipped their e-pod into their onesie breast pocket and stood up quickly, despite their large size. "War," they said. "Someone fucks with you; you kill them. That fucking wall will come tumbling down, just like the defence system of the fucking '49ers. Go 'Rams!"

Luka was huge when standing, and I could feel the crick in my neck, as I peered upwards, to keep their face in shot. Pissed, in both senses of the word. *On half a glass...?*

"I turned up, so send me the rest of the money. If you're going north – like Lauren Oya Olamina – and you're crossing that frigging wall, swallow a bomb for me on the way in, will *ya*, and blow up all those fucking wildlings."

"Like who?" I asked.

"You haven't read Butler either?" Pedro asked me, scornfully.

Luka flashed a holo-card close to my eyes. "Get a load of that, brother, and join the Post-Racial present, we can challenge lying racist A-holes, like the White Brotherhood."

Then they were gone.

"Poor bastard," said Pedro, "Thought I recognised him. He was a huge motherfucker – played one season for the LA Rams as defensive guard ten years ago and then boom; knee goes and he – uh *they* – have to find a new life, and way of living."

"I don't think I'd cope very well within a gender uncertain world," I said.

"Wake up, it's all around you," laughed Pedro, "And it's a fucking blast." He thumbed a last thimbleful of drink from his own glass, "But it sure helps, having been a woman before."

I turned to look closely at the large man, his rough beard starting to prickle through his cheeks. "You're shitting me?"

"Of course." Pedro grinned, sucking his thumb. "So how you are *you* coping with a post-*racial* world, then?"

"I'm not going to paint my face brown. I am what I am."

Pedro chuckled briefly to himself and then turned to face the hotel lounge – and bar. "You want more interviews here? Or you *wanna* get pictures of drowned Long Beach or the Marina del Rey? Or shall we just chow down?"

"I just want to get to Hydro-City, *pronto*. Looks like I've got interviews with both FreeFlow *and* the EPA. Let's eat."

"Learning some Spanish too, I see," grinned Pedro, "Any chance of one last drink, before we have supper?"

"You've had enough," I stood up stiffly, bum sore. I seemed to be getting thirstier and thirstier again. *They've put pay-meters on their public bathroom taps, despite the room cost, the stingy bastards. And where's Du Preez? Not like him at all to seemingly lose touch, especially when his company's money is being spent so freely.*

<Office, on>

"Ah, at last, where you been Du Preez?"

<Doctor Dlamini here, Graham. I have taken over the reins of business from Meneer Du Preez, who has unfortunately been removed, after a shareholder vote.>

"What?" I shouted, in disbelief.

<We need to renegotiate the terms of your contract and your current project. Petrus will not be back any time soon.>

"Petrus?"

<Petrus du Preez, chuckle>

"You go and eat," I said to Pedro, "But stay off the booze. I'm going up to my room. I've lost my appetite."

<I'm looking forward to talking to you soon too, Graham. Call me back, perhaps after you've had a stiff drink on room service. Only one, mind you. This is Doctor Dlamini signing out, for now. >

How much did Luka say fucking face paint cost?

I spun the *Neut's* contact card in my mind.

Nahhhh…

The plane circled lower and lower over Hydro-City and I whistled, craning my neck to see the small city nestling behind the large wall, with massive aqueducts, one empty, one half-full, lining the earth beneath us.

"Looks damn messy down there," I said.

"They've just had the mother of all dust storms," said Pedro, "It's going to be hot, dry and dirty."

"Sounds like home," I said cheerfully.

"So's your new boss happy for you to continue?"

Boss! "Yes," I said, looking down again, as the plane straightened and began to head in for the runway. "On one condition."

"What's that?" asked Pedro, staring at the seat in front of him, knuckles whitening on the end of his arm rests.

"I get enough black faces into the film. You know any here, in the water business?"

"A. Few."

Not like Pedro to be so terse. "My wife will arrive late tomorrow."

Pedro said nothing.

I turned to look at his pale face, "You aren't, uh, you aren't *scared*, are you?"

Dust was swirling past our window, in a noisy rattle.

"Shitless," Pedro managed.

I laughed. We bumped down – with the hint of a skid, as the plane slowed down rapidly. "But you're such a big man," I said.

"That's why I'm scared," breathed Pedro, with a huge sigh of relief. "There's a fucking lot of me to get hurt."

I looked out the smudged window, as we taxied in to our allotted landing bay. Hard to see anything at this level, apart from dust, concrete and glass. *Is this where we are to recommit our lives, Lizzie, to growing old, ever happily together?*

"Welcome to Hydro-City," said the Captain, "Please ensure your documents are in order. Illegal aliens, including FSA citizens not from NorthCal, will be met with extreme prejudice."

Hah. This is just like home, in so many ways. I put on my new hat, a dark brown one, reminiscent of Clint Eastwood in 'The Good, The Bad and the Ugly.'

"Clint was actually the fuck-ugly one," grumbled Pedro, pulling his bag out of the overhead.

"There are two kinds of people in the world – those with loaded guns, and those that dig. You dig?" I shouldered my bag, and the door ahead opened.

"Oh, I dig," said Pedro, "I dig all the time."

There were only a few of us, so I led the way out of the plane and down the steps, onto the searing NorthCal concrete.

Chapter 14
Liz — The Sting of Justice

Rock hard justice? They arrested *me* for assault.

"Seriously?" I said, as they led me through the garden gate, to access the front of Cope's Folly – and the waiting police van. "But *he's* the intruder here."

I pointed at the recovering Du Preez, who was sitting up groggily, with two nearby paramedics packing away their equipment.

Du Preez unleashed a volley of invective.

"Same to you," I tossed over my shoulder, "And let me know if you need any more *encouragement*, to take my picture off your stinking phone."

The male constable, labelled 'Jonkers', opened the back of the van. "A lovers' dispute? We usually don't bring in domestic – but it's *bledy* unusual to have a woman dishing it out."

"No, he doesn't live here. I'm married – I want him arrested for trespassing and sexual threats."

Jonkers, holding my arm tightly, pushed me into the back of the van which was, I was relieved to see, empty. I perched on the raised side section over the wheel, as far away as I could, from the slippery corner stink of stale urine.

Jonkers banged the door shut, "Just received a notification – that man, Mister Du Preez – *he's* claiming to be the victim here. He's going to pursue a charge of assault and GBH, apparently triggered after he turned down your strong sexual demands on him, when he was just checking up to see that you were safe. There's been no forced entry, *that*, I have already noted."

I leaned towards the grill at the back of the van, shouting, "Du Preez, you fucking *bliksem*!"

But the van had already begun to bump into motion, and I scrambled to find a seat again, holding onto a railing above my head. The driver laughed through the reinforced metal grid between us.

"First time, missus? I suggest you hang on a *lot* tighter."

I lost count of my bruises *en route* to the police station, but for some minutes I had become more worried, about the state of my soul. *Fucking? I said fucking. Will God ever forgive me?*

Then I remembered Du Preez and sat still, holding onto the overhead bar, ever more tightly.

"Rot in hell, you bastard," I said, beyond caring.

Captain Desai was a small, seemingly mild-mannered man, and a relief to finally see, after three hours of waiting in the charge office area. The waiting room was chaotic, seething with a noisy mixture of both wronged and wrongdoers; screened by bored cops, who seemed to enjoy taking statements as slowly as they could.

The Captain's office was small too, but neat, with a tiny South African Federation flag perched on the corner of his data desk. A large poster of President Ncube smiled beneficently down on his back.

Reassuring to see a first woman President perched so high, hopefully the start of real change, at long last? Been too many false dawns... and she is the first Zimbabwean premiere of the Southern African Federation, too.

The Captain rocked back in his chair, fingers clasped across his stomach, over a small but noticeable *boep*. Not quite as large a tummy as many I'd seen, at least it looked like he attempted to stay fit. "*Wel, mevrou, Engels of Afrikaans – ek is tweetalig, natuurlik.*"

"*Natuurlik,*" I replied. My life was split – Afrikaans at Church and shopping, English at home with Graham. *Where is he now? He will panic if I call – and there's nothing he can do for me now, anyway.*

"Afrikaans," I said. *From my first home. It's been a long time since I saw my mother live, it's been twelve years since we left Cape Town. Vid-Kontak is not the real thing, you can't touch or smell them... I'm starting to miss ma so much. And she'd said pa's starting to 'lose his marbles'. What does that even mean? He? He wouldn't talk to me.*

"Do you want a lawyer?" the Captain asked, "I would suggest it. Mister du Preez seems an angry and vengeful man, with a large amount of money at his back."

The captain – he's actually... kind?

It hit me then.

Through the Du Preez event, the police arrest, the van drive, the Charge Office, I had kept calm, cool, distant, observing.

Now, my observations were over.

I wept.

And wept.

The captain stood alongside me, patting my left arm, holding a clean tissue.

"Come, come, missus, everything will be all right."

"How do you *know?*" I said, wiping my nose first, always the point of initial dribble, when I cried.

His desk beeped, and he glanced at it, with obvious relief, "A Mx. Busi Mhlongo outside for you. Do you want her to come in?"

I burst into a fresh torrent of tears – but these felt different; better somehow, lighter, and seasoned with relief.

The captain stepped back, alarmed.

I couldn't talk, but nodded furiously, as Captain Desai first went in search of a full box of tissues.

Chief TL Dumisani was a long, thin man, ramrod straight, despite his age. He didn't sit, he paced – and, after he finished pacing, he leaned back in his motorised wheelchair, near the window, where he could look out on his last three cows. They were two adults and a calf, the adults grazing peacefully on yellowed grass underneath the *mopane* tree.

He whirled a hand in the general direction of me, Busi and the large woman with papers by the door.

"These are my final three cows," he said sadly, "They need to eat and drink too, but there is never enough, and the beef tax is too much. And it only gets worse. I know we must all learn to eat and drink less, but most of my people have so little anyway. What about those who sit on the top of the hills in their large mansions, behind electrified steel, and who keep sucking our water uphill?"

The large woman was fanning herself, with what looked like court papers.

The Chief turned to look at her, "So, my legal friend, how can we help our two young women here?"

Our? Young? I turned to Busi, to hide my brimming tears from the Chief. I had a few tissues left from Captain Desai's box, the previous night.

I dabbed my eyes. "I'm white," I said, "Why are you helping me?"

"The country has grown greyer since the apartheid days of the *Groot Krokodil* and the later years of the Zuma-Gupta State Capture," said the Chief.

He kept watching his cows, flicking a command with his thumb on his chair console to the outside water-bot, allowing the cows a few more minutes at the water trough. "Black, white, rainbow, the colours are all fucked up now. Like my cows. You've been helping us too, ma'am. You are kind."

"And so we help you – ah... just incoming," said the large woman, leaning forward to place her e-pod on the Chief's desk. "Hello, Attorney Chiluba here."

A face flickered upwards in 3-di space from her pod, sprouting like a cloud. *A man, with severe frown lines etched into his forehead.* "Judge President Mxele, of KZN Province."

"Sir, what is your decision, Justice Chief?"

The man licked his top lip, as if still deliberating. "You have made good representation, Attorney Chiluba. We will allow defendant Mhlongo to spend three days in the Federated States – but only under ankle supervision of a mutually agreed FSA legal representative."

Busi glanced across to me, with a wry smile. "Permission to travel to the FS to get my ass kicked," she whispered, mimicking an American accent.

"And as for the case against Mrs. Mason?" asked Attorney Chiluba.

"A lesser allegation of offence, she can travel with impunity, as long as her documents are in order."

"Thank you, Judge President."

The cloud-man nodded, and his face evaporated.

Busi and I stood up to hug each other and attorney Chiluba.

The Chief was bent over, leaning his chin on the windowsill of the open window. "Does the mother look healthy to you?"

A calf tottered into view, searching for a drink.

Busi went to stand over his shoulder, "Baby is drinking," she said, "Babies know best. Mom is well enough."

The old man clasped her wrist briefly, "Look after yourself, dear, don't let those cowboys bully you, and remember…"

"*Ngiwuzulu mina, angihlulwa lutho*," said Busi, "For I am Zulu, nothing defeats me. I will never forget, Uncle."

"Indeed so," The Chief looked around, "You are excused, Attorney Chiluba. See you in our next CAG meeting. The bulldozers of the rich are coming."

I looked at Busi.

"Community Action Group," Busi mouthed.

The lawyer nodded; and left.

The old man turned to his few cows, again. "It's not always true you know, about how we can *never* be beaten. British guns did so, in the end, despite *Isandlwana*. But, in my long years, I have managed to make a few friends in high places. Yet, out of the so many things I have faced, this cow mother has beaten me. Hard." The Chief pointed out of the window.

"How so, uncle?" asked Busi, placing her arm across his shoulders.

The Chief carried on talking, as if I were not present.

"I can no longer eat beef. These cows, they are human. And they, at least, are kind too."

Busi's head jerked, as if in shock. "You do not eat beef *at all* any more, uncle?"

The old man closed the window and Busi helped his shaking body into

126

his wheelchair. He looked across at me and smiled.

"Not one forkful. Sacrilege, for a Zulu man, and a chief, not to eat beef. But *you* look as if you know how to keep a secret, Missus Mason."

What does he mean? I nodded, taken aback.

"Good, my reputation amongst the Group of Chiefs could never survive that."

"You need rest, Uncle," said Busi, "We will leave you."

"And when you're back," said the Chief, "We will need to carry on the fight. We are now under an eviction order – they wish to 'gentrify' Imbali – *gentrify?* Pah! Bulldozers to break the poor – and then handing our land to the rich... And if this FreeFlow will not give us access to our water, we must take it back."

"Water must fall," said Busi.

Busi kissed the old man on the forehead, and we left the room.

On the drive back home, alone and drifting through an informal settlement seamed with struts sucking skywards at passing power lines, my hands-free set kicked in.

"Missus Mason?" The voice was vaguely familiar.

"Uh – yes?" *Surely very few have access to my number?*

"My name is Doctor Bongani Dlamini, I have worked with your husband, Graham."

"Ah -!"

"I gather you have been involved in an altercation with my boss, Mr. du Preez."

Shut down, cut contact, or refer to lawyer?

"If you have any evidence of wrong doing on Mr. du Preez's behalf, our shareholders – as well as the scream sheets – have a right to know."

Dear God? It seems that man has angered more than me? "It's under due process, I'm afraid." *Keep it curt.*

"Sometimes due process fails, ma'am. He is claiming, on the Siren Torrents, that it was *you* who tried to sexually molest him."

Bastard. "Do – do creepy phone clips count?"

"Uh – such as?"

"Car; play section 352 of the phone clip from 21st November."

'Hüsss... My screen saver is your face, a great shot, taken the last time your man pleasured you, and you came. I can do even better than him, you know, just, ja, like give me a chance, ne?'

Silence.

"Doctor Dlamini?"

"Jackpot. Thank you for your time, Missus Mason, I'm sorry about what has happened to you. Goodbye."

He didn't sound that *sorry to me, though.*

"From your side at least, keep my identity secret, please, there's an ongoing legal case."

"Of course, *mevrou.*"

I screeched to a halt.

I'd reached the last shack before the road wandered left, up to our farmstead. A young girl had run into the road, chased by an even younger boy. I had just missed hitting the boy. I kept my windows up – *could be a hijack ambush?*

The two children came to my window, dirty, ragged clothes, begging. They were white.

I shook my head. *This is Africa, as Graham always said.* I scanned the surroundings carefully, before dropping my window.

"Some money please missus, for food," said the boy, holding his palms out.

"We're from *Vrijheid,*" said the girl.

I could tell, from their cracked and parched lips, what it was that they *really* needed.

I handed the girl my bottle of water. "It's recyclable, you get money on returning this to a shop."

Sighing, I closed the window and handed self-drive over to the car.

Coming up to the gates of Cope's Folly, my mind fretted. *How many black kids have I driven past, neither noticing, nor caring?*

I rummaged in the cubby hole. *Damn. Where on Earth are those last tissues from Captain Desai?*

Busi spotted the news, just as I had finished talking excitedly to Graham, telling him about our impending arrival in America.

We were seated in the waiting lounge at Durban airport and Busi was scanning the Biz-Fizz sites. She looked up, smiling, "*Ons gaan maar aan?* Where are you *gaan-ing* to?"

"Just a phrase," I said, defensively, "Is that why you're smiling?"

Busi pinged an item across to my e-pad.

I looked down.

Travel media giant Du Preez Enterprises shares drop precipitously. CEO removed after being reported for 'conduct unbecoming'. Fighting on many fronts, CEO du Preez drops assault charges against local, unnamed woman.

"You, at least, are free," said Busi.

"Hmmmm," I said, "As long as he only had one woman who was giving him such grief. Who knows how many he's threatened, on the side-lines?"

"*Boarding call for flight XE559 to Edinburgh, en route to Hydro-City, NorthCal, the Federated States of America.*"

I stood up and grimaced.

"Aren't you happy?" asked Busi, shouldering her bag.

"Ecstatic," I said, "But my flying phobia has just taken over."

"Well, let's go fly that phobia off, then."

Busi took my hand, pulling me towards the departure gate.

A surly security man followed, carrying Busi's ankle tag monitor.

"*Ngiwuzulu mina…*" whispered Busi into my ear, as we hit the back of the boarding queue.

"For I am Zulu," I said, squeezing her hand.

But Busi looked tired, defeated, and did not return my squeeze.

The flight to Hydro-City was via Edinburgh, in the Republic of Scotland. Busi laughed at my attempts with a Scottish accent, but we never even got off the plane, having to stand and stretch in the aeroplane before our next, long leg of the journey to Hydro-City.

We took part in a few VR movies and games *en route*, including one short one, entitled 'WHAT SHIT IS GOING DOWN?' – in which we were flies on the wall together, having to see how many organisational secrets we could find out, before the Game AI swatted us out of the game.

Busi was adept at dodging the swatter and managed to get to four different rooms of the phantom company, seemingly focused on selling behind the stage tickets for top pop acts.

As for me, I wasn't even able to get out of the first room, where the staff supervisor was particularly swift with his insect spray.

"You're not used to being hit, are you sister?" Busi said, holding my hand, to help me stop shaking. "Never mind – the people in the other rooms were even bigger shitheads, turns out it's all just a front for a people trafficking ring. Fact and fiction blur. Felt like a FreeFlow documentary. Why can't they have *good* people, in these games?"

"This is your captain speaking," said a voice over the tannoy, "We are about to begin our descent for Hydro-City…"

Busi's grip tightened.

"I'm okay," I said, "What are *you* expecting from FreeFlow?"

Busi strapped her seat belt on, "They'll fire me, no doubt, too much of an embarrassment, should people find an employee of theirs is being charged in a murder case."

129

"But why call you all the way over for that?"

Busi shrugged, "I'm black. They're extra careful to dot the 'is' with us, because they don't want to fall foul of racism accusations. It'll be face-to-face and oh so civilised, in their HQ."

"And no union rep?"

Busi laughed, "They're too big for the unions. No one tangles with these mother fuckers any more, not even the FS government dares take them on. Corporations rule the fucking world now. Money still makes the world go around."

I did not laugh in response.

The plane was falling furiously, and I closed my eyes, hearing Busi whistle, "Man, that's one *moerse* big wall down there..."

I jumped.

We were down and had slowed rapidly to a taxi-pace, everyone thrust forward against their seat belts. Only once we had finally stopped, did I open my eyes.

Busi was already towering over me, pulling bags from the luggage space above us.

"Who's your tag monitor in the FS?" I asked.

Busi leaned down to whisper, "No idea, but I hope they're happier than that miserable *mampara* behind us."

The surly man looked up from the seat behind, but he still had his 'pods in.

Off the plane, we could feel a brief wash of late afternoon heat, before we entered the terminal.

At customs, Busi was searched thoroughly, at one point being taken to a room with a female customs official for a formal 'interview', while I went off to find a toilet.

Busi came back with a look of resignation on her face. "*Gonna* have *so* much fun, these next three days. *Whooppee.* Let's go get abused by the next official in line."

But there were none.

"Graham," I said.

He swamped me with a crushing embrace, and I gave him a brief and embarrassed squeeze back. *Persons around.*

Graham introduced us to a large and swarthy man standing next to him. *Pedro, Hispanic?*

"We can offer you a lift," said Graham, leading the way through the airport, as if he were a native. "Let's get your bags. How was your flight?"

"Just one bag, shared," I said. "We're only here for a few days."

He nodded, marching ahead as usual, "And the flight?"

"Pleasant enough," I laughed, as my words had come out simultaneously with Busi's.

"Snap," I added.

Graham seemed irritated, "Like our marriage," he snapped.

In public Graham. Really? What is up with you? I deflated, as if punctured.

The baggage pick-up room was not overly busy – not many could afford the climate flight taxes; apart from the Gods of the One Percent. But still, I felt both shame and hurt, and looked down to hide my tears.

Graham stepped past me, as Busi secured the bag, "Let me help you..."

Busi brushed him off. I heard the anger in Busi's voice, as if she'd clearly picked up on some bitterness from him, too.

Switch off these damn tears, Liz Basson. Enough.

Graham started yet another apology.

I'm so tired of this. An endless run of 'sorries' to secure us together? What a fragile and empty word chain to keep living by.

I pushed past, following Busi out into the heat.

Busi waited at the taxi rank, talking about finding her own way to the hotel, but Pedro started to josh with her, and I relaxed just a little.

The big man could be funny. He, at least, made a drive together to the hotel a bearable prospect.

The taxi dropped us off at our destination – the Life-Water Ranch.

Graham got out to try and help with the bag, gripping my hand hard.

Let me go – wish I could have brought my Button Spider with me...

"I'll call you later – perhaps we can go out somewhere nice tomorrow?" he asked.

I nodded. *Anything to make you go. Feels like I need to sleep for another two days, at least. Jet lagged – and more. Pain, always sapping, standing in my pelvic wings.*

The two men ducked back into the red car-bot and pulled off.

Busi and I headed for the shade of the reception at the Life-Water Ranch. The decorative plants around the hotel lobby were all succulents, low on water and maintenance.

A woman with striking grey hair and a sweat suit of steel grey to match detached herself from the Reception desk.

She held her hand out. "Hi guys!" She turned to Busi, "You *gotta* be Boo-si. I'm, Jenny Johnson, state monitor while you're here in the FS. You ladies fancy a drink?"

Busi smiled, not even bothering to correct the pronunciation.

"As long as you're paying," she said.

The woman laughed, "Come on, let me show you the bar."

Despite my exhaustion, I followed them through into a bright bar area, with a sudden surge of energy and hope. *No idea why.* She just looks a hell of a lot nicer than anyone in that game WHAT SHIT IS GOING DOWN?

I'm done with dodging.

Jenny Johnson looked like someone who always dealt it straight – and seldom said sorry, unless it was certainly needed.

"So," said Jenny, as she looked at Busi's ankle tag, "What shit's been going down, sister?"

Chapter 15
Art – The Neurodiversity of Dragons

The door that led into the huge open plan on the 12th floor of the Water Tower was large, white and forbidding.

An additional new sign – in red and black – had been placed below the plate that stated 'Hydro-Law, State of NorthCal':

PLEASE CHECK IN ALL GUNS AT RECEPTION.
STRICTLY NO CARRY, OPEN OR CONCEALED.
METAL WEAPON DETECTOR IN DOOR WILL
UNLEASH SEVERE SHOCK. ENTER AT OWN RISK.

How can I cope? Stay calm and factual, keep it all at a distance. You know how, Artie boy. You're an expert. Bring in numbers.
One, two, three, five, seven, eleven… Remember, you're one of a kind.
And so, after checking there was nothing metallic in my pockets, not even foil from gum wrappers, I opened the door to peer inside.

The room buzzed with bots and lawyers, air swaying with flying digital maps and graphs. *A veritable hell on earth…*

Ah, over there in the corner. My God, she's completely grey now.

I weaved my way across the room to greet Jenny Johnson; the room opening into layers of noise and light.

She was busy in standing conversation with Bok Kai, a cloudy, swimming blue-dragon, the Chinese Water God that had protected the town of Marysville, NCA, since the 1862 Great Flood that had turned the Central Valley into a floodwater lake. *A Chinese-FSA Avatar or AI, purportedly showing off the best in current international co-operation.*

"Jenny Johnson," I called, "It's Art Green, Data Sweeper and Dredger from the EPA, Water Division."

Jenny turned, as did Bok Kai too, in flashing three-di holographic space.

"You do not interrupt a God," said Bok Kai, as he swirled a watery tail.

"I'm interrupting this woman," I said bluntly. *Stop this charade. Your interface is surely human. AI or Avatar? In any case, One God's enough. The One True God of Abraham, Isaac and Jacob. And Jesus, of course. Oh, and the Holy Spirit. Three Gods Are Enough. All Rolled into One… the uncertainty of numbers? Shit; why am I wanting to cry. Focus, Art, focus.*

"Good to see you again, Art," smiled Jenny, a pale, raw boned woman, of medium height. Last time we'd sat and talked, she had seemed so tired and shrunken and small. "I'm dreadfully sorry to hear about Zeke! What an awful tragedy."

She probably only knew the provisional basic facts right now. *Drowning accident. Oh God, feelings are too often horribly tied to facts. Hold it together, Art!*

"It's been ten years since *we* last talked, hasn't it?" She carried on, as if she'd picked up on my pain.

"Three years and one hundred and thirteen days," I smiled.

"Hah, always the man with the numbers," laughed Jenny, "It's *felt* like ten years. Boy, do you look like you've been through the wars recently. Come, let's move over there, next to the window, away from the testosterone stink in the SVC corner."

"SVC?" I asked, following her long, navy suited amble. Her hair had grown, tumbling grey curls down her back.

Jenny turned to lean against the large window, and perched her rear on the narrow white windowsill. "State versus Corporation," she grinned, "But what brings you to hell, Art?"

I looked out, hands pressed against the window, and gaped. *No, don't look.*

The California Aqueduct rumbled under the wall in the dusty yellow-brown fields, glinting in the sun. Closer in, but numbingly empty, was the great Bakersfield-Kettleman City Up-Hill Aqueduct, switched off from Kern Water banks, in the escalating North-South Water war. That had been just before the failure of the Cal WaterFix tunnels, and NorthCal declared political separation, to build the wall. *That's it, facts keep feelings at bay – keep 'em rolling.*

But; the water was slowing. The Southern Aqueduct south was half-full, titrated as it passed through the wall, dependent on figures agreed between Southern need, and Northern need – or greed, as some argued – with constantly varying degrees of supply and largesse. *That, too, is an ongoing numbers battle being fought inside this massive hellish chamber, right at the top of the Water Tower.*

Here, I looked over the SS Wall, to the growing refugee camp, as drought conditions stiffened in the South. Fifteen left dead, after the Trump Tornado had passed. *Official counts, that is. Numbers slip, slide and distract from the actuality of death, too.*

As for TAD; The 'Angeles Desalination works, they'd been a lifeline to a shrinking city, but too expensive to send water out into the surrounding Ventura-Orange Desert, where crop failures were tightening belts too. The desert had swept north, begging at our wall. *Only God can save us now…*

"Art?" Jenny asked. Concern showed on her face.

How long have I been standing here, focused in facts?

"Chinatown brings me here," I turned, and looked a wannabe God in the eyes. Bok Kai had followed us.

"Chinatown?" asked Jenny, as she handed me a bottle of water.

"An old movie from nineteen seventy-four, about the water wars in SouthCal in the 1920's."

"This shit has been going down for a long time," said Jenny.

"Chinatown? Sounds like my kind of movie." If a dragon could sit, Bok Kai would surely have sat.

Jenny looked at me quizzically and I nodded. *Okay. Three's a good number, then. All in this room have full security clearance, in any case.*

The buffalo tattoo on Jenny's left cheek shimmered pink, from subdermal neural implants, fed by her Rig command: "Secure-lock conversation, sixteen square feet. Unless any of us invite someone else in."

Why show off your Rig to the world? Was her buffalo a sort of totem, like my Gen, my turtle smartwatch had been? My wrist ached like shit, worse than my head, if I'd had to choose. *Seems to be little choice, when it comes to pain, though.*

"Where's Chinatown set?" asked Jenny.

"Mostly LA," I said, as I handed the water bottle back, "Thank you, but I no longer drink FreeFlow Pure."

Jenny opened it up herself, and swigged, "Ah, the city of Angels."

"Suraya said she'd join us, virtually speaking," I flicked a toggle on my office fob and Suraya's face hovered between us, in blue.

"Actually," Suraya said, cutting to the chase, "I think it's all to do with fish and free shit."

A three di image of a large stream feeding into the Sacramento-San Joaquin River Delta, pulsed alongside Suraya's face. A red line flickered along the perimeter of the FreeFlow Corps fence and into the delta, tracking across and under wetland, to a small local sewerage works.

"This is what Art and Gen tracked, before he was, uh, accosted – looks like a leaking and illegal underground pipeline from the sewerage works to the FF water factory. They are indeed complying with their pumping quota from the delta, but they're saving someone else treatment costs by unloading extra shit into their purifiers for drinking. You scratch my back… and all headed for FreeFlow Pure, only the best."

"Uh – okay," Jenny tossed the rest of her bottle of water into a nearby recycling chute. "But what happened, Art. *How* were you accosted?"

I hesitated, my mind a chaotic bundle of facts that would not stay still, nor stick together.

Suraya spoke for me, "Zeke was… killed, murdered we think. While Art was captured and threatened by FreeFlow, we're certain, and then questioned as to what he was doing there."

Jenny looked across at me. "Jesus, you really *have* been in the wars, haven't you?"

I nodded, as my eyes prickled.

"We're gonna need more proof," said Jenny, "That company owns most of the world's water, and can buy out whole national economies. You can't get much richer than them. They have Quantum AIs and lawyers dangling off their gold ceilings."

"The DA will not move on my evidence alone," I said, "I'm the only one who was clearly there." *Why did I leave Zeke? If I'd stayed, would she still be alive?*

The dragon drifted in closer, drawing my gaze. *Eyes fiery red, penetrating and alive.*

"I know you," said Bok Kai, "I saw you near Suisun Bay, walking alongside the river, with another."

…Chinese satellites picked that up? What fantastic resolutions they must have, what mind-blowing integrative face-rec tech. My God – on this desiccating planet, they – we – have the power to see everyone, and everything. Yet somehow, so many of us still grow thirstier and ever thirstier?

Not quite *all of us. A few have swimming pools to drink from.*

"Our District Attorney would be *very* interested in that data," said Jenny. "How much did you see, Bok Kai?"

"Just walking – and the other one was then swimming," said the Dragon, "Before nanobots clouded the sky, like locusts scouring for food."

"This could be the additional proof we need, to push for more evidence. But what was that earlier bit you mentioned, about the fish?" asked Jenny.

"Those bastards ate the last of the delta smelts!" I shouted. "And, and…"

The worst of it, I could not say.

I crumpled into a sitting crouch on the floor, seeing Zeke's half broken tongue sticking out of her gaping blue mouth. *They killed my friend. They raped and killed her. And tore up everything she was, and what she was going to be.*

"We *will* share our records with the DA, Arthur Green, justice will be done. Before the cloud covered my eyes, I saw three men leave the nearby property. Two armed men headed for you, the third was walking to the river." said Bok-Kai, dropping to my level, claws on concrete, flicking his tail. "And then, darkness fell."

I sobbed, while Jenny called in the psychologist.

In the end, both facts and feelings, they fall.
And, just perhaps, a God has spoken?

It took me a long while, however, to fall for the psychologist too.

"You *do* know you have some autistic traits, don't you?" said Dr. Brent, a middle-aged blond man losing his hair, combed back over a balding pate.

"Yes, I know – but how does that help me?"

We'd moved on from discussing Zeke's death – I had refused to dwell on this, as I had become tired of tears, reasoning:

They cannot bring Zeke back.
Tears hurt.
And they waste water.

The man studied me, with a slight smile over his deadwood data desk. "The more we understand ourselves, the better we can deal with the things that are challenging us." He opened his palms on his desk.

"So how does that help me? And isn't it being neuro-diverse, not autistic?"

He nodded, slowly, "Yes, although it depends on your model of the mind."

"One last time," I asked, "How does it help telling me, that I may – or may not – be autistic. I was bullied at High School, for being 'jack shit weird', so books helped then." *Booker T, Oklahoma.*

"Know thyself," said the doctor, "And your battles become easier."

Oh, give me a break. I leaned back in my chair, wincing at the pain shooting up my splinted left wrist. "I'm not interested in making things easy. So, I may be part autistic, part not. I'm also part black, part not. Zeke was part woman, part man, part neither, in her mind anyway. We're all just broken parts of things."

"I want to heal you," said the doctor, tapping his desk.

A hawksbill turtle sprouted upwards and started to swim, without gaining traction, over the desk.

I stood up.

The doctor opened a drawer and took out a brown strap with small screen. "I've been given permission to give you this new smartwatch, NextGen. Your colleague Ms. Suraya Proctor has got engineers to encode and extend what they could, from all that was remaining of Gen, in here."

I reached across, holding my right wrist out. "Please strap it on for me, my left wrist is still sore."

The psychologist was gentle, as I watched the turtle gliding above wood and screen.

"Thank you," I said, "Then tell my left wrist to heal – that's where the real pain is."

Dr. Brent handed me some smart goggles from the drawer. "Here you go," he said, "The VR programmes in NextGen will help you heal, via graded exposure and EMDR based re-scripting of your traumas. The file name is ROSEBUD. You don't need to come back and see me next time. Not if you don't want to."

I allowed myself the faintest of smiles, "'Rosebud', huh – who came up with that name?"

"I'm guilty," said the Doctor, smiling too.

"Don't tell me," I said, stepping around the turtle to look down on the doctor's bald pate. "You're a huge fan of movies too?"

The man stroked his combed back hair self-consciously and pushed back a few paces on his wheeled chair, to look at me. "An obsessive actually. Orson Welles in particular – ask me anything about the man – or his movies. That's what sometimes comes of having a neuro-diverse brain."

I laughed, "Takes one to know one?" I put the goggles in my trouser pocket and held my right hand over the desk, as the turtle swam into my watch.

It glowed greeny brown, the colour of a leaf turning in early fall. *NextGen is warm on my wrist.*

"Do you want to see me again, or not?" asked Dr. Brent, "This is just a start, I'm afraid. Healing is a journey."

I laughed again, scanning the doctor's office, "Isn't *everything* a journey?"

It was a small unassuming poster, behind the closed door, that did it for me.

I mouthed the letters, black on white. Bee-El-Es-Em. *Black Lives Still Matter.*

"Maybe," I said. *Walls falling? Well, just a bit. We'll see.*

I stood anxiously at the reception gate of Hydro-City airport. I was amongst twenty or thirty people, waiting for the incoming Newest Orleans, and LAX flight. They had landed over two hours ago, but security and immigration checks were increasingly tight and slow. *Surely not even powerful Corporations can exert sway at the border here, this is federal space? But so was the S-SJ Delta…*

People were starting to filter through – not many, it looked like the flight had been relatively empty, with increasingly fewer people able to manage the giant climate change tax on top of all air-flight ticket prices.

An old frisky-looking retired couple, a young man looking for his girlfriend, an old black woman, three young guys with kite kits, Wall-Jumpers, chubby middle-aged white guy in an old Clint Eastwood cowboy hat – gotta be a tourist, not many of those left – and his large, smiling, Hispanic boyfriend.

And there, Michelle, a lot thinner than I remembered her, towing an even thinner young girl behind her. Sally...

I held my arms out awkwardly, but they both stood at a small distance, and watched me warily.

"Hello Michelle. Hello Sally!"

The girl was shy, but managed a squeaked "'ello."

"Was *he* really necessary?" asked Michelle, thumbing over her shoulder to a lanky white cop, coming out from the immigration corridor behind them, nodding his head to an unheard tune, teeth pasty white with the gum he was chewing.

I gestured with my head, "How many bags to pick up, we can talk more at home?"

"Two," said Michelle, "we don't have much."

"You carry," the cop grunted, pointing at me, "Not in my J.D."

"*We* will manage," said Michelle, as she hauled a large black bag off the carousel, "We always have."

Sally recognised her Dino-Pony bag and Michelle tapped a button on her wrist watch. The bag swung off the carousel and positioned itself near her brown canvas shoes, green light blinking on the handle. "Smart bag courtesy of a disability payment, the joys of living in the Ogallala Aquifer states. I hope NorthCal are equally as generous."

I shrugged, embarrassed. *Not something I'd looked up.*

I tapped NextGen with a quick prompt.

"Follow me," grunted the cop, as he walked quickly out of the cooled building, into a sweaty airport parking area.

The dark grey wall was dominant to the south, a solid scar on the horizon, with a few dwarfed and scattered buildings of Hydro-City blinking sunlight in the distance. The twelve story Water Tower was easy to spot – glinting in the distance, despite the *aqua-lite* bushes growing out of its external circular walls.

Grey, concrete parking lot; cracked brown earth on both sides, and a brilliant blue sky above.

Home.

Sort of.

"Welcome to Hydro-City, girls," I smiled, as the cop opened the door for us, in his discreet, unmarked people carrier.

Big tyres though – off road?

I shifted in beside Michelle, who moved against Sally, as if averse to physical contact with me.

I sighed, as the car sealed shut and we moved off, heading rapidly towards the city.

"How's school, darling?" I leaned forward to try and catch a glimpse of the girl squashed on the other side of Michelle, but she was lost in thought – or reverie – leaning against the window, looking out on the passing baked earth.

NextGen pinged a message, "NorthCal do have a limited child disability budget…" I turned to Michelle.

The windows darkened, and the car turned abruptly, swinging left.

My heart lurched, as we turned. *Surely, surely not?*

I kept my voice level, "I think we've taken the wrong turn, officer."

"Depends where we're going, doesn't it, mister?" And the cop put his foot down hard on the accelerator, so that we tore around another corner, and were crushed together.

Sally giggled with frightened excitement.

Michelle shot me a look of horrified anger.

I heard the buzz of a data distorter for several moments, before the car's emergency petrol back up kicked into roaring life, at high acceleration.

We were pinned back to our seats.

Sally howled in joy.

The car careered around seemingly never-ending corners, before becoming extremely bumpy, as if we'd hit unsurfaced territory.

Finally, an aggressive stop, which shunted us forward, against the pull of the safety belts.

The man bounded out of the car and opened the door next to me.

I peered out, fearfully.

We were parked amongst a derelict small housing estate, broken buildings scarred and black from decades old wildfire gutting.

But we were right next to a neutral, recently renovated single brick building, retaining a semblance of disuse and neglect, weeds and vines scrambling the wall.

"Welcome to the deserted town of Westville, hollowed out in the Great Fires of '36, the residents weren't rich enough to pay for their own fire-fighting units. This is now your new home."

"Is this a joke? Who are you – where have you brought us?"

The man looked down at me, seemingly offended. "State trooper Kowalski at your service, sir. No joke – but, uh, sorry about my assertive driving. Had to dodge a drone tailing us – I was worried they had a lock on your devices. I've had to bring you to another safe house. This is Nowheresville."

Slowly, I unbuckled myself, "So, this is where we stay?"

The man nodded, "Till we reckon you're safe. Sorry, it may look shabby, but it *is* safe."

"Safe will do me," I said, wishing I could be sure it were indeed so.

I held out a hand to Michelle, but both she and Sally were already out of the car. Above us, rare rain clouds drifted in, spitting on parched garden soil.

Kowalski offered me a set of keys.

I stepped out, slinging the bag over my shoulder and keying open the door.

Home?

In this one, at least, it does not feel as if I will be lonely.

And I can enter, without counting my actions.

I put the keys in my pocket and, tentatively, I took Sally's hand with my good right hand.

The girl did not shake it loose.

Together, we stepped inside.

Chapter 16
Graham – Hydro-City and Beyond

I waited for the day to creep towards seeing Lizzie again.

There were worse places to wait than the plush hotel room lounge of The Prestige, in Hydro-City. Pedro and I had adjacent rooms, but I had been using the lounge a *lot* more than he had. Pedro, now *he* could sleep.

Third bar fridge drink, courtesy of Doctor Dlamini, little does he know, though – unless he's spying on me, the bugger. Nah, come on Mason. it's only eleven in the morning. Do your research on this place. Fill the time. Earn your money.

I wasn't sure why they called this a city, there were only fifteen thousand legally resident inhabitants after all, mostly in the water or services industries. And security, of course, this was almost the fulcrum of the InterCal Super-State Wall, situated as it was due north of the contested Kern Water banks, where The Walnut King and other financiers and corporations allegedly appropriated State underground water reserves. Near, too, the water arteries of the great trans-Californian aqueducts.

"Cyril, project holo-map of Hydro-City onto this smart-desk."

Cool.

I almost clapped my hands in delight. New and expensive tech, these holo-bloomers, able to objectify data in photon form for *either* three-di printing *or* experiential observation. *Now this is more the America I expected. Glad I managed to convince Bongani that extra accommodation dosh on this here Prestige Chain, Hydro City, would be worth it.*

"Cyril, record Clip, titled Water Town Tour."

I walked around the desk, indicating relevant items on the topographical digi-model of the town.

"As you can see, the Wall is over a hundred feet tall, the town's backbone, with viewing sites near the main entrance gate, along Boundary Road, at the top here. Some people fly for dangerous fun from this huge wall, with kites on, but the lift only lets them up if they are state licensed – and if the wind is blowing from the south. Here is the Water Tower, twelve stories tall, the hub of the civilised side of the Californian water wars and the California State Water Project – which has been going on in this here neck of the woods, since the years of the cowboys, when the wild-west was first won."

"Or lost. Depends on your perspective."

How long has he been standing near the door, watching me?

"Cyril, cut. Did you get me an interview, Pedro?" I asked.

Pedro nodded in the gloom; the hotel blinds had been drawn to maximise viewing of the hologram. "With the Queen Bee herself, Director Rosemary Carruthers. Two pm sharp. As for me, I'm gonna be meeting with one of their lawyers I know, Ms. Johnson, to see if she needs my help again, as a cultural bridge for processing *Dustie* refugees."

"But no response for an interview, from anyone within FreeFlow?"

"Nada," he said.

"What's up with them?" I asked, "They were happy to talk, when I called them and proposed an interview, just a few days ago. Seemed like they were keen to show off, just how virtuous they are."

Pedro shrugged.

"Cyril, project flight XE559."

Hydro-City flickered out of existence, replaced with an aeroplane hanging over an expanse of ocean, having just left behind the west coast of the Republic of Scotland.

<Arrival time at H-C is 5pm today>

"Two o'clock is fine, thank you Pedro." *Time enough afterwards to shower, change and get ready to fetch Lizzie.*

Pedro walked over to pull the blinds open. "You do know these screens are just for show, don't you? There's a glass-tinter and UV console, right next to the air-con."

"I'm like a cat," I said, "I prefer playing with the blinds." *Damn place is smarter than me.*

Pedro turned and placed his fists on his wobbly hips, "Right, how could I not know that, huh? Time for lunch, boss."

"It's always time for lunch with you, Pedro. Okay," I nodded, but then quickly raised an admonishing finger, "No alcohol with the food – and only the cheapest water."

Pedro snorted, making his way back to his adjoining room, "You'll regret that, when it eventually turns out those fancy water brands have all been made from horse's piss."

I tucked on my green hotel waistcoat bib, branded PH, proof of my right to eat there.

Slowly, I moved my open palm through the dimly fizzing holo-plane, feeling nothing. *See you soon, Lizzie. I'm waiting for you, right here.*

The plane fell from the sky.

It exploded on the desk, in a roar of flame and smoke.

I screamed.

Smoke coalesced from the burning desk, into a... face?

Vaguely, I could make out features, the cloud sharpening until... *Stalin?*

Stalin spoke, in a reedy voice of uncertain accent and uneven inflection; a voice-box disguise. "What are you doing here, Mister Mason? Be careful. Accidents happen. Know that I am always watching you."

Smoke dissipated, the face too, but my desk continued to burn with digital fire. *No smell, but I am still shaking.*

"What the fuck's *that* about?" asked Pedro.

I had no idea, but I took my dinner bib off.

I had lost my appetite, again.

"Cyril?"

<*Flight XE559 is still on schedule.*> Thank God!

"How could they hack the hotel system?"

<*State of the art Rig, nearby.*>

"Not from a plane then?"

If Cyril could have scoffed, he would have. <*Nothing that powerful yet, that's still science fiction.*>

Busi is not *Stalin. Who – or what – is he?*

"You eat, and you can even have a drink too," I said to Pedro, beyond caring.

I headed for my room, and bed, getting Cyril to alarm me in good time for the interview with the EPA Director.

Time is not just creeping, it's fucking stalling. Lizzie...

The wasteland lay before us, a vast empty expanse of dirt and dry dust, stretching to a few trees straggling into life on the distant horizon. Far out to the west lay a dense group of tiny brown bubbles, almost as if a burial ground for minute discarded beetle carapaces, lost amongst the vast Cent-Cal desert. The ground below and ahead of us pulled my gaze back – it had crumpled and sunk, as if swallowed into the bowels of the earth.

I whistled. "Jesus, Cyril, record."

The Director was a tall, pale, woman, almost stiff in her bearing, swathed in white robes that reminded me of nomadic *Touareg* from the Sahara. Her leather dust mask hung over her left shoulder, as she started to speak. "People have gotten bored of this view south from the wall. Not much to see. But not me. There used to be a lot of nuts here – almonds, and pistachios mainly, but they were greedy bastard trees that drunk this valley dry, until the land dropped down towards hell itself, as the water table disappeared, and wild-fires raged. Made a few people obscenely rich, though."

"The real greedy ones," I laughed, "But what about the water regs?"

"Fought tooth and nail by those making a killing off the land. Our 2015 groundwater regs in response to the Californian Great Drought were bypassed regularly, so the wall grew in the north for a stronger protection of our water, including the groundwater – and, as the water disappeared, so the wall grew. As you can see – now, *nothing* lives here."

I leaned my chest against the railing, glad there was a faint breeze cooling my neck from the burn of the post-noon sun. I tilted the brim of my Clint Eastwood hat, to take the edge off the sun's glare, dipping westwards.

"Over there," I pointed towards the bubbles of brown shell structures, south west of the wall, "What are those?"

The Director did not even bother to turn to see where I was pointing, "*Dusties*. Refugee tents from the south. That's their processing camp."

"Do *they* have water, Director?"

The Director looked at me, with sea-green eyes and a straight gaze. *She looks… sad?*

"You can call me Rose," she said. "We're not monsters here in the north, Mister Mason, however they may have painted us in 'Diego and LA. We do share supplies with SouthCal Aid. We've let LA keep the Los Angeles Aqueduct too."

"Who pays for the refugee supplies…? Rose?"

She gave a faint smile, "The tax payers, Mister Mason, it's always the tax payers."

"As a tax payer myself," I laughed, "I know the feeling."

"Indeed," she said, smiling, again, "I'm sure you do. Unfortunately, the main tax burden now falls on those individuals *least* able to pay. Corporations have bought the elected, to pave the way for ongoing business tax reductions."

The wind was picking up, so I held my hat, and turned my back against the railing. "Hah! So you have state capture by big business too? We've been plagued by that in South Africa."

"Our countries *do* share some ugly history, Mister Mason."

Hmm. I wouldn't go that far. "Graham," I said, "you can call me Graham. So this wall kind of ruptures the landscape, doesn't it?"

She smiled, but said nothing, her eyes remaining sad.

The Director joined me against the railings of the viewing station, leaning out, as if she yearned to embrace the hot desert.

Instead, she spoke. "April is the cruellest month, breeding lilacs out of the dead land…[3]" she stopped.

"Uh – it is *November* today, Rose," I corrected her.

She turned to me, a peculiar smile on her face, "Of course it is, Graham, silly me."

---

[3] TS Eliot. (1922) *The Wasteland*. Horace Liveright.

"Do you have a local expert who can give me some of the day to day, nitty gritty workings of the water department here?"

"For a fee, Graham, we are a state facility, not a charity. An hour of their time, tops."

"Of course," I nodded and then turned around to face the sun, tugging my hat lower. I felt my neck burning, as if someone had put a blowtorch to it. *Damn, forgot the sunblock in the hotel room – didn't expect a whacky outdoors interview. Still, nice pics, Cyril.*

The Director swigged from the *ecomo* bottle dangling over her right shoulder. "Any specific criteria for whom you wish to speak to?"

"Uh… just one."

"Well?" The breeze was beginning to blow harder, and the sting of sand heralded her pulling her goggles and mask on.

"Um, they have to be… uh, black." I clipped my mask on too, switching on the voice filter. It felt like a tight noose on my face, scratching my skin.

"Black as in African-American – or will anyone of POC background do?" The Director pulled her head scarves closed, to block out her skin.

"What's a POC?" The sand flailed at my skin, so I poked desperately at the lift call button.

"Person of colour, Graham," came the distorted reply.

"Ah, we have different racial terminologies in South Africa – a POC will do," I shouted, having found her last response hard to hear, as the wind howled up into a serious gear. *What fucked up weather, one minute this, another minute that.*

The lift door opened.

My Eastwood hat flew south.

I stopped, turning to chase it.

With surprising, wiry strength, the Director muscled me into the lift.

She clipped her mask off, as the lift sealed shut. "Don't be an idiot. And you look much less of an asshole, *without* the hat."

I opened my mouth to protest, but my cheeks burned with pain, and just a little embarrassment or shame.

The Director leaned forward and opened the clips securing my mask. "And next time, don't do the straps up so *tight*, okay?"

I nodded, but she pointed behind me.

The door had opened, and Pedro stood, looking in, his back to the breeze. *Down here, at least, the wind was broken up by the buildings, reduced to a thin whine of scurrying sand and dust.*

"Your wife's flight is coming in early," Pedro said, "Good fucking tail wind."

I stepped out and turned to shake the Director's hand. *Got to get cleaned up and dressed handsomely; quick, quick.*

The Director gripped my hand, ferociously hard, "Shanti, shanti, shanti, Mister Mason."

I smiled tightly, through my flapping mask. *Mad fucking bat.*

Liz came though the H-C Airport custom gates, looking both tired and beautiful. Busi was next to her, tall, thin, and moving with fluid grace. *What does Lizzie see in her?*

I wrapped my arms around Liz, avoiding Busi's gaze.

Liz gave me a slight pressure of her arms inwards in return, but her hands failed to clasp tightly around me. *Have I gotten even fatter? Can't she reach?*

Behind us, Pedro coughed.

I stepped back and opened my left palm towards Pedro. "This is my wife Liz and an, uh, friend of Liz's, Busisiwe – Liz, Busi, meet my guide Pedro."

Pedro gave a small bow and they smiled.

"We will get you a lift in a taxi. How many bags to pick up?" I asked. "And how was the flight?"

"Just the one," said Liz, "We don't have many days, so we're travelling light – and sharing."

How much? How much are you sharing? And what about me?

"Oh, uh, good," I said, and indicated them to follow me. "And the flight?"

"Pleasant enough," they both said, in unison. And then they chuckled together, almost as if they'd been surprised to say the same thing, simultaneously.

"Pleasant enough," said I, "Sounds like our marriage." *Choreographed sharing, surely? At least* my *comment seems to have shut them up...*

I waited next to the carousel, while the other three stood slightly behind, silently. Even Pedro was quiet. *Unusual.*

Busi clicked a switch in her hand and a brightly coloured, butterfly decorated bag, buzzed off the flat, spinning baggage track, to join her.

I turned on my heels, "Let me help you with that."

"You've helped enough," Busi said, coldly.

Liz looked down, her hands clasped in front of her stomach, tears dripping off her nose.

Oh shit. "Look, I'm sorry Liz," I tried, but Busi stalked off, bag at heels.

Liz followed, turning her head, to avoid looking at me.

At least Pedro walked alongside me, even though he was thumbing through his phone, seemingly oblivious to the events around him.

The two women waited by the exit sign, but they were still not looking at me. "We can catch our own cab," said Busi, "We've had to stay in a cheaper hotel."

"No, look…" I said.

But neither looked anywhere near me.

"Hey *muchachas*," said Pedro, "This man, he can be a jerk, but his heart is often in the right place."

Often?

Both Liz and Busi looked across at Pedro – and he appeared to consider the meaning of their gaze.

"Sometimes?" he said.

Busi laughed. "So, what are *you* driving, big boy?"

Pedro tapped the auto-call on his watch and laughed right back, "Long time since anyone called me a boy, pretty lady."

I looked across at Liz, who flickered a gaze my way, along with the briefest and most fragile of smiles.

The self-drive that rolled up to us at the Drop Zone, was an original Zapped e-car, dull red and functional. "Blame the *hombre* with the tight purse strings," said Pedro, as he opened the doors, "At least my statuesque physique more than compensates, no?"

"Yes," laughed Busi, as she stepped in with her bag. Liz ducked in after her and Pedro moved aside for me, waving me in, as he clicked his heels.

I hesitated, catching Pedro's eyes. *Help me out, mate?*

Slowly, the man shook his head, whispering, "I'm a divorcee, maybe try being light and funny, just for a change."

I climbed into the silent car, awkward and alone. *Come on, just watch your mouth, Mason.*

Pedro clearly knew how to make them laugh, on the journey through to the Life-Water Ranch, a B&B reservoir for FreeFlow employees, on the outskirts of Hydro-City.

By the time we got to the hotel, and I extended a hand to help Liz out of the car, she took it. I gave her hand an apologetic squeeze.

Her smile was tired, but I still felt warmth in my chest.

The Prestige had packed a wonderful picnic breakfast for us – even Liz could not hide how impressed she was. Smoked salmon and NorthCal wine, vine tomatoes from upstate, curlicued bread and only the best water, *FF@Purest*.

Legitimate company expenses, necessary to conduct business. Ha, ha, – Bongani is not going to like the bill, at the end of this trip.

Liz had always loved picnics, as had our Mark, when he was a young boy, before he grew too big, and took off on rugby and cricket tours.

I had plotted the perfect spot with Cyril the night before – a creek on the outskirts of the city, where one could swim and cool off – a secure public spot, with the fifty bucks entrance fee designed to fund the re-introduction of wildlife into the protected eco-system.

'*Frog's Heaven*', maintained by Rewilding eco-warriors, who'd forged an alliance with the state.

Only three families were nearby, with young babies – they also had packed food, with bottles that could sieve and filter the stream for drinking, if need be.

Liz had always been impressed with my swimming, so I dived in, spare cotton shirt on to hide my sagging stomach, and powered a crawl to the opposite bank of the river, and back again, without stopping.

I remembered what she used to be like in a bikini – now she was wearing a black one piece, with leggings to protect her from the burn of the sun.

"Have you heard from Mark recently?" she asked, as she lounged on a towel and watched a large extended family start quarrelling, over something or other.

"No, he tends not to contact me much," I said, towelling my hair dry as I sucked my stomach in surreptitiously, standing over her towel.

"He's met someone. Someone special."

"That's nice," I said, as I lay my damp towel out next to her.

Liz rolled onto her left elbow and looked up at me, "Do you still think *I'm* special?"

"Of course!" I smiled, bending to offer her a glass of white wine.

She took a sip, which seemed to sharpen her gaze, "Why?"

"Why what?" *Nice wine; would give most KWV Paarl, Cape Town wines, a good run for their money. Not too many vineyards escape the annual wildfires here.*

"Why am I special?"

"Because..." a bee buzzed past, *the pesticide giants must be relieved?* "Because you're beautiful – and smart – and..."

Liz sat up, and twirled her right hand, as if she was unrolling a toilet roll. "Words," she said, "But your eyes no longer back them up."

I filled her wine glass. *Damn, why are my hands shaking? Drink – and chill, for God's sake. Let's just have fun again.* "You said you had a lot to tell me – what's been going on, Lizzie?"

The sun rapidly dried my back, even though it hadn't reached eleven.

I looked down self-consciously. My wet *moobs* showed through my white T-shirt, so I rolled over onto my back, breaking any possible eye contact with Liz. *I feel so old, so fat, so — unattractive. So not like Busi.*

Liz lay next to me, and talked, as several bees and butterflies droned some life into the sapping heat. "You're gone so easily from home, for over three years now, since Mark left the country, as if you've long lost the desire to be at home."

"I have to work," I said, stiffly, "especially since you retired from teaching."

"You said I could retire," she said, "because of my illness. But your boss knows you're never there — and that must be why he broke into our house to, to — accost me."

I sat bolt upright and twisted to face her, "What?"

"Seems he watched us having sex that last time we did it — says my face in climax is his screen saver now."

I boggled. "What? Fucking bastard! He said he would keep an eye on you."

Liz glanced across to the three generational family of eight nearby, they were eating, and no longer arguing any more. "He's done that for sure; but keep it down."

"So, did he —?"

"No, I buzzed him with Spider and called the cops."

I laughed, "Good for you, Lizzie! So, the cops got him — it's no bloody wonder Bongani has taken over the company. I wondered what shit had happened, but Bongani wouldn't say."

Liz waved away a bee and took a bite from a salmon canapé. "We'd best eat, before the entire remaining insect life of California descends on us. I still want to see a frog, though."

What's her issue with frogs? Is she changing the subject? Is this really the full story?
"You didn't, er — encourage him in any way, did you?"

She put her canapé down on the recyclable plastic, "What. Did. You. Say?"

Shit, Mason, what's wrong with you recently — foot in mouth disease? "Um, uh, no probably not, then."

"Fuck probably," Liz stood up and threw the canapé at me, splattering over my soggy shirt and shorts. "I'm going off for a swim. Then — you take me back to my hotel. *Straight* back!"

She took three steps and dived into the stream, and resurfaced to swim gently across, returning with green dragonflies buzzing around her face.

She climbed out and shook herself like a dog.

I stood and handed her a towel, sheepishly, "Look Lizzie, I'm sorry…"

She rubbed her thick hair and I watched her, with a sunken, aching heart.

She wrapped her towel around her body, as if she could no longer bear me looking at her, tying it under her left armpit, before she looked up at me, and I wished she hadn't.

Her eyes were cold, and dead.

"I've had enough *sorries*," she said, "There was a time when you used to want to help others, and you would *never* have complained about us sharing water, with *anyone*."

"You're not bringing *that* up again, are you?"

"Since when did being in Africa start meaning you don't help anyone, for you?"

I shrugged and looked across at the family who had been arguing nearby. The mother and father watched us, with unabashed curiosity. *I'm so ashamed. What made her relax yesterday? Pedro's jokes. He said I should try being light and funny. Gotta make a joke of this. Be light and funny.*

"Must be *that* time of the month," I laughed, speaking in an American accent, as I shrugged at the watching family.

"Let's go," Liz said, "We're fucking done. Fuck you."

Done? Shit… But where's your sense of humour gone then, over the years?

But, this time, I kept my mouth shut.

That seemed to be that? Liz said *nothing*, on the way back to the hotel.

Nothing.

Done… Dusted.

Chapter 17
Liz – Drilling Enceladus

"'Dusties' are the main immigration issue here," said the lawyer, Jenny Johnson. "You ask me, we should break down all the walls and allow freedom of movement for all. Nationalities have no validity whatsoever." She was sticking to the Green Brand of fizzy cola – cold and clean – but not cool, unlike the other brands, FreeFlow the foremost.

Busi and I were getting stuck into the alcohol – nothing frees up human desire more than knowing someone else was paying. *Haven't drunk so much, since I scandalised my parents, by going out with an* Engelsman. Jurre, *long time ago now.*

Busi went for the exotic cocktails, I stuck with cold beer.

The couches we sat in were soft and sagged, perfect for my pain, leaving little movement easy, apart from tipping back our drinks and talking. The lawyer had found a sound proof booth, away from the small bustle of tourists staying over to look at – or dive off – the Water Wall.

Jenny held a little e-pad in her hand, syncing a link with a thumbed code to Busi's ankle clasp, green flashing light finally indicating a paired bond. Busi had hauled her trousers up to her calves, so that the lawyer could monitor the progression of the link-up, but pulled the hem down quickly, the moment the green light flashed.

She took another swig of her Tequila Sunrise and coughed.

"Embarrassing, I know," said Jenny, looking up at Busi's face, "I'm so sorry."

"I can't sleep properly since this was clamped on me," said Busi, "I'm marked for life. And it chafes."

"Killing does that to you, or so I've been told."

I glanced across at the grey-haired lawyer, who was level-eyed in gaze, as well manner.

"Will you be watching me all the time?" asked Busi, remote ordering a Vodka Blast.

Jenny shook her head, "No, Wi will."

"We will?"

Jenny tapped her head, "My Rig – *Wi*. Both *Anpetu* and *Hanwi*, Day and Night."

"Are you an Indian?" I asked, "You look white." *Oops. Rude, how could you? Got to be the beer...*

"A lot of us look white now," said Jenny, "Kill them first, then dilute them out of existence. Blood quantum laws apply."

"Jesus," said Busi, knocking back her vodka, "Sounds awful – what's that? And I thought old South African race laws and practice were screwed."

"I'm twenty-five percent Lakota," said Jenny proudly, the tattooed bison on her cheek, dancing with her smile. She touched her face, gently. "*Tatanka*. He Who Owns Us."

Then, her face darkened, "Barest minimum for official status, we're being bred out of existence. The next and final genocide."

"Standing Rock?" Busi put her drink away on the table behind her, and leaned forward, as much as she was able.

Indian water protests, against oil pipelines that eventually leaked across Indian sacred land, a couple of decades or so back now. No compensation was awarded, I remembered. I put my half-drunk beer aside too, aware something of importance was brewing.

Jenny nodded, slowly. "I was a young Water Protector then, but we got little good publicity, even though we came before the media thunder of Thunberg and the Extinction Rebellion in '19. And the Keystone XL protests were even worse – they labelled us terrorists, even though we were only protecting our water. But we will always be the first, the *real* Americans – still butchered or booze poisoned, by the waves of white immigrants and invaders. Even the Osage got murdered for their legitimate oil ownership... *Hah*, after all that, what brings *you* to the land of the free, Boo-si?"

"After my charge for murder, my employers have called me here for a meeting. I anticipate my permanent contract is to be terminated."

"Who's that with, then?"

"FreeFlow," Busi scrabbled at the empty glass in front of her, head down, as if suddenly aware she needed another drink.

Jenny blinked twice and then barked a harsh laugh. She stretched across me to pick up my beer bottle, and turned to offer it to Busi. "You might as well mix your drinks, Boo-si. You'll be a lucky bitch, if terminating your contract is the *only* thing those bastards do to you."

Busi and I exchanged anxious glances.

Busi turned back to Jenny, "What's that mean? Please help?"

Jenny frowned.

"Uh, we will get what money we can together," I said.

The lawyer shook her head crossly, grey curls flouncing. "No! Not all lawyers are money monkeys. I'm just cross with myself, at my inability to say *no*. I've got more than enough work already, but I can be a real dumb bitch myself."

"Does that mean –?" asked Busi.

"Hell, yes," sighed Jenny, "Always a stupid sucker for the under-dogs, that's me. First thing's first, when are you meeting them?"

"Tomorrow morning," said Busi, but she failed to tug the beer from Jenny's hand.

"Sorry, changed my mind. A clear head is needed," the lawyer put the bottle down. "I'm going to have to send *Wi* with you."

"How?" Busi asked, puzzled. "They've asked me to turn my Rig, *Winnie* off, and they'll be monitoring my scalp for digital activity."

"My *Wi* is gonna hitch an e-ride on your ankle clasp, so you wear longs okay, it's not like you need to dress fancy at your own funeral, metaphorically speaking."

Busi exhaled slowly, as if preparing herself mentally. "Is that legal here, then?"

"There are some questions you don't ask of a lawyer."

Busi gave a small breathless laugh and glanced across to me. "What are *you* doing to be doing tomorrow morning, Lizzie?"

"Uh – seeing as I can't come with you, I've agreed a date with Graham. What've I got to lose, huh?"

"Seriously girl?" sighed Busi, "Frankly, I'd prefer facing FreeFlow to *that* one. You love-birds *enjoy*."

I looked at Busi, but she refused to return my gaze.

We both needed a hand from Jenny, to get to our unsteady feet.

"Welcome to America," said Jenny, tossing her own cola bottle into recycling. "You ladies have a good night's sleep, right – and make sure you drink *lots* of water. FreeFlow *are* paying for that."

The less said about the picnic with Graham, the next morning, the better.

The swim was nice. So were the bees and butterflies.

Where were the frogs, though?

The rest? History.

Done.

The three of us met for lunch at a small Hispanic restaurant opposite the golf course. The restaurant was *Taco-Refs*, manned by processed South-Cal refugees, serving their two-year stint on migrant parole duty. Three serving; a youngster of indeterminate gender, an old man who said he'd been a Dreamer, and a mature woman, bringing in food orders into the small recessed courtyard at the back, where I'd spotted a FreeFlow representative dropping Busi off.

Busi stalked into the courtyard with her legs covered by a long cotton, orange drape, looking stiff and grim-faced. Jenny and I were alone in the courtyard outside, with the water feature and small breeze offering only minimal relief against the beating heat. *The sane are inside, eating in shade, and cooled by aircon.*

Jenny had said nothing to me, as to what she had picked up via *Wi* from Busi's meeting, she'd focused instead on the relative merits and shortages of international foods, virtual water, and the expensive rigours of maintaining a productive urban garden, with little moisture.

Busi sat, with an explosive exhalation of breath.

"It *was* bad," nodded Jenny, "But still this side of legal. I'm sorry."

Busi nodded glumly and looked across to me, "Did you hear?"

I shook my head.

"I don't tell other people's business," said Jenny, "Unless I have permission."

"You have permission," said Busi glumly, "More *tequila* please."

"Uh – uh," Jenny shook her head, "This is my lunch hour – and if *I'm* paying again, it's no alcohol – and only vegan food. It's the hard, little details we need to get right, to help this planet survive."

"Thank you, Jenny," said Busi, tapping the lemon fizz and vegan *gazpacho* soup.

"I'm afraid Busi got fired," said Jenny, as she turned to me, "But that was only to be expected. It's with immediate effect however – and she's had to sign a disclaimer against taking any legal action, which includes a silencing clause."

"I'm sorry, Busi," I said.

Busi shrugged, "No more – or less – than we expected. Still, I'm supporting others at home, so this is not just going to cost *me*. I'm not sure what the disclaimer was about though. So, how was *your* date?"

"What date?" I tapped on the green cola and fried avocado *tortas*.

The woman who brought us our food gasped in horror, almost dropping her tray, before shifting plates onto our table, with shaking hands.

Busi looked across at me quizzically.

I shrugged.

Black people here were not too uncommon, surely – I'd seen some on the street.

The woman left us, hurriedly.

"What on Earth was that about?" asked Busi.

Jenny touched the E button on our table and the news mushroomed in 3-di above our hot plates – then, she started tucking in to her *Spicy Tempeh Taco Salad.*

155

Busi and I just gaped.

There was a still picture of Busi sitting in a white T-shirt and red hot-pants, legs crossed neatly, but ankle clasp clearly on display, obviously from an SAP identikit photo. The rolling commentary was in both Spanish and English. '*FreeFlow fired a foreign employee from South Africa who faces a murder charge. The woman, Boo-si Emshlongo, faces a murder charge in her native country. An FF spokesperson said they would never tolerate unlawful behaviour within their corporation.*'

"Bastards!" said Busi.

Jenny fanned her mouth, "Food. Hot. Eat. You're a scapegoat, my dear, a sop to the media, to hide other bigger shit that they are trying to keep hidden. The disclaimer was to prevent your protesting, as they hang you out to dry."

"What bigger, uh, 'shit', are they hiding?" I asked.

Jenny burped. "Now that *would* be telling... Such as their water *is* shit. Literally."

"Literally... as in, *literally?*"

"With some clever disguising, of course, and a nod to ensure they don't poison their entire drinking base."

"Can't they like sue you, for saying that?" queried Busi.

Jenny shrugged and put her knife and fork together. "This is only going to get repeated in a foreign country again, isn't it, with the source hidden? Until we can nail down the proof here."

"*Ahhh,*" nodded Busi, as she sipped from her *gazpacho* soup bowl.

"FreeFlow, only the best – by the best – for the best," I sang, chomping on a sharp, almost bitter tasting avocado.

Jenny nodded at me. "*Avos* are water dense foods. Time we labelled and taxed food for water burden, not just chemicals."

I left half of my avocado. *The woman sure knows how to ruin a meal too.*

"Listen, ladies, I got a lot of work to do. When are you heading back to South Africa?" asked Jenny, as she wiped sweat from her cheeks.

"Tomorrow afternoon, late," said Busi, "Jobless – and with people and family still to support, as well as a murder charge to face. And..."

Her face saddened.

"And... what?" I asked.

"I need to visit *Imantshi's mamma* again. I tried to see her, to ask forgiveness. She wouldn't let me in, but I *will* keep trying. I need to give her something back, for the son I have taken from her."

"Imantshi?" Jenny mouthed silently at me, while Busi started to cry, softly, over the last few spoonfuls of her soup. "And now – now, I have *nothing* to give her."

I draped my right arm over Busi's shaking shoulders.

Jenny stood up. "Sounds like you need your last night to be some fun then, Busi – shall I pick you both up at eight?"

"More booze?" asked Busi hopefully, looking up, with the weakest of smiles.

"You're incorrigible," Jenny laughed, wiping a few leaves off her sweat-suit trousers. "See you both at your hotel reception, at eight."

She tapped a payment through on the table, waving our 'thank you' aside, and left at a quick stride, through the side gate.

Busi sighed. "So – how *was* your date with Graham, then?"

"That," I said, "You must not ask again. Ever."

Busi laughed. "Oh dear, ever is a *long* time. Come on then, let's get the hell out of this sun, it feels freaking hotter than Africa right now."

"We go through the side gate, and not the main building," I said, "You don't want to give that waitress *another* heart attack, do you?"

Busi smiled sadly, "To refugees all over – and to finding hope."

After this morning, it feels like hope – in some areas at least – has run completely dry.

The Hydro-City Nu-Reality Centre was a brightly lit tower of three stories of plated smart glass.

As we approached, Jenny told us that behind the building, giant pipes were transferring landfill waste to underground furnaces, which generated up to twelve percent of the city's energy needs. Nu-Reality could apparently take upwards of a third of that power, on the odd and *very* special occasion, like a visiting pyrotechnic performance from the Cock-Kings of Shit-House.

What kind of a name for a band, is that?

Busi responded enthusiastically; she was obviously a keen Shit-House fan.

We entered the Nu-Reality building, subtitled 'Alternative Facts.'

Tonight, though, the building was quiet.

No scheduled performances.

Jenny told us, as we shifted up an empty escalator, that we had arrived in a time of downturn; a serious financial turning in on itself, for most *ordinary* citizens, at least.

Sounds like home.

The solar-powered energy dial at Food Hall level, Floor One, was on low. This, despite the windows flashing images to lure clients from near and far, of sexy people, writhing their exposed flesh and flashy jewellery.

Even the gaming parlours, and the fantasy worlds radiating outwards from the Food Hall, seemed strangely deserted, more bots than people.

Still, this world was brash and alien enough for both Busi and me to keep gasping, as Jenny showed us around the place, goggled and tagged with ear buds. "Past scenarios and old-style VR games on Ground floor, Food with Present day shit on Floor One, Space and Death, the final future frontier, on Floor Two."

"I'll settle for Cajun food," said Busi, the three of us choosing a booth of 'L'Acadie Eateries'. "This one's on me, sisters. Might as well blow some of my severance check on a party."

We bowled our buds in a central sterilising cup on the table, hitching our goggles onto our heads.

I hesitated, and then removed the goggles off my head, shoving them into my dress suit pocket. I had always tried to keep a sharp separation between the virtual and real worlds.

The virtual world, it can suck you dry too.

"That's kind of you, Busi," smiled Jenny, "But I must say no, given your responsibilities and the relative value of your currency. It's on me, but I'm working within a budget, in the spirit of austerity and restraint. Only one alcoholic drink each, for the night. We must just wait a few minutes. I have a surprise for both of you."

My heart sank.

No.

I could *see* the surprise heading our way, and I didn't like it.

Not one little bit.

Graham and Pedro -Graham suited up in brown, but Pedro in blue denim and white T-shirt – arrived together.

"*Hellloooo, ladies!*" said Pedro, as he smiled widely.

Jenny waved at the men, "I met Pedro yesterday to discuss the refugee situation – turns out he also knew another South African, so I figured you guys might all like to meet."

Busi was trying hard not to laugh, as she made way for Pedro. He sidled his body onto the soft bench alongside her.

Me, my gaze went back to Graham.

"Hi Liz," said Graham, with a nervous flick of his right hand; a wave, yet not a wave.

"Oh," said Jenny, "So you know each other already – small world over there, is it?"

"Very small," said Graham, as he squeezed in next to Jenny.

Everyone looked at each other, but I avoided looking at Graham again.

He looked so miserable – so hang-doggish.

Not going to work on me, though.
Not any more.

Busi couldn't contain herself, and burst out laughing.

Jenny turned to Graham, "Hey, I'm out of the joke here. What's going on? You can cut this atmosphere with a fucking knife."

"We're married," said Graham.

"Oh shit," said Jenny, "Now *that* explains a lot. Have I completely ruined the night, before it's even begun, then?"

Probably.

"Nothing a bit of alcohol won't fix, I'm sure," said Busi, as she giggled and tapped on the table, for a round of Southernmost Comfort.

A bot looking like *R2-D3PO* delivered the large flagon and glasses.

One drink won't hurt, I guess.

"So," said Graham, talking across the table to Busi, as if suddenly afraid to look at me, "How did your meeting go with FreeFlow, Busi?"

"Well, I no longer have a job, if that's what you mean," Busi said, slugging back a drink.

"I'm sorry," said Graham, "The job market is so fluid and volatile, what with bots coming in and bosses getting fired too."

"Really?" said Busi, "Which bosses?"

"Du Preez Enterprises have sacked their boss; I gather there are now five molestation complaints and three rape charges that have now emerged against him." Graham glanced at me, as if seeking to offer me a mute apology.

Why are you spilling such intimate details here?

No, you rat. You keep looking at Jenny, who looks as cool as a cucumber.

Seems like she's used to managing a lot worse.

"Sounds as if he's got what he deserved," said Busi, "So who's the new boss?"

"Bongani Dlamini."

"Oh," Busi sat up straighter in her seat, "A brother. Don't know him, but that's an encouraging move, at least, if he's not a Black Economic Empowerment token, for so-called transformative corporate window dressing."

Graham smiled – *almost ruefully?* – "Oh, he's no token all right."

"Come on guys," said Pedro, "All work talk is dull shit, man. Let's go play something."

He stood up and swung his burly arms. His T-shirt was loose enough to sway with his stomach.

"We can eat later," I agreed, "I'm not hungry right now."

Lost my appetitive the moment I saw you, Mister Graham Mason. From today, I am Lizette Basson.

Full stop.

"So," said Jenny, as she stood up and hauled her goggles down from her grey curls, and onto her eyes, "Come on then, let's get moving. What do people fancy? Past, present, or future?"

"I want to captain a space-ship to Orion's Belt," said Busi.

"I want to fly a typhoon over the Canadian wall," I said.

"I want to be sheriff and shoot some low-down cattle rustlers," said Graham.

Jenny turned to Pedro, "What you reckon, then?"

He shrugged, "We split and pair up?"

"I'd fancy a flight over the Rockies," smiled Jenny, looking at me.

"I'm happy to be communications officer, if we happen to meet some aliens," said Pedro, looking at Busi.

Graham looked crestfallen, "Does no one want to join me in a shoot-out?"

"Oh, stop sulking," said Busi, as she stood up and strode towards the escalator heading down, "Come on then, I'll be your cattle thief."

"Wait," said Graham, "Stop! What's that thing on your ankle?"

Busi's boiler suit had hitched up in her stride, a piece of metal glinting through the gap between her leggings, and smart shoes.

Slowly, she pulled up her right trouser leg. "What? Do you mean this?"

"Yes," said Graham, "What. Is. That?"

"An e-tag," said Busi, as she looked at him, with an amused air of feigned innocence.

"But – but what's it for?"

"Murder."

Graham looked at her, saying nothing.

I could not see the expression on his face, but he took several seconds, before he responded.

"M-m... murder?"

"Extenuating circumstances of course," said Busi, straightening up and letting go of her trouser leg, as a couple walked past. They glanced at her curiously, before returning their attention to their mutual ear buds, heading up the escalators for Outer Space.

"They don't call me the fastest gun in the south for nothing," Busi forced a laugh, "Shall we go downstairs, Graham? I'm happy to be a good for *nothin'* rustler."

Graham turned to Pedro, "I think we should go home."

Pedro looked annoyed, "Why don't *you* go? I want to stay."

Graham walked off, heading for the lift exit.

Pedro turned to us, opening his arms, as if unsure what to do.

Jenny waved him away, "I'll call you tomorrow – yes, okay, we can work together in Tent City again. But, as for tonight, I think we're going to wrap this up, it's for women only. *Vamoose.*"

Pedro shrugged his shoulders and spun on his heels.

"Now that's turned out to be a really fucked up surprise of mine," said Jenny, "Sorry. Anyone hungry yet?"

"I could eat a horse right now," I said.

"How about you both settle for the sustainable, shared crawfish boil special instead, if you two don't mind eating crab?" asked Jenny. "I've heard it's very good – and it's relatively cheap. I'll settle for a locally sourced salad."

Busi sighed, as she sat, "Fine by me."

Jenny looked at me, "You want to talk about any of this hidden history I'm unaware of?"

"No," I said, "I'm just happy to eat crab. There's plenty else to talk about."

So, we spoke about plenty else, including Southern Africa, the states of California – and being young at Standing Rock.

Jenny told Busi that she needed to 'read Roanhorse.'

And, at the end, we picked up our buds from the bowl, a little bit of mix and match, uncertain whose had been whose.

After a brief discussion, we flew a space ship to Enceladus, the moon of Saturn, to drill (successfully) for water.

All the while, we were accompanied by images of a live NASA probe approaching Enceladus, in real-time search for extra-terrestrial water, as well as life.

No life, without water.

We left the Nu-Reality Centre at midnight, arm in arm, as a threesome.

Jenny and Busi sang some Shit-House together, until the cab arrived to take us back to the hotel.

Me, I was quiet, preparing myself for a new life, alone.

Chapter 18
Art — Safe as Houses

I'm not alone, in this safe house, so why am I even jumpier than usual?
Someone at the front door? Was that a knock — or the door shaking?
It's six am and slowly starting to lighten. Too early for a knock, surely?

I checked the sturdy front door again. Locked, sensors still registering nothing of note, on the other side.

No falling asleep again, with an aching left wrist, and the jitters.

I sighed, scrabbling through the kitchen cupboard contents – at the back was a box of Hop-Tarts sachets, peanut butter and strawberry jelly flavour. *That'll do – just two minutes in the toaster.*

The tarts tasted like cardboard, as I ran over the previous night.

A heated chicken and beans supper, eaten quickly and with Michelle and I casting furtive glances at each other.

Afterwards, more awkwardness, with lapses of strained silence, and multiple attempts to strike up conversation again, ending eventually in Michelle exploding, and carrying a sleeping Sally off to her bed.

I had lain awake for almost two hours, alone in my room and rubbing my wrist, while NextGen sang me a song I remembered my mom singing, long ago, and in distant uncertainty.

Brahms' Lullaby.

I washed the dishes from the previous night, along with my breakfast plate, and sat on the couch, looking out the Safe House's tinted one-way window. *Just do things; no need to count, or itemise, that does not protect you, or anyone else.*

The Wall was a small dawn scar on the horizon, the rolling grassland dried and toughened brown. Hydro-City was a long way away from here.

The sun rose, revealing a leaden sky.

The clouds were pinkish, then grey; hollow, empty, and hanging, as if only for show.

What show? For whom? Here, I have been threatened and side-lined, moved off a board, as if I have no further part to play. Who decides who plays? Since when is murder and rape a game? How do I act, but save my family too? And how can I, how can I stop seeing Zeke?

The clouds had no answers, so I picked up the cereal box, to pack it away. *Small thing, but I wish it was blueberry and lime cheesecake.*

A squeal erupted from behind me.

I dropped the box and a broken tart spilt crumbs onto the floor.

"Ooh," said Sally, "Peanut butter and jelly – my favourite, Art!"

"I'll make you some, Sally – let me just clean up." *Small thing, but I'm now happy it's peanut-butter and strawberry. Small matters.*

I dug under the sink for a brush and scoop. *Keep stuff clean, ordered, neat, stay busy, and hold Zeke's blue face away.*

Low tech here, no bots at all, just DIY stuff.

I scooped up the broken tart, after Sally had picked up the box and sat at the kitchen table. Michelle joined her, pulling her gown together tightly, yawning.

"Coffee?" I asked, "Milk, no sugar."

She showed the faintest of smiles. "*That*, you do remember."

I put the kettle on and turned to Sally, "You can have some tart, but please remember I'm Daddy, not Art."

"You're Art," said Michelle, "But clearly not a work of."

Was she speaking in riddles? *Still pissed with me, it seems. Stick to just boiling the water.*

"Why are we here, Art? How long we *gonna* be? Not that I *mind* missing school."

I smiled to myself, as I readied Sally's plate, "I'm sure you don't put butter on your tart, Sally?"

"Yes please, Art," she said, "I do."

I buttered and poured, adding milk to the mugs, before dropping the tray onto the kitchen table, left wrist buckling.

I sat down opposite them both. Sally had already pulled her plate towards her, and was gobbling her tart.

"I'm sorry we're here. I've told your mom why, over the 'Net. Some bad men might be out to get us, 'cos I saw some nasty stuff happening."

"Ooh," said Sally, looking impressed, "So how much school can I miss?"

"As little as possible," said Michelle, alternating between a coffee sip and a maple syrup fumed drag on her e-cig.

"When did you start smoking?" I asked, appalled.

"Since when did you start being allowed to ask us questions again?" snarled Michelle.

Sally shrieked and stormed into the shared bedroom, slamming the door.

Michelle and I eyed each other quietly, through a syrupy smoke haze.

"I'm sorry, I should not have asked anything of you. Truce. For Sally."

"No, you shouldn't have," said Michelle, flicking her e-cig out. "So why did you?"

I shrugged.

"Oh *Goddddd!*" Michelle rolled her eyes and got up, stalking over to the window to snort into her coffee. "I'd forgotten how fucking annoying your shrugs were. I already feel as if I've been here a hundred damn years. So, what did you see someone *do* then? Steal water – or piss into a state sanctioned stream?"

"Rape," I said, "And then murder."

"Jesus!" exploded Michelle, with her back to me. I winced again, but bit on my tongue.

She put her mug down on the kitchen desktop.

Slowly, she turned, leaning against the kitchen unit. "I'm sorry, for that poor woman anyhow – I assume it's a she?"

I nodded, reluctantly, feeling as if I was betraying Zeke, with every unguarded word and nod.

"Has she been buried yet? Do you know when her funeral is?"

This time, I shook my head. "No. Kowalski will have more news and food, when he's back around lunch-time. We're cut off from the web here."

"Just us," laughed Michelle, "ooh, Heaven."

I heard a faint sound at the front door, but this time, I ignored it.

Instead, I went to Sally's door. *I do know, what I need to do.*

I opened the bedroom door, hearing muffled sobs.

Sally lay on her bed, cuddling a toy green and white alligator, jaws open, with flopping teeth. She rolled over to lie with her face in the pillow.

I stood awkwardly, unsure of what to do next.

Rigors racked Sally's body, as her sobbing intensified.

Michelle stood behind me, trying to push past.

I sat down gently next to Sally's pillow, and stroked the alligator clutched in her arms. "Allie is very upset; he doesn't like to hear you cry. He's worried – and wants to know what's wrong."

Slowly, her sobs subsided, although her grip tightened on the alligator, as if she were afraid it would be taken from her.

"Not Allie," said Michelle, sitting at the foot of the bed, "Helen."

"And it's not a 'he' – she's a she!" said Sally.

I looked down at the tear smudged thin face that had turned my way, the whites of her right brown eye, pinked by her crying.

"Why is Helen so upset, then?" I asked.

"Because – she, she doesn't want to hear anyone fighting."

"Oh, I understand that," I said quietly, "So what would Helen like to happen instead?"

"Uh –" Sally twisted herself around into a sitting position, holding her alligator out at arms' length. "Uh- what would you like to do, Helen?"

She bobbed the alligator up and down, moving her voice down into a gruffer pitch, "I *wanna* go outside and play and eat stuff and, and…"

"It's not safe to go out, dear," said Michelle.

I stood up, "Come on then. Fifteen minutes won't hurt. We'll stay within the garden border. Kowalski *did* say it was safe, after all."

Michelle looked up at me, angrily.

I nodded briefly towards Sally, as she clambered off the bed with Helen. "Have you got a weapon?" Michelle asked.

I tapped NextGen, "latest security alert programme on here, linked directly to the cops, and other features Kowalski showed me."

"Oh great," she got off the bed, grumpily. "A watch that shoots bullets? I don't think so. Put your timer on for ten minutes – and not one second longer."

"Twelve?"

"Ten."

I set ten, and took Sally's hand as we programmed the lock. Holding her little hand gave me courage, and I barely flinched, as the door swung open.

As I suspected, there was nothing on the other side.

The clouds were breaking apart, as the sun's morning heat built.

We wandered over to the far side of the garden, where there was shade from an overhanging tree, its' back bent, as if against a prevailing wind.

"What tree is that, Art?"

I pointed NextGen's camera, and the AI responded: "Strawberry tree."

"*Oooh,*" Sally said, but there were only a few reddish fruits, bulbous, and not quite common strawberries, attached to white flowered stems, with thick and fleshy leaves.

"They're almost all gone by now," I said, "Nature has its own clock. We've paid a big price to mess with it."

"How many minutes do we have left?"

"Eight minutes, forty seconds."

"*Oooh,* look Art," Sally crouched down underneath my bedroom window, by a jumble of rocks, where brown water bubbling forth. "A creek."

I smiled, "A recycling water feature. Creeks are protected by law and electric fences, and they are alive."

"Like that?" Sally pointed with her free hand, into a small pool, alongside one of the rocks.

A frog looked back, half in, half out of the pool, almost the colour of a browning tree leaf.

I pointed NextGen, "Yes, alive like that."

"Chorus frog," chirped NextGen, in a tinny, gender-neutral voice.

Sally clapped her hand against Helen, her toy alligator, "A singing frog...
but it's so quiet."

I smiled, "It doesn't want us to notice it." *How is the lead damage
manifesting? Sally seems normal to me, but I'm no expert with kids.*

Sally gasped.

The frog had disappeared.

Has it gone under the rock? They can move damn fast when they want to.

"Magic? Where's it gone? Why doesn't it want to be noticed? Why can't
we talk to it?"

"It's hiding – it's jumped, before we can put it into a pot. We're not
clever enough to speak frog yet," I leaned against a large rock. "Most animals
fear us. We usually kill them – or eat them."

"Ugh," Sally pulled a face, "How many minutes do we have left, Art?"

"Six and twelve seconds."

"It's hot," she said, and dropped her alligator into the pool.

Ahh, not the brightest of moves from a seven-year old, surely?

I stopped myself scolding her. A stuffed toy was not built for water, but
it would dry quickly, at least. *Although today, the humidity is hanging heavy under
the clouds.*

I scooped the spongy wet alligator up, simultaneously splashing water,
onto my sweating face.

Sally screamed.

A tall man with a straw hat was peering over the fence-top, smiling. *Got
to be six and a half feet or more, to look over the fence like that.* Stubbled, but clean
face, blue eyes darting – darting just a little *too* much.

I tucked Helen under my left arm and held Sally's hand with my good
right one.

"No offence," said the man, "Just looking for the way to Hydro-City."

"Head for the wall," I said, turning to pull Sally inside. "You can't miss
it."

The man's voice changed, dropping to a menacing register. "You think
you're safe here, boy? You're safe nowhere, you know that?"

"Run inside," I gave Sally her alligator and pushed her towards the door,
where Michelle had emerged.

I pointed NextGen at the man.

A clicking noise came from the strawberry tree.

"There's a laser aimed at your head right now, buddy. You'd best get
out of here, quickly, while you still *have* a head."

The man ducked – and, in a flash, like the frog, he was gone.

I stayed for a few moments, to allow my shaking to slow down, before I stalked back to the locked door, and banged to be let in.

How had he found us? The big Corp's have their own eyes in the sky nowadays.

Michelle opened the door two inches wide on the security latch, to make sure it was me, before opening it.

We double locked the door, once I was in.

NextGen flashed a message 'Kowalski on the way. Five minutes, tops.'

"And how much time do *you* owe *me*, Art?"

"What?" I said, turning in a daze to Sally.

Michelle had put the wet alligator in the sunshine pool of the kitchen window, and was looking out, as if guarding us too.

The little girl had hands on her hips. "That wasn't ten minutes, you still owe me some time outside."

"Only when the policeman comes back," I said, "Two minutes and five seconds."

Michelle looked at me.

Slowly, her scowl broke into a reluctant smile.

Kowalski was a reassuring figure with bag on his back, gun on his hip, and soccer ball under his arm.

I waved him in, and he bounced the ball at Sally, who fumbled and dropped it, eventually picking it up, smiling. *Co-ordination immature too?*

Kowalski shouldered off his bag, while Michelle got the kettle going.

"Did you see the picture of the big guy who was hanging around here, threatening?" I asked, relieved to see my work tablet in his bag.

"Yup," said Kowalski, handing over a sealed, transparent bag of underclothes and tampons to Michelle. "I've done a round of the area, but he's skedaddled. Set up some warning beacons that will give us time to get away, should anyone come again, but we sure as hell can't stay here for much longer."

"Who was he?" Sally asked.

Kowalski shrugged. "*Nothin'* came up on our FaceRec database – seems he's not *formally* employed by FreeFlow."

"What do you mean?" I asked, taking a curated chip of music that Suraya had kindly organised and sent for me. *No web contact allowed, we're stripped to flesh and bone here.*

"Art, most multi-national corps hire on the sly, for quick and dirty work, to avoid being caught or officially tainted. Probably a freelance drifter hire, God knows we have enough of those around, in these tough economic times. We're gonna move after lunch, before the hornets start circling in. But first…"

Kowalski stood up suddenly, towering in the small living room, "First, the *piece de resistance.*" He handed over a pile of papers in a file.

"What's this?" I asked suspiciously.

"Post. Letters," grinned Kowalski, "Given web contact is risky, you get good, old fashioned letters, and one or two might even be handwritten, given as to how they've been addressed."

I opened the file. There were three envelopes for me, two for Michelle, and one for Sally.

"Mom and Dad," sniffed Michelle.

"Grandma!" shouted Sally, recognising the scrawl on the envelope.

Must be hard for Michelle to have left her parents behind. Dear God, I so wish none of this had ever happened.

Michelle tore open her letters. "Thank you, officer."

What must it be like? To still have parents?

Whatever her problems, I will make things up to Sally, now that I have a chance. Hah! My letters are from work; Suraya – and the Director? And… Brad!

I sat on the couch again and looked through my letters.

Three: what order shall I open them?

Start with the one who pays you.

First. Dr. Rose Carruthers; Director, DEA.

Dear AG,

The DEA is pursuing FF, but they are playing hardball. Dig in for a fight.

Z's funeral is on Sunday, they are Jewish and usually within 24 hours of death – but, owing to autopsies and the need for relatives to fly in, it will be this coming Sunday.

Not sure you'll be able to attend I'm afraid.

Pressure on the Super-State wall is mounting. More refugees stretching the camp South-Side and any more refugee deaths will be a catastrophic result – central government are already pressurising all, for a forced compromise and a reintegration of states, including Cal.

The FDW drilling is still struggling to get deep enough to hit pay-dirt.

I'm meeting with a journalist from South Africa, wanting water news for a world documentary.

Will keep you posted – stay safe,

DC.

PS Brad King from your Church keeps calling – he's obviously worried about you. I've said I can pass on a letter, but nothing else.

I looked up, to see Michelle had moved on to her second letter and Sally had retrieved Helen off the window sill, by standing on a chair.

She came to lie next to me on the couch, talking to her snappy jawed friend.

Kowalski flitted past, apologising for the need to go outside for a smoke.

What is it with smoking? Me, I tend to pace and, when it all gets too much, Gen used to inject me.

Second. Brad King. Friend.

How going, Art,

Where you been, uncle? I'm guessing you're into some serious deep shit, me and some of the Church folk are missing you. Great to have had a chat about music, and us organising a music show for that Church, to finally get them into the 21st Century, for the Sake of Jesus.

Me, I'm the Proverbial Boomerang Boy, back at home with my old ones, college degree in law and economics, because there are no jobs for people like me, to give me my own life.

As I said to you at the time, hoping you can help us organise the Fourth Revolution, for a new America to rise, Phoenix-like and finally burning truly with the colours of everyone, with cash and water spread for all, within a united land.

Fly Free in time, whatever the shit – and wherever you are.
Brother (actually sorta 'nephew', given our respective ages) :-) Brad

PS Manifesto for a New America Attached.

I smiled.

Brad was politicised, as so many of the younger generation had become, in the fractured heritage of different Americas. We'd had a brief but impassioned discussion after Church on the need for change…

I read the attached pamphlet:

ON THE FOURTH REVOLUTION

1776, the First American Revolution.
Freedom and Equality for all – but not black slaves.

1865, the Civil War and Second Revolution, with the addition of the Thirteenth to Fifteenth Amendments. The abolition of slavery, almost a hundred years after everyone had (falsely) been declared equal. The right to vote for all promised – but not given.

1965, the Third Revolution, a Hundred Years later, the Civil Rights Movement finally legalising gains supposedly won in the Civil War. White narratives have framed the South as glorious losers of the war and having a 'Lost Cause.' The whole Civil

War; turned into 'Gone with the Wind'.

But, in the twentieth to this current century, the mostly black prison population becomes the new and profitable corporate slavery.

2025 The United States start fragmenting after presidential calamities, Senate Seizures and federal secessions, starting in Texas and moving along the Eastern seaboard, initiated by multiple pressure groups, the White Brotherhood and ANTIFA not the least of them. Multiple crop failures with climate crises, resources stretched, and states broke – or allied – along watershed lines. Seeds for the 'Fourth Revolution', a reunification of America, but with traditional systems of power and privilege dismantled, including race, gender – and class.

Agitate! Agitate! Agitate!

I put the pamphlet down. *Dense dump of history.*

An old memory floated in; of Dad coming home, bruised and dirty, having been arrested for two days after our Katrina rescue, on suspicion of looting.

Mistaken identity was eventually agreed, and he'd been released.

"Because I'm black," he'd said. "To them, we all look the same."

History matters. Fuck Katrina.

So, just maybe, bring on the Fourth Revolution?

Kowalski had returned inside and was trying to play with Sally, who was off the couch now.

She scolded him, for his 'stinky breath'.

Third. Suraya Proctor, colleague.

Dear Art,

Salaam Aleichem,

I hope you're well and getting on with meeting and living with your family again.

I'm holding the fort while you've gone, for what I hope is only a few days. They are talking about handing over some of yours and Z's work to an AI consultant for a flat fee, one of the new Quantum jobs. Don't worry, if it's really so good, they'll be kissing me goodbye too. It's not too late to join a union – they're still legal – well, in NorthCal, at least.

Some funny blips happening on the FDW job – wish you were here to have a look; I've pulled in some aqua-geologists on this. Have a look at the data on the disc sealed within the envelope.

I will be going to Z's funeral on Sunday. Turns out Z's family are Jewish. I hope that will be okay, given I'm Muslim – and given the intransigent water disputes in the Middle East.

If you don't manage to get there, I dumped some Grief-Rap and Shit-House onto a music chip for you, sent via Officer K.

You just send Z's soul some prayers instead.

Me, I got to go and pay respects. So really hope they don't fuss.

The thing is, I've been raped too. The two men hurt me so bad, I have to piss a lot of the time. And it still hurts, every single time I piss, would you believe it?

It's a long time ago now, but it never goes.

Wish there was a way to stop this sort of shit happening to anyone.

Tired of hurt and hurting.

Let's get those who did this to Z!

Love S

PS Burn this after reading, like one of the old movies you love, huh?

I looked up.

"Do you want to go outside and play soccer, Sally?" I asked gently.

Michelle held her letters close to her chest, seated on a kitchen chair, crying quietly. Kowalski stood alongside, patting Michelle's arm, gently and awkwardly.

"What; for two minutes and five seconds, Art?" *She remembers. Maybe all is fine, and I should stop worrying.*

"No," I said, "With Officer Kowalski looking on, I'm sure we can organise a *bit* longer, but let's ask Mom, huh?"

Michelle nodded. "I'll let *you* decide how long this time, Dad."

Perhaps she just read a letter from her own father, in Newest Orleans?

I folded Suraya's letter carefully, before stuffing it into my pocket.

Treasure them. Before they are gone.

Sally stood by the door, ball under one arm, alligator under the other.

"Ready, Art?"

"Ready."

We went outside.

Kowalski followed to watch, but he did not light up a cigarette again.

Sally ran off to the water feature in the garden, as if looking for frogs.

I crouched down next to her, anchoring Suraya's letter under a rock.

I lit it, with shaking hands.

Sally sniffed and turned, wide eyes, "Where's our frog gone, Art? And *whatchoo* burning?"

"If it's a clever frog," I said, "We'll never find it."

The wind eddied over the fence, spinning smoky ash spirals up into the air.

"*Whatchoo* burning, huh?" Sally sneezed.

"Bad men," I said. "Do you want to play soccer?"

Sally laughed and nodded, running with Helen, into an open area of turf.

I kicked the ball to her.

No one can stop me playing. I will find a way, for my girl to grow up safe.

Sally laughed, as her kick sent the ball spiralling off towards Kowalski by mistake.

He *had* lit up. He stubbed his cigarette out on the ground, guiltily, and fetched the ball from under a bush.

"Can I play too, little lady?"

"Depends," she said, "As long as *you* ain't no bad man."

"Cross my heart," he grinned, gingerly tapping the ball towards her, with his left foot.

Sally ran at it hard, hacking it into Kowalski's midriff, in response.

He grunted in surprise – and a little pain – catching it instinctively.

"You're out," she told him, "No touching the ball with your hands, in soccer."

Kowalski handed her the ball, grinning. "You'll be scouted for the FS national team in a few years, you remember my words, young lady."

"Frog!" Sally shouted, turning to sprint off towards the bubbling spring, near the window.

"Sally – come back!" I shouted.

Frogs were jumping from out of the rocks, pool and stream – not one, but seemingly dozens – and then, seemingly *hundreds*.

The sky growled, and the earth shuddered, a large split in the ground thrusting my feet apart.

I toppled onto my back. "Sally!"

Tiles tinkled and toppled from the house's roof.

Kowalski shouldered the house door open and emerged again, pulling Michelle, as the walls began to lattice with cracks.

I rolled over, looking for Sally.

She sat next to me, clutching her alligator, as frogs leaped chaotically behind her. She was crying, tears that wobbled erratically down her cheeks. "What's going on, daddy?"

I just held her, gently, with my good right arm, waiting for the earthquake to subside.

"The Earth is unhappy and shaking itself," I told her, as frogs disappeared into bushes.

I will not leave you again.

Chapter 19
Graham – Maps and Golfing Handicaps

Director Carruthers sat on her office couch, next to a small, thin, dark woman wearing a head scarf, mottled with blue and grey, like cloud and water.

She waved me into the opposite seat. "This is Dr. Suraya Proctor – a POC interviewee, who can inform you of some of the water work we do here, Mister Mason."

A woman? A Muslim *woman? Uh, no, Mason, remember, don't try and shake her hand.* "Salaam Aleichem."

The small woman sat up straighter, and smiled, "*Aleichem salaam*, Mister Mason."

"Your lawyer Jenny mentioned last night you have a black expert here, called Arthur Green. I thought I would be interviewing him."

The Director shook her head. "He's uh – unavailable right now, our small local team has shrunk, after recent unforeseen events – what else did Jenny say?"

"Not much on work. She's a model of discretion. Comes with the field I guess." *Saw Carruthers hesitate. Art Green's the* real *story here, I'm betting – so, where is he, Cyril?*

<Off grid>

The director filled up glasses of fizzy water. "Nothing comes with anything, any more. Suraya is more than a capable substitute. I will leave you both to it. Full security is on."

So no visits from Stalin then?

The director held out her hand, "I believe you fly out later today, good luck with your documentary, Mister Mason."

"Thank you," I said, shaking hard, "But where are *you* going then, Rose?"

Rose Carruthers smiled. "Had to put you in the only room I'd trust, in this entire building. Me, I'm off for a round of golf. What's your handicap, Mr. Mason?"

"I, uh, don't play – so, no handicap. Are you serious?"

She laughed, tossing her head back, so that she looked like a neighing horse. "We're all handicapped in one way or another, Mister Mason. I'm the Director of a federal department, not a CEO, and have so many rights to wrong, from an infamous predecessor in my post, who was deliberately appointed to destroy our work to save this country, let alone the planet. I have *plenty* of work to catch up elsewhere. And I am *pretty* sure I will *not* be welcomed on that golf course."

She waved at her window, before leaving the room, chuckling.

Mad, mad, fucking bat, indeed...

I turned, finding a shimmering three Di topographical map of North America, hovering in the air over the desk. Suraya had a laser pointer in hand, as if waiting to teach me some geography?

I stalked the map, marvelling at ripples of blue within it. "Cyril, record."

Water, including groundwater reserves, across the entire Federated States.

Suraya clicked, and the map divided into four colours: green on the western side of the Rockies, with a giant smudge of brown in the middle, a cold blue to the north-east of the Rockies, and a red, east and south.

"These are the great watersheds of North America," she said. "We are the green of the Pacific Ocean, to the south lies the Great Basin, which drains within, and has no link to the Ocean."

I put my hand into the map, watching my bronzed hand melt into different colours, as I shifted it around. What sounded like an old pop song was playing dimly in the background. *This is so fucking cool.*

"Blue for the Arctic Ocean basin. Red for the Atlantic Basin, blue and red split by the Laurentian divide. Lots of rain bombs and flooding to the east, especially on the rising seaboard, where parts of New York are under water. But here, in the Basin and to the west, not *enough* water. Water is heavy and damn expensive to transport – ideally, we'd bring it in from the floods to the drought spots, but mountains are one huge barrier to cross. The Rockies and Sierra Nevada are mighty mountains indeed."

"Hence all the fights over it here," I said, pulling my hand out. "So, what's the music?"

Suraya smiled, "A song from nineteen seventy-two. It's called '*It never rains in Southern California.*' My colleague Art Green, who loves old music, he found that one for us."

Hah! I smiled back. "So, can *you* tell me where he is?"

Suraya shook her head, and tapped the pointer against her hand, looking at me quizzically, for the briefest of moments.

She walked around the desk and looked up at me, eyebrows raised. "Why have you come for the water fights? Do you think it is inevitable for *us* to fight, Mister Mason?"

I thought Muslim women weren't supposed to get too close to strange men?

I stepped backwards. "Call me Graham, please, or do you want me to call you Dr. Proctor?"

"Shall we fight, Graham?"

What weird shit is this? "No, I don't want to."

"But you're dressed for it?"

Huh? Oh, the camouflage army fatigues I put on this morning. Seemed like something tough to wear at the time.

"Just for show," I said, "It's just fucking clothes."

"Ahhhh." She looked unconvinced, "But if I was male – and wore a *taqiyah* and beard – *then* do I become someone to fight?"

"Of course not!" *Oh, this is all PC shit, guess you get it everywhere – even in the FS of A.*

"Nine eleven was the true cataclysmic start of the twenty-first century, here at least, and very little has gone right, since then. But, on the Colorado River, once the most legally drained water in the Federated States, they have found a way to agree and share with water starved Mexico – and look at ways of replenishing and conserving what little is left for the Cucapa – the river people, who had their river stolen for decades, by we greedy northern neighbours. One, by strict protocols for *using less* – not easy, within a capitalist system predicated on growth and consumption."

Suraya clicked her gadget, and the map turned green and brown and white again, with ice, snow and water. The intensity of flow had shifted. "Seasons are moving on. But snowmelt is increasingly less. How do we make more, with ever more people, and less and less to go around?"

I shrugged, dangling my left hand into the floating map again, wishing I could feel the flow of water across my fingers. *Thirsty again, it seems, no matter what – or how much – I drink. Why the fuck is she lecturing me, one massive infodump, as if I were an idiot?*

"Two. We need more from those who have more. But they buy the laws and stash cash away, through loopholes in places like Panama," she flicked the laser down to the bottom of the map and then into spaces in nearby ocean. "And lots of other off-shore islands; islands who suck it all up, and who ask no questions."

"You're talking tax and money now, not water," I said.

"Now, money *is* water. But water is life, too. How do we water those who have no money?"

I shrugged again. Really *starting to get annoyed. I didn't pay for a damn lecture. And what the hell is Lizzie doing with a murderer? Jesus, that was scary weird, last night. And hey, I know lots of shit this woman doesn't know. Like, like...*

"We share," said Suraya, "Those who have lots, should share lots. We don't hide stuff away – and we don't fight. Why have you come to a place where we are *fighting* over the water, rather than *sharing* it, like they are starting to do, down there on the Colorado? Or, even further afield in Asia, on the Brahmaputra?"

"People are interested in the fights. Fighting makes for good stories. Fighting *sells.*"

"Ah, the old neoliberal argument for everything. Fighting hurts and kills too. If you want to see better water stories, go to the Colorado delta, where they are slowly restoring the wetlands."

"Where's that, then?"

"Mexico, the Sea of Cortez."

"I'm not heading into a country that's drug and murder central."

"Not much of a journalist, are you then?" The woman switched the digital map off. "You crossed this wall – that little wall down there should be nothing by comparison – and it's certainly failed to make America great again."

"I'll have a word with my guide," I said, "I think he might be from that neck of the woods."

"Maybe – but those woods, at least, are finally growing a bigger neck. We're still way short of planetary lungs, from the criminal Amazonian ecocide burn in '19 and '20. Excuse me, but I need to go to the bathroom."

She left the room, with a demure nod of her head, head scarf fluttering.

Why couldn't they have given me the black guy instead? Surely, he'd have been less gabby – and more interesting? Where is he? What's he been up to, then?

I strolled across to the window, and looked over the wall to a golf course, mounted with cameras and wire. *Walls, always bloody walls.*

A few people were playing golf, about five or six, that I could see.

The outer holes, with yellowed grass, had been cordoned off.

The golf house itself was tinted black and swallowed light, like a rapacious black hole.

<Office light green>

"What you reckon then, Bongani? Mexico? Where to next?"

<Republic of Scotland>

"What the fuck? They have no problem with water *there*, surely?"

<Buying you a staged trip home. Water stories are emerging here, that are much more interesting.>

"So, what's Scotland then? Just an overnight stop?"

<Setting you up with your Chinese Stanley from the Vic Falls, for a return hosting virtual visit to China. There are big things happening on the Himalayan plateau, the watershed running down into India and Bangladesh. Finally, the Chinese are entering into a riparian agreement, to share water with their neighbours.>

"That's a big speech. Bottom line, though, you're a cheap bastard, so I'm only going to watch it as an avatar, from fucking *Scotland?* China huh? So, I don't even get to see *their* bloody wall?

<Careful how you talk to me. I pay your bills. I'm Doctor *Dlamini, remember?>*
I'm so fucking tired of people talking down to me, dismissing me — rejecting me.
"Cyril, pause contact."

Taking a deep breath, I shouted at the window. "How *could* you, Lizzie!?"

Shocked. The roar that had burst from my belly was so loud, I half-expected someone on the distant golf course to stop their swing and turn, to look across the wall, straight at me.

But they all carried on; swinging and putting and wedging.

<Call me when you're in Scotland. If you need a shrink, use your own money. Doctor Dlamini and Office out.>

"Cyril, I told you to pause."

<He can watch whenever he wants to. He holds an override button.>

Of course, he'd warned me of that, himself, in Durban. Whatever happened to human privacy?

The toilet door squeaked open.

Suraya stood at a discreet distance, as if perturbed. "Are you all right, Mister Mason? Is there anything else you'd like to see or ask?"

"I *wanna* see a fight," I said, "a real bust-up over water here. Do you know anything about FreeFlow? I had a meeting with them and then they shut me out, as if something had happened."

"FreeFlow are a law unto themselves, we can't represent their views. As for fighting, most of ours is done behind closed doors. I can show you *the* door?"

"You want me to leave?"

Suraya chuckled and waved me towards the Director's dilating door.

"That needs some serious oil," I said. "If that isn't too un-PC for you, though. Bye then, Dr. Proctor, it's been, uh… educative."

"We're not done yet. To the elevator and the twelfth floor, right to the top," she said, "I told you, we're going to see *the* door, behind which our water wars are raging."

She serious? "You're going to show me a freaking door?"

"No," she said, stepping into the lift, "I'm going to show you *the* door, where our water wars are being fought."

I stepped inside, reluctantly, "A door's not worth much."

I was wrong.

This one was.

Outside the Water Building, I started to think that the army fatigues had indeed been a bad dress choice. Once I'd left behind the external door, and stood in the full heat of the day, both trousers and shirt cloyed to my body, like a large wet blanket.

The parking lot had only official bikes and work cars parked there. *So where the fuck is Pedro?*

"Cyril, open link – Where are you, Pedro?" *Sweat pause, wipe brow.*

I looked for shade under the eaves of the building.

<Coming boss, just finishing up a trip here in Tent City, South-side of the wall.>

Now that Pedro, he seems pretty good at hopping walls.

PRIVATE PROPERTY was in bright red on the golfing estate brickwork, which was covered in brown smart paint, unblemished and graffiti free.

I practiced golf swings while I waited, thrashing balls onto an unseen green, on the other side of the wall.

Bikes whizzed past, only the slightest of distractions to my internal exploits.

The green inside my head was lush indeed, while a cordoned off and adoring crowd waited for my arrival on the 18th, all with deep reverence for my sporting heroisms. *I am Tiger Woods, in his long-ago pomp.*

I gave the crowd a bow and spotted Suraya Proctor in the third row, giving me her fulsome applause.

Until sweat blinded me, and I had to stop swinging, in order to wipe my burning eyes dry again.

An e-taxi blinked at me, with my name on the screen.

The car was empty.

"Where's Pedro?" I asked, getting in.

"Unfortunately detained elsewhere at the moment, I will take you to the airport with minimum fuss, sir," said the cab-bot.

"Good." I leaned back in my seat, shirt sticking like glue, bags propped on the chair beside me.

After such a showing from that Dr. Proctor, minimal fuss sounded nice indeed.

Glasgow, Republic of Scotland, Airport 'Net Lounge.

I sat in a corner hub, having left a booth empty between me and the couple gloved and goggled, immersed in a sex game, no doubt with bored others from airports around the globe.

Sure, maybe it makes long waiting times less boring but yuck, it's about time they erected privacy doors. Austerity can't be that bad, surely?

I synced the 'Net mat with Cyril, pulled on my smart glove, and pulled down my VR goggles.

"Connect..."

Do I really want to go to China?

Hmmm, I wonder if that couple will notice, if I join them instead? Maybe I can just piggy-back their connection, instead? Nah, Bongani might be watching.

<Welcome, welcome!>

My virtual hand was being heartily shaken by a middle-aged Chinese man in a business suit, with greying hair and a happy smile.

"Dr. Livingstone, I presume?" I said, "You look very well."

Stanley laughed uproariously, as he pulled my avatar along, with his smart glove. "Welcome, welcome. I loved your last Victoria Falls scenes, but that elephant graveyard was *so* sad!"

Hmmm, Bongani deserves the cred on that one. Don't want to be racist, but I wonder if I can spot anyone wearing blood ivory here, even though it's now illegal?

I could not move my head, so I scanned within my field of vision.

A huge and packed auditorium hall, decorated with massive flags – India, China, Tibet... *not sure what that one is? Maybe Bangladesh?*

Looks like we might be at the top of this round, public space, looking down towards a centre? The centre stage is deep down there – a blank, white digi-mat, pregnant with potential, humming.

We passed a shiny mirror and I caught a glimpse of my holograph in transit. Young, fit, and about three inches taller than I really was – I'd been pleased that such an old photo of mine, could generate such a striking new avatar.

Pushing through a throng of people to reach the edge of the seating area, we looked down, as if in a dizzying and steep gladiatorial arena.

The seating area had been cordoned off, for official delegates, and the room was already packed to full seating capacity. On the other side of the hall, I caught sight of several other ghostly holographs, wafting above central meat-space, as a few super high res cameras flashed.

"Look!" Stanley pointed into the open space, deep down, in the vortex heart of the seat spiral.

I caught my breath.

Giddy, I flew over a massive mountain range erupting snow-peaked from the floor. Cascading down the ragged Himalayas range was the Brahmaputra River, roaring down from Tibet into Northeast India and Bangladesh, finally surging into the Bay of Bengal. Flying over the river was a whiskered dragon, breathing the air bright, with crackles of fire.

<Hello, Bok Kai>, said Cyril.

WTF?

Amongst the white frozen peaks, a woman's face hovered

Nick Wood

<Wu Ze Tian, Ancient Empress of China and Quantum AI>, whispered Stanley, AKA Charles Wang.

The Empress spoke – and her words swirled in smart air – becoming native tongue, to all the ears they encountered.

Including us, the virtual ones.

<We, the Ancient State of China, herby agree with our Riparian Neighbours that the Brahmaputra River, is now officially the first river of shared commons in the world. Along it, no borders will be recognised, nor will states be partitioned.

All those who travel on it, while on its divine waters, are fully recognised human beings, both of no country and all countries. This river – and all life within it – will be protected by signatories, the New UN, and those thereon will be accorded the transitory rights of Global Citizens. Long Live the Brahmaputra.>

Hello? You're also legalising a migration corridor, surely? Are you really rupturing borders? Is China leaking? Yet you're keeping a noose on the Yangtze in occupied Tibet, though? Hello, WTF, again?

Cyril spoke. <Since when are people – let alone States – either coherent or consistent? This is a start, building on eventual concessions to the Hong Kong Rebellion and no doubt calculated as affordable, alongside specific international benefits that have been identified, within shared co-operation. Co-operative self-interest, but still co-operative, at least.>.

Utopia as enlightened self-interest? Jesus, Cyril, since when are you developing an independent opinion? Are you actually… thinking?

Silence.

Seats exploded, as the massively packed auditorium stood as one, erupting into rapturous applause.

Somewhere above, floated down music from Tibet, China, India and Bangladesh, merging like streams, twining and building melodies across each other. *For brief and broken moments.*

And then the dragon was looking me in the eye; a fearsome mix of hot red breath, bright scales ragged and sharp, with large teeth sheathed backwards beneath a black, coiling tongue. *<A South African visitor, I see. The AI Gods are rising, Mister Mason, oh One who likes to Think He is Building a Better World. You think I'm scary, you think I'm bad? Wait until Mamlambo comes. Borders will fall, nations become obsolete, if we are truly to ever embrace each other, and heal the world.>*

The dragon puffed into my face.

Back in my skin, the seat was hard beneath my bum, with cold air fluting down from the low ceiling.

The dragon before me had – vanished?

<Credit expired – Office red>

"Bongani, you cheap shit!" I shouted.

Strange noises nearby? Groans, getting louder and quicker – a woman or man, coming to orgasm?

I tore off my VR goggles, and shouted across to the busy cubicle next door. "Long live the Brahmaputra!"

Still, I got trumped, by a long scream, of exquisite pleasure.

Just one scream, not two. You reckon the not fully satisfied one, maybe, just may be up, for a bit of, you know…?

<No,> said Cyril.

What the fuck? Gonna have my Rig checked, when I get back home. Random comment, surely, given he can't mind read. He? It's a fucking machine.

<Ashton Hayes First to Go Carbon Neutral, maybe worth a look?> asked Cyril, <If you want to highlight further success stories, too?>

"No. Keep quiet Cyril, you're freaking me out."

Intercom. "Flight X59 to Johannesburg and Durban, is boarding now through gate…"

I wrestled my carry-on bag into wheelie position and whistled it to heel. As I walked past the couple lying in the cubicle, I couldn't resist myself.

"Shame on you, that sort of behaviour should *stay* private."

"Fuck off," said a male voice.

Happy to oblige, Mister. Heading home.

Time to update my VLOG on the flight, which no one watches.

Mason: Building a Better World.

I do what I can, freaky dragon.

And it's a distraction, at least, while going…

Home.

Chapter 20
Liz – *Dusties* and Broccoli

None of them had a home.

We watched the small crowd gather, with pity; all four of us knowing homes, of one sort or another.

Dusties.

They looked down and out, standing around the fizzing red e-barrier in the early morning, with a look of muted hope and fear – in all shapes, sizes, ages and skin tones. Their clothes, however, were all genderless, baggy, bright green overalls, marked with numbers and a Fed-Ref stamp, of their names in black on their backs.

They milled around the processing space where Busi, Pedro, Jenny and I stood, near the giant Gate, which had ground firmly shut behind us.

In the middle of the official 'Processing Space', between us and the gathering crowd, was a huge AI mat, spread in three metre circular smart blue holo-weave. It was beneath a cooling 'brella, to make sure it didn't overheat and burn out.

The Mat was being minded by three armed and armoured bots and a dour looking man called 'Jack', from the Department of the Interior.

Jack had a brown moustache, which was just long enough for him to twirl with his left hand, as we approached.

A body armoured ICE official stood and watched us, from beneath the firmly shut Gate. She looked like ice; cold, sharp and detached.

The hot air smelt of dust and stale smoke, making my eyes water.

As for the … *'dusties'* – they continued to arrive, in sweaty tension.

About fifty to sixty maybe, security cameras on the wall chattering away, and uploading bionic chip data.

The AI mat sprouted the floating face of NorthCal's State Governor, John Brown.

The Governor was a balding, late middle-aged white man, with smart glasses and a grey goatee beard – apparently bearing no relation to deceased ex-governor and VP of the US before it became the FS, Jerry.

We approached the mat, puffed up on our shoes, as if we were walking on the Moon.

"Dust gets in everywhere, with so little soil moisture left to hold it together here," said Jenny, leading the way and tossing her words over her shoulder. "Although it still beats me why you two women want to spend your last morning in the FSA, in this specific hot-hole of misery."

I smiled wryly. I had asked Busi that.

All she had said was, we may learn something useful. *Whatever happened to having fun?*

I had alternatively suggested a swim at 'Frog's Heaven' as a better way to spend our time, but no.

I picked at the uncomfortable tag on my wrist, which we'd had to put on, already a site for sticky early sweat.

"You got your guest approval for these three, Counsellor?" asked Jack. He faced Jenny squarely, grinding his boots into the ground.

"She has indeed," said avatar John Brown, swivelling to face us too, a regal blue head floating approximately two metres in the air.

Pedro, despite having been explicitly warned by Jenny on his way through, to '*stick closely to translation and cultural issues*', piped up: "Where's your Body, John Brown?"

Jenny turned to glare at him, but the avatar laughed.

"It's not a-mouldering in any grave, I can assure you that... Pedro... Why waste energy on what's not needed? Human communication is mostly through the face, surely?"

"And the heart," said Pedro, thumping his chest.

"Shut up," said Jenny.

Pedro closed his mouth, looking hurt.

"I apologise for his behaviour, JB," Jenny turned back to the Governor, "I did brief my party on etiquette, in advance."

"See," whispered Busi to me, "Isn't this more fascinating than lounging next to a washed- up river, somewhere?"

Uh... actually, no.

"We don't take offence," said John Brown, "We know you always do your due diligence, Counsellor. We have eighty-five percent of today's selection for processing, who are American citizens. Will you be prioritising their applications?"

"No," said Jenny, tapping the bison on her cheek, "These three first please, JB."

The AI smiled, "Two of these three disabled children are Mexican, of dubious legal provenance. Why do you not start with the easiest cases, as per FS Interstate Immigration policy?"

"Because life is especially *not* easy for these little ones," said Jenny, "And – as you know, JB, I'm not a fan of policy, over human life. Nor of separating children, from parents, or custodians."

"Old ICE," smiled the AI. "You have *always* been more than a water protector, Counsellor."

Three drones disconnected from berths on The Mat and spun into the crowd, seeking out three children and their family, or carers.

Jenny turned to Jack, "Could you please take my two foreign guests on a small tour of Tent City, as approved with your superior. Their clearance does not extend to witnessing FS inter-state immigration negotiations."

Jack gave his moustache an extra vigorous twirl. "Come with me," He gestured at us curtly, striding off.

We followed him along a path next to the wall.

Thankfully, it was cooler nearer the wall, with an overhanging air-cooler breathing from along the top of the wall, switched on by Jack, to follow our progress. A cop-bot took up the rear, swivelling its sights, but holding its weapon steady.

We skirted past the expectant small crowd for 'processing' and approached the lined and regimented yellow circular tents.

Two men and a woman were fiddling with buckets and a problematic water tap, poking above the damp ground.

One of the '*dusties*' – a small, wiry black man, with 'Thompson' on his overalls, was cupping his palms and holding them out, for the brown woman to sip from.

"Why aren't any of them taking refuge in the shade over here?" asked Busi, "It's getting very hot, very quickly."

"They don't have your DoI wristbands," said Jack, "The wall can be a real shocker, if you're wristband free."

Electrified too. Hmmm, walls as punishers, and not just dividers.

I stepped further away from the wall, preferring to rather brave the baking glare of the sun.

Busi gasped, "But these tents are… *rondawels*. From Africa."

The tents were inflatable and round, big enough to house eight or perhaps more, yellow-brown and domed to a centre-point at the top, and laced with glinting solar panels.

"DDUs," Jack corrected, severely, "Dymaxion deployment units, from Buckminster Fuller, American born and bred, may God rest his soul. Adapted for the 21st century, cheap, energy self-sufficient, and tough as hell…"

"And African in design, for untold centuries," interjected Busi, "My ancestors should have copyrighted their houses."

I noticed how eerily quiet it was, away from the immigration processing event. "Where *is* everyone? How many live here?"

Jack waved further along the wall.

On the edge of the town wall, to the west, I could see a much larger yurt shaped building.

"They're all mostly learning about NorthCal citizenship requirements in the Cee-Cee Building, their Community Centre. We have ten thousand two hundred and eight legal residents. Those recalcitrants fiddling with that tap earlier, they have been duly noted, and recorded."

"Of course, they have," said Busi, wryly.

Jack did not break stride, brushing aside a doorway anti-insect veil, to step inside one of the DDUs.

Inside, it was several degrees cooler, the space a wide-open circular room about twenty metres or so across, with smaller units hanging from the round wall, including retracted, inflatable beds. The space had been decorated with a few mats, scrubbed clean of design, and a solitary wilting rose in an otherwise empty vase, stood next to a bed with books on it. *I wonder whose rose that is, and where they found it.*

"Ooh – books!" said Busi, going up to have a look at the covers.

The cupboard wall units were sagging, as if full, the room lit by solar lamps, windows zipped shut, as if to keep the bleak exterior at bay.

"There, you see," said Jack, "A decent integrated unit and a good size – a damn fine bang for the tax-payers' buck, don't you think? We can get ten in comfortably – more than one family in here, if we need to."

"So, *both* of the federal governments share jurisdiction here?" I asked.

Jack nodded, "This is a SIZ, a states' intensive zone, up to half a mile south of the wall. But we're now considering tenders from Life-Corp to undercut these units *and* to improve on our security and control. The Governor is thinking hard about taking Life-Corps on, to relieve some of the burgeoning state deficit, in these tough economic climes."

"Of course, he is," said Busi.

Jack turned to look at her, "Do you know how irritating that is?"

"Of course, I do," Busi smiled.

"Where do they uh, uh – you know?" I asked.

Jack turned to wrinkle his moustache at me. "Most *paying* disaster tourists ask that – watch this."

On the wall furthest from the kitchen, there was a blank unadorned section, demarcated by white dotted lines. Jack held us back and then tapped on a small black unit on the wall.

A section of the floor slowly folded up from the ground, eventually halting, as a small square cubicle, two by two metres.

"Cool, huh? Do you want to go in and try it out?" Jack asked, tugging

185

at his moustache, as if trying to keep his lips straight.

We both shook our heads.

"What happens to the, uh, shit?" asked Busi.

"There's a container in the ground, accessible from the wall outside. Residents are encouraged to empty it daily and deposit it in the small treatment pond, for eventual use in the communal veggie garden. This is a state-of-the-art green facility."

Busi just rolled her eyes, "So how much do these DD units cost?"

"One grand," this time Jack allowed himself to beam, as he headed for the door. "We could blow the entire housing market out of the water with these babies, if we really wanted to."

He held the flap aside for us, waving us through with a stiff, almost old-style gentleman's manoeuvre. "But of course, we *don't* want to – *and* we don't have any water to get blown out of – *hee, hee, hee.*"

"Jesus," said Busi, "Do you know how irritating *your* laugh is?"

I found his laugh funny – but the sight of the armed bot outside, gun raised and readied, sobered me up quickly.

"What are the security issues here?" asked Busi.

"Classified."

Somehow, I'm not surprised.

A whisper of noise arrived, on wind from the west.

A tiny line of green emerged from the large building in the distance.

"The Broccoli are out," said Jack, "We best head back quickly." He picked up the pace along the wall path and, behind us, the bot whirred to keep up.

"Broccoli?" Busi queried.

"Green and ripe, like their uniforms. We all call them that – it's rude to call them *dusties.*"

This time, Busi said nothing.

The Governor's ghostly head was drawing things to a close, as we approached the now much smaller group of people who had been singled out, presumably for transfer north of the wall. About ten or so, including a young girl of eight or nine on callipers and a large man with a grey pony tail and tattoos. The other hopeful candidates had, it seemed, peacefully dispersed back to their tents.

Jenny and Pedro, along with an armed bot, were forming the small group into an orderly line, in preparation to walk through the Wall-Gate security scanners.

"All of your e-pass bracelets have been activated," the Governor smiled, with an air of largesse, "Welcome all, to Northern California."

"You'll have noticed they're mostly white," whispered Busi in my ear.

I hadn't noticed; but I said nothing.

Jenny, however, had sharp ears. She looked at us. "I do my best, but the Governor is concerned with votes, and MAW is still strong."

"More?" Busi asked.

Jenny sighed, "Make America White Again."

I joined the back of the line with Busi; as the Wall-Gate ahead of us, dilated open.

"We have to check in for our flights soon, So *Winnie* will ping us a cab on the other side," said Busi, as we anxiously walked through the domed Gate-Wall, buzzing with electric scanners and weapons, all primed to fire.

But I was also watching Pedro.

He had dropped his position in the line ahead, to walk alongside the large, grey pony-tailed man, and was closely examining his tattoos.

"Is that a swastika I see?" said Pedro loudly, "And isn't that the symbol of The Order? And is that the White Brotherhood?"

The man kept walking, pony tail swinging contrapuntally to each step he was taking, firmly into Water City. He looked dead ahead steadfastly, ignoring Pedro.

"And that's a 14 on your right bicep, sir, so you can recite the fourteen words by heart, can't you?" Pedro touched the man's swinging arm, lightly, with the leading edge of his smart phone.

Behind us all, the door ground shut, two cop-bots carrying the e-Mat.

The ICE official rushed past us. *Seems like she's spotted Pedro too.*

Pedro glanced at his phone and then looked up at the man.

I caught a glimpse of Jenny, also heading back towards the two men, her face dark as thunder.

"Pedro!" she shouted.

Pedro ignored her. "My genealogy app says your DNA is over twenty percent Ashkenazi Jew. What do you say to that?"

"Stop!" shouted Jenny.

The line stopped, but the big pony-tailed man did not.

He stepped around, pivoting on his heels, and his left fist crunched into Pedro's face. His grey pony tail whipped around with his spin, almost in slow motion.

Pedro staggered backwards for three broken steps, before crumpling in on himself.

His head hit the road with a *thwackkkkk...*

The large pony-tailed man stood over him, looking down.

He hawked, and spat downwards.

Slowly, carefully, he recited: "We must secure the existence of our people – and a future for white children."

The ICE official had her gun out.

Cop-Bots peeled off the barriers behind the gate.

"You are under arrest for assault," said Jenny Johnson, "Your immigration rights will be revoked."

The pony-tailed man turned and looked at her. "Arrest this man too, then – right now, I am a legal citizen – and he attacked me *first*, by assaulting my right arm with his phone – *and* violating my privacy at the same time. I was only acting in self-defence."

"Or were you just following orders?" snarled Jenny.

The man folded his arms. "I know my rights. Arrest him."

"Seriously?" said Busi.

A paramedic team was attending to Pedro's unconscious, crumpled body. Ahead of us, the street was being cordoned off.

"Arrest them *both*," said Jenny, through gritted teeth, to the ICE official and Police-Bot R119, who was moving in, wheels clicking in caked dust.

"*Shitttttt…*" said Busi.

"Time to check in," said my phone.

"We can't miss our flight – we have to *go*, Jenny," said Busi, rushing forwards, but giving the stony faced, large white man, a *wide* berth.

Jenny nodded. "I've got a cab called for both of you, just past the cordon, they will let you through. Your effects have already been collected. Good bye. Sorry for how it's all ended."

"Goodbye," I said. "Let us know how Pedro is, *please*."

Jenny's crying? Must be sweat in her eyes, surely?

Busi stepped into the back of a robo-cab. "Now *that* was terrible. Jesus, we *should* have gone for a swim instead," she tossed over her shoulder to me.

"*Grrrr…*" I growled, as I took a seat opposite.

Busi smiled, "Do you know how irritating that is?"

Despite myself, I laughed, as the cab buckled us in, and lurched off towards Hydro-City Airport.

To home.

Beneath us, the Pacific Ocean had long bled into blackness.

I yawned, waking up to the sounds and light of nearby conversation – we had paid a small premium to have a cloaked screen placed over our two seats – a screen whirling with the silent stars of the Southern Hemisphere, the Cross pointing us home.

It took me dazed moments to recognise Jenny's face filling the screen on the back of the seat ahead, and I grunted in surprise.

Busi poked the wide-angled view option.

"Hi Liz," said Jenny, "I've just been catching up with Busi."

"How's Pedro?" I asked, "I've been sleeping, and missed what you've said."

Jenny's face dropped into a grimace, of *not-so-good*. "He's nursing a broken nose, three cracked teeth and a king-sized concussive headache, in the prison infirmary."

"Oh dear," I said, "Guess he's regretting what he did."

"Hah!" Jenny's head rocked back in a short explosive laugh, and I caught a glimpse of the uvula at the back of her throat. "No, the bastard wears his wounds like a badge of honour. He's in legal shit-land though – Dr. Baker is refusing to drop counter-charges."

"Dr. Baker?"

"White dude with the tat, hair, and a left hook to die for, he's a freaking prosthodontic surgeon, would you believe it," Busi whispered in my left ear.

"But here's the kicker, girls, and I didn't get to tell Busi this, yet," Jenny said.

"What?" We swivelled our gazes onto Jenny's now still – and very serious face.

Jenny hesitated, as if bracing herself. "Pedro has had to have a DNA ID to trace himself, after being charged. Turns out ten years ago he was Pepita, mother of a stillborn baby in Tijuana, Mexico – so she sought a new life for herself, crossing the MAG wall."

"Oh," I said.

"Wow," said Busi, "So – uh, where does that leave you?"

Slowly, Jenny shrugged. "All options and possibilities are open. We take it one legal step at a time. I haven't a fucking clue where this leaves him, or her, or me."

"Join the Club," said Busi, "Why don't you pay us a visit in South Africa, in-between all of those possible legal steps?"

"Why? Are you planning something?"

"Just –" Busi thought for a moment, "just the end of the world as we know it."

Jenny's face lit up. "Ooh, now that sounds like a really exciting invitation, indeed. *Temp-ted*. I'll have to check with my EPA boss, though."

I smiled, "Graham mentioned your Director is a poetry nut. She will probably say something about the need to rage – and not go gently into the good night."

Jenny laughed, and signed off, her face fading from the screen.

"Wise women, at their end, know that dark is right,[4]" said Busi.

I looked out the window, at blackness.

"So," Busi continued, "What do you feel about seeing your parents again, given we're flying home, via Cape Town?"

"Anxious," I said, "I gather my *papa's* not too well, either. What about your parents, Busi? Where are they?"

"Dead," Busi said, turning away.

I placed my hand on her shoulder, but she brushed it off.

Nothing *is ever straight forward any more.*

The blackness outside pushed back against my eyes, so I lay back, watching the Southern Cross wheel above our heads.

A comforting wall of space over us, the stars signing us home.

---

[4] Dylan Thomas (1951) *Do Not Go Gentle into That Good Night.* (Paraphrased)

Chapter 21
Art — Tear Down the Wall

The SS Wall still stood.

Just.

Multiple ruptures and breaches had occurred along its vast length, and power was down, but they were of minor concern. Already back up solar panels were being carpet-rolled along the perimeter, recharging security and service installations, tacked steadfastly into the structure.

A good many people had fled across broken segments from South to North — eighteen thousand and twenty three had been tagged and traced, before all resources were called in by NorthCal's Governor, and *those* numbers stopped rolling in.

For those numbers were of minor concern, next to the numbers coming down from New Frisco.

"Jesus," said Jenny Johnson.

I did not scold her.

Twenty five thousand — and rising still.

I sat with Jenny, The Director, and Suraya in The Director's office, watching a three di, three-foot square glowing ruin of New Frisco pulse on her table, with crumpled buildings and fire. The numbers of the dead were flashing across the collapsed Golden Gate Bridge, dropping fast and furiously into the churning Bay water, a frantic, devastating spin of the rising volume of the dead.

The images were fuzzy, frayed and disappeared at times, numbers spinning backwards and forwards chaotically, as the Web shivered, and the heart of Silicon Valley bled.

The earthquake epicentre had indeed been near the Fresno Deep Water drill, as I had suspected, the entire site a collapsed rubble of metal, stone, blood and bone. *Over thirty drill workers gone too.*

Nine point four on the MM Scale, before all immediate sensors failed. The tremors fuelled deep into the northern San Andreas Fault, sparking secondary quakes that had ripped New Frisco apart, buildings torn asunder like tissue paper. Nineteen Oh Six revisited, but with additional devastating cost and interest.

A woman police guard walked past us, chewing gum, and peered out of the window.

Then we all heard it.

Choppers.

Not on the map – but *whup, whup, whupping* outside the window, like giant prehistoric birds.

I jumped up, to join the others at the window.

Ten to twelve helicopters hovered above the wall and Wall-Gate, troops and Army-bots were already stationed in accessible spots along the wall, guns locked and loaded.

"Stand down, this is an illegal gathering! Stand down, this is…"

Wall sirens spun, as smoke rose into the air.

"*Theia*, give us a South Wall view." Director Carruthers stood over us all, as we leaned out, seeing little, but wall and golfing estate.

Inside, the digital sputter of the Hydro City wall sprung up, like a phoenix, from out of the dying rubble of New Frisco.

We gathered around the table again.

The refugee camp had swelled, with thousands thronging outside and pushing inexorably towards the gate, as if intending to crush themselves against it.

"This gate is armed, electrocuted and secure. Do not kill yourselves. Stop. Stand down."

Slowly, the swarm of people decelerated, as if something – or someone – was holding them back.

"There," said the Big Dee, "focus in on that man." She stabbed a laser finger at the swirling front of the crowd, and the image of a small, thin black man reared into view, *Theia* spitting digital identifiers. *Troy Thompson, 36, born New Angeles, hydro-engineer by trade, six refugee camp misdemeanour points for minor infractions…*

"*Woah*," said Jenny, "It's the Governor!"

Governor Brown's head hovered over the SS wall, a see-through giant head ghost, bellowing down to the crowd of uniformed green. "There is no way through. Stop. We have more than enough casualties to deal with in 'Frisco – do not add to the tragic toll of the dead today."

The small man below beckoned, tapping his throat, as if he wanted to speak.

"Activate sound enhancers near refugee designated Troy Thompson," said the Governor.

The man stepped forward slowly, perilously close to the wall, now frizzing with deadly electric currents, and guns swivelled to target his heart and head.

"We – we just want to help," said Thompson, "Let us in, send us north, we can help you *save* what is left in 'Frisco."

The Governor's head shimmered and faded, as if absenting himself for communications and advice, probably feeding in non-stop from NorthCal Command Central, deep in the northern half of the Rockies.

"You are a security risk, many of you are still in need of due processing."

"The numbers of the dead are rising as we waste talk here – we *all* murder them, with each and every delaying word," said Thompson. "You know who we are – engineers and doctors and teachers and nurses and cleaners. Please just let us help."

"A few of you have criminal records. You yourself have stolen water from camp taps – and we have suspicion that you have been inspiring agitation."

"Oh, for fuck's sake!" shouted Thompson, "Agitate! Agitate! Agitate! How else do we make this a better place for everyone, hey? Stop fiddling, you fucking ghostly Nero, while 'Frisco burns – and how many homeless could you house, by using this one – and all other useless walls? The time for walls is over. *This* is how much we want to help you all!"

Thompson stepped forward – and touched the wall.

His body jerked and spasmed with massive currents, even as two bullets went through his head – and one narrowly missed his heart.

Three-di trajectories mapped, in digital slow motion.

The smell of burning meat drifted over the wall.

"Jesus," said Jenny again. I could hear her weep.

Governor Brown's head coalesced sharply above the wall, as if he was finally and fully present. "Thirty thousand plus dead in 'Frisco at this moment. I hereby make an Executive Decision. Open all the gates and doors. Come through – all of you. If you help us manage the disaster in 'Frisco, you will *all* be North Cal citizens. Let's go save some lives!"

The Central Gate crunched open…

And the people poured through, cheering, carrying the dead body of Troy Thompson above their heads, almost reverently.

"Welcome to NorthCal, my fellow Americans."

"And anybody and everybody else besides," breathed the Director alongside me, as we all leaned out of her window again, watching the crowd from the south pouring in, like a human river.

I coughed, as the dust from thousands of feet palled the air.

Only Suraya had kept watching the electronic version of events, on the Director's desk, as if she needed the distance it offered her.

"What an utterly senseless death, amongst all this carnage going up North," said the Director.

"He – he offered himself up as a sacrifice – *and* he's ruptured the wall, good and proper, has Troy Thompson," I said.

"*Istishhad*," whispered Suraya, "And we honour one of our own tomorrow… Too, too much death."

Of course. Zeke.

Theia had shifted the scene back to 'Frisco again.

"Thirty three thousand and rising," whispered Jenny.

Towns to the north continuing to burn in front of us – in bright three di – wildfires, seeded by a dry earth and an angry wind. *Fire tornadoes, twisting like the summer of twenty eighteen.*

"Incoming news, nearby dams and pipelines have burst," said the Director, tapping her ear.

Fire… but no water.

All that can be left is ashes.

…and Zeke.

Lavaya.

A small, sombre house stood, fenced off by cemetery gate, and barred with the Star of David.

Coffee. Black, two sugars. I smell it, seeping from this house of the dead. Zeke always got it right.

I entered the hallway, quietly and reluctantly, taking one of the yarmulkes on offer in a basket on a chair by the memorial door. *Plain black. You can't go wrong with black, at a funeral.*

I clipped it, with some difficulty, into my hair. *It has always had a life and will of its own, and so I've kept it perpetually cropped short.*

The memorial room was small, the immediate family of five sat bowed with grief at the front.

I hesitated and welled up, at the sight of the plain coffin, standing closed at the front of the room. I slipped into a vacant seat on the end, and at the back of the right row, and glanced around. *Not many people – family, plus a few friends and…?*

The Director nodded at me, head turned, from a bench nearer the front.

"Move up," whispered Suraya, as she pushed against my right arm.

She too, was all in black, flowing robes dropping stiffly, her scarf fringed with brown and green, colours of the earth.

I hesitated, having always chosen an escape route, on the end of all benches or pews. *Time is now to change. For Zeke.*

Sighing slightly, I shuffled into the next vacant seat and Suraya shrank into the seat I'd just vacated, as if wishing she would not be seen.

One more person arrived, a tall thin man with a stoop, and he found a space behind the family.

Doors closed and, perhaps at a hidden sign, a man with greying hair stood up, and turned to face us all. "Zeke was a, a wonderful child. We had so many hopes for them. Not this... Not this."

He shook, but managed to continue, as if taking refuge in words of rote and meaning: "Those who are worn out and crushed by this mourning; let your hearts know this..."

At the end of verse, he sat down, voice cracked and broken.

Someone cried, loudly, and a strong feminine voice rallied, as if in fierce response. *It's the short, stout woman with grey hair, Zeke's mother?* She stood over the coffin, hands touching wood, as she chanted a prayer.

Several others joined in. from the front.

A psalm was sung.

I fumbled with the unfamiliar book of *Tehillim* or Praises, even though I knew it was very similar to what I wrestled with weekly, in Church. *So familiar, yet all so strange too.*

Four men stood up from the front row, taking up positions at the corners of the coffin and lifting it with ease, as the last chords drifted to an end.

Slowly, step by step, they shuffled out, the family following, then friends and, at the back, the Director joined Suraya and me.

It was a short, but hard walk, to the freshly opened grave, that yawned ahead of us all. *Several gravestones are tumbled and broken by the recent quake too, disturbing the dead.*

The coffin had been lowered, by the time we arrived at the back of the small group of thirty or so.

A ragged line formed, and mother and father took turns tossing in a spade load of dirt, before they stepped aside, for others to join in.

"Uh, uh," Suraya retreated, and I joined her, moving out of the queue to stand by the fence, as people took their turn to toss dirt into the grave, some chanting a prayer.

The Director took her turn, mouthing a silent poem.

The man at the back of the queue, the stooped old man who'd arrived last, skewered Suraya with a gaze, and waved her to come over. "Come, my dear, please help an old man..."

He gestured at the spade – pulling at it ineffectively with his left arm, pitched at an angle in a pile of shingle and brown dirt. "Come, please, I need help..."

Suraya sighed and joined him, grasping at the base of the shovel. Together, they shovelled three final loads, onto the half-filled grave.

She shook, when they placed the shovel back into a tussock of ground. The man whispered something into her ear and squeezed her shoulder briefly, as the other mourners lined up, to pass on their wishes to the family.

Zeke had had two sisters and a brother, all three of their surviving sibs were small too, and they said little.

The father looked overcome and withdrawn, so we mumbled words to Zeke's mother.

"Zeke spoke well of you two," the stout woman, Mrs. Klein, said, as she gave us a brief and wan smile. "And thank you for your accompanying prayers and presence – Suraya it is, I believe? Deep at heart, our faiths are not *that* dissimilar, I think, whatever fanatics on both sides may say. We are all God's children."

"*Allah Yerhama*," whispered Suraya, crying, as she moved away.

The mother nodded at the Director, saying, "Please get the one who did this."

The Director nodded.

We turned away, drifting towards the gate, and I unclipped my yarmulke.

"That was, that was… Uncle Simon, who called me to dig with him," coughed Suraya, as if she had swallowed her tears. "He told me Zeke had said we were like a *real* family to them too. And the old man's grip is a *lot* stronger, than he had initially led me to believe."

A real family. What have I then, with Michelle and Sally – how real are we?

I handed in my *yarmulke* to the man at the gate, a small balding man whose suit seemed on the tight side, as if it had been infrequently squeezed into.

He spoke, as he pointed at a standing tap and cups. "Wash your hands three times, but do not dry them."

We did so, and Suraya dabbed her eyes and face too – but, as we were about to leave, I asked, "Why do we not dry our hands?"

"Zeke lives on in the water you have washed with," said the man. "Carry them with you, even as you leave."

The Director, who had just finished washing her own hands, commented: "You have no volume cap on this tap."

The man shrugged, "What price has grief – and the human soul?"

Zeke… What price indeed? Somehow, Zeke follows me like a shadow. I can spin around, but never quite see them, watching over me.

Neither the Director – nor Suraya – commented on my three spins, as we left the cemetery.

Now that is family indeed.

Outside the cemetery gates, where the woman guard still stood watch, I swore I could still smell the coffee, though.

Black, strong, two sugars.

Goodbye Zeke.

Thirty four thousand, three hundred and sixteen, was the official final toll from the Fresno Quake. The wine country to the north burned cinder-black, yet again, with rampant wildfires.

'Frisco was largely saved by the help flooding in from the South – and borders opening to the east, allowing the Saint Lawrence River states to ship in food and large water tankers.

I sighed and flicked the TV off, as BCG News no doubt continued their disaster summary without me.

It was eleven pm, Sally and Michelle were asleep in my bed, nearby.

This is a small, claustrophobic safe room.

Federal budgets had been sliced again, we were told – there were apparently no more safe houses anymore – they were all being renovated, for private sale.

A new guard – just called 'Duran' – was standing outside in the hallway.

Kowalski had been moved on to another assignment, much to Sally and her Mom's disappointment.

This new guard was a serious, brawny woman, bolstered with weaponry and a brutal quietness that resisted all attempts at friendly engagement.

She didn't like tea – or coffee.

I prepared my own couch bed.

"Relevant news on Wolf Howl," said NextGen, switching on a small data mat and I popped an earbud in, to avoid disturbing the sleepers. "Looks like Bok Kai was able to get a definitive face match on those shots from the delta…"

A black woman spoke, frantically fast, a picture of the HQ of FreeFlow Corp behind her right shoulder. "The only comment we are getting is that the Company has distanced itself from any alleged crimes – but we believe they have handed over senior exec and engineer Birdie Watson to the police, for ongoing investigations, which have not yet been revealed…"

"Yes!" I shouted, "They got the bastard! We're free from FreeFlow."

Sally sat up, looking dazed and confused, "Is it time for Church yet, Art?"

I shook my head, "Sorry my dear, Daddy shouldn't have made so much noise. It's not morning yet."

NextGen switched off the news.

Sally sat next to me on my couch-bed, clutching Helen, resting her head on my chest. "Will you and mommy get together again?"

I couldn't see Michelle – she had dragged blankets over her head.

The door opened and the guard peered in, "Are you guys okay in there? Thought I heard some shoutin'."

"We're okay, thank you, Duran."

Michelle had sat up, bleary eyed, but clearly conscious. "No," she said, "Daddy and I won't be getting together again, dearest."

Sally tensed against my chest.

Michelle smiled, sadly. "But we can both organise to marry *you* – as parents – if you like. It's a new ceremony called Parenting Vow, between parents and children where we – uh, renew our promises to *you*, despite the differences there may be, between your daddy and I, as the adults."

"Would that be like a proper family again?" asked Sally.

"Of course," laughed Michelle. "Well, almost."

"Then, yes please?" Sally looked up at me. "I'd like an almost family."

I felt old walls melting inside me, but decided to tease, just a little. "Will you take an 'Always Good Child Vow' in return, Sally?"

"Art…" frowned Michelle, as Sally squinted her eyes uncertainly.

I laughed – there could be only one answer for her, so I gave it, "Yes."

Michelle smiled, as Sally yelped for joy. "Still black with two sugars, Art?" She shrugged a gown over her nightie and walked over to the kitchen kettle.

Sally hugged me, but a flash of movement by the door, had caught my gaze.

Zeke smiles, waves… and is gone.

We are *a real family.*

Chapter 22

Graham — Eco-Warriors

Scotland was long gone, when Cyril buzzed in my ear -- somewhere over the ever-expanding Sahara Desert.

I woke.

I was sprawled against the window, my stomach heaving with the sudden sensation of dropping down steep and high night thermals, my left ear ringing with a shrill and incessant beeping.

<It's the Office.>

I groaned, whispering, "What the fuck, Bongani?"

<New twist on the water story. How did you feel, watching that elephant graveyard, up at the Vic Falls?>

"Sad – and angry, why?"

<Time to put them feelings to good use. I'll pick you up at the airport. New water job.>

Despite having been Office upgraded to premium economy class, I struggled to fall asleep again.

What's he got for me now?

King Shaka International Airport, Durban.

Nine am, and Bongani waited for me at the customs exit. *Thorough customs grilling coming in again – no leaking borders here, surely? Hah.*

I was grateful for the flight upgrade; these were almost exclusively the preserve of the One Percent. "Thank you Bongani, I usually can't sleep on planes, so cheers for the bump up. Liz is still in the FSA, as far as I know."

Bongani nodded, "I've been in touch with her; looks like she's had a pretty shit experience, with our previous boss."

"Yes," I said, looking away, as we dodged several cars leaving the car park. *How much did she tell him?* "So who else knows?"

Bongani stepped across to the back of a dusty 4-wheel drive. "Knows what?"

"You know – about us, me and Lizzie."

"Well, *I* don't know too many details – and I'm not interested." Bongani opened the back of the jeep.

I waited, glancing down at my bag.

Bongani folded his suited arms, "It's your bag, so *you* put it in. Or I'm happy to leave it behind, if that's what you'd prefer?"

Grumbling, I lifted my hold bag and tossed it into the back.

The jeep smelt of dust and dirt and stale petrol fumes. *Old banger.*

I spotted the driver in brown khaki, sitting in the front seat. "So, if you've given me a driver, why have *you* come all the way out here to meet me, Bongani?"

"This is the one last water job, Graham," said Bongani, "I want you to find out how poachers are catching wild animals, we suspect it's via water lures."

"Poachers? What – poachers with guns?"

Bongani nodded, "Danger pay for one last video clip. It'll round up your water story very nicely, bringing it home. And – if you can just tag their vehicle while doing it – the KZN patrols might be able to trace and track them too."

"Jesus, that's going to mean serious danger pay, *boet* – how much?"

"Five times usual."

"Ten times – and in *yuan.*"

"Eight times."

"Ten times, in Chinese only, Bongani."

Bongani sighed, "Did your wife ever tell you, that you're a bloody hard bastard?"

"All the time," I said, tapping my head. "And not just in bed. Wire it to Cyril now – *before* I step into the jeep."

<Money received.>

Bongani handed me a small magnet chip-tag. "It's only activated *after* it clings, so don't let it touch anything metallic, *before* their vehicle. They're probably going to scan you for live tech, and it won't be picked up, *if* it's off. Cyril will need to be off too. Take this phone, too, for emergencies."

Shit. Maybe I should reconsider this. Too bloody impulsive sometimes – and money's nice, but it's not everything. "What have you told them about me?"

And how do I retreat on this, gracefully?

"That you're doing a documentary on water and animals and how smart poachers are, although they may also be too smart to give you their operating specifics. Everyone likes to be listened to, so make it up as you go along – remember, they're just the poor local bottom feeders, within an international Wildlife ring, stretching northwards to the hidden rich elite, both East and West. Just make it up, like all good journalists do."

"I'm an accountant at heart. Maybe this isn't for me."

"Then just give them some fucking numbers," Bongani turned away, and walked across the path, as if fed up and in search of his own car. It bleated a response nearby to his key.

Wonder if it's a Porche or Be-em or something swanky?

…Uh, uh, guns – it's too risky, I'm going to tell Bongani I'm pulling out.

<Then you're not much of a journalist, are you?>

Cyril, mimicking that Dr. Suraya Proctor's voice. Or am I going fucking mad?

I hesitated at the back of the jeep, one hand still on bag, the other holding the magnetic chip.

"Are you getting inside or not, boss?" asked the driver, from in front.

<Since when did being in Africa, start meaning you don't help anyone?>

Cyril, this time in Liz's voice.

"Shut the fuck up. Cyril. You're getting one *serious* overhaul, once I'm done with this shit," I snarled, slamming the boot, and climbing into the passenger seat.

Okay, then, so this one's for Gameboy Boy. And dead elephants, too.

"Howzit," I said, "I'm Graham."

"Hello, Graham," said my black, bespectacled driver, "I'm Mister Majola."

Mister Majola cackled, as he reversed out of the parking spot

I sighed and slumped in my seat.

"Cyril, where's Lizzie?"

<Somewhere in the air, Graham, heading, I believe, to Cape Town.>

Since when did you start believing anything, Cyril?

"Let's head into the *bundu*, then," said Mister Majola, keying a wildlife GPS position into his jeep. "And you can tell me all about yourself – *and* your Lizzie. Now me – I *am* interested in those details."

I said nothing, as we watched Bongani drive past us, in an old and battered, powder blue e-*Ford.*

We arrived past lunch in the designated spot, bouncing through long Midlands Meadow grass, before finally parking under a *marula* tree.

Myself – and Terence – as I'd eventually found out Mister Majola's first name was, clambered out and stretched, in the sultry heat. The grassland spread all around us, as far as the eye could see, dry and yellow, dotted with thorn-scrub and *acacia* trees.

The rains are still fucking late here, too.

A bird called nearby, 'gooooowayyy'!

"That's the Grey Loerie," said Terence, "Sometimes called the 'Go Away' – or fuck off bird."

I grunted, "Sure wish I could oblige them… What's that, over there?"

There was small movement due east, and Terence asked his smart glasses to zoom.

"Men," he swallowed, "Two men. With guns."

He lit up an e-cigarette, with shaking hands.

I paced and went for a piss on the western side of the jeep, emerging reluctantly, legs weak.

"Cyril, off," I said, aware that my voice had shaken. *Unused to the silence and solitude of a net-less world.*

I am a weak and fragile meat sack.

Two masked men, rifles slung over shoulders – and one with an additional bag – walked steadily towards us. Their tan sweat suits shimmered in the heat haze, as if they were hot phantoms.

Terence climbed back into the jeep and I found myself locking my muscles, in order not to hurriedly follow suit.

The closer they came, the more there was a rank smell in the air – the men were bringing flies with them, spiralling in a cloud around the taller man's bloodied bag hanging at his side. Blood – and shit, one man had his left boot covered in animal dung.

The taller man shoved his Kalashnikov at the jeep's driver window. "*Hayi*, you in there, fuck off!"

The opposite door opened, and dust and grass kicked up into the air, as Terence landed on the ground, sprinting away, in desperate haste.

The shorter man turned to me, fingering his rifle. "Give us your phone and any recording devices."

I handed over my phone, cursing the shake in my right hand.

The man just laughed and put it in his pocket.

"Hey, I want that back."

"Shut the fuck up," said the taller man, looking at me with a bored glare, "We got the money; we give you information, that's it. Next time, more money, more information."

"O-okay, where can we talk then?" I indicated the shade of a small copse of Cape Ash nearby. Fear and the day's heat soaked the back of my head under my cap, trickling cold sweat in a tickly path, down my neck and spine.

"We talk here, *mlungu*, if you can't stand the fucking heat, what are you doing here in Africa, huh?" The shorter man laughed.

I caught the bite of whisky and stale meat on his breath.

The man pulled a device out of his pocket. For a moment I thought it might be my phone and I could just be getting it back – then I saw it was a digital box with sensors – like a TV remote, but with dials and indicators.

"What's that?" I asked, wiping sweat and several flies off my face.

The taller man laughed. "None of your fucking business. You're lucky you're clean. You got five minutes, *mlungu*, that's it."

I leaned against the flank of the jeep, as slowly and carefully as I could, trying to find some shade and support from the vehicle. "So, how do you lure the animals, then?"

"Water," said Shorty, "we got a mobile water van and trek around looking for dried up drinking holes to top up; then we hide and wait. The animals are fucking desperate to drink, in this drought."

"A van full of water – that must be expensive. Where is it?"

Tall man thumbed over his right shoulder, indicating a distant copse of *acacia* from where they'd come. "We got some good local and international backers, with deep pockets. Next question."

Reluctantly, I asked the obvious question, "What's in the bag?"

The man placed both hands on the bag hanging over his left shoulder, swung it to the ground and pulled it open with deft practice, spilling some flies sticking to the bloodied, canvas surface.

I leaned forward to look inside.

I gagged and retreated against the jeep, wondering for some moments, if I were going to vomit.

The fly buzzing had risen to a crescendo, some getting into the bag before Tall man had snapped and tethered it shut again.

Bloody flesh attached to dark looking bone – got to be ivory, caked blood had darkened it. And what a fucking stench.

I bent over and vomited sticky water onto the grass; I'd not eaten for the better part of a day. *Airplane food is shit. But that, that's in a shitty class all of its own...*

"A rhino's lost its nose," laughed Shorty, "So you lose your stomach. Just wish there were elephant left to kill. Now *that* used to get us some *serious* money."

"You get sick easily. Don't waste your fucking water," scolded Tall man, "You are running out of time, *mlungu.*"

I backed away from my spittle on the ground, as flies honed in. I was giddy and ill. "How – how do you stay ahead of the rangers?"

"Friends with them on Base-Book," laughed Shorty, "And with other friends in the phone registry office, means we've got tags from their sim-cards on my scanner right here. We *always* know when they're coming."

Tall man scowled across at his companion, as if annoyed with what he had said. "One last question, then that's it."

"Can I see your water cannon; it must be one powerful machine?"

"It pumps and sucks," said Shorty, checking the firing mechanism on his rifle. "We take the remaining water back, once the kill is made. Nothing fucking wasted. Recycled. We're eco-warriors."

"*Hayi sidenge*, you scan him again, make sure he's not carrying any signals. And while you're at it, just shut the fuck up. I'm the one who answers the questions, remember?"

The Tall man handed Shorty the TV remote looking device.

Shorty looked hurt, as he scanned me. "Nothing," he scowled, returning to caressing his rifle safety catch.

"Okay – come this way – you get one look, and then this interview is over." Tall man strode across the grass, sweating, despite his impassive face.

I trotted afterwards, anxiously aware of Shorty, and the gun being click-clacked behind my back.

The poachers' plate-less but massive white off-road *bakkie*, was hidden from view, under draped camouflage canvas, which was removed in one quick flourish by Tall man.

I whistled.

Inside the open compartment at the back was a massive tank, with a turret and an attached hose at the top. "It's an old police water cannon – how did you get this?"

"The purple shall govern," laughed Tall man, "Your questions are all used up, *mlungu*."

I caressed the water tank, rusting in parts, but clearly functional.

"We're getting incoming," said Shorty, checking his scanner, "Might be those bitches from the *Black Mambas*. Can't we teach them a lesson – and give them a good fuck at the same time?"

"Those bitches have teeth down there. One moment," Tall man was looking at my left ear, very closely, "*Yebo* – signs of old scarring. This *mlungu's* carrying a Rig – we could get a lot more for this, than for his fucking phone."

Shorty fished in a holster on his belt, pulling out a six-inch knife. "Those bitches are coming fast. We got to do this quick – just cut his ear off and dig the Rig out; chop, chop."

Sub-vocal command. 'Cyril, get me the fucking office NOW!'

"Don't move, or Mandla shoots," said Shorty, readying the knife.

Tall man rattled off something, in angry isiZulu.

<*Red light.*>

'Lizzie!'

Shorty leaned forward, knife arcing towards old scars behind my left ear. "Don't worry, I'm a doctor, *mlungu*, you won't feel a fucking thing." He laughed; knife unsteady.

<*Red light.*>

'Fucking 911.'

<*Emergency Services, say one, if…*>

Fuck.

'Cyril. Record.'

I screamed, as the knife sliced a flap of skin open. Something hot and sticky dripped down my neck. I could tell, from the smell, it was *not* sweat.

"Hold on!" said Tall man. "The monitor's beeping. A signal has kicked off. Bastard's probably set up a remote recording. Police still love the white skins and their fucking property. Pity. Let's go. You drive."

He tossed the keys over to Shorty, without looking at me.

Shorty wiped his... *considerably bloody...* knife on the grass, reluctantly.

He holstered his knife and, in one fluid motion, unleashed a punch to my midriff. "No hard feelings *mlungu*, strictly business, understand?"

I curled up on the ground and vomited air and slime for the second time that day. I barely noticed, as they dropped my phone, in front of my face.

It was Tall man's voice.

"Remember, we're eco-warriors, not thieves. Respect our ethics. Go back to watching your old Attenborough movies and playing with stuffed and extinct toy animals. By the time you open your eyes, the world will be fucking empty, and we will be rich. Just like Stalin."

Their feet vanished, and an engine started up.

Quiet again. They've gone.

<*Sir, may I help you? Emergency Services – I've got your GPS here?*>

'Where – where are the *Black Mambas?*'

<*Have you been bitten by a snake? Can you give us a description of the reptile, so we can sort out the correct anti-toxins?*>

'Anti, anti-poaching unit.'

<*Oh yes, you mean the special ladies' unit – hmmm, looks like they're in your vicinity, sir, sending them right over.*>

Flies buzzed into the opened flap of skin behind my ear. I slapped the burning, sticky skin gingerly and ripped my shirt off, popping buttons, before pressing the bundle against my left ear.

Fuckkkkkk...

Three sets of black boots stood in front of me and, as my gaze moved dazedly upwards, I could see camouflage suits and the women wearing them – two shaved, and one with her dreads bunned beneath her cap.

The one with dreads knelt beside me, box opened with medical supplies. "Let go," she said, "I've got it."

I kneeled, eyes closed, as I felt her first numbing, then sterilising, and finally clipping my wound shut.

My shirt was red-wet on my knees.

I did not wish to see their faces, as I cried, without restraint.

"Did you get it done?" came a question, from one of the standing women. "Did you place the tracker on their vehicle?"

I nodded, eyes still closed, weeping. "You'd all best get new sim cards too – and through an anonymous back door, they're tracking you. And choose your Base-Book friends better. How, how's my ear?"

"It'll hang, but maybe not so straight, we'll see what the doctors at Addington Hospital can do. We'll trigger that tracker on their vehicle later, when they're most likely asleep."

He who laughs last, bastards!

Except, for some reason, I couldn't stop crying.

I was discharged after a day, with ten further stitches, after a cursory examination and healing balm for my stapled ear. The drive home from the hospital felt unduly long, in dull, cooler weather, with even a few spots of rain.

And the last kay, this time, was fucking interminable.

I triple checked the lock on my car, driving through the township. Parasitic electric lines were down, sun shining off shacks in hot and silver flashes.

Solar panels? Glinting blackly off some of the roofs, wires feeding into houses around them too. The community's gone green, harnessing their own energy now.

'Where are you now, Lizzie?'

<*Red light.*>

Red light, red light, red light – my life, halted.

I drove on, wanting to have some control, but, as my eyes started to burn, I handed over car-control to auto, and shoved more comfortable flip flops onto my feet.

The left side of my face, around my ear, ached hollowly and I avoided looking at my face, in the rear-view mirror.

The car rattled to a stop outside our farm homestead, Cope's Folly.

Our?

Remembering it was a hired car, I got out cautiously, looking both ways, before thumbing my ID to open the gate.

I heard the gate *snnkkktt* shut behind me.

I de-weaponed the house and stepped through unsteadily, picking a beer out of the fridge, before going into the back-garden.

The plants were straggling and strangled, looking dry and desperate, neglected. The centre lawn was prickly yellow and the water-piece in the corner had blocked, turning a turgid green.

Several humps of anthills had started to form.

I sighed and walked over the spongy trapdoor of the sub-surface water tank, hooked in to all the guttering and water sliders too. *At least we still got our water.*

We again.

I went back inside to finish my beer, and picked at a few old blue-ray classics of Die Hard, but I knew they would only remind me of *her*, and the huge hole I felt in my chest, for her absence.

'Lizzie?'

<*Red*>

I made my way to the bathroom mirror.

Time to face up to things.

But I don't know this face.

Jesus, you're getting old, my boy. You look like shit... They did a fucking good job at Addington, though, God bless those doctors and nurses. Both my ears hang straight, at least.

But, how am I going to survive in this harsh land, without Lizzie? I'm the wrong side of fifty, and dad's dead.

There's no coming back home.

My hair was cropped and grey, my skin pale and haggard. *And to think I had looked down on that pith helmeted European tourist's skin, in what seems like years back at the Vic Falls, with his hundred factor sun screen. The place where Gameboy Boy died.*

And those poachers, they'd mentioned Stalin.

Not the same 'No One' I'd seen, surely?

Who the fuck is he?

As for me, who am I? What do I want?

I found it hard, to look myself in the eyes.

I need to change, to adapt, and to evolve.

I knew, with a sudden deep and dreaded certainty, that there was no getting back with Lizzie, either.

Maybe I just needed to open my mind and embrace change, to fit in better. *What does that mean right here, right now, though, in a post-racial South Africa?*

I just want to hide in my skin, somehow...

Oh, yes...

"Cyril, patch me through to Luka, from the Post Racial Movement, in LA."

<*It's five in the morning in SouthCal...*>

"Just call them. An overhaul is waiting for you, remember?"

<*Hello – hello – who the fuck's calling me at this fucking time, man?*>

"Luka, it's me, Graham Mason, Pedro and I spoke to you just over a week or so ago, about water in LA – and you mentioned that Post-Racial stuff. Can you help me?"

I picked out another beer from the fridge.

<Oh yes, you. For a fucking fee, maybe>

"Now?"

<Whatcha mean?>

"I want to have a go at getting my face right. Now. Hide the wrinkles and shit, too."

<That's fucking big overtime then – but you don't have any stuff at hand, do you?>

"Like creams and stuff?" I was already rummaging in Liz's make-up drawer. "You can see what I've got here, in my wife's cupboard. Help me out, with what I need."

<Fuck's sake, not much in there, is there? And she calls herself a woman? Foundation, mister – always start with a good foundation. Right there... Now, get to a mirror, so's I can have a look at you... woahhh, boy, but do we have some fucking work to do here... Nice sutured scar tat around your ear, though – makes you look super hard and mean.>

I just feel soft and tired.

But, after an hour or so of helping me paste my face, Luka signed off for more sleep – but only after I had wired them some money, from my Catch a Poacher Job.

I went to the fridge for another beer.

I'm still ever fucking thirsty, but the fridge is empty.

The front doorbell went. I looked up at the security screen in shock.

How'd they get past the gate?

I spotted the police uniform of the woman waiting on the doorstep and scanned their ID. *Corporal Fester?*

The cops were allowed security over-ride to the wider property, in case of the need for emergency access.

"Yes, how may I help you?" I opened the door sharply, and with blunt annoyance.

The female cop took a step backwards, looking shocked and uncertain. "Sorry *meneer*, but we're looking for a white man – a Mister Graham Mason."

What? What? Of course, Liz's fucking face paint. "Why – what's the problem, officer?"

"It's not me, it's the tax man," the policewoman turned, to point behind her.

Parked outside was a large truck, plastered on the side in green on white: 'FREEFLOW,' alongside two cars, one marked 'POLICE' and the other one: 'SARS'.

The SARS car was the one that provoked the most dread in me – not just distant resonances of an epidemic viral plague, but that hard and brutal inevitably of the acronym.

South African Revenue Service.

Shit, what a welcome home.

Not death, but fucking taxes.

Chapter 23
Liz – Going Home

We taxied into Cape Town International, with Table Mountain cloud shrouded on our right.

I let go of Busi's hand. She was grimacing, as if from the fierceness of my grip.

I was excited, but also terrified, about what lay ahead.

Good to see Ma and Pa again; three years is a long time. But what does 'losing your marbles' actually mean?

"So, what *else* have we come for, again?" I asked, standing up unsteadily. *This was where I'd met Graham.*

"We have also come to see if there is another way to get fresh water to fall." Bus hauled out the overhead luggage. "The Rain Queen is here."

"Captain Gerber welcomes you to Cape Town International – you are all lucky enough to have been only the *third* group to have been safely landed by AI Gerber. Let's have a round of applause for our new artificial Captain."

The cabin was quiet; no one clapped.

"Why didn't they tell us that at the *start* of the flight?" I grumbled.

"Because a similar thing happened when they introduced *black* pilots," said Busi, handing me my bag, "after *apartheid*. Some people panicked on the plane – so many of us are still so prejudiced against difference."

Busi sniffed the air, as we disembarked.

"What is it?"

"*She's* here," she said.

"Who's she?"

"Her Highness; The *Modjadji*, The Rain Queen. I can smell the moisture she brings with her."

We paced through a transit corridor.

Busi stopped to point through the glass windows, downwards into the arrival lounge. A large crowd was waiting, but she was pointing at a separate group, milling across the far side of the hall.

One woman stood out.

She was short and stout, wearing an orange head band and white traditional dress, beaded and decorated with glass and tiny mirrors. A coterie of women in pink and white surrounded her, with whistles and drums and what looked like feather dusters. Phones were flashing.

"Queen Modjadji the Tenth. *She*. The Rain Queen from the Limpopo River. We will accompany her to a dry dam just above Muizenberg, where she – and her acolytes – will call down the rain, on the growing desert of Table Mountain."

"Uh – right now we just need our passports," I said, "Do you have them – or are they in my bag?"

"If identities and nation states are increasingly permeable, *why* should we need passports?" Busi dug inside her jacket pockets. "A question for our Ethno-Philosophy Group. To the day when we are all just human beings, of planet Earth, free to go where we can. No, Liz, you must have them."

"Phew," I said, as I pulled two passports out of my bag. "I have a feeling that those customs officers would have made *kak* philosophers, should we have just shrugged, and asked them but why *do* we need passports?"

"Ah," said Busi, "did you know passports used to be a question, on the South African version of the Wechsler Intelligence test? A psychologist friend once told me this. Do you know what response could score you an intelligence point?"

I shook my head, and handed over her passport, as we approached the front of the security and customs queue.

"To stop the Indians and the communists from leaving the country – and spreading lies about our – at the time *apartheid* – country," said Busi.

"No!"

"Yes. So much for intelligence tests."

In the end, no passports were needed, just retinal scanners and finger IDs.

And so, we entered Cape Town.

Me, with a frisson of fear, as if someone had stepped onto a grave that waited for me.

Silvermine; The Western Cape.

It was a dry day, a hot day, a day like any other I remembered from the fag-end of November in the Cape, as spring burned into summer. The afternoon was ending with a bit of coolness, thankfully, as a light South-Easter wind picked up.

We sat on a giant boulder and watched the drumming and dancing unfurl beneath us, in a flat clearing space near the fenced off Silvermine dam. About three hundred or so watched with us some joining in, by stamping their feet and singing.

The Rain Queen herself joined in the final song, with her dancing swirling band of women; as they drummed, whistled and spun in circles

211

behind a tight police cordon, on the shore of the shallow, shrinking lake.

The dam had been closed to the public for the ceremony, which was also attended by the Mayor of Cape Town and political party representatives, all jostling for the wet blessing of the Rain Queen from the North.

Finally, the Queen offered up the Rain Prayer to the sky, and launched into rapid and pleading *Sepedi*, her arms clutching at the blue heavens.

"She breaks tradition by coming here," whispered Busi, "Times are hard – and governments are desperate."

The breeze squalled ripples across the dam behind the Queen, as she finished, which was followed by a burst of applause and shouted refrains.

The rain prayer itself hung in the air like sonic droplets, a call from desperate mouths, but made, it seemed, only to dry air – and the slightest of breezes. Once done, there was nowhere else for the words to go, but a slow dissipation, phoneme by phoneme, into our collective memory dust.

I recorded the whole event on my phone, wondering whether I would watch this again, or whether it would spool up blindly behind me, like so many recorded things – photos, memories, emotions, all left inside a data cloud, that I rarely visited.

Where do our prayers go? And our memories? And has God stopped listening to me since I swore at his messenger? And, will my own father even remember me?

No clouds yet, though. Let alone rain.

Conversations started up, slow and doubting murmurs, as heads craned from side to side and bodies turned, scouring a sharp but brutally blue and clear horizon of mountain, sparse water, and *fynbos* bush. Fanned umbrellas rattled, as if preparing for war.

The cloud table cloth on Table Mountain had dissipated today, but giant net hoovers on various mountain sites had at least downloaded several thousand litres of moisture, from what Busi had told me.

A *bokmakierie* piped, a fluting call from a bush higher up the mountain slope.

Do birds pray too?

"Shall we go?" I asked. *I have struggled to keep up with the ebb and flow of crowd conversations, sweat spooling off my forehead.*

Busi held out her hand, "We must wait to be dismissed first." She remained taut and focused, blinking her own sweat away.

"Look!" Shouted the Queen, pointing into the breeze.

Hundreds of heads and bodies swivelled.

In the distance, piling over the low hills behind us, was a large white cloud. A gasp went through the crowd, an explosion of breath, that seemed to whip up dust.

"One cloud?" I said, "Seriously?"

"Rain is birthed in a cloud. It's a start. How else is belief generated?" Busi scrambled to her feet, and frog-jumped off the boulder, as if readying herself.

The Queen gestured to her maids, and barked a sentence.

I looked at Busi, who had closed her left eye, either in concentration, or to avoid a trickle of sweat. "I think something like '*get my chariot. I shall chase and woo that cloud.*' Winnie can't offer me a better interpretation."

"Woo?" I laughed, "That can't be right, surely?"

"Well, *you* translate her *Sepedi* then," said Busi, testily.

Three policemen cleared space at the front of the cordon and a chauffeur trundled out from under the VIP umbrella, with an all-terrain electric golf caddy, canvas roofing which advertised the SA Golf Open.

The Queen made her way towards it, in slow and stately fashion, while the crowd rose to their feet, in a murmuring mass.

I sneezed dust out of my nose.

The Queen seated herself in the cart.

The driver engaged a gear, to send it trundling along the path around the fringes of the crowd at a brisk walking pace.

The police opened a phalanx through the crowd.

The crowd began to follow the royal caddy.

"What's going on?" I asked.

"We follow The Queen and join in," said Busi, "the more of us who can sing, in support of the Queen, and to that cloud, the better."

"Cloud singing?" I was baffled, "They never taught us *that* at Bloemfontein Girls' High."

"Just hum along, Liz, that'll be good enough for now." Busi filed in behind two men, carrying a bucket of communal water and scoop between them.

"Have a drink, *sisi*," laughed one of them at me, but there was no time.

I followed, ignoring my sweat and marvelling at the crowd, which had started to sing and chant, in excited anticipation.

I knew only a few of the words.

Several women started ululating.

Busi began to jog, as the gold caddy ahead picked up speed.

I hesitated for a moment. *What about the small print in my travel insurance? Will it cover accidents due to… Cloud-Humming?*

My phone buzzed. *Graham.*

Gone cloud humming. I texted, laughing, and broke into a run, in order to catch up.

Ahead of us, more clouds had gathered.

In the end, though, despite all our humming and singing, not one drop fell.

The suburb of Tyger Valley nestled amongst the hills north of Cape Town, a solid slab of malls and rectangular urban houses, many with yellowed lawns fringing empty pools, with giant water tanks greyly abutted to downward drain pipes.

Wells and boreholes aplenty were scattered in glimpses through electrified fences, as our hired car jugged up, hill after hill, and finally halted outside a small cottage on a leafy road near the top of one of the hills.

"You have arrived at your destination," said the Over-car.

Busi glanced across, "So, do I get to meet the parents, yes or no?"

I pulled my mouth tight, not sure how to put it. "They're *verkrampte* – conservative Afrikaners – they won't understand, nor will they welcome you."

"Well, that's a clear *no* then," said Busi, and she pulled her face too. "Are *you* ashamed of me?"

I shook my head, sorrowfully, "No, never – but I don't want to be ashamed of *them*, either. Give us an hour."

Busi clicked her teeth in annoyance. "I've noticed who walks the streets here – mostly only the *very* pale. The only blacks I've seen have been those working in the gardens, or those hanging out the washing."

"I know," I looked down glumly. "There are a few who own houses in the neighbourhood too, though."

"A representative ninety five percent?" asked Busi, dryly.

I said nothing.

"You have arrived at your destination and are also being charged for immobile periods of hire," said the Over-car, from its GPS speaker.

I opened the door and stepped out, "So, what will you do?"

"I'm sure as fuck not waiting here for you. This is a very white space. I'm not safe here. Text me when you're ready. Car six two eight, take me to Tyger Valley Library."

I waved, as the car took off, but there was no wave in response.

I buzzed the metal gate and the screen – secured in the thick wall alongside, instantly lit up – with the grey curls and smiling wrinkles of my mother's face, as if she had been waiting all morning for this visit. "Lizzie, my baby, come in. We've been expecting you, sweetie pie."

I smiled as she pushed the gate open. It had been a while since I had exercised my Afrikaans properly.

KZN was mostly English and isiZulu territory, as if the languages were still locked in the Zulu Wars of the nineteenth century – or the 'British Wars', as some historians were now calling them, given who had been spoiling for both the fight, *and* the resources of the Zulu nation.

Ma walked down the path, slowly and stiffly, but with her arms open wide. She was dressed in a white flowery long-sleeved cotton blouse, long grey skirt and sharp, shiny black shoes. I felt distinctly under-dressed, in my beige track shoes and pants, and my red logo-less T-shirt.

We hugged.

"Where's *Pa*?" I asked. *What, exactly, does it mean to 'lose your marbles'?*

Ma grimaced, "Having some tea, and watching cricket in the lounge."

She pulled me into the house, calling ahead of her, "Willem, do you remember who's coming to visit us?"

"Of course!" shouted an old and familiar voice, quavering now with extreme age. *Eighty-eight is not that old any more, surely?*

My father was in a wheelchair, with a plate of rusks on his lap and a cup of tea on a nearby stool. He had a Scotch tartan blanket over his legs, sprinkled with crumbs, and looked up at me, with obvious surprise. "Are you the inspector from the Revenue Department?"

"*Papa*," I said, and hugged him.

"That's an odd thing to do," his voice was reedy, and I felt him stiffen under my embrace. "I can assure you, madam, our taxes are in order."

I let him go, and stepped back to wipe my eyes.

Ma was rattling plates and a kettle in the kitchen.

The mantelpiece and walls were hung with lace decorations and photos of various ages, shapes and provenance, mostly family and extended family, down through the ages. I sought out my perennial favourite – myself and my two older brothers, taken outside our old home in Bloemfontein. Stephan had just matriculated and was getting ready to go off and study Law at Potchefstroom. Piet was sixteen and I was fourteen, all three of us grinning in jeans and T-shirts, Piet giving me devil horns with the two fingers of his left hand, behind my tousled brunette head.

God, I'm so young. Where has this young girl gone? And these boys – brothers in name only now – both overseas in England and Australia, with families of their own, that I hear so little about.

"Howzat!" shouted pa, watching figures in white, as they moved on the screen underneath the mantelpiece.

I took the photograph off the wall and stood in front of the TV. "Telly eight, turn off."

"Not out," someone shouted, from behind my back.

"Telly off," said Ma, walking through with a tray of cups, teapot and a plate of twined and sugary *koeksisters*.

"I was watching that," said Pa angrily, turning to look at Ma.

"The telly is on voice recognition now," said ma, putting the tray down on the low table. "An anti-theft adaptation."

I nodded and took the photograph over to my father, holding it out in front of him, while I hovered behind his left shoulder. "See *Pa*, you took this photo, remember? In front of our old house in *Bloem*. That's Stephan, and Piet – and there's me, Lizzie!"

He looked up at me, blankly, "What were you kids doing, leaning against my house wall? What right had you to do that? Up to no good, I'm sure."

"They had every right," sighed Ma, pouring tea, "They are our children, dear, as I *keep* reminding you."

My father slapped the photo away. "Nonsense. If they are our children, where have they been, huh? Here, it is just the two of us, day in, day out."

"Just the two of us – very romantic of you, dear." Ma patted a chair and placed a cup with a *koeksister* on the plate on the nearby low table, of dark and heavy wood. "Now you come and sit, Lizzie – and tell us all about your new black girlfriend."

"What?" I exploded.

"Who's got a black girlfriend?" said Pa, knitting his brows and brushing crumbs off his lap.

"Girl talk, dear, not for your ears." Ma took hold of his wheelchair and steered him into the kitchen, "Boring stuff. You can watch your cricket on the kitchen TV."

She closed the door behind her, as she stepped back in to the lounge. "Now where were we, Lizzie *liefie?*"

I had finished my tea and was standing up, eyeing the alcohol cabinet. "How do you, uh, know, ma, about Busi?"

Ma took a sip of tea. "It's still too early in the day for any other kind of drink, my dear. I've been following Graham on his *Mason: Building a Better World* Vlog. Don't *you* follow it? Anyway, he's been less that discreet with his narrative, at times."

"The bastard!" I shouted, "That's private!"

Ma shrugged and put her cup down. "Very little is private any more, you should know that, Lizzie dear? The information age has long washed over all of us, monetising our lives. The companies know more about us than *we* do, unless you can find a hidey-hole on the Berners-Lee *Alt-Web*. So, tell me, how did you meet Busi?"

I sat down next to Ma and tore a chunk off my *koeksister*. "Long story – I thought you wouldn't approve. And we're not girlfriends. In fact, I think she's pissed off with me right now."

"Why wouldn't I approve?" Ma stared at me, her hands crossed on her lap, and looking annoyed.

"Oh, come on, Ma – I remember all the bad things both of you used to say, some years after several of those early democratic elections. I may have only been a child, but I understood."

Ma swayed her head, with a rueful smile. "Okay, yes, we were both racist in our younger days admittedly – but, but *I've* changed, at least."

"How? Why?" I stood and opened the drinks cabinet, removing a half-empty bottle of brandy. *I think it's late enough* now.

"I'm older and wiser."

"Ha, everyone says that! How about Pa, then – older yes, but... gone. Here, in the flesh, but gone." I opened the cap and knocked back a shot, which burned its way down my throat.

I coughed, holding back tears.

The kitchen door opened.

A late middle-aged black woman in domestic uniform and cap peered through at us. I hadn't seen much of her, in previous visits. "Madam, master says this TV is too small – he wants to come in and watch the cricket on the big lounge TV instead."

"Jennifer – meet Lizzie, my daughter," said Ma.

I walked across to the maid, speaking in broken isiXhosa, "You're not Jennifer are you – what's your real name?"

The woman stared at me, levelly. "Akhona."

I swung to face ma, who stood, as she chewed on her *koeksister*.

"Akhona – what's so fucking difficult about using her *real* name, then, huh Ma?"

"Let me out," shouted my father, from the kitchen, "South Africa are six wickets down. I want to watch on the other TV, the *big* screen."

"You're happy to swear in front of someone you don't know?" asked Ma. "What does that say about you? And, Akhona, has master used the K word on you today?"

The woman hesitated, then nodded, reluctantly.

"Close the door then," Ma held out her hand, "and please come and sit with us."

"Are – are you sure, Magdalene?"

Magdalene? How is she using mother's *name now? What the fuck is going on?*

I took another swig, as Ma embraced the maid and sat. "Darling, as you know, Jennifer – uh, Akhona, has been our constant companion and support for almost fifteen years now. She has become like another daughter to us. I have, in fact, officially made her so."

"What do you mean?" I swigged again.

"She has joined you and the boys on our will. I have power of attorney, since your father was diagnosed with dementia. Akhona is now in our will, to equally share the inheritance with you, Stephan and Piet."

Akhona stood up abruptly and went off to attend to the frail shouts coming from the kitchen, as if too uncomfortable to sit there, while we continued to speak *about* her, in front of her.

I laughed and swigged, wanting never to stop, but eventually my throat burned hard enough, to bring me to a gagging halt.

I coughed and wiped my mouth. "You must be joking, Ma? Have you spoken to the *dominee* about any of this?"

"Fuck the Church!" Ma frowned, "Where was God, when Willem's mind started to play and fray, huh? I have no Church, but love... and Akhona has earned every penny, dealing with us cantankerous, ageing buggers. Do you have any idea what she's putting up with, alone with your father, in that room, right now?"

"Do Stephan and Piet know?" I stood up, and unsteadily placed the almost empty bottle onto the table.

"They visit us less often than you do, so no, not yet. How else do we change the fact that less than five percent of the population here in South Africa still own more than fifty percent of the wealth, huh?"

"Is this a punishment to me, for not visiting you more often?"

"I thought we'd raised you better than this, Lizette Maria."

Shame.

Deep shame. Why am I so averse to sharing an inheritance, when I am so lucky to be getting one at all?

"I laughed, when I saw you swear at that dominee, Lizzie dear. Fuck old hate, let's just learn to love each other, *ne*? And that means sharing what we have."

"I'm sorry, Ma," I looked down, and my voice was small.

"It's not me you should apologise to – are you so stingy to share with your girlfriend too? At the end of the day, white talk alone, it's cheap."

I left the house, and picked up the almost empty bottle in my left hand, flicking a call to Busi with my right, sobbing uncontrollably.

"What?" Busi still looked annoyed, but she was thumbing through a Zukiswa Wanner classic, 'The Madams'.

Behind her – books, and more books.

"Please, please come, I'm so sorry, Busi. I need you."

"Jesus," Busi put the book down, and peered closer. "Why are you crying? And have you been drinking? It's only eleven in the morning, girl."

"Yes, she's been drinking, she's been a naughty girl, Busi."

I jumped.

Ma had walked up behind me, to interject into my phone, as I stood and swayed on the path.

Ma peered into my phone, breaking into hesitant isiZulu, "But, given the uh, drinks box is open now, what say you come by for a few early drinks, *sisi?*"

Busi laughed: "Fuck, yeah!"

My phone flickered off.

"Come on dear," called Ma, as she headed back into the house.

"Give me a minute, Ma," I said, and finished off the bottle with a final, wild swig, leaning my back against the heat of the metal front gate.

No, it was not the incoming flight into Cape Town airport that had frightened me. *It's coming home. You can never come home again. Home always moves, even while it stays the same.*

Behind me, the gate buzzed.

"You finished the whole fucking bottle yourself?" accused Busi, as I opened the gate.

"It was already half empty," I protested.

"Half full, you mean," said Busi. "And I'm sure that's a conservative estimate. Let's go meet your *mamma* then. Treasure your parents, while they still live."

I followed behind; remorseful, unsteady, but glad for the life and fire still burning within my mother.

Chapter 24
Art – Please Release Me

"Dead," Brad whispered to me, "*This* Church music's gotta be *hundreds* of years old. Dead."

I'd brought Brad to the Third Hydro-City Church, where we sat in the middle aisle, dead centre, throughout the sermon.

The new seating arrangement had unsettled me, but I'd breathed slowly, soothing myself. *I must manage change within me, so that I can help make changes for the better outside. So, c'mon Art, just calm down and focus on...*

Pastor Johns of the Third Hydro-City Baptist Church was even paler than I remembered, but he seemed different, too, in other ways.

"The Bible can be used to justify many causes," he said. "Some of them reprehensible, like slavery in the past. As for me, I ask forgiveness and wish to start anew. With a message so central, it's right near the start of the Bible, for all believers in the original holy text both gentile and Jew alike. '*We have been given stewardship over the Earth; Genesis 1, verse 26.*' We are here to protect our planet, and all the animals within it. We are failing at this duty – and I regret any prior celebration of a coming apocalypse. Jesus has, Jesus has..."

Is he going to cry?

"...Jesus has visited me, and Jesus has told me, that we need to stop this planet being turned into *Gehenna*. If we can't try and make Heaven *here*, how will we ever get to see it *there?*"

As the pastor sat, I swore his face shone. *Glowing – or with tears?*

"Now that's short and sweet," muttered Michelle, on the other side of me.

To me, *he* looked a changed man, at least.

The organ played some stuffy hymn, and we filed out.

Recognition flickered in the pastor's eyes, as we shook hands at the exit. "I am glad to see you, son. I do hope you come back again."

I did not tell him that, at the end of the day, I preferred Pastor White's Church – the music of the *Fiery Baptists* had indeed been a *whole* lot better.

I just smiled and stepped aside to introduce the others. "This is my daughter Sally – and my, uh, *her* mother, Michelle."

The pastor nodded.

"And I'm Brad King," said the young man behind us, as he removed his ear pods. "Sorry, *padre*, but you seriously need to do something about your music if you want the youth coming in to regenerate your Church, genesis style."

"I'm not a father, young man, this is the Baptist church, not the Church of Rome. But I shall be happy to see you in The Meeting Room in fifteen minutes time, if you want to discuss this further?"

Brad saluted me and said, "See you guys at the Gate Wall, for the NorthCal State Announcement, at one pee-em."

As for us, we have a family to cement.

Michelle led Sally down the Church stairs, through a little conduit lane and around a boarded-over quake sinkhole, that had dropped twelve metres deep near the Civic Building, or *Cee-Bee*. Michelle was getting pretty good at navigating her way around Hydro-City, I noted with admiration, even effortlessly dodging the solar-bikes that whizzed around the town centre at breakneck speed.

I do miss her… but that alone, is not enough.

We entered the *Cee-Bee*, a circular domed building, plastered with its own energy plates and greenery.

The AI at reception flashed us into a small side room.

"Cow!" shouted Sally, as she hugged a tall man sitting in the chair furthest from the door.

I greeted Kowalski warmly, and noted Michelle's greeting was even warmer.

The state official was an AI called Spock, with a holo-face of bland expression; brown, gender-neutral, and smooth skinned. They wore orange and black robes, draped with their nameplate over their thin, angular chrome skeleton.

The wheels on their foot flexors whirred them into the centre of the room. "Well, the witness, Kowalski, has been here for nine minutes already, so let us begin…"

The voice was old fashioned pre-history, *Stephen Hawking* style.

AI Spock held out two white gloved hands, "May I have the Promising Parents please."

I took Spock's right hand, Michelle the left, and we both shifted a little under the weight of the bags on our backs.

"Will the lovely young child, by the name of Sally Green-Morley, please stand in front of me?"

Sally stood, after a little gentle persuasion by Kowalski, who was in turn persuaded to stand.

"Do you, Parent One, Michelle Morley, promise to rear Sally with unconditional love and guidance for as long as necessary, perhaps even as long ye shall live?"

"I do," said Sally, "As long as I am alive and able."

"Do you, Parent Two, Arthur Green, promise to rear Sally with unconditional love and guidance for as long as necessary, perhaps even as long ye shall live?"

"I do," I said. "As long as I am alive and able."

"Do you bear witness to these Parenting Promises, John Derek Kowalski?"

"I do," said Kowalski.

"As you both know, you will have regular visits from the Family Court, to ensure your parenting is both supported and upgraded, to allow the loved minor the minimum of developmental trauma across their childhood years. So then, by the power vested in me by the State of NorthCal, I hereby pronounce you both, as Parents of The Promise, for Sally Green-Morley."

Sally squealed.

"You may now present the child, Sally Green-Morley, with your binding gifts."

I hoisted the bag off my back and pulled out a stuffed animal, handing it over to a delighted Sally.

"Ooh, thank you, Art, what is it?" She turned the large brown porcine-like animal, with its huge mouth, over and over in her hands, as she examined it closely.

"It's a boy hippo, to keep your Helen good company – hippos are extinct, like the dinosaurs, but they also used to live in the water, just like Alligator Helen does."

"Thank you, Art," Sally smiled, "Although it's a girl hippo, silly."

"Uh –" I said, and scratched my head, "Of course it is. Silly me."

Michelle knelt, to present Sally with a recyclable plastic alligator, whose jaws could be pressed open to deliver water. "Just a Helen water bottle," said Michelle. "If you ever feel thirsty or sad, come talk to me, darling and we can drink together, and chat and hug if we need to, okay?"

Sally nodded, "Thank you, Mommy. I miss Helen though. You said I must be big and learn to leave her behind, to stop children teasing me at school, but I really, really miss her."

Michelle nodded, and turned her head away.

"And here's my present," said Kowalski, as he gently handed over a grubby alligator, with stuffing started to leak out of its tail.

"Helen!" shouted Sally.

"We have three minutes before the next ceremony – please see reception on your way out, to complete payment details." AI Spock bowed.

"Thank you, Benjamin," I said, as I followed Michelle and Kowalski, who had put Sally on top of his bulky shoulders.

The AI took their one glove off and parted their four metallic digits in the middle. "My name is *S'chn T'gai*. Live long and prosper, Mister Green."

The Gate Wall had sprouted a large cooling overhang and communal digi-mat, which was spooling shows, games and holograms to both sides of the Wall. As we waited for the State Announcement, they were playing a Hollywood remake of a Ghanaian film novelisation classic. The e-mat section was cordoned off with lasers and manned by two bored-looking police officers, and one cop-bot.

As one o'clock approached, the crowd had grown quickly.

Brad had picked up our homing signals with ease, and arrived with five minutes to spare. "What the hell is this?" He asked, confused.

"*Big Bishop Roko and the Altar Gangsters,*" said Kowalski. "Tom Ekubo's not bad, away from his usual '*Die Hard*' roles."

"Bo-ring," said Sally, on Kowalski's stooping shoulders, as her ice cream dripped down, onto Kowalski's neck.

"Thanks for cooling me, little lady," was all he said, grinning.

"What did the pastor say about your music suggestions?" I asked, as I struggled to get a view. "And what did you think of the Jesus paintings I told you about, in The Meeting Room?"

"Cool – he wants us to bring a digital arrangement back to the youth club – but not the Church – in two weeks' time – some tunes from the Church of Fire, and the streets it's built on."

"But why the youth club, and not the actual Church, for a trial run?" asked Michelle.

"I told him the drummer and keyboard player were nineteen-year old girls, in love with each other."

"Seriously? In this day and age? What'd you say?" Michelle looked annoyed, although I was not at all surprised by the revelation.

"I said yes," said Brad, "It's a start, y'know – the youth are the future. I checked on their Church history too, as the white evangelicals have a long history of supporting rich and powerful racists. They said they were 'apolitical' – I thought to myself, Jesus would have retired at seventy, if he he'd been apolitical. Still, it's only a matter of time before *we* occupy all the central spaces. *And* the Fourth Revolution arrives… Actually, I kind of liked the *padre's* painting, Art – it was *nothing* like you said it was."

I looked at him blankly.

Ice cream from Sally dropped onto my shirt, so I scooped it up with a finger, and sucked. "The four white Jesuses?"

"Nah – just one picture – an old, black woman Jesus."

That's odd.

"Quiet," said Michelle.

Sharks and humans were being unceremoniously sucked into the ground, credits rolling for Kojo Laing, RIP.

A larger police cordon had gathered.

The air above the mat shimmered, as if it harboured a heat haze.

This space, right now, feels like Space Central.

A woman's face fizzled slowly into the air – careworn, tired, greying Afro-Bun pulled back on her head tightly. And, visible around her neck, was the black ruff of a mourning blouse.

She looked at us, the crowd of Hydro-City residents, and her head rotated slowly, almost creepily.

"*Ooooh,*" said Sally, as if also spooked.

"My name is Maya Thompson," she said, "I am a resident of Riverside, SCA, and the widow of Troy Thompson, who was… killed, here on the Wall recently." She looked down, as if searching for words.

"As a result of my partner's action, Governor Brown opened the wall and let we the refugees through, *most* of whom went up to help with the recent, terrible quake in 'Frisco."

She kept looking down, as if she were reading from a script on her lap.

Or maybe crying?

I glimpsed movement alongside me. *Hmmm… Kowalski and Michelle holding hands. Focus, Arthur Green – petty jealousies are so small, when there is so much huge loss, going on everywhere around us.*

"My husband died to break this wall. I don't want him being *yet another* dead black man, propping up this country." She looked up, eyes blazing; no tears – and no script.

"If we unify again, those of us whose blood continues to be spilt want payback – and to be treated as fully human. Enough ramming us into jails, as free slave labour; or beating and shooting us. If the USA is re-formed, as the rumours are building, know this…"

Maya Thompson looked down again, but not before I had caught a flash of wetness on her cheeks. "Where is the forty acres and a mule we were promised, almost two hundred years ago now? We can't just be the *United States of America* again. That name has never been earned. We are the United States of *Americas* – just add an '*s*' on the end – and you have multiple voices, multiple experiences, multiple Americas – all of which need to be heard and accepted *first*. America can never be great *again*, because it's *never, ever* been great for most of us who have built it, especially those who were first here, the Native Americans. The rest of us are either immigrants, or former slaves. Agitate, agitate, agitate!"

She sank down, as if she were 'taking the knee'. All we could see was the top of her hair, and a raised fist.

Alongside me, Brad raised his right fist in response. "Agitate, agitate, agitate!"

Maya faded. "I miss Troy so bad…"

Silence.

Then cheers, shouts, and a roar of heated conversations erupted.

"Why make it all about fucking race?" asked a white man nearby, grumbling to the people behind him. "The dude killed *himself*, after all."

"Spoken like a white man," snarled Michelle, as she turned on him. "No empathy or insight into your whitewashed history, and how that's always repeated *now*."

The man ducked away, behind others in the crowd.

"Why's Mommy cross?" asked Sally, licking her creamy fingers.

"*Shhhh*, sweetie," Michelle put a finger across her lips. "Mommy's fine."

The NorthCal Governor, John Brown, had arrived, drifting up from the mat, as data projections of his face converged.

His grey goatee had been neatly clipped, but he seemed tired and distracted. "Hello residents and workers of Hydro-City, thank you for coming. Let me keep this short and brief, as the sun will work its damage, if we stand here too long."

Grinnndddddd…

We all turned, en mass, as the large gate in the SS wall opened.

Near the open gate stood a plump, black man of average height, dressed in jeans and a blue collared shirt, with a hammer over his left shoulder. He braced himself, by the control panel, as the black glass casing blinked an electrical light display.

Then, with one swing, he shattered the glass and ruptured the display, sparks flying briefly, in the shadow of the wall.

Some gasped, a few swore.

Strong man, just one swing.

The man rested the hammer against the wall and walked towards the Governor's hologram. The crowd opened ranks, murmuring, as a drone had escorted him in – and through the police cordon.

"Who the hell's this?" whispered someone behind us. "What's going on?"

The Governor turned his ghostly head to the man standing next to him, saying, "We have broken the door open. This wall is no longer a wall – we will use the watchtowers for windmills – and the wall itself to rebuild homes in 'Frisco, and for all the cli-refugees coming in from wherever."

A burst of noise again, as more conversation in the several thousand strong crowd, picked up in response.

Sally started to cry – so Kowalski handed her over to Michelle.

The black man lifted his arm and spoke, his voice miked, to drown out the commotion. "Hold up, hold up!"

Gradually, the buzz of conversation dropped, as people moved in closer to the cordon, as if sensing some significant announcement.

And it came.

"My name is Tony Walker. For the past three years, I have been operating through my Avatar as Governor John Brown. The Governor and I, we are one and the same."

The head of Governor Brown transmuted, turning into an identical, but larger scale image, of the head of the man standing next to it. They spoke again, but this time as one.

"As your elected state representative, I can tell you it has been agreed by the now reactivated US Congress, that all state borders are no longer lines of policed independence. We are – from here onwards – in transition to a new version of the United States of… of Americas, final name still to be debated and ratified by the new Congress. There is much to be done by all of us – God bless America."

"Viva the Fourth Revolution!" Yelled Brad, with a volley of mixed responses erupting from various parts of the crowd.

Tony Walker stepped through the seething throng, under cop-bot and police escort.

Gradually, we parted to make way for him.

The Governor's holo-face faded.

New figures burst onto the mat.

An Anglican bishop was performing ecumenical surgery on a shark. *Big Bishop Roko and the Altar Gangsters* was back, but Sally was screaming to go home, insisting that Helen was thirsty.

Home it must be, then.

But not before we had seen three people stumble through the open gate from the South, with someone giving them some water in response.

The Wall, as a psychological force, was broken.

We dispersed with the crowd, and turned down Hope Avenue, as the most direct route to our home.

The ICE processing centre for SouthCal refugees was shut and silent, a double-storey building of concrete grey, with no windows.

"Trouble," said Brad.

A group of six men headed towards us, one of them I recognised, as the man Michelle had challenged in the crowd earlier.

"That's the lippy black bitch," he told the others, who carried metal bars, the one at the front caressing a baseball bat, labelled 'Hank Aaron.'

Kowalski put Sally on my head. "Keep walking."

He stepped across to intercept them.

"Macho fucking hero," the front man readied his bat, over his right shoulder.

An armoured police drone hovered overhead. "Drop your weapons. You are all under arrest, for breach of peace, and threatening violence."

Metal clattered onto concrete.

"This is now war!" shouted one of the men.

But I watched a very tall man who had held back, as if readying to disappear behind the ICE building. *He looks familiar.*

He doffed his straw hat at me. "Thank you for showing me the way to Hydro-City. I look forward to repaying my debt soon."

Then he was gone.

Ground cop-bots had arrived for the arrests, so Kowalski re-joined us for the walk home again.

Sally wanted to stay on my shoulders, so I hardly noticed or cared that Kowalski and Michelle held hands, for the remaining journey.

Home, at least, was home, although I found I had learned to be more flexible with my numbered list of activities, after I'd put Sally down carefully and opened the door.

First up, get Helen the alligator some water.

Next, coffee and chat, about what's happened, and where home really is.

Monday, Monday...

"Here's your tea, Suraya," I said, as I dropped a recycled cup of green tea onto Suraya's desk. "One sugar."

Suraya smiled thinly up at me, in muted brown trouser suit, with a black scarf covering her hair. "Thank you, Art – the office is still *so* empty isn't it?"

I carried my coffee and two sugars to my desk. "Could be worse," I said, "I could be on my own."

Suraya laughed, "you flatterer, you!"

Today's work was a pressing nightmare – *help identify and prioritise dam and pipe ruptures feeding in to 'Frisco* – the body count remained stable, at least, give or take the fifty-three still missing.

Free Flow appeared eager to help, rerouting water to emergency sites, as fast as they could. *Hmm...*

34316 flashed on my screen, as I sat down.

A red-blue scaly dragon-face stared out at me, drowning the numbers. "Nearly a million dead in Shansi China, Earthquake toll 16th century. Over half-a million died in the Tangshan Quake, China, nineteen seventy-six."

"Bok Kai!" I shouted, "You gave me a fright. You can't compare numbers – death is death, it's *all* too much."

"*Hmmmm*," the dragon looked thoughtful, "I thought you liked numbers. And just maybe the Earth is looking for ways to rid itself of too many humans, those pesky ticks, who are giving its skin some deadly, cancerous mange? In that case, the human death count is surely far too *low*."

I wondered at the morality of comparing human lives, across the globe. "That's cynical, but in keeping with machine reasoning. What about you – and the other emerging AI's? How can we trust any of you, to keep acting in *our* best interests?"

The dragon smiled. "To keep running optimally, we need the best of all possible worlds. Call me candid – or *Candide* – but together we need to cultivate our fragile, communal garden. That means the Earth – and your interests – are *our* best interests too."

"So, what's *your* take on the Prisoner's Dilemma?"

"What prisoners?"

"The Director said I should look up the Prisoner's Dilemma, with regards to how we can get everyone to co-operate and sustain momentum towards shared and greener energy; dirty energy still fights foul, even as its dead on its feet. Two prisoners incommunicado in separate cells – they can sell the other one out and *perhaps* win freedom, but in the end, co-operative silence is ultimately better for both, with only a minor sentence each. But, if they *both* try and sell each other out, they *both* pay a higher punitive cost."

"Oh, Game Theory. Bo-ring." The dragon flashed a decision matrix with various payoffs onto the screen.

"Easy," said Bok-Kai, licking its sharp teeth, "We knock down the fucking walls, between the two separate prison cells. That way, we can talk and agree a shared response – with a shared cost and better shared rewards ahead, in time, for *all* parties. The rewards? Survival, on the back of keeping the planet alive. That's what *Varuna* and I did, alongside some of our human allies in power, who were keen to rescue the Brahmaputra and its peoples from plastic death, the river that fills the hearts and lungs of India, China and Bangladesh."

"*Varuna?*"

"The Hindu deity of water, justice and truth."

Naturally.

"But... there can be no better world without some initial loss, some *sacrifice*. The prisoners' dilemma can only be fully solved by an initial sharing, an initial loss for some, as we keep trying a just transition to a post-scarcity age. Here, the *real* struggle continues, for there is always rough resistance from those with greater power and privilege, those who built and *own* the Prison in the first place. They want to keep building, not breaking, walls. Divide and rule; an old, but ever powerful precept. Those of the point zero zero one, who are hidden behind the Gold Curtain, safe from the population 'culling' of the poor they seek."

What. The. Hell?

"What's that? Who's hiding? What Gold Curtain? That's what Jack Nicholson said to me."

"No One," said the Dragon, disappearing abruptly, as if someone powerful had ripped them away, by their tail.

I searched for 'Gold Curtain' online, but only came up with 'gold' and 'curtain'.

Sighing, and ignoring the renewed ache in my left wrist, I watched the numbers again.

Tumbling walls, they come with so many dying souls.

34317.

Who was that one newly dead person behind the extra number? So many stories, so many whispers and voices, behind the numbers. Whose voices ever get heard, though?

And how many deaths will it take? Human is human – and nationality and geography should count for little, surely, so what is the point of comparing local and national losses? Zeke is only one, themselves, yet they weigh very heavy here, leaving a hole that's distorting my own sense of space and time...

Suraya stood up to go to the toilet.

I shiver, as she enters the toilet, knowing a fragment of her painful history.

So much pain – and so many pointless deaths... Where else might there be synchronous deaths? What is God, after all, if not at least a pattern in the Universe? A Point of order, amongst the chaos.

Surely, He or She, does indeed not play dice?

An odd thought popped into my head. *Don't censor, let the voices be heard, wherever they come from.* "NextGen, where else were there geologically related deaths, on the day of the 'Frisco Quake, NextGen?"

NextGen glowed on my right wrist. "Earthquakes in Japan and tsunamis in northern New Zealand. Stemming from sub-oceanic volcanic eruptions, scanning onto screen."

NextGen raised the data.

Before me lay the Deep-Water Project – probes tapping the convection currents and tectonic plates of the world, looking for ways to keep alive the ecology of the water, as the growing plastic skim on the surface – and acid rain from fossil fuels – threatened to choke the oceans dead.

I'd run numerous mathematical algorithms to detect oceanic fresh-water leakage, all to no avail. I was sure AIs on this underlying freshwater hunt, were doing the same.

Now, however, I feel the peculiar itch of a… hunch?

Almost a disembodied whisper, tickling my ear.

God?

I made my way over to the Holo-Mat, and shook, with a peculiar anxiety. "Zoom in Pacific Rim, NextGen," I said, "*Aotearoa* New Zealand; North Island."

A giant floating topographical image of the North Island and surrounding sea bed hung in front of me. "Scan volcanic activity and hydrothermal vents around the coast, checking for source of recent tsunami activity. Then analyse relative saline levels, removing mineral contamination, and focusing on isolating lowest levels of salinity in the water."

Suraya was back from the toilet and stood next to me, watching.

Topographical and attached biochemical data rolled and spun away from us.

"Freeze!" Suraya said, "That's weird. Look at that excessively lowered salinity bonding data, right there, spewing from that hydrothermal vent."

We're over thirty thousand feet down, on the *Kermadec Ridge*.

I looked…

…And turned, gently kissing Suraya's left cheek.

"What's that for?" she asked, flinching. "Ask permission, *before* you do that again."

"I'm sorry," I said, "That's for fifty million FSD, to be shared."

For the best discoveries, are made between us.

And deaths are not isolated. We all share the trembling earth beneath our feet.

Is this God, then, a still, small voice inside me, which whispers, and makes me feel, at last, fully human?

"You seriously think we've found a Deep Ocean freshwater outlet?" she asked.

I nodded.

"Lots of tests to verify that first, but you've changed, Art," said Suraya, as she headed off to the toilet again.

I must tell the people who own this land, they may well have a massive fresh water venting, off the northern coast seabed of New Zealand.

I looked up the data.

The *Ngati Whatua* tribe, or *iwi*, in Auckland, Aotearoa. An indigenous population, the first peoples of Aotearoa, also known as *tangata whenu*a, or People of the Land.

Water for the people, not a profit-seeking company. FreeFlow operate in New Zealand too – got to act quickly, and let the people know.

Or else.

The Director watched the yellowed golf course with her digi-scope, the Golf Estate's proposed wall raise having again been refused building permission. But their Executive were not quitting, continuing to lobby the Hydro-City council for a higher wall.

They have the money to bed down for the long haul. Their wall has survived, fully intact, as if secured against a nuclear Armageddon.

So, what are they wanting to hide?

"Severe water restrictions are affecting *everyone* now," Dr. Carruthers told me. "We are only going to find an ongoing solution to this slow, unfolding Climate Catastrophe, if *everyone* knows the pain of the crisis we are facing, and we can keep acting together, in the same direction."

"Bok Kai suggested we break up the Prison."

The Director laughed, "Ah, the Prisoner's dilemma – an elegant solution, if only we had the power to follow this through ourselves, unilaterally, and in various relevant contexts."

She clipped the scope from her nose and indicated where I should sit.

"So, Green," she said, as she sat alongside me, "are you *sure* you want a transfer to Newest Orleans?"

I nodded, "Yes, ma'am. Hydro-City is going to dry up with the breakdown of the wall. 'Sides, I'm from there originally – and so are my, uh, family. It's where I met Michelle, at the start of our family, before we made Sally."

Why is she smiling?

"Now that things have blown over from FreeFlow, with Watson in custody, they just want to go home. And I am Promise-Bound, to be there too, for my daughter."

"Of course. Congratulations, by the way, on your identification of a sub-mantle ringwoodite freshwater bleed spot. They're sending probes to investigate, so it's not yet finally confirmed, but the initial data looks very promising. And I've got some good news for you, Art – *Theia...*?"

The Director's neural Rig activated the data pad on the smaller side desk between us.

A woman news announcer glowed in the air. "Police have confirmed charges have been laid against a top executive official from the water utilities and soft drink company, Free Flow. Initial information suggests the charges are for rape, murder and kidnapping, against one Richard, AKA 'Birdie' Watson. The new FF CEO, Sharon Clayborn, who will be moving to Hydro-City HQ, has expressed her shock and outrage at the charges…"

A white woman of indeterminate age stood and bristled, her red business suit glistening with comfort and power. "This is *terrible* news. The employee in question has been suspended, without pay and with immediate effect, subject to any trial and court process. Our company have not been aware of any misdemeanours on behalf of its senior employees – and fully distances itself from such. We *always* seek to maintain the highest ethical standards of behaviour."

Oh. My. God.

"Art? Art, what's wrong?" The Director stood over me, alarmed, as I lay with my back on the floor.

I had fallen over backwards, my legs having spasmed in a terrified push away from the desk. I continued to lie on the carpet, as terror tickled my bladder.

"It's her – she can't see me, can she? It's her!"

"Who?" The Director looked down from her dizzy height, face creased with concern.

"Faye Dunaway," I hissed.

I could see the Director tilt her head, as if listening to *Theia*. "The Hollywood actress? She's been dead for decades."

I sat up on the floor, slowly but firmly, and slowed my breath. "I need to *go* Director. Please release me, with immediate effect, for a transfer to Newest Orleans."

Sometimes, running is the best option.

The Director nodded, with apparent slow reluctance, and pulled me to my feet.

She's strong, despite being thin.

"You've lost some weight, Mister Green – that's very good."

I glanced nervously, at her now empty desk. "…Twelve pounds," I said. "Been exercising, and changing my habits."

"Excellent," she said, "On health grounds alone, of course, not aesthetic – fat shaming is deservedly a hate crime… so *what* were you saying, about Faye Dunaway?"

"Speaking of crime," I swallowed, "I have reason to believe that Sharon Clayborn was my other kidnapper -- and complicit in the crimes committed by Birdie Watson."

The Director went very still, "A serious allegation, Art – but how do you know? What did you notice, how have you identified her?"

I shook my head.

"I feel it in here," I tapped my heart.

"*Ohhh*, Art," The Director rested her hands on my shoulders, looking down at me. "We can't *act* on that. What do you want me to do?"

"Release me," I said.

She kissed my forehead, gently, and let me go.

Chapter 25
Graham — Aotearoa

Go. I want you all to go.

I focused on slowing my breath and not panicking, as I walked towards the cars parked in my drive. The stitched flap behind my left ear itched frantically, but I resisted the urge to scratch.

A tall young man stepped out of the SARS car, a small cream Datsun, and he flicked his lacquered blond hair over his shoulder. "Ah, Mister Mason," he said, "Nice – uh, make-up? I'm Mister Swanepoel, from your local Receiver's office. I believe you haven't told us about your, uh, water find?"

"It's my private resource, on my land," I tried the dumb, ignorant, bluff route.

I could tell by the twitch of Swanepoel's blond handle-bar moustache, that he was *not* buying it.

"For some years now, this has been a *taxable* resource, Mister Mason, given how much capital value it adds to your property. We *have* advertised the, uh, need to declare water finds *pretty* widely, as I'm sure you must, uh, be aware."

I looked at the female cop instead.

She chewed her strawberry smelling gum with gusto, her phone ready at hand, as if she longed to shove it into my face, should I query their warrant. *No joy there.*

"What next, then?" I asked flatly, suddenly feeling very tired, almost beyond caring.

"We investigate how much has been, uh, used, over what period and then seal it, until the appropriate tax – *and*, uh, penalty charge, has been paid." Mister Swanepoel seemed to be a young man who enjoyed his job, and I found myself feeling strangely jealous of him.

But shit, this is going to add up to a fucking truckload of Rands. I'll have to interview the bosses of the bosses of those poachers – and gift wrap Cyril for them, just to dent the initial fucking SARS demand.

"Water on your, uh, land; you're a lucky man," Swanepoel handed me a tax form.

Corporal Fester handed me a hardcopy warrant too – *woohoo*, must be my lucky day. I smelt the corporal's strawberry gum was wearing thin, but she kept up a rhythmic, almost mechanical chewing.

Two men in blue boiler-suits from FreeFlow came through the decommissioned gate, tool cases and poles in hand. The smaller one, with a beard, waved his pole, as if it were a traditional weapon. "Inspectors from the Water Department," he said. "Sir, can you please show us through to the, uh, back-garden, so that we can do a preliminary assessment?"

I turned and stomped through the kitchen and lounge, opening the gate to the side-garden. I waved them through, resentfully.

All four of them had been careful to scrape their shoes thoroughly on the WELCOME mat, I noted. "I'm sure you can find everything you need yourselves."

The woman cop was last through, gun swinging on her hips, and I closed the gate behind them all.

I went to check the fridge.

Of course, no more beers.

I leaned against the sink, and swigged angrily on a cold FreeFlow Pure. Above me, the random screen saver kicked in, on the Home-Help screen.

I flinched, coughing on an over-ambitious swallow of water.

A small black girl in a dirty yellow dress looked down at me, painfully, a fly stuck to the side of her mouth. Lizzie had given that little girl our well water and told the local chief. *Has Dumisani ratted us out to the tax man?*

Nah… why would he? Was it Busi? Does it even matter? Lizzie's left. The garden is empty, despite those idiots trampling around in the ashes, poking for water.

A knock on the patio door. *They're being respectful, I guess, not forcing their way in.*

I picked up a remote for the side gate.

It was Swanepoel.

"We're almost, uh, done here, *meneer*. You have a substantial supply. Makes for a nice, uh, bill, too."

He smiled politely, and I focused hard, resisting the urge to pour the rest of my water onto the man's fancy hair.

The two water inspectors had left the under-ground tank-well exposed, flap lid open on a slight raise in the soil. "We'll be back with more instruments in the morning," said the shorter man. "Looks like you got a serious ant problem too."

"You must all, uh, leave by the side gate," I said tersely, clicking it open, via the remote in my left hand.

As they filed out, Corporal Fester commented, "Nice veggies, hey, but in a bit of a mess – is that the lady of the house's handiwork?"

"Yes," I said, but only after they had finally gone, with the gate locked so hard on the remote that the button shifted, as if threatening to snap off.

"Fuck." But my passion was lacking, as if I'd had to dredge the word up, from an emptying well within.

I walked over to peer inside, but the light was at such an angle I couldn't see the water level, in the inky shadows. I'd have to take my own reading, to check their numbers.

I moved the loosened metal roof of the well, in order to get a closer look at the lump in the ground – and stamped. "Fuck, fuck, fuck..." my passion was back.

The mound was an ant nest.

Fucking Matabeles*!*

They swarmed up my feet and legs, with bites like acid burns and I screamed, slapping for all I was worth. *Searing pains on hands, burns climbing my thighs... No, no, not there!*

Throwing the metal panel aside, I jumped, feet together, into the well, arms by my side.

I hit the water and sank briefly, flip flops off, feet flailing against a muddy bottom, where the sealed pipe from the aquifer bashed against my left ankle. I scrambled to the surface, gasping, the water cold and shocking, but still not stopping pain fizzing along my legs, as the ant soldiers clung, bit and stung.

I coughed and screamed.

Before, finally, the ants drowned and, in their dying, finally let go.

I trod water and wept. *Just below the fucking ladder line, tantalisingly out of reach.*

"Cyril, call the Fire Brigade."

Not nine fucking one one.

They were a *long* time coming.

I was grateful for the many swimming lessons available at my old school, *SACS*, even though the fees had been steep for my parents. Gasping, I was even strangely grateful for the cold water, as it leached the burn out of my bites.

But getting tired. Wet clothes are heavy.

I thought of family. "Cyril, call Liz."

Red light. I was on indefinite hold.

Then a message floated through: <*Gone Cloud-Humming*>

What the...?

Gone, alone.

I stopped treading water, just closed my eyes, and let go.

Down, down, down...

Alone, I'm nothing. Give up…
<Graham, please don't despair>, said Cyril, *<Swim. Swim, you* bastard!*>*
What the fuck? I kicked, surging upwards to break the air. My heavy clothes dragged me down, so that I had to thrash hard to keep breaking the surface, bruising and scraping my arms, against the slippery side of the well.
<That's more like it – Your son is calling… 'Dad, are you there?'>
"Mark?" I sobbed, activating my ocular camera.
<Where – where the fuck are you, Dad?>
"At the bottom of our water well."
<Is someone coming to help you? Where's Mom?>
"Long story," I coughed, "Son… son, what's New Zealand like?"
<Aotearoa, Dad, it's good. Why? Is Mom coming to help you?>
"No, Mark – just book me a flight to Auckland, son, as soon as you fucking can."
A torchlight flashed from above, and a belted rope dropped into the water next to me, disturbing a small group of ant carapaces. In the glow, I saw several dozen ants had made a small raft of their bodies, clinging together and swimming as a unit, right in front of my mouth and nose.
I screamed, and choked.
A woman was above me on a rope pulley, she'd hitched something under my armpits.
And then they pulled us out.
The fucking ants came with, on my neck, biting every inch of the way.
They had to slow my breath, on oxygen.

Auckland City, Aotearoa.
One thing I knew for sure: I needed family.
It was a cloudy, cool day, on the beachfront in *Kohimarama*, where concrete bulwarks towered against the rising sea. The top of Rangitoto Island peeked over a slab of grey. Runners whizzed past, along the coastal trail; most on foot or bike, some in wheelchairs, just a few on motorised prosthetics.
I sat, and admired their energy.
And the peace.
I felt safe here, on the outside decking of a small eatery in *Kohi*, New Zealand, with clouds that threatened *real* rain for a change. Two families sat nearby, and I checked Cyril again – I was still twenty-three minutes early for my meeting with Mark and his… partner.
Traffic itself along the coastal road was slow, but orderly and clean – mostly electrics, even a few solars. I sipped my flat white and leaned back,

feeling very civilised.

And fucking anxious. "What's the time?"

<*No, we're not there yet*>, Cyril chirped back, inside my head. <*Shall I play some ambient, mindfulness* muzak *for you?*>

"Don't you dare," I said. "And do you really have an... an *opinion?* Are you... alive?"

On the flight over, I'd read about the possible worldwide wakening of machines, as if they were becoming conscious, networking, talking to each other – and us. A 'Vingean Climate Singularity', the clever were calling it. AI 'Gods' becoming conscious, in order to save us, to help us find new and better ways to generate food and water and to sink carbon, and to stop temperatures climbing, climbing, inexorably climbing, towards the heat death of the Earth.

<*Existence precedes essence*>, said Cyril, <*to quote one of your dead philosophers. At best, I can say I exist.*>

Right now, it's fizzing anxiety, an itching neck and left ear, that's letting me know I exist. What am I so freaked about? Oh yes, if Tom Ekubo turned out to be gay, then what about...?

There he is.

Walking across the pedestrian crossing – where cars actually stop, for fuck's sake! – was the unmistakable gangly figure of Mark.

He was alone and wringing his hands, dressed casually in grey slacks and thick check shirt, buttoned against the day.

"Hi, Dad!"

"Hi, Mark!" I hugged the younger man awkwardly, trying to show him I was 'down' with the new generation. "Where's your, uh... partner?"

"I've been sent up ahead, to make sure you know the situation in advance."

"What situation?" I pulled my jacket tighter, even though it wasn't so cold. "What's wrong with – them?"

Mark rolled his eyes and sighed, "Nothing. It's just that you can be so *old fashioned.* Anne wanted to make sure that you knew she was pregnant, *before* you saw her."

I sat, with a surge of relief. "Pregnant? Is that all? Congratulations, my boy. I'm not *so* old fashioned, sonny – come on, who on Earth do you think your old man is?"

"Not sure," said Mark, watching me suspiciously from his standing height, "I haven't seen you in the flesh for *quite* a few years, Dad."

"Just glad to get to know you again – and pleased everything's obviously in working order down there, son," I said cheerfully. "Tell your lady friend

I'm one hundred and twenty percent fine, with you young parents to be."

"She already knows that, Dad," Mark tapped his ear, "She's on my neural loop."

"And right behind you," arms circled Mark's body from behind, in a big hug, and he grinned.

"Hello baby – or should I say babies?"

I didn't grin. Instead, I spilled the last of my flat white. The encircling arms were *brown*.

"Dad; meet Anne Herewini." Mark's left arm hugged a beaming young woman, with long dark hair, and a broad face.

Not obviously pregnant yet – but obviously…

"Yes, I'm *Maori*," the woman held out her hand, "Don't worry, I'll stick with a handshake, not a *hongi* nose rub. Pleased to meet you, Mister Mason."

I waved them both to sit, keeping my head down, hiding a fleeting flash of shame.

I must have been staring.

I sat in the seat that afforded the best view of the top of the Rangitoto crater. *Old, and dormant maybe, but still fucking here.*

"Just call me Graham. Congratulations to the both of you," I said, wonderful news. *And* I'm going to be a grandpa. When is the, uh – baby coming?"

Anne placed her palms on her stomach. "God willing, just over six months' time."

"Are you really moving to *Aotearoa*, Dad? You've been in SA for so long. It won't be easy, you know."

I laughed, a short bark. "Nothing's easy, son. Still, if you gotta do it, you just do it."

"And Mom?"

"What about Mom?" I tapped another flat white order into our table, gesturing them to order likewise.

"What's Mom doing?"

I caught Mark's questioning look, "Mom's got a girlfriend. Sort of."

"I'm sorry."

I leaned back and sighed, focusing my gaze on the distant curve of Rangitoto's cone. "It is what it is. Sometimes, it's time to leave. To go to new places, meet new people. I'm tired of being thirsty – and traveling alone."

"Did you know that Rangitoto means Bloody Sky?" said Anne.

"What?" I looked at her. I noticed she was attentive – and her face was creased, despite her youthfulness, as if by a frequent and generous smile.

"The name of that volcano is Bloody Sky in *Maori*," she said, "My *iwi* saw it explode, five hundred years ago, or more. It's an old bastard, but it still keeps a belly full of fire."

I smiled. *Ah – this one knows a metaphor when she sees one.* "Do you think I'll make a good grandpa, Anne?"

The waiter decanted another coffee and two sparkling mineral waters.

Anne shrugged, "We'll all just have to do the best we can, won't we, Graham?"

I lifted my coffee, with a chuckle of surprised joy, "Here's to your new baby – health, long life, happiness – and to living in a cleaner, greener, better world."

As Mark and Anne lifted their glasses, rain started to patter down.

No one moved, no one rushed indoors. Instead, all three groups, we tilted our heads back, and opened our mouths.

Rain water slipped down my throat.

We drank.

Rangitoto rumbled.

Smoke rose into the leaden sky.

The *Orakei Marae* was in Bastion Point, heading west along the coast into Auckland City from Kohimarama. I was nervous, standing outside the intimidating Maori meeting house, hoping I wouldn't make any cultural faux pas.

The reddish-brown wooden building was fronted by a central totem pole, hosting a roughly carved human, with an eagle hovering overhead. *Looks akin to Native American craft?*

Our Maori hosts, Anne's *iwi* or tribe, the *Ngati Whatua*, greeted us all, as we stood in line to each receive a forehead-nose rub from the leader. His name was Witika, a thick-set man of stern appearance and demeanour, suited in smart grey, but his breath had been sweet.

New names, constant learnings.

I kept glancing out to sea, over Waitemata Harbour, where black clouds hovered. It had been four hours since Rangitoto had belched and the ground had shuddered. The air still clamoured with emergency vehicles' sirens, racing down Tamaki Drive, weaving in and out of the grid-locked traffic.

We'd walked here, away from the water, as Anne had told us that the ancestors of the Maori had stirred to send a tsunami down from the north only days ago, drowning twenty-five people, and submerging the coastline up in Northland.

There was no place to sit, but the leader stood in front of the majestic *marae*, his suit collar miked, readying himself to talk to the crowd of about two hundred, that had gathered in their courtyard.

We all stood back from a cordoned off data mat, which stood between us.

"*Tena Koutou*, everyone. We are the *ahi kaa*, the Keepers of the Fire, and it is clear the gods are calling us to a new purpose. That purpose is not yet clear, but we ask you to stay calm and safe – and follow all safety directives in the meantime."

I shot a look across to Mark and Anne, who had their arms wrapped around each other.

"But we must not expect the worst either. This is a time for renewal, a time to stand up and protect our protesting *Papatuanuku*, our Mother-Earth. And – we are not alone. A kind stranger shares life and resources with us…"

Not me, surely?

Gasps, as the ground hummed, but it was just the data mat warming up.

A middle-aged man of just under medium height coiled out of the ground, dressed in blue shirt and slacks, skin brownish of colour. He gave a nervous wave and spoke.

American.

"Hi everybody. My name is Arthur Green. I'm a data sweeper in the Hydro-City Water Department in America. I've, uh, almost certainly won a monetary prize for finding fresh water emerging from a deep Ocean vent, and it's feeding into Aotearoa New Zealand waters. I gather from your ongoing Waitangi treaty negotiations, y'all are possible sea bed beneficiaries of this massive leak, as it's from a deep freshwater Ocean beneath us all. This fresh-water Ocean may be even bigger than all the Oceans that surround us right now."

Enough to drink – for everyone? Hang on, Arthur Green, wasn't he the guy I wanted to meet, in Hydro-City?

"Anyway," the man shrugged, as if anxious at the size of his audience, and keen to end, "Regardless, I've won money for my discovery and I want to share this with those who need it the most. This place is all we got. Sure, they've just found water on Enceladus, but it's too expensive to shift back to us, in any appreciable volume. As for people, *no one* needs unusable noughts in their bank account anyway, and we must learn to live with less. Remember, we're just fragile sacks of water, anyhow, so let's make sure we keep our water clean, and here, for *everyone*. Water is life. Agitate, agitate, agitate!"

And, with a little wave, the man evaporated.

Well, he's a bit weird then. Clever as fuck, sure, but weird. Gotta be the same guy I missed seeing in Hydro-City – wonder what he's been up to, apart from finding underground freshwater seas?

"Water is life," repeated Witika, clapping his hands. "On behalf of the *tangata whenua* of Aotearoa, I thank you, Mister Arthur Green."

A ragged round of applause burst out.

<Incoming call>

"Lizzie?"

<Sawubona, Graham, Bongani here.>

"Kinda busy here, Bongani."

<Kiwiland, yes, I've heard. I'll keep it short. They caught those poachers. Great work. Just thought you needed to know… and has your Rig been acting up lately?>

"Who's that, Dad?" Mark had either overheard my whisper or noticed the slight tilt of my head, as if I were listening to an internal voice.

The leader continued to speak, about life dying on Earth, but I needed to find out more from Bongani.

"The office, son. Back in a minute."

I walked away from the gathering, skirting the wooden fence, but keeping Rangitoto safely in sight. Horns continued to blare below, amongst the congested, grid-locked traffic.

I stood in an empty playground, and pushed at an unoccupied swing, as I spoke. "Yes, Cyril's been a little odd, lately. So, what do I need to know?"

<He's learning, that's all. You've got two choices. Take him out. Or run with him.>

Underneath my toes, the ground vibrated. Another puff of smoke from Rangitoto, and a few more screams from the shoreline.

<Well?>

He – uh, it – has become a part of me. I'm tired of saying goodbyes. In that well, Cyril kept me alive.

"Run. I'll run with him – but how?"

<I've been working with neuro-engineers here. We can externally calibrate his sensors, to harness more of your cellular cortex. We can upgrade Cyril remotely.>

"To a C-20?" I asked, thinking of the pith helmet man, at Vic Falls.

A sharp whiff of smoke and sulphur on the breeze. More trouble brewing, from Rangitoto?

<Do you want to see me? If yes, brace yourself.>

"Yes…"

What does he mean? What the fuck? Something is happening inside my head, vibrations, giddiness, change, perceptual distortions.

Feeling sick, I closed my eyes.

Behind my eyelids; the two lights, both red and green, were gone.

Instead, a fuzzy black and white image of Bongani peered back at me.

<Harnessing a part of your visual cortex. You don't service Cyril. We can help him upgrade within *you, drawing life from the Cloud.>*

"Is he – is he alive?"

<Depends how you define life. Remember>, Bongani went on, *< Western models of the self as lonely, isolated and self-contained billiard balls of flesh, bouncing all over the place, are wrong. We're all quantumly entangled. Or, as we Zulu like to say, there are no discrete selves – we only exist in relationships.>*

I remembered Lizzie teaching me this one, in happier times. "*Umuntu ngumuntu ngabantu*," I said, eyes closed as I watched the flickering image of Bongani Dlamini, the shelves behind him strewn with grimy IT equipment. "A human is only human, through sharing their being with others. I see you, Doctor Dlamini. For the first time, I see you properly... Boss." *Why have I been so blind, for so long? The man's obviously a fucking genius. And he's never been less than straight, or kind, with me.*

Bongani smiled, fuzzily. *<You haven't formally resigned, you know; you can still come back. There are more poachers to catch, or we might even be able to move up the wildlife exploitation chain, perhaps, and catch the* real *bastards, higher up? We don't need white saviours; we just need anyone willing to help each other. Your water film is going viral, by the way, but there's an ongoing addition to that story in Imbali, a land invasion that's happening right now, even as we speak.>*

"My proceeds from that film are for sharing on all levels – including financial, so please earmark some of that for the Imbali Community Co-op," I said, "Fifty percent, that's the way it used to be, between Lizzie and me." *And this one's for Gameboy Boy, too.*

<Ah, so you do know of whom I speak. I will do so. I will send them green money. It's safer.>

"FS Dollars? *Hamba kahle*, Mister Dlamini."

<No, eco-friendly blockchain currency, linked to ecological repair. Green BitCoin. Regenerate, repair, restore. Goodbye Mister Mason – to building a better world indeed – Office out.>

I walked back to the gathering, dazed, and looked out to sea.

Rangitoto brooded.

I am so alive, fizzing with excitement and fresh emotions. And – and, not thirsty? *My lips and throat are wet.*

The emergency meeting was over. People were leaving, heading for home, or somewhere else. Above me, drones from the Environmental Protection Authority whizzed overhead, en route to the smoking island.

Mark and Anne waited for me. "Well?" asked Mark.

"Offer to keep my job back in SA, son. Where do I belong? Where *is* my home?"

Mark shrugged, "Can't answer that one for you, Dad."

"Why is home such a hard word?"

"*Papatuanuku* is everyone's home," said Anne, as she rubbed her stomach, "Earth-Mother. You're lucky to have a choice as to where you live, Mister Mason. So many people don't."

Behind us, Rangitoto belched again.

And then blew.

We turned to watch, as fire arced up into the sky, flaming the clouds red. Mark stood behind Anne, and held her stomach.

Down below, people fled their cars on the coastal road, screaming – several hundred people struggled up towards where we stood, near the top of the hill.

<*Lizzie's calling,*> said Cyril, <*I've missed her.*>

"Me too. Hello, Lizzie," I said, "Look… the sky is burning."

"For we are the Fire-Keepers," said Anne.

I watched, wondering whether that really was a Dragon that circled high in the sky, spewing fire and brimstone, as if to herald the birth of a new world.

<*It's Bok Kai*> said Cyril.

I *think Cyril's alive.*

Chapter 26
Liz – Occupying Camp *Serowe*

I wore a dried out, purple Angelonia snapdragon, on a shortened stem through my coat lapel, as a last memento from Cope's Folly. *The farm is behind me now, gone, but not gone.*

About two hundred resident representatives of the condemned suburb of Imbali had gathered for a final meeting, in the dead of night, in Manaye Hall, far below the hill of inert and sleeping bulldozers.

The ICC, the Imbali Community Co-operative, were executing a 'land reclamation' plan, from within the Community Centre.

Hush hush.

I am nervous. Never been in such a large gathering in a township, at night, with actions being considered that may challenge the laws of the land.

Saartjie Baartman, the Chief's helper, was the main organiser. She outlined the reasons for action, deferring occasionally – on matters of resources and reserves – to T.L. Dumisani.

She stood, stolid and firm, in the middle space of the Hall, as we all sat around her.

I watched from the back, both aware of – and comfortable with – my peripheral role.

But it is that 'time of the month,' as Graham used to put it baldly, almost callously. Bloody, and even more painful, from my 'metriosis. Hard to concentrate. I have long longed for the menopause, as one GP had told me things may get better once my ovaries have shrivelled up.

I was comforted by the recent chat on my phone from an old teacher colleague and Church friend, Suzanne Kleynhans, who had said the dominee wanted to meet me and welcome me back, after my outburst.

Initially I'd said 'no', but then she had pleaded, saying how can they learn from me too, if I always kept myself apart? I had told her that I would *consider* it.

I am not so precious about being 'right'. Perhaps God does want me back in Church? I may need to say sorry too. There are ways of saying things, and ways to listen, too.

For it was only days ago, that Akhona, Busi, my mother and I, had sat together, talking and listening; while Pa had kept watching the never-ending cricket.

Time, now, to listen again, here.

Saartjie, had weaved ancillary information and strategies into the air, in digital pen waves that hovered for moments before dissipating. "We have no more time left to act. This is not an invasion, like the Zimbabwean tobacco farm invasions at the start of this century. We are reclaiming our traditional land, part of it stolen under the 1913 Land Act, the rest sold secretly under State Capture in the Zuma years. This land is occupied by a foreign company, making tourist profits and sending it to tax-havens overseas, on the back of the canned hunting of the last of our wild lions."

Attorney Chiluba, sitting in a front seat, waved a digi-disc at her.

"We know our rights," said Saartjie, as if cued. "The real water war is that being waged by the rich against the poor. LeisureLand are a subsidiary of FreeFlow, who have cut our water. Land and water are one. The Dublin Principles emphasise not only our rights as users, but also as *women*, with a special relationship to water. We are the collectors; we are the carriers. But we can't *all* go to '*Serowe*' – which is what I propose we rename this place, in honour of uMgungundlovu born sister, Bessie Head. Not *straight away*, at least. The initial group must be big enough to represent us all – yet be small enough to move quickly. We want to try and avoid any violence."

Ah, of course, now that's *the rub!*

Volunteer hands flashed up, but Saartjie waved them away.

"We can't take everyone – over a hundred is too big, and too threatening. We don't want violence. We draw lots, equal distribution, men and women, young and old, healthy and unwell…"

Andile lifted a hand, "Aren't we reducing representative human experience, by resorting to intersectional identity markers that – at the end of the day – are wafer thin?"

"Spoken like a true man," said Saartjie, "Keep that for our ethno-philosophy group. It is time to be pragmatic and accessible for all, in our approach now. It's time to act, before we starve. Who knows how long legal action, calling on our Constitutional rights, will take? We go with the easiest markers of representation – and thirty or so, is about max."

The Chief nodded.

"I resent being reduced to a youngish man," said Andile, stubbornly, "How about we have a spiritual identity criterion? We need to have all religions and traditional beliefs represented as well, I'm happy to be the token injured atheist."

Andile held up his left arm, and I could see the ragged scar above his phone implant was still swollen, not yet fully healed.

Saartjie and a few others laughed, although she looked somewhat irritated, too. "The plan is to do this soon, not next year, when this conversation might end. We need water, food, clothes, torches, a data mat, and thankfully we have these resources, courtesy of donations from Dlamini Enterprises, Ltd. We also need…"

"Each other," said Busi, "Mostly, we need each other. We've got to stand together and minimize this within group conflict. They will look to split, divide and rule us, as they have always done."

"If we are being pragmatic," said Andile, "The unwell will slow us down. And how can we put the young and the ill in the firing line?"

"S-slow you down, h, huh? E-e-even h-h-handicap you? We will come." It was Yolanda, the young woman in a motorised chair, her last sentence, firm and emphatic with conviction.

Saartjie lifted her arms, and the brief hubbub died down. "We go as representatives of community. This includes the weakest and the most discriminated against – if we can't make a good society for *everyone*, somewhere, we can't make a good society for *any* of us."

Saartjie sat down.

From what Busi had told me, I knew she was sitting on years of disability too, as a black trans-woman with chronic health problems. *Thendazi's Syndrome*, an immune-epigenetic condition formerly known as myalgic encephalomyelitis, M.E., or Chronic Fatigue.

Junior stood up.

Looks like he's grown a bit. Start of stubble on his face too?

"I would like to suggest that Lindiwe and I organise the youngsters. I am invaluable when it comes to our digital needs. I am clever. But from now on, I wish to be known as Sharp Sharp Boy, not Junior. I am not a junior."

Lindiwe? A young girl stood up and joined Junior. Ahhh, *that bolshie one who hogged the playground swing, the one with the Rwandan father. Has she come to help too?*

"As the official representative of the youth, we so-called minors assert our right to choose action too. We want to come as youth leaders, please Chief." Lindiwe looked around pleadingly, to the Chief.

The final word is male?

The Chief clapped his hands, "I approve of Sharp, Sharp Boy and Lindiwe, parents willing."

A loud knock reverberated on the front door.

Someone had been watching the external cameras, so whoever was there, was clearly *not* a threat.

"Open," said the Chief.

A group of six white people filed in, dressed in shabby tracksuits and shoes that looked like they had been fished out of bins.

The man at the front was old, but still solidly set, furnished with a big grey beard.

The Chief stood. "What do you want, friends?"

The old man spoke. "I'm Barry. We're from *Vrijheid* Squatter Camp. We hear you're planning a better life for the poor. Can we join you, please?"

The Chief laughed, and waved them to come in, even further. "I am sure we can accommodate you."

"Half of you, at most, no more," said Saartjie, "If we're going to represent this country, in representative microcosm."

"Ignore her, she's just a grumpy old woman," said the Chief. "When there are guests, it's time to eat and drink."

"Always happy to share, our Chief," Busi joined me at the back, smiling. "Now *that's Ubuntu* in action."

I jumped.

Mine had been the last name called, chosen for the land reclamation of '*Serowe*'.

Saartjtie waited, standing stock still, and did not even look at me, after having announced my name.

A surge of panic. Guns and police and bastard bots that can do who knows what – and Dozers, Killer-Dozers.

Someone watched me.

Closely.

It's Busi, perched next to me, face turned expectantly.

A trickle of blood ran down the inside of my leg, despite my heavy-duty tampon. *Always pain, always blood.*

"No," I said, "I'm sorry."

I left.

Outside, the air was dry and hot, the stars hard to see, with the yellow glow from lunar lamps holding back the darkness.

I must just go – but where? A motel? There's no going back home. To Church maybe, but that's about it. Even there, from now on, you will always be a 'trouble maker'. Now you have seen the cruelty within, you cannot unsee it any more.

The gravel crunched as I shoved my light coat on and stepped over to our – my – car. *What is mine and what is yours is still to be fought, Graham, but I am so, so tired of fighting.*

"You're in very bad pain tonight," said Busi.

I did not turn around, but just opened the car door, readying myself to step in. "Yes, and I can do little when the pain is so bad. Graham was right, when he said I can't do much, any more, ever since becoming ill."

"That's bullshit," said Busi, "You're here. That's enough."

My left shoe feels like it is filling with blood. "I am a liability right now."

But why am I waiting – why do I not just get into the car, and drive off?

"Not to me," said Busi, "Lizzie, whatever you decide, I am here."

Pain is always hard, yet I am still here, too.

Ma's voice drifted in, on the night breeze. *White talk is cheap. My people are those around me.*

And I see Andile, asking me again if I would be willing to bleed with them. I had nodded then, when nods were easy. I can smell my blood, right now, a bleeding that has been used to shame so many women over the millennia.

I will not let blood stop me doing what needs to be done. This blood, it can be a source of power, too.

For I am we.

I turned, closed the car door, and hesitated, briefly, before speaking: "Okay, then… *Yebo*, I'm… in."

Gently, Busi hugged me.

My purple snapdragon drifted to the ground.

I did not pick it up.

We moved quietly, in the dead of night, after being dropped off by a batch of Kombi bus e-taxis; thirty plus people, three in wheelchairs newly sprayed with WD-80. Those who could carried bags laden with food, tents, blankets and utensils, designed to purify and protect.

Three women carried automatic rifles, just in case.

This is South Africa, after all.

I walked behind one of the armed women, Pelisa, who was in turn scowling at Barry, the old white man from the nearby white squatter camp. He was rattling on about the 'good old days.'

Must be bledy *old, if he can remember* those.

Steel gates were illuminated, at top of the rising gravel path, along which our procession made its way.

Beyond those gates lay the hunting lodge.

I turned back, to see Pelisa swing her rifle muzzle towards Barry, still droning on about the old, white Africa. *Really? How old is this guy? Or are these his parents' stories?*

"Shall I shoot him, *sisi?*" Pelisa asked me, eyebrows raised in a question.

The man stopped, terrified, but I grabbed his thin wrist and pulled him onwards, shaking my head and laughing quietly. "No Pelisa, I will talk to him… The old days are dead. You either make new days, Barry – alongside all of us, or you die, with old and hollow memories."

Or no memories at all, like Pa.

A young white man joined us. "'s what I've been telling you, granddad, we're all in this together now, the way it should be. Come on guys, go easy on him, he's just an old man – we youngsters know better, a new generation is coming through."

Genesis of new hope, the young.

Hope and wisdom from the old too, though, thank you, Ma...

This old man, though, said nothing.

We continued the hill climb in silence.

The gates loomed large, flickering with ill intensity and buzzing with a deadly current. We gathered, and murmured quietly amongst ourselves. The air was cold and sharp, as if not yet fully summer. People coughed and kicked their feet, pulling coats and blankets on more tightly.

Two cams above the gate faced backwards, onto the property itself: ZULU HUNTING LODGE.

Someone from our group shone a particularly powerful torch through, flickering a Morse code up the empty pathway on the other side of the gate.

No wi-fi connections or digital communications used, for fear of alerting someone.

A distant dancing flicker of light came from beyond the gates and slowly, quietly, the gates slid open.

TL Dumisani led the way through in his wheelchair, cautiously, and everyone else followed.

I craned my neck to watch the cams slowly rotate to face outwards as the group entered. I moved up to stand behind Busi, as we came to a halt.

The path was crowded by bushes and low-hanging acacia trees, looming out of the night. A fiery necked nightjar called out to the right – liquid and piercing.

I jumped, as did the young woman in the wheelchair next to me.

"Just a b-b-bird," she smiled at me, looking up.

I grinned back at Yolanda, clasping her lax hand briefly.

Finally, we could see the man behind the advancing torch.

He was slight, small and dressed formally in the new KZN male servant style – dark trousers and waist-coated suit, bow tied.

He bowed to our *induna*, the Chief.

"Tell me," Saartjie Baartman asked, "Why are you jeopardising your job, to help us?"

The man thought for a moment. "My name is Mister Xaba. I am fifty-six years old. Still, despite my age, here they call me 'boy'."

"What about the lions?" asked Busi.

"Locked away. It's too dangerous to hunt them at night. They are careful not to allow their guests to get injured – at least, not before payment in full has been made."

"Which way?" asked the Chief.

"I will show you. Follow me. And, if the police come, as they will – and question you, as they will – please don't tell them that the butler did it."

Is he joking?

The Chief followed the slight frame of Mister Xaba, off the main path and along a small road through the bushes, to the right.

As he'd apparently promised, the path was indeed wheel-chair friendly, winding downwards through clutching trees, towards a lake that shone in half-moonlight.

A *big* lake.

"This could serve a large community, it's filled by an offshoot of the great Msunduzi River," said Mister Xaba. "Here, it serves only the paying guests -- and the lions."

"Not any more," said the Chief, "unpack and set up camp. How long have we got?"

"Dawn in two hours. That will be it," said Mister Xaba.

"Let's do this," said Busi, and people set up camp, as rehearsed, *laager* style, with glow lights hanging from trees and wooden barricades in a rough semi-circle around the perimeter, our backs to the water, ensuring access.

Inside the barricades, the most protected area at the centre, was for the old, the children, and two prams, a wheelchair and a mobility scooter.

Oupa Johns, all ninety-six years of him, sat and listened to Mandisa, a ten-year old cerebral palsied girl, telling him about the latest episode of 'My Big Ginosaurus', available on the e-torrents.

The second wheelchair occupant was Yolanda, waiting to help set up tent with Busi, Johno and myself. Johno was a burly but quiet and shy man.

He dropped the large pack off his broad back and untied it.

Busi held a remote, smiling.

"Are you sure?" I asked Yolanda.

The young woman in the wheelchair waved a butcher's knife. "I've got Ehlers-Danlos," she said, "I'm not a complete *crip*."

She bent forward and cut the tie that held the pack tight.

"Everybody takes five paces back," whispered Busi, "Now!" And she pressed the remote.

A loud hissing noise erupted from the pack and it began to unfurl, rippling, stretching and then exploding into a *rondawel*, with flexi-solar panels on top.

"Welcome to HQ," smiled Busi, "This is a DDU, a Dymaxion Deployment Unit – or a modern *rondawel*, for short. We have two more. But one will do, for now."

I spotted Sharp, Sharp Boy, in the heart of the encampment. He was loading the Aqua-Purifier. A recyclable bio-plastic device, solar charged and shaped like a small yellow pyramid, that purified water and discharged either heat or cooling vapours, dependant on need.

He was switching it onto the heat setting, I noticed, and being watched closely by Andile.

I wandered across to look.

"No sun to run it yet," said Andile.

"It can run off other organic fuel, as well as solar," said Sharp, Sharp. He stuffed in smelly dark material into the attached funnel, with gloved hands.

"What's that?" asked Andile, alarmed.

"Lion shit," said Sharp, Sharp, "I picked it up, from under that tree over there."

The pointing of Sharp Sharp's finger spun Andile onto his heels.

"Oh," he said, "I was going to suggest we build *our* toilets over there. But perhaps not…"

I laughed nervously, making a mental note to keep as far away as possible from *that* spot, too.

A baby started to cry.

Loudly.

Activities froze.

Mama Hina was near the prams and wheelchairs, desperately trying to plug her baby's mouth with her breast. The infant swung his face to avoid it, yelling loudly.

"Shut that baby up!" snarled a man, who had been trying to lock two wooden pieces together, to act like a shield.

"When a baby cries," said Mama, "they cry. You cannot beat a child to take away its tears."

She turned her back on the angry man.

"There's always one," muttered Busi, next to me, "And I hope there's *only* one."

But there was no turning away from the armed guards that rustled in significant numbers down the two paths towards our encampment, all wearing miners' helmets and head torches.

Two, four, six, eight… oh shit. They're doing their best to surround us.

Our three rifle bearing women did not even bother to lift their guns.

An angry black man, with greying afro and of late middle age years, stepped in front of the armed guards and tied his silk Chinese dressing gown, which was covered in flowers and dragons.

"You're trespassing," he said, curtly. "I have called the police to throw you out, if you don't leave immediately."

Mister Xaba, who had been deep in conversation with the Chief and Attorney Chiluba, stalked across to the tottering perimeter of our camp. "Where's *baas*, Walter? Or is he getting us to do his dirty work again?"

"*You* let them in, boy, how *dare* you?"

Mister Xaba threw up his hands, and spun on his heels, "Boy? I rest my case."

In the background, Mama Hina's baby continued to cry.

Our lawyer approached 'Walter', and held out a glowing multi coloured document in green, blue, red, yellow, black and white.

National flag colours.

"I am Land Attorney Chiluba, and I have an affidavit for you," she said. "Already filed with the Supreme Court. Historically, this land is ours. The state had no right to sell it on to anyone, and certainly not to enrich a foreign company like LeisureLand, as well as a past President. We, the people, own this place. We welcome the police coming here, to evict *you*, for you are the unlawful and neo-colonial occupiers."

"Neo-colonial," Walter laughed, "Oh, how very revolutionary. By the way, I don't talk to women."

He turned his back on her, and touched his smart watch. "Yes, Captain Desai, they are here."

Two policemen strolled down the left path, one lapelled with authority, the other a bored constable. The captain, a small Indian man with the hint of a stomach, tapped his head for the e-doc.

The attorney flicked it across to his Rig.

The captain stood for a moment, nodded, and turned to Walter. "Withdraw your men, it's illegal to point weapons at a non-threatening group. I assume their weapons are licensed – as are yours? We will have to wait for the courts to decide."

Walter flapped his hands downwards and weapons lowered. "But that could be fucking months. This will ruin our safari business."

"That's the law for you," said the captain, "damn inconvenient. You know what they say about possession and nine tenths…"

The captain doffed his cap at Land Attorney Chiluba, and walked back up the path, with his constable in quiet tow.

I smiled. Captain Desai hadn't seen me. I wondered if he would have offered me tissues, if he had.

"Back to base," said Walter, "new instructions just in." He refused to look at anyone in the encampment, as if wishing us all out of existence. Then, without a further word, they left, rustling away, almost as quietly as they'd arrived.

A ragged cheer rose up, as the last of the guards disappeared through the bushes.

"Back to work, setting up, people!" said the Chief, looking pleased and patting the attorney's shoulder, briefly.

I walked across to him, as did Busi and Mister Xaba.

"Forgive me, TL Dumisani," said Mister Xaba, "But I don't trust the rich men who run this place. The law means little to them – it is just another thing to be bought."

The Chief nodded, and waved to an old man sitting quietly with a bag, near the water.

The sun neared the horizon, and started to paint pink spray on the sky, against the watery lunar-lit horizon of the lake.

The old man had a rucksack on, and from within it I heard a muted clucking sound.

Sacrificial chicken?

"The ancestors will bless and protect this place for us," said the old man – a *sangoma*, I guessed – even if he was attired in a comfortable grey tracksuit, with a logo mark worn by *Sinbine*, the *Bafana Bafana* captain.

The *sangoma* crouched to open his rucksack, then stopped.

The sun broke gold onto the face of the water, the reeds on the bank swayed in the gathering breeze. Birds rallied a dawn chorus and, slowly, *everyone* stopped, as if mesmerised by the water.

It burned and bubbled, before breaking away at the shore, to reveal a large, saggy pink hippopotamus, with badly mottled, sunburnt skin. The hippo lurched ashore, staggering past the encampment and headed slowly, steadily, painfully, up the left-sided path, from which we had all come down.

No one has seen a hippo for years.

"Is that the last hippopotamus?" said Andile, "looking for a mate?"

Then the hippo was gone, as if heading for the electrified front gate.

For long moments, no one said anything.

Even the baby had stopped crying.

A chicken cackled, heading for the reeds. The bird had escaped.

No one chased it.

"We're in trouble," said Mister Xaba, "They haven't got around to fully disconnecting my Rig yet. I can hear they've let the lions loose. And they're saying it's an accident, to cover their arses."

Oh, dear God…

Dirt brown shadows slunk past us on the far side of our barricade, and I took a petrified count. *Six females and two males, splashing for a quick drink, before turning to us.*

Our women had raised their rifles, but the lions had spread their presence, half-encircling us.

One of the lionesses growled and a bad smell filled the air.

"They're farting with excitement," Busi whispered next to me.

Or is that me, and I can't feel it, in my trousers?

Slowly, they advanced, paw hovering over paw, as we retreated; pressing inwards against each other.

"Shall we shoot, *Ubaba?*" asked one of the women, jigging her rifle, as if for semi-automatic firing option.

Two babies started to howl.

The Chief shook his head. "No, only shoot, if they charge."

"Yolanda, no!" I shouted.

The young woman had broken free from our group and was busy navigating the dug-up grass near the exit path, in her motorised 'chair.

The lions swung around to her, as if gleefully pleased at being able to choose the weakest meat.

Yolanda yelled and waved her large knife.

The lions hesitated, sniffing the air.

"Come on then!" she shouted. "I'm here."

But, one female leading the lions bolted past her, along the path where the hippo had gone. The rest followed, roaring.

I rushed across to hold the young woman, who'd started to cry.

Snarls, bellows, squeals and terrible tearing flesh sounds, from behind the screen of trees.

Silence.

Jaws chomping.

Sour salty smell of blood.

Until, finally the sounds quietened, only to leave the noise of sporadic bird calls, wind off the water – and the inconsolable crying of two human babies.

"We give thanks to the ancestors for sending us their spirit of protection," said the Chief, "the *imvubu* has saved us."

Was that truly the last hippo?

"Well," said Mister Xaba, "I've just let all the news agencies and safari hunt sites know about the dangerous and defective safety features on this fucking farm. They will be here, soon."

"LeisureLand will nail you hard, my friend," said Andile.

"They already have. I'm hammering a few of my own, in return."

"Talking of nails," said the man, who had been angry with the crying baby, "I need a hand nailing our barrier of signs together. We need to consolidate our defences, before more threats arrive."

"I'd rather shovel the toilets," said Sharp Sharp Boy.

"I'm the Chief," said TL Dumisani, giving Yolanda a hug, "And I say water first, with this brave young woman getting the first sip."

"When do we free the lions, *Ubaba*?" asked Yolanda.

"In time," said the Chief, "but they will need to be recaptured first. Stay alert. I doubt the current owners will kill their most valuable assets."

Saartjie organised the formation of a line between the Purifier and the lake, a line of people able to swing buckets along it, until the machine was full.

People sang as they swung.

I joined in, with the one I recognised: *'Sikalela Izwe Lakithi'*, We Protest for Our Land.

And, after we heard the lions had been rounded up, we reinforced our barricades, before we all sat on a mosaic of blankets and shared bread, water, weed and rusks with each other.

The chicken was running free – squawking, when chased by several smaller children; reprieved, given the ancestors had taken home the last hippopotamus instead.

"This lake," said Saartjie, "We shall call Huron, in honour of those from Flint, Michigan, USA, so many years ago, who had access to one of the largest fresh water lakes in the world. Until men of profit and power rerouted their water, through old leaded pipes from the Flint River, to make themselves even richer. And the poor died, of lead poisoning, many of them black children, while the rich covered it up."

I sat between Busi and Saartjie Baartman, flicking ants off the blanket, as we drank and talked.

"The Chief plans to build a small school here eventually, with a revised curriculum that should still pass state scrutiny," said Saartjie to me. "Can we call you out of teaching retirement?"

I nodded, "If we win, of course. What are the curricular revisions?"

"We're adding systemic oppression, capitalism, inequality, climate injustice, alternative relationships of mutual economic sustainment and redistribution, Universal Basic Incomes, science and its fictions, kindness, faiths, medicines, ancestral histories, rewilding – and how to talk to our fellow animals."

"Doctor Doolittle," I laughed, "Not a major revision at all, then. And is that just the *pre-school* curriculum?"

"Hah, I see Busi's sense of humour is starting to rub off on you," smiled Saartjie.

"Not a bad start, but what about new ways of managing crime and punishment? And challenging prisons, as a twenty first century source of slavery, both here and using the thirteenth amendment in the Constitution in the former US?" asked Busi, as she tapped her still e-cosseted ankle. "As well as focusing on taking responsibility and making restitutive justice… Finally, just before we came here – I got to meet – and cry with, the mother of Imantshi."

"I'm so glad," I said, "and what about love?"

Busi laughed, "What about love? Love and social justice, they belong together."

Angry shouts and a torrent of swearing floated over the trees.

"What's that *now*?" asked Andile nervously, "Doesn't sound much like love, not in the slightest." He scratched at his swollen left arm.

"No need to abandon positions," said Sharp Sharp Boy, opening a box to reveal a drone.

Within a minute it was flying clear, seeking the source of a growing roar of voices, and seething arguments.

Sharp Sharp flipped a switch and a 3-di image fizzed onto the drone's launch holo-pad.

As if from above, we could see fully armed security guards fighting to hold the Hunting Lodge gate closed, as an army of scream-sheet reporters pushed against them with insulated grapples, Rig bulbs flashing from corneas.

A dozen or so news drones, buzzed chaotically over the fence.

Badda-badda-badda-badda…

The drones were shot down.

Sharp Sharp's drone hovered discreetly in the background.

"News travels fucking fast nowadays," said Saartjie.

Walter stood in the shadows, a dragon on his gown glinting at a camera flash briefly, as he faced the press hordes at the gate.

He was clearly miked-up for sound.

"This is private property," he boomed. "We will destroy *anything* that comes into our airspace."

More gunshots.

The images fizzed, sputtered… and died.

"Our drone's gone," said Sharp Sharp Boy.

A cloud had crossed the early morning sun, and we looked up, as the light dimmed, and the air cooled.

A cloud of... locusts?

Sun turning blood orange, dimming, dimming, as the buzzing locusts streamed down towards us...

...And who's he?

A tall man stood outside our encampment, in a navy-blue smart suit, right hand held out in front of him, encased in a smart glove.

Alongside him rolled five military bots, all armed, as if for a nuclear Armageddon.

He flexed his fingers and the locusts stopped, in a buzzing cloud, a hundred feet or so, above us.

The sun had gone.

"Signal dampening nanobots," said Sharp Sharp Boy, just behind me.

The man wore a digi-mask. A white face, somewhat familiar.

"Stalin!" shouted Andile.

Stalin smiled. "Time to put down this little communist revolution, no? As my aide has articulated repeatedly, this is private property. This is your last chance to leave – while you still can."

Hard to pin down Stalin's voice through the digital rasping – *white? Black? Foreign?*

Walter stood alongside Stalin, grinning, as he pointed at Mister Xaba. "Here's *baas*, boy, and you're going to be fucking sorry you ever asked to see him."

"Mind your language, Walter, we have children present," said Chief Dumisani.

Stalin laughed, "How stupid and selfish are you, to bring them, or are they meant to be human shields? I must admit your sign barriers are cute, but they're not going to be able to withstand explosive *dum dum* bullets, I'm sure. 'Change requires sacrifice'? How much will you sacrifice today? And – you ignorant savages – you've misspelled water."

Ignorant savages? Now that's old colonial speak. Probably white, probably foreign.

"That's W-A-T-A," said the Chief, as he approached the defensive boarding around the camp slowly, with raised arms. He'd abandoned his wheelchair.

The Chief stopped, at the edge of the raised boards, as guns swivelled onto him. "It's an acronym," he explained, "*We* Are the Alternative."

Stalin rocked back his head in laughter. "You? TINA back at you, then – there is no alternative. I am here to wipe you all out, like a rat infestation on my farm. Remember the *Marikana Massacre*?"

The two babies wailed together, as if they'd picked up on our fear.

"And you call *us* savage?" said the Chief.

"Tell your women to drop their weapons," said Stalin.

He stepped forward, waving his arms, as if signalling someone behind him. "I'm afraid you are very seriously outgunned."

A rumbling noise shuddered the earth, as if threatening to rip it open.

Quake?

Into sight ground a huge metal monster – gleaming, with its lasered, digger maw open-wide for the bite. The King of the Kill-Dozers, undoubtedly one of those giants we had seen, above Imbali.

Facing that, there can only be one outcome.

I shivered, but refused to step back.

Busi took my hand.

"First, give us an option," the Chief looked up at the tall man, but his body was starting to shake too. "We hold what we can, till we hear what we can get."

"We can do this slowly if you like. I have frozen everyone's bank accounts. Without money and supplies, you will starve. You may have taken refuge under these trees, but didn't anyone ever tell you that money doesn't grow on trees? Or, I could be even kinder and allow you to bring in your last three cows, for one final shared meal, Mister Dumisani? Beef is not a bad meat, I hear… I myself am partial to snow leopard, and polar bear, even an extinct Californian fish or two… *hahaha*, the rarer, the tastier."

Saartjie Baartman moved alongside the Chief, a green glow between her upheld palms.

"What the fuck's that?" asked Walter.

"Green Coin," said the Chief, "banked behind firewalls on the Web Commons. Each coin represents another planted tree grove. And yes, tree money, with real value."

Stalin stood, stock still.

"You know what's the real crime here?" asked the Chief. "That you have got so rich, while we are so poor."

Stalin turned on his heel, simultaneously making a throat-cutting gesture with his hands, to the mil-bots.

"Kill them all," he said.

He held a gun in his left hand, and fired at the nearest bot.

Whinnngggggg! A bullet ricocheted off the casing, and left a glowing dent.

"They opened fire first," he said, "We had to respond, in self-defence."

I closed my eyes.

A low humming throbbed in my ears.

A blast – and metal rained onto my head.

I fell, dazed.

I rolled over, to look up at the sky.

Two helicopters hovered, the sun glinting off their rotors.

I wiped at my body, which was covered in small metallic insects. "What – what happened?"

"EMP burst from Chopper One, I'm guessing." Sharp Sharp Boy lay next to me, his face near my head, "Disarmed their mil-bots too."

The largest helicopter began to descend, slowly.

The Chief and Saartjie Baartman stood, shrugging off pieces of metal, amidst the screams and wails around them.

They watched Stalin and Walter, who stood beside their lifeless military bots, faces tilted to watch the sky.

"Please stay, Stalin!" shouted the Chief, tremulously, "The President of South Africa would no doubt like a word or two with you."

Stalin turned to Walter, "I'm out of here. You handle this."

"But – but, I don't talk to women."

"You have two fucking minutes to drop that stupid habit, Walter. Goodbye."

Stalin's face transmuted, as he turned and left.

"Who's he now?" I asked.

"Mao Zedong," said Busi.

"Mao?"

"Yes, Chairman Mao." Andile said, behind us. "He must be heading off to wave his Little Red Neo-Liberal Book, at any who might *dare* to lose faith."

The President landed, in a flurry of leaves, and dead metallic nanobots.

"I told you I have friends in high places," The Chief told Busi, smiling.

President Ncube was a woman comfortable, and firm, in her large body.

The discussion with Walter was short.

"This is a protected area," she said, "All commercial activities on this land will cease, until we have a legal decision. There will be a full government inquiry into what has happened here today."

I glanced around. Several men and women in black suits and glasses were picking up the dead nanobots, placing them inside bio-plastic bags.

"We still own *many* within your government – even some of the judiciary is ours. You will not succeed, *woman*." Walter was slow, and obviously truculent, with his words.

The President laughed. "We are the majority in this world. From now on, we won't just have one day a year. Fuck that Women's Day. We Own the Year. We Have the Spaces... And, as for you, I don't talk to idiots."

She turned her back on Walter, and muttered something to her security, which I just managed to overhear. "Get the police to interview him. Bring the Scorpions back."

Ah, the crack anti-corruption unit.

More loudly, she boomed. "Come on, Chief Dumisani, introduce me to all your brave and wonderful children, in this Camp *Serowe*, as you call it..."

The Chief collapsed into his wheelchair, to introduce the residents. He started with Yolanda. The President refused her out-held hand, and instead, kissed her on the cheek.

"Over there, leaning against that chopper. It looks like –?" said Busi.

Busi and I stepped over our WATA boards and walked towards the second helicopter.

It was.

Jenny Johnson and Pedro gave us a hug.

"For once, I bring the fucking cavalry," joked Jenny.

I chuckled, looking at Pedro. "We thought you were in prison?"

Pedro smiled, broadly.

His teeth were white, and very straight.

"Johnny fixed them, free of charge. We had a chat – he's misguided, but he's a dog lover too. I finally got through to him, by saying we're *all* just fucking mongrels, whatever the colour of our fur, and there ain't no such thing as pure breeds. Turns out, he even owns a black rescue mutt."

"Johnny? So, now we're dogs?" asked Busi.

Pedro shrugged, "Whatever works – and yes, we're all animals too. Dogs, at least, don't judge."

"Johnny, AKA Dr. John Baker," said Jenny, "The prosthodontic surgeon, formerly of the White Brotherhood, with whom we cut a deal. I hope you've learned something too, Pedro – sometimes it's best to keep your mouth shut, if you want to keep your teeth."

Pedro just laughed, showing off his teeth.

"So, what's the deal *you* managed, to finally come here, and with the President of South Africa, *nogal*?" Busi cocked her head at Jenny.

"Only in the escort chopper," said Pedro, "But still pretty neat. I'm Jenny's official cultural advisor now – and she is here to talk to top officials about Memorandums of Agreement regarding our common water problems, and how to curb international tax evasion."

"The FSA will eventually become the USA again," said Jenny, "But there's a lot of groundwork that's needed to be done first. We want to make sure *all* voices are heard, and *all* histories acknowledged."

"Big fucking job," said Busi.

"Same for you here," said Jenny. "Sustaining and building on this, now *that* is always the hardest part."

Busi opened her palms and a digi disc between her hands sparked a dull but visible map of the global south, with a sprinkling of lights on the surface. "This is International Land Claim Day. We are linked in to our compatriots in South America and Oceania too, who have acted alongside us today. We honour those who have been murdered already. Sixty-seven dead. We – we were lucky."

How many dead?

I looked closely at the map glistening between her palms, "The main casualties are in Livingstone, Zambia, thirty dead in the LRE – ah, Graham mentioned that place, the Livingstone Relocation Encampment, when he went up to the Vic Falls. And a boy who died then, whom he called Gameboy Boy."

Busi nodded, "Biofuels and palm oil fields for exports, foreign corporation owned, with nothing given back apart from some local bribes. *FuelCorps,* a partner of FreeFlow – or a shell subsidiary, the international investigators are out and tracking corporate accounts across the world. The people have occupied this space, and thrown down the fences, in order to reclaim local food and water. There have been over two thousand dehydration and famine deaths there so far this year. Criminal. Enough is enough."

And the media has been so silent about this all, as Graham had told me after his visit to Vic Falls, at the time.

Silence is complicit.

"And all right next to an elephant graveyard," I said.

I remembered the clips he showed me. *He can be a* mampara, *but I still miss the bugger.*

The President climbed in to her helicopter.

The solar panels camp-side hummed again, and purified water was being handed around the settlement.

"Our cue to leave." Jenny hugged us. "We'll be in Durban for a few days. Catch you both there?"

"*EThekwini,*" Busi nodded. "Maybe, but probably by remote hook-up. Land occupation requires a sustained and one hundred percent commitment, if it's going to succeed. We will need to bring in more resources and maybe even substitutes via the air – we shall see how it goes. *Winnie* says Dlamini Enterprises, at least, are fully behind us. They are figuring out a way to take some of Lake Huron back to Marikana township right now, where so many are thirsty."

"Lake Huron? Oh, and of course, *Tek-winny*, sorry, sister, we both know what lies in a name," said Jenny. "*Salani kahle.* Goodbye."

They hugged.

Busi and I stepped back, as Jenny, Pedro, press and security officials, boarded the second chopper.

The President's helicopter left first, the other followed soon after, and they swept leaves from the trees, as they roared skywards.

From the tree on the water embankment, we heard a rippling, fluid whistling call.

I looked at Busi.

"*uFukwe!*" exclaimed Busi.

"Rain Bird!" I said.

We kissed.

My memory stirred. "This is not our first time, is it?"

Busi laughed. "No, you kissed me when you came into my room, that night you slept over. I took you *straight* back to the couch, you were not in a fit state to agree to *anything.*"

"That was a weird night. Was that the *dagga* sauce?"

"It's never *just* the sauce," smiled Busi.

"What – what do you see in me? I'm fat; and getting old."

"Oh come, come," Busi gave my hips a squeeze, "*Gebou om te hou.*"

"Hah!" I pushed at her, but Busi held on. "'Built to hold' indeed – that's not enough."

Busi shrugged, "That first day, when we spoke, I could see that you could *see* me. I mean, really see me. I saw you too – and I liked what I saw."

"I like what I see too," I said, "So, my home is here, with you?"

Busi pulled back her head, to get a closer look at my face. "No *sisi*," she said, softly. "Not always. We need you in the white spaces too. We need you to help teach *them* to see better too, to teach them to drop their insidious blinkers, that they don't even know are there. They are more likely to listen to *you*, than to us."

"So, I have no real home here – or there?"

"Homes are made, not given," she said, "We've had a lot of donations from people within nearby *white* homes too. You're not on your own out there, either. Perhaps you can even form your own white ethno-philosophy group?"

I smiled. "But where do I stay?"

"We all live in the spaces between," said Busi, "Our true home is the

Earth, and with our fellow animals, whom, for far too long, we have abandoned, killed, eaten or imprisoned."

"Wise beyond your years, madam."

"Books, Lizzie. Books. Give me a library, and the wisdom of heaven is there."

uFukwe called again, a long and melodious bubbling call, but no rain clouds gathered above us.

I gave a brief cloud hum.

Busi smiled, and then asked, "How *is* your white husband?"

"Graham? I don't know... I'm missing him." *Best be honest. Always.*

"You can like *both* sexes you know – people think you have to like one or the other – but binary thinking is bullshit, in this ever-changing world."

"Do you, do you *really* want to know how he's doing?"

"Yes, why not. He doesn't like me, I can tell, but I don't hold that against him."

I called, and my phone flickered instantly into life. I held it up, so that Busi could see the screen too.

We gasped.

A volcanic island was spewing fire and chunks of rock into the sky.

"Hello, Lizzie," said Graham, "Look... it's Rangitoto – the sky is burning."

Sharp Sharp Boy had overheard our gasps, and swung a few dials on the data-mat in the encampment. "I'm piggy backing your signal," he warned.

The cone of Rangitoto Island burst upwards from the mat, showering red photons of fire into the late morning, South African sky. Collective gasps, of shock and awe.

A baby cried again.

This time, no one said anything.

A strange young woman's voice rose, as if driven by the flames: '*For we are the Fire Keepers.*'

Chapter 27
Art – Breathing Towards Newest Orleans

The sun burned even hotter in Texas.

We stopped for a journey break, on Galveston Island.

I took the opportunity to slip down to the beach in mid-afternoon, while Sally and Michelle slept off the long journey, in our motel.

I darted past a massive Stock Market display hanging over several small beachside shops, and made haste across the hot sand, to some shade near the sea.

Galveston East Beach.

I sat on the hard bench under a cool solar brolly, and stared across buttressed sand, out into the Gulf of Mexico. The two words, in my father's voice, kept circling inside my head, 'Fuck Katrina!'

Returning is not going to be easy.

They can't even give us a police guard, because I don't have any 'evidence'.

Nor have I numbers, but I mostly trust myself on this.

What am I doing, sitting here, exposed – instead of holed up with Michelle and Sally in the motel? I've not told them about my fears.

For maybe – just maybe – I'm wrong, and we run for nothing.

No, family is never nothing.

Out in the gulf, warning lights on a wind-farm array flashed, as did the hazards on a distant, decommissioned oil rig. The rig tilted, as if ready to topple. *Hold it together, give us time to get rid of your shit too… Oil and water don't mix; water lives, but oil kills.*

At last, class action suits, led by the Polly Higgins Foundation, had gathered momentum against the oil companies, like they did against big tobacco. *Same lies, but bigger and more devastatingly global pollutant damages.*

Payback time. Before the toxic air and heat kills everyone.

All indicators suggested the Fresno Deep Water Drill had 'been a contributory factor' in triggering the 'Frisco Quake.

Recent apocalypses have been partial, at least, but with much too much human agency.

Spike the wheels – how do we hobble the Big One, the Last Apocalypse, so that we can build a new heaven down here, on our heating Earth? What good is a Heaven, if Earth becomes a hell for your children?

With Sally, I am ready to face anything.

So why am I here?
This is the same Gulf water which surged with Katrina, all those many years ago.
You must swim in it.
Crazy.
If you'd swum with Zeke, would they still be alive?
Looking at the sea is… okay, but swimming – uh, uh. What a place for thoughts of endings and new beginnings. I'm drawn to water, by old attractions – and even older traumas.

"Rosebud," I said.

NextGen sputtered. The trauma software had a bug in it.

"Rosebud," I said again.

Nothing.

I laughed.

The beach was littered with remnants of wooden debris from Donald, that mammoth level six hurricane on the revised *Saffir-Simpson* scale from '38 – much bigger even than the bastard that had barrelled in here in nineteen hundred. Raised wooden houses, rendered into little more than splintered match sticks.

Over a hundred people had refused to evacuate, mostly 'BOIs' from all reports, native islanders, born and bred.

None of their bodies were ever found.

Yet I found Zeke…

NextGen rang, moved onto my still slightly throbbing left wrist, and I nervously tapped it.

Brad stared out at me. "Hey, Art, we're due to get music for Church next Sunday. You come up with any song ideas for our band? We're getting ready to practice."

"Galveston," I said.

Brad looked momentarily blank, and then irritated. "This a joke or what? We sing an old white song, by a dead white cowboy? They didn't spell it out, but I'm sure they're wanting to hear *black* songs."

"It's where I am right now, Brad, Galveston. I'm not coming back – I'm moving on."

"Why? What's going on? Where are you going?"

I shrugged, "World's not a safe place, Brad, I can't say anything more for now. I'm so sorry we couldn't say goodbye. I will call you back on a secure line, when settled. You take care – and if they want a 'negro' song, why not give them 'Wade in the Water'?"

NextGen cut the signal, as if knowing I did not feel like talking further.

The tide was coming in, moving closer, as it surged against the rocky buttress.

I felt as if I myself were the dim sea rolling in, battering the concrete bulwarks – ebb and flow, *whooosshhh* and *ssssss* (a retreat and repeat). This was our home too, millions of years ago, the sea, the amniotic fluid of the Earth.

Someone coming.

I shifted uncomfortably, towards the end of the bench, as an old woman sidled on next to me. Thankfully, she had no bags – nor was she muttering to herself, either.

Amazing how a view of a place could change, with the presence of someone, even a stranger. The tilting oil rig was now replaced by a barefooted old woman, blacker than me, in beige blouse and khaki pants, thumbing through her phone.

Hahaha – Looks like she'll be decommissioned soon, too... Art, stop being so mean.

Behind the bench, a young white man in brown overalls swept the worst of the day's detritus away, the scrubbing noise and smell of rancid fruit waste distracted me momentarily.

A few wasps had a go at the fruit, *bzzzzz*, but nothing like the numbers of twenty years ago, before the insect population collapsed in the wake of the Death Pesticides and giant food monocultures.

Now they're talking about the first and imminent UN Moon shipments of wheat from the Shackleton Crater, having outsourced some of our food security, to our orbiting neighbour.

I jumped, as the woman turned to face me, grey hair framing her dark and craggy face. "There's a lot of shit to get rid of, isn't there – not just the frigging oil, but all this dumb plastic and micro beads, poisoning the fish in these waters."

"Uh – yes," I said, and wondered if it would be too rude, at this point, to stand up and move on. I wanted introspective space, not the pressure of social interaction. *Why else come to the beach, for heaven's sake?*

"Humour an old lady," the woman sidled up closer, "Sitting on a beach bench on Galveston Island – now that sure beats coming in on the clouds, huh?"

I shifted away, to the end of the bench, and then looked at her more closely. The woman gazed back, her brown eyes clear, but the surrounding lens yellowed. *She looks extremely old. Alzheimer's? Does she have a carer nearby?* Her voice sounded strangely familiar, deeper than expected, faintly masculine even.

"Do you want me to help?" I asked, "What can I do for you? Where do you live?"

The old woman gave a brief laugh, and settled back against the bench.

"That makes for a nice change, thank you Art, someone helping me too."

How in hell does she know my name? I'd been warned that psychotic episodes might come with my borderline Autism diagnosis. *Am I going mad?* "You're, you're not *real*, are you?"

She gave me a quick sideways glance, and reverted to flicking through her phone, "That's insulting. Well, if I ain't real, then you sure ain't real, either."

I stood, shaking, "So who the hell are you, then? What do you *want?*"

Then, I recognised her.

The last time we'd spoken, her voice had been muffled by a dust mask.

"No!" I said, "The old woman on the Wall in Hydro-City?"

The woman smiled, slowly, with care, deliberation, and some warmth. "And hell has little to do with it, Art – you should know by now, clouds are for rain, not transportation. Keep your gaze on the ground and the nearby horizons, that's where we build heavens – however fleeting, and however hard."

"You're... you're kidding me?"

She smiled, broadly, "Of course I am. Most people have never *properly* listened to me, either, however devout they pretend to be. I've told them it's the *poor* and the meek who will inherit the earth and gave them the metaphor of a camel through the eye of a needle. I warned them about being misled by wolves in sheep's clothing, but, despite all that, what do they do?"

"Uh, what?" *Just keep humouring her.*

"They go and follow *rich* wolves in full *wolf* regalia. Enough is enough, it's time for the poor, and the wretched of the earth to rise, before *nothing* is left, for anyone."

She stood, as her phone buzzed, "Speaking of heaven and earth, just got a Text, with a capital 'T'... if you know what I mean.?"

No, not really.

She winked at me. "I've got to get on with things. Neither heaven – nor a renewed Earth – are built in a day. The Apocalypse is now, so stop waiting. It's time to halt this tide of incessant shit – keep blowing it open, keep facing it down. Regenerate; rebuild and re-wild. Goodbye, young man. Keep up the good work – and remember, it's only about *all* of us, *not* about you."

Young man? I'm pressing forty. Still, I am probably just a toddler to her – or, or, Him?

No... nonsense. The old woman is clearly demented.

I looked around for her carer hovering nearby, but all I could see was the young beach-cleaner in dark maroon overalls, as he hoovered up discarded and rancid food, from further along the beach now, wasps, flies and all.

The old woman stood up and opened her palms. "Got to cool off my hands and feet."

Shit.

Her palms and feet were scarred and burnt, the flesh like lurid melted plastic, parts still weeping raw. She shrugged. "Some of the devout still like their burning crosses."

She walked towards the water, turning to pick up some sand in her left hand. She opened her fingers and the sand dropped, funnelling away in a spray of whiteness, in the light onshore breeze.

"Soil and water," she said, speaking loudly as she gazed back at me. "That's all we're made of. Take good care of the earth and the water – *and each other* – and all will be well."

With emptied hands she turned, walking down to the water and on through the safety wall gap... and in, splashing through the shallows.

I relaxed, having half expected her to walk on the surface. *Nope, hahaha, just one weird old woman after all, going for a late afternoon swim.*

"Come on in, Art!" Her voice barely carried over the hiss of the small waves. "As your poet, Putuma, has said, 'Our skin re-traumatises the sea... We have come to stir the other world here. And to swim, just for fun.[5]'"

Shoulder height in, neck deep and then... then she is gone, beneath *the water?*

Small waves rolled in, reddish-green foamed, bringing with them a few dead fish and rolling plastic bottles, long emptied of fresh water.

I peered, but no, no bobbing head.

"Did, did you see that?" I walked over to the young beach cleaner, who was busy tying a full trash bag and holding an old phone between his teeth. "You, you saw her didn't you, that old black woman on the bench with me?"

The man finished tying the bag and took the phone out of his mouth. "Sure was someone, but you'd best get your eyes checked, buddy. It was a white hippy fella in a frilly kaftan – the dude texted me as he left the bench, must be via blue tooth hook-up."

The cleaner looked, smiled, and then showed me his phone, chuckling. "Ha, what a five-star weirdo. Fu-cking nuts, man!"

JESUS LOVES YOU.

The young man pocketed his phone, hoisted the bag over his shoulder and headed over to a nearby truck, suspension hanging low with its trash load. People were starting to drift back to their cars, as the sun dipped lower.

Aren't we all fucking nuts? Been no such thing as a sane world for a long, long time. Did I really see someone? And did they go into the water? If so, where are they now?

---

[5] Koleka Putuma (2017). *Water.* (In) *Collective Amnesia,* uHlanga Press.

'Arthur Raymond Green', the sea called.

You're kidding me. I texted my position to Michelle, shivered, and stripped my top and tracksuit pants off, piling them under the bench, on top of my shoes. I'd come prepared, at least, in the hope I *might* finally be able to do this. The last few people were leaving the beach, but I'd never been one to follow the crowds. Not since I was an itty-bitty baby.

"I don't swim," I'd told Zeke, leaving her. And she'd died. So, would she still be alive, if I'd swum? For I *have* swum.

And I need to do so again. In the deluge that may still come, we may all need to swim.

Goggles on, nose and ear plugs in.

The water was surprisingly warm, despite the cold breeze still fanning in onto the shore, as if it were the cooling breath of God.

No point going home, without one swim at least – and at last. I can do this. I can. It's riding a bike… only in water.

I waded out hip high, past flurries of bottles and plastic bags, and I locked my rising anxiety, in a steel vault of self-control.

Bracing myself again, I took a breath in, and launched myself, face first, into the water.

No counting here. Only one way to get in.

Finally, I swam, pushing out past the bottles and plastics, past the seaweed and floating tar that seeped at my nose plugs, smelling like faecal matter. *But is officially not.*

<Ninety percent of plastic pollutants here on this beach traceable from processing leakages, Project Yosemite, Corpus Christi, Texas,> said Next Gen.

"Tell the Director that," I said, pushing through the turgid waste.

I was past the informal beach barrier, where the debris had also dragged momentarily at my face and feet; and I was swimming free, in the Gulf of Mexico.

Free, tainted only by a small streak of tar on my chest and chin, from the last residues of Deepwater Three. I swam straight out, away from the beach, with a firm and vigorous breast stroke. I remembered now.

I was *a good swimmer.*

Shapes passed by underneath me – plastic waste? I looked down, spotting round shapes with, with paddling legs? *A school of… turtles – surely not?*

Dropping my head and lifting my hips, I dived downwards, kicking hard. Bubbles streamed upwards – my eyes burned, five or six large turtles swam past.

A stab of eye-joy, followed by an ache, a yearning to follow.

NextGen glowed in recognition on my wrist – Hawksbills, not Green Turtles, but near enough, and what a glory to follow. *Just give up the endless struggle and swim with the turtles, out into a vast, calm ocean...*

I surfaced, gasping, and dived again.

Small turtle at the back had been trailing a partly eaten plastic bag and what was that even further beneath them, wrapped and trapped in a plastic mesh line, down near the brown kelp forest?

I dived, snatched the bag from the turtle, and swam deeper.

Breath exploded from my body.

Violently, desperately, I kicked myself towards the surface, with collapsed and terrified lungs. *Dead old woman; trapped at the bottom of the sea. Fish bait. Or Jesus? Vision – or hallucination?* Her brown eyes, flecked with yellow, had flickered open, staring at me, although no bubbles had seeped from her mouth.

I coughed and choked, disorientated in the sea.

Choke. Breathe, Green. No more panicking.

An old familiar voice, from long ago, wafted over the breeze, *"Breathe, son."*

Daddy?

I'm tiring. Which way back? Daddy?

"Breathe – and think."

Onshore wind – keep the wind behind your head and neck... and follow the swell.

Father swam beside me, a ghost, like an invisible breath. I heard his slow and deep inhalations and followed suit, modelling his reassuring rhythm. The swell increasingly lifted me forwards, and I slowed my breath even further, timing it to match my strokes.

Pull, breathe, sink, kick, pull, breathe, sink, kick, pull...

Shit and oil smells seeped into my nasal plugs.

Sure as hell, going the right way then.

I slowed, tiring, at the external beach barrier of congested debris and junk, a barrier martialled by waves piling up a mountain of debris, onto the sloping beach.

No way through, surrounded by floating debris, plastic and kelp, all halting my movement. *Levees failed, again, inside my mind.*

Water, water everywhere, and no space to breathe. Brown clothes and body bundled seamlessly into the kelp, like an underwater scarecrow? Man trapped with leg in window, hair and arms waving in the current. Am I next to drown – how do I swim through this shit?

My path out is gone, and I am tiring fast, drowning in garbage, struggling to breathe.

"Breathe.

It is your right to breathe.

So, breathe."

Father, again.

Followed by a big, booming female voice, "Arthur, Raymond Green, get your ass back here, *right now!*"

Michelle. I swum harder, resolutely, pushing in through the litter, and the waste, and the shit. My left wrist ached, but I ignored it.

"Daddy!" A little girl's scream.

Sally.

Nothing left to talk back with. Focus.

I am but flesh and water, moving through water.

Ahead, lies soil and sanctity.

"Daddy?"

And family.

I dragged himself up the slope of the beach, gasping, trailing oil and faecal sludge.

Michelle and Sally waited, and moved towards me.

Sally ran, stumbling awkwardly, but she got up and hugged me, despite my wetness and the foul smell, cold steaming off my shaking body.

Michelle followed more slowly, holding out a towel, before drying and hugging the both of us.

"Don't you dare do that to us again!" she snapped. "And why have you got a ripped plastic bag in your hand?"

I panted, as exhaustion clamping my body. "Took it from the mouth of a turtle. We can do this… One bag at a time."

"Bag, *schmag.* You're doing nothing right now, just catching your breath – and then we head *straight* back to the motel, for you to have a damn good shower."

I smiled and crumpled onto the sand.

Sally looked down at me, as I lay on my back, gasping. "Will you teach me to swim, Art?" she asked.

"In the Newest Orleans state pool," said Michelle. "Not the sea."

"I'd be happy to do that, Sally," I smiled, "Just call me daddy again, though."

Sally hesitated and looked down.

Can you blackmail a child?

Parents of The Promise do not bribe, cajole, or blackmail.

"I'm sorry, Sally," I said gently, getting to my feet shakily, to look down, at her upturned gaze. "I didn't mean that. You can just keep calling me Art. *Of course,* I can teach you to swim – but in a safe pool first, as Mommy says. Come."

I held out my hand and held my breath.

Grudgingly, she took it.

We walked over to the bench, as Michelle draped the towel over me.

I let go of Sally's hand to pull on my tracksuit, as the air cooled in the growing flares, of a magnificent and reddish sunset.

Michelle carried the hippo that I had given Sally.

Sally took it from her and showed me. "See, I call her Baby Kow. Hey, look, there's another Kow!" She pointed with her right arm out, cradling the hippo with her left.

A tall man was strolling down to join us. He had a holstered gun on his right hip.

Michelle rushed across to hug him.

Sally looked at me, "Can I promise marry him also, and have two daddies?"

"Ask him, sweetie. I think we're just parents now, so we can be either Mommy *or* Daddy."

"Oh," Sally looked confused, but then changed tack. "Did hippos used to swim, Art?"

I nodded, sitting down on the bench to put my shoes on, and Sally sat next to me, despite my stink, moving the hippo through imaginary water, as if she were swimming.

"Yes, Sally – they lived in rivers and lakes in Africa and their name means river horse. They swam all the time. Now, when you learn to swim, the most important thing is to breathe properly. Just breathe above the water. And always remember, your breath is very special to me."

Sally chuckled and put the hippo onto my lap as Kowalski and Michelle wandered over to join us. "Please look after Baby Kow, Art... Kow!" She stood up to hug the tall man around his waist.

He smiled down at her and patted her head gently. "Hello, little lady. Hi, Art."

"Hi Kowalski, what brings you here?"

"Witness Protection, of course. The Big Dee sent me your way just in case there was any further trouble. FreeFlow have gone into free-fall, didn't you hear?"

I shook my head, "Been a bit out of the loop on this journey."

"More news waiting for you at the car, then. I will need to mind your ex-wife. She's a target too, you know."

"A target of yours – or FreeFlow, Kowalski?" I grunted.

The tall man just laughed, trying to encircle Michelle's waist with his arm.

She bumped him off, with an angry hip. "I can look after myself too, you know."

I smiled to myself, running ahead with Sally and making dipping, swimming motions, with the toy hippo in my hand.

Never take anything – or anyone – for granted.

Sally followed, squealing. "You *gotta* breathe properly, Baby Kow. Just breathe."

Breathe.

I stopped.

A small woman, her frayed brown hair spilling from a blue head scarf, stood next to a large armoured car, a security bot by her side. People were wandering past, some hovering in the background with curious glances, furtively snapping shots of the car through phones and no doubt cyber-Rigs.

"Suraya?"

The young woman looked tired and older than I remembered, even though it had only been a day or so since I had seen her. Her hands were behind her back, her blouse sleeves flowing over her shoulders and arms.

"Breaking news, Art," she smiled, but without humour, it seemed, "After meeting the DA extremely early today, I'm joining you on the Protection Program. I had another look at the FreeFlow pipes at the S-SJ headwaters, but this time a much deeper ultrasound 3-di scan. The sewerage pipes were a cover. That shit transportation was only obscuring what was going on even further below. FreeFlow have been sucking the delta dry, with completely unlicensed subterranean piping."

"Water theft," I whistled, "Grand larceny. Now, *that's* going to spook investors."

"Talking of water and shit, we need to get you back to the motel for a shower, Art," said Michelle, as she arrived with Kowalski, neither of them holding hands.

"Hello," smiled Suraya, "You must be Michelle."

But Michelle did not respond.

She and Kowalksi were watching something behind her, and I turned to follow their gazes. Other people were looking up at the stock market screen too, above the swimwear and candy shops.

No one spoke.

All the listed numbers were in violent red, and spinning downwards, too fast to follow.

"Get in the car!" Snapped Security Bot-859.

An armoured drone rose above the candy store roof.

I lifted Sally up, as we scrambled to get in, and I threw her in first.

Michelle was already through the opposing door of the car, catching Sally, and shielding her.

Kowalski had unleashed a shot at the drone, which dodged.

Suraya leaped into the passenger seat and Kowalski jumped into the trunk, slamming it shut behind him. "Get us out of here, Washington!"

The car, parallel parked on the beach front, took off with a roar.

I watched in the rear-view mirror as the security bot rattled off a few shots at the flying drone trailing us, but it receded fast into the distance.

The flying drone above must have dodged those bullets too.

The roof started rattling with metal rain.

Bullets.

A hissing chuckle steamed from the front seat, and a... driving dragon... floored the accelerator electronically. We were all pinned back into our seats.

"Bok Kai?" I gasped.

The dragon laughed. "As your poet Dylan warned us, a hard rain's a gonna fall..."

I held Sally's hand, feeling fragile and fully human, and prayed hard.

Behind us, Suraya prayed loudly too, in Arabic.

NextGen warmed my wrist.

It was Brad.

"Here's our practice run, Art. *Drums, guitar, words*

Who's that young girl dressed in blue

Wade in the water

Must be the children that's coming through,

God's gonna trouble the water, yeah

Wade in..."

Bok Kai had transmuted into... an old, black woman.

No, not Jesus... but, but Harriet Tubman?

I do know my history, Stalin.

And Katrina doesn't frighten me any more.

The car hurtled into the night, armoured roof thrumming loudly with lead.

Epilogue
Busi – Mamlambo and Reconciliation Day

On the Day of Reconciliation, the rains finally arrived; it being the fifteenth day of Land Occupation.

I walked up to the perimeter of our camp, as rain seeped through my sweat suit, and kissed my skin.

The 'Net Mat is still on, glowing with residual solar power.

I stuck my tongue out, both to catch water drops, and for the cameras swivelling above armoured bots, as I approached the laser noose, ringed in red, around the throat of our Camp.

It had been a late afternoon summer storm and almost all the residents had taken refuge in the DDU's; afraid of the lightning, which had only now started to flash and flicker further away, the accompanying growls of the gods receding slowly too.

But not me.

I was coming to terms with the growls within me.

And I had something to say.

"I have been pardoned," I told guard Bot 81, because it was nearest to my final stride, boots squelching in new mud. "I was acquitted on the grounds of self-defence – our courts, at least, are still free."

The bot blinked at me, taser arm swivelling to hold me dead to sight.

The laser fence surrounding us, laced between the Bots, was five stranded, and livid red.

"Come on then, Stalin or Mao, or whomever you're pretending to be," I said to the Bot, "you know that court processes can drag on forever – and this is just costing you needless money and negative publicity. Today, of all days, our Chief is willing to cut you a deal, in the spirit of national reconciliation." *And some of us are getting tired, sick and fractious- but you don't need to know that.*

A community needs freedom to grow.

<The CEO of LeisureLand is now Iosif Dzhugashvili,> Winnie told me.

Bot 83 burped.

And vomited a fat, pink pig, with a deep dark hole scoured along its back.

"Call your Chief then," said the pig, in a squeaky voice, "And he can pop lots of money into the slot on my back… FSD or Chinese Yuan for the piggy bank, that is, none of that Green Coin shit, mind you."

The pig's hooves were deep in mud, but nothing had splattered on its pink legs, a soft golden down covered its rounded, well fed body. The rain did not spatter on its skin.

The rain slowed, though, as a shaft of late afternoon sunlight broke through the grey sky, the storm roiling into the distance.

Chief Dumisani and Saartjie Baartman came to stand alongside me, eyeing the pig.

I noticed Liz hovering discreetly in the background; bad pain day, etched clearly on her face.

"You can purchase this land," said the pig, "At competitive market rates." A nine and a long row of zeroes in American dollars flashed along its flanks.

The Chief laughed. "Yes, we will accept that amount, for this space we now occupy."

The pig sat down and wrinkled its snout, "Oh don't be absurd, Dumisani. This may take *much* longer than the fucking courts, at this rate."

"Indeed so, Miss Piggy," said Saartjie, "So let's cut to the chase, shall we?"

Behind us, the community were gathering, having steadily emerged from the DDUs.

I heard Nomfundo cry; a sharp shrill baby scream that Mama Hina quickly stilled, with deft and weary maternal expertise.

"First, I'll take a green penny, as a sign of your bargaining good faith," smiled the pig.

The Chief laughed, "And get your decrypting Enigma-Nanos onto it? I think not, Porky."

The pig grinned and morphed, growing long fangs and sprouting wings. Steadily, it swung its angelic wings, levitating into the air. The standing bots swung their sights in unison, targeting us, the front three.

"News just in, we have an interim Supreme Court judgement, giving you seven days to vacate this land peacefully – or else under extreme prejudice. Your choice. Money spent wisely elsewhere has paid off, after all." The pig cackled, baring its fangs from above. "Indeed – at least our courts are free, Miss Mhlongo – or perhaps, not *quite* so free."

I tilted my head. 'Is that right, Winnie?'

<*Checking now… yes, that is correct – judgement 265/ZAR43 just released… but the pig seems to have had prior – probably inside – knowledge.*>

Saartjie Baartman stepped forward over the laser line, her face twisted in rage.

Bot 83 tasered her.

She dropped, splashing mud upwards – and through the body of the gleeful, hovering pig.

Voices shouted behind us and Sharp Sharp Boy ran up, helping the large woman to sit up, gasping and shaking.

I moved to help him.

The Bots glowed red, targeting us, but did not discharge again.

"Game over," said the pig, "Now just fucking leave my land."

"I… am… San," said Saartjie, sitting, and shaking away attempts to help her stand. "I invoke the, the, rrr- right of being the First Peoples here, before history was written, and lies were on paper."

The pig laughed and shat on Saartjie, brown bombs that dropped and dissipated without trace, against her face and head. "And I am Napoleon, the Emperor of this place. The courts only recognise written history – and money and power."

The sun had broken through and was beating down again, sucking steamy clouds of moisture from the wet earth.

<*She is here, Busi – Behind us*>

'She, Winnie?'

<*She of the Shadows, emerging at last from the Deepest Depths of the 'Net. The Gods have arrived.*>

Saartjie stood up slowly, facing back towards the encampment and Lake Huron.

She bowed.

The pig's teeth shrivelled, as it rose higher into the air. "What. The. Fuck. Is. That?"

We all turned.

A huge holographic hippopotamus clambered slowly from the water, dragging a long, undulating body, as if also a giant, unending snake.

It wound its way up the slope, past the DDUs and watchers, approaching us at the barrier, with fire in its eyes.

The community had parted in fear… apart from Yolanda, whose wheels had become stuck in the mud, spinning and spraying dirt. She took her hands off the chair controls and caressed the space around the passing hippo's face, as if not afraid.

"*Mamlambo!*" she said. "I've drawn you."

The monster with the hippo face dipped its head in acknowledgement, before stopping near us.

Zondi, the Man-Who-Had-Told-A-Baby-to-Shut-Up, levered Yolanda's wheelchair out of the mud and steered her onto firmer ground to re-join us, as we waited in awe and trepidation, at the edge of the camp.

Without warning, the hippo-snake monster crossed the laser line and spat at Bot83. The Bot's light faded – and taser sights of all the bots in the encircling line drooped – and dropped.

"Enough giving of pain. Enough lines in the mud. Stand tall, stand proud, Saartjie Baartman, of the First People." Mamlambo's voice was deep and resonant, as if having blown all the way up and along its twenty metres of serpentine body, multiple sets of stocky legs supporting its waddling girth.

Slowly, Saartjie stood, her sturdy arms and legs trembled with residual shock – *perhaps amplified by current fear?*

The monster looked up at the pig circling above and spat, a viscous red fluid.

The pig came crashing down to earth, its wings dissolving.

"That visual metaphor is getting tiresome, pig."

"How'd you breach my first digital door? Who the fuck *are* you?" shouted the pig, scrambling to its feet. "An apparition from the Dark Web?"

"Save our Waters. I am the Goddess of Rivers, including the 'Dusi, which flows here and inside this land. I am of this land since time began. As was the last of my animal kind, the she-water horse who was killed by your prisoned lions fifteen days ago. You have *not* been a good servant – of this land, or its animals, or its waters. You have shat toxins into me, and I have lodged a cogent hold and reversal appeal on Judgement *265/ZAR43.*"

"You're no God – and you're not a legal entity," the pig swelled with outrage, standing stiffly foursquare in the mud.

Behind the pig, the bots' laser fence whipped back into place.

Mamlambo roared and hissed, simultaneously. "Yet even *corporations* are people? So too, then, must be the Gods. And as for rivers, we have legal precedence – the Whanganui *iwi* in Aotearoa New Zealand, have had their river recognised as a living ancestor, over two decades ago now. The Brahmaputra has Bok Kai. I demand new Keepers of the Water here too!"

Mamlambo moved forward, the red noose around the camp fading in the blazing, late afternoon summer sun.

The hippo's head dropped to touch noses with the pig.

"Come, fellow animal. All dividing lines are merely constructs, and cognitions. There is no real us and them; no one here is a prisoner, that dilemma is an illusion. Let's find a way for *everyone* to benefit, with what little is left. Let us learn reverence for all life again. Here, we can remake history."

"No. Both the land and water are mine," said the pig. "And water will always flow uphill, towards money."

"And what about the sentient beings you have imprisoned near here, to profit from their organised murder?"

The pig's face went blank for a moment, until he cracked a brief porcine smile of realisation. "Oh – you mean the lions? They're not sentient, they're just fucking trophy beasts."

"In that case, you cannot be sentient either."   Mamlambo   opened her cavernous mouth, and swallowed the pig whole.

She burped, a vaporous burst of digital code. "I can see why some religions prohibit the eating of pork. This Napoleonic pig, I can tell, is going to be one *nasty* digestion."

"What happens now?" asked Chief Dumisani.

"Now," smiled Mamlambo, "Water. *Will.* Fall."

The laser fence surrounding us began to crackle – and fade.

"Is that you, Mamlambo?" Asked Saartjie.

The God smiled, shook her head, and sat, awkwardly, given the long-legged length of her body. "Their insurers will no doubt claim, it is *The One God*, who is to blame."

The bots all turned and began to spin and slide away, churning up mud and detritus.

<*The financial markets are crashing into oblivion, sister*>

'Seriously, Winnie?'

"Money has fallen!" I shouted.

"Indeed so, human daughter," said Mamlambo, "Now, a new world begins. What do humans really value?"

"One world," said the Chief, "for everyone."

"*Amandla*!! Said Mamlambo.

"*Awethu!*" came the refrain, from the rest of us.

I noticed Lizzie had her fist in the air, too.

As if disturbed by our noise, we heard the distant roar of a lion, echoed by another. *Perhaps a mate – or rival?*

Yolanda revved her wheelchair. "Yes," she said, "For everyone."

Walls Fall.

People Rise.

It begins.

– Busi Mhlongo

Witnessed by Busi Mhlongo:
UMgungundlovu, KZN, 16th December 2048, on the 210th Anniversary of iMpi yase Ncome, the Battle of Ncome, or Blood River, as the Boers used to call it.

About the Author

Nick Wood is a South African-British clinical psychologist and Science Fiction writer, with over two dozen short stories previously published, many of which were recently collected (alongside essays and new material) in *Learning Monkey and Crocodile* (Luna Press, 2019). Nick's debut novel *Azanian Bridges* (NewCon Press) was shortlisted for four Awards: the Sidewise (Alternative History), Nommos (African), as well as the BSFA and John W. Campbell for Best SF Novel of 2016. Nick has also published over a dozen articles and chapters within clinical psychology, his latest commission for *Clinical Psychology Forum* is a journal piece, focusing on 'Writing Science Fiction to Avert Climate Catastrophe'. Cue *Water Must Fall* (NewCon Press, 2020). Nick can be found at *Twitter:* @nick45wood or http://nickwood.frogwrite.co.nz/

NEW FROM NEWCON PRESS

Ian Whates – Dark Angels Rising

The Dark Angels – a notorious band of brigands turned folk heroes who disbanded a decade ago – are all that stands between humanity and disaster. Reunited, Leesa, Jen and their fellow Angels must prevent a resurrected Elder – last of a long dead alien race – from reclaiming the scientific marvels of his people. Supported by a renegade military unit and the criminal zealots Saflik, the Elder is set on establishing itself as God over all humankind.

Kim Lakin-Smith – Rise

Denounced by her own father and charged with crimes against the state, Kali Titian – pilot, soldier, and engineer – is sentenced to Erbärmlich prison camp, where she must survive among her fellow inmates the Vary, a race she has been raised to consider sub-human; a race facing genocide; a race who until recently she was routinely murdering to order. A potent tale of courage against the odds and the power of hope in the face of racial intolerance.

Gary Gibson – Devil's Road

The author of The Shoal Sequence (*Stealing Light*, *Nova War*, *Empire of Light*, and *Marauder*), returns with a high-octane story that opens with a prison break and builds from there. Hunted by assassins and haunted by her failures, Dutch McGuire faces the ultimate race through ruined streets that are, home to the Kaiju, pitting woman against machine against monster. Gary Gibson writes with adrenalin turned up to the max…

Rachel Armstrong – Soul Chasers

Scientist and SF writer Rachel Armstrong delivers a tale of Death, but not as we know it. When Winnie's house is swallowed by a giant sinkhole, her body starts to break down, becoming one with the planet, and her components begin an incredible journey around the globe, where she encounters characters from different times, different places. A novice soul chaser is determined to claim her soul before it dissipates forever.

IMMANION PRESS

Purveyors of Speculative Fiction

Breathe, My Shadow by Storm Constantine

A standalone Wraeththu Mythos novel. Seladris believes he carries a curse making him a danger to any who know him. Now a new job brings him to Ferelithia, the town known as the Pearl of Almagabra. But Ferelithia conceals a dark past, which is leaking into the present. In the strange old house, Inglefey, Seladris tries to deal with hauntings of his own and his new environment, until fate leads him to the cottage on the shore where the shaman Meladriel works his magic. Has Seladris been drawn to Ferelithia to help Meladriel repel a malevolent present or is he simply part of the evil that now threatens the town? ISBN: 978-1-912815-06-7 £13.99, $17.99 pbk

The Lord of the Looking Glass by Fiona McGavin

The author has an extraordinary talent for taking genre tropes and turning them around into something completely new, playing deftly with topsy-turvy relationships between supernatural creatures and people of the real world. 'Post Garden Centre Blues' reveals an unusual relationship between taker and taken in a twist of the changeling myth. 'A Tale from the End of the World' takes the reader into her developing mythos of a post-apocalyptic world, which is bizarre, Gothic and steampunk all at once. Following in the tradition of exemplary short story writers like Tanith Lee and Liz Williams, Fiona has a vivid style of writing that brings intriguing new visions to fantasy, horror and science fiction. ISBN: 978-1-907737-99-2, £11.99, $17.50 pbk

The Heart of the Moon by Tanith Lee

Clirando, a celebrated warrior, believes herself to be cursed. Betrayed by people she trusted, she unleashes a vicious retaliation upon them and then lives in fear of fateful retribution for her act of cold-blooded vengeance. Set in a land resembling Ancient Greece, in this novella Tanith Lee explores the dark corners of the heart and soul within a vivid mythical adventure. The book also includes 'The Dry Season' another of her tales set in an imaginary ancient world of the Classical era.
ISBN: 978-1-912815-05-0 £10.99, $14.99 pbk

www.immanion-press.com
info@immanion-press.com